OneWay

THE MESSAGE

Robin L. McClellan
Deborah K. Mark

Mechanicsburg, Pennsylvania USA

Published by Sunbury Press, Inc.
50 West Main Street
Mechanicsburg, Pennsylvania 17055

www.sunburypress.com

For information about special discounts for bulk purchases, please contact Sunbury Press Orders Dept. at (855) 338-8359 or orders@sunburypress.com.

To request one of our authors for speaking engagements or book signings, please contact Sunbury Press Publicity Dept. at publicity@sunburypress.com.

ISBN: 978-1-62006-551-8 (Trade Paperback)
ISBN: 978-1-62006-552-5 (Mobipocket)
ISBN: 978-1-62006-553-2 (ePub)

Library of Congress Control Number: 2015930518

FIRST SUNBURY PRESS EDITION: February 2015

Product of the United States of America
0 1 1 2 3 5 8 13 21 34 55

Set in Bookman Old Style
Designed by Lawrence Knorr
Cover by Amber Rendon
Edited by Ruth Marie Kast

Continue the Enlightenment!

1

Philadelphia, Pennsylvania
March 1902

Reginald and Margaret Hamilton were recognized within the business community and societal circles of Philadelphia as successful and abounding in God's blessings for their lives. Reginald had climbed the ladder of success, achieving his fortune through hard work, perseverance and a steadfast belief in the Golden Rule: *Do unto others as you would have them do unto you.* The couple had an unwavering devotion and a deep, abiding faith in God, dutifully placing God first and then believing all else would fall into place. Now in their early forties, their station in life reflected this belief. Their deep spirituality and honorable work ethic was a testimony to the Bible verse Ephesians 3:20: *He who is able to do exceedingly abundantly above all that we ask or think, according to the power that works in us.* They had been blessed far beyond their wildest dreams, except in one area of their lives.

Margaret Hamilton's heart longed for the day when God would bless them with a child. Year after year, she had seen the best physicians Philadelphia and New York had to offer, each time being reassured and encouraged that physically she was capable of becoming pregnant and delivering a healthy baby. But as one year moved into the next, it seemed that this was not God's plan for them, at least not in the customary way. The couple had discussed adoption from time to time, which now was looking to be their only option of ensuring their hearts' desire of bringing a child into their family. Night after night, instead of praying for God to bless Margaret with a pregnancy, now their prayers were for God to lead them to the child that He had chosen for them—a child not only in need of a loving family, but one who was in need of help due to life's trials and tribulations.

On the first of the New Year, Margaret scheduled a meeting with the Head Master at the prestigious Greenwich Adoption Agency in Philadelphia. And within a few days, the Hamiltons were approved and raring to go on their search for either a son or a daughter to complete their family.

By the end of the first week of meetings, Margaret and Reginald were introduced to a young girl from Egypt. She immediately captured their attention and soon would capture their hearts as well. Even though the Head Master found her to be well-behaved and quite pleasant, he strongly urged against adopting her due to her vague past and lack of family and medical history. At best, she was most likely the bastard child of a poor, uneducated woman who lived in a small, remote village near Cairo. And in his opinion, she wouldn't be the ideal fit for an affluent couple such as themselves.

He went on to further explain that a few years earlier, during an excavation trip to Egypt, a group of archaeologists from the American Institute of Archaeology in Philadelphia found her among the ancient ruins of the Great Pyramids of Egypt. It had been reported to the Egyptian government officials that on that day, a bright fireball with a vapor trail possibly hundreds of kilometers long streaked across the sky at noon. Within seconds of seeing the first flash of light, the archaeologists watched as a second fireball streaked across the sky and exploded somewhere behind the smaller pyramid in the group. A shockwave resulted, launching sand and rubble (or meteorite fragments) through the air. Fearful for their lives, and thinking that the world was coming to an end or that the earth was about to open up and devour them, the archaeologists turned to run. Then, suddenly, amidst the flying debris and chaos, a small child emerged from behind the pyramid where they'd seen the second flash of light. No one in the group spoke a word as the men watched this small, delicate child take one unsure step after another until she emerged from the dust to stand directly in front of them. This solemn-faced child appeared exhausted and only a day—or even hours—away from dehydration and starvation. Her lifeless and tired eyes indicated to the group that she was possibly suffering from a past traumatic event. Her skin was dry, sun-scorched and cracked; her clothing was torn and filthy. In short, it was undeniable this small child had been alone in the desert for some time. However, with the village deserted, there was no way to confirm or deny their suspicions, and there was no way to track down her identity.

For a moment she stood frozen, glaring into their faces and looking as if she was quite demented. Clutching a notepad tightly in her hand, she then pressed it to her chest, threw her head back and screamed. A wild, savage sound exploded from her lips.

When the fight seemed to go out of her, she slumped down to the ground, just as a man who had moved in close to her caught her by the wrists and pulled her in close to him. Instinctively, she flung her arms around his neck and buried her face against his chest, sobbing so hard, so inarticulate with grief that they could not understand what she was saying. Finally their own tears came as they made out what she was saying over and over again.

"Kata Kata," she cried passionately. "Mama, don't let me go into the light... Hold me, Mama... Don't go... Hold me!"

The following day the group of archaeologists wasted no time when it came to contacting government officials, both in Egypt and the United States, concerning the future of this little girl. The only information she offered to them was her name, Iana. And by week's end, arrangements were in place for Iana to travel back to the United States with the group of archaeologists. Once in the US, she was placed in Greenwich Adoption Agency, which happened to be governed by the brother of one of the archaeologists who had found her.

Iana's instructors were constantly amazed at her pleasantness, considering the fact that at such an early age she had already suffered through more adversity than most of them would face in a lifetime. She had adjusted well to her new life at the orphanage and was excelling in all of her studies, particularly in the subjects of mathematics and art.

One afternoon during a recess break, Iana watched as a young boy twisted and turned the multi-colored panels of what she presumed to be nothing more than a colorful little box. The more he twisted and turned the panels, the more frustrated he became. Now completely aggravated and at his wits' end, he launched the little box up and into the air, sending it right in the direction of Iana, who had returned to her seat and was vigorously drawing in her notepad. Out of the blue and without taking her eyes from her pad, Iana reached her hand up into the air, snatched the box in-flight, and then sat it down in front of her.

She said nothing, only narrowed her eyes and pursed her lips as she picked up the box for a closer look. Then without pause and in record time, Iana arranged each square panel to successfully solve the puzzle. Each side of the cube was now a solid color.

"Congratulations Iana!" Mr. Quinn, the class instructor, gave her an admiring pat on her shoulder. "I have never seen anyone decipher the puzzle as quickly as you just did."

As he turned to scold the young lad for his tantrum, he caught sight of the drawing Iana had just completed. Amazed, he picked up her notepad, then half-stated, half-asked out of disbelief, "Iana, this picture is of a child grabbing a cube out of the air?"

"Yes sir, I know," she replied, smiling at him sweetly.

"That's exactly what just happened." Mr. Quinn looked at her quizzically as he placed the notepad down on her desk. "How did you do this?"

All eyes were on her as she looked around the room, scrambling inside to figure out how to explain her drawing.

Timidly, she covered her face and whispered, "Pictures just come into my mind and I draw them." She shrugged her shoulders and quickly handed the notepad back to Mr. Quinn. "See? I have lots of them."

Leafing through her notepad, he stopped at one very detailed illustration of a stormy day. The image depicted a downpour of torrential, driving rain with layers of thick black clouds. At the bottom of the page, *"Exodus 10:22, 'Thick darkness in all the land of Egypt... three days'"* had been written and underlined.

The following series of illustrations portrayed a child, happy and at play, with a small black dog, and then concluded with a drawing of the dog standing in the middle of a dirt road. Then the little girl was pictured alongside the animal, with closed eyes, appearing to have passed away. In the next picture, the child was weeping; in the next, stroking his head; and finally the child was drawn with her head lying on the dog's motionless body.

The sorrow and grief was palpable. Mr. Quinn took a deep breath and continued on.

The following pages were of a woman with the small child—possibly Iana and her mother, he thought. A deep crease formed between Mr. Quinn's eyebrows, and he suddenly noticed that he was frightened. A woman on her knees was pictured with wide black eyes, tears streaming down her cheeks as she looked up to the sky, fear flooding her face as she held the small child in her arms. This illustration was unique in that it displayed what looked like Egyptian hieroglyphics at the bottom right corner along with the words "*Flying bird... to disappear.*"

He quickly turned to the next page, on which Iana had drawn a flash of bright light streaking across the sky above the frightened woman, with these words from Exodus 9:24: "*So there was hail, and fire mingled with the hail, very grievous, such as there was none like it in all the land of Egypt.*" Later on in this section, the woman was shown alone, lying on the ground with her eyes closed.

Mr. Quinn remained silent, dumbfounded by Iana's exceptional artistic ability, the Bible verses and what he believed to be Egyptian hieroglyphics that accompanied her drawings. He sensed he had just witnessed a child's emotional diary of experiences; whether they were fact or fiction, he didn't know for sure.

Mr. Quinn looked over at Iana. "*Who exactly is this child?*" His mind was instantly prompted with the questions of where and who had taught Iana the Bible or the meaning behind the hieroglyphics. "*Could it truly be that these images just come to her?*" he wondered.

After a moment he heaved a sigh. *"It's almost as if Iana has been inspired by some sort of mystical energy."*

"Mr. Quinn?"

Startled at the sound of his name, he let out a quick breath and turned to face Iana.

"What do you call this little box?" she asked.

Bringing himself back to reality, he explained, "It's called a Magic Cube, Iana. Each of the six wooden panels is painted with solid colors: white, red, blue, orange, green, and yellow. An internal pivot mechanism enables each panel to turn independently, thus mixing up the colors."

After having mixed up the colors, once again Iana proceeded to twist and turn the colorful panels to solve the puzzle, possibly quicker than she had done previously.

For the first time since her arrival at Greenwich, Iana sensed acceptance; now she was considered a part of her class. Rather than going off by herself during the recess periods, Iana spent the time entertaining her classmates by solving the Magic Cube puzzle again and again, each time enjoying a round of applause.

After various meetings with the Head Master, the Hamiltons knew all they needed to know about Iana, and they were well aware that the possibility of future emotional difficulties with her might be present. However, in their hearts, minds and souls there was a peace that passed all understanding, and to these deeply religious people, Iana was the child that God had chosen for them.

The following day, the official papers were drawn up for Iana's adoption. The little girl without a last name, who was going to require all the love and help the Hamiltons could provide for her, finally had a home to call her own.

From the first day Reginald and Margaret brought Iana home as their daughter, they acknowledged that, while she may not have had a great start in her life, they were determined that she would have a great finish! The Hamiltons honored that promise every day of Iana's life.

Growing up as the daughter of an affluent family, Iana had what could most definitely be described as the life of a child who had the proverbial "silver spoon." It was overflowing with everything a child could wish and hope for, but as the years passed by, Iana remained untouched by the authority and power money often made available to a human life.

During her teenage years, she developed a strong sensitivity to the pain of others, especially children. By the time she entered The University of Pennsylvania, she knew what her life's work would be all about. She remained captivated by the perplexing aspects of those children who lived with disturbing nightmares in their heads, the violence and perversity that words could not explain. Children suffering when love would never be enough, children who lived without the dignity granted to animals. She dedicated her four years of study to emotionally distressed children such as these. Their young lives were merely an existence, absent of any hope of a future, yet they endured courageously day after day. Like all of them, Iana was a survivor.

In the spring of 1915, Iana received her Bachelor's Degree in Child Development and Psychology. Reginald and Margaret commemorated her achievements by presenting their daughter with a Bible designed especially for her. The black, leather-bound book boasted hundreds of colorful maps printed throughout its pages, making the events and places it described come to life. Each tissue-paper-thin page was adorned with gold edges; in the back of the Bible was a section for documenting Iana's future family's life events. What made this Bible exclusively hers, though, were the blank pages inserted throughout the scriptures. Each was an empty canvas solely reserved for Iana's illustrations, which she had drawn from the beginning in the notepad Mr. Quinn had seen and had continued to draw throughout her life in notepad after notepad.

In a calligraphy script, a heartfelt inscription from her parents was written to Iana on the presentation page inside the front cover of the Bible.

To our darling daughter, Iana.

This passage of time with you has been God's greatest blessing in our lives. We never imagined the amount of love one could feel for another human being until you came to be with us. We fell in love with you at first sight and will love you forever. We have never been as proud as we are on this day.
We honor and celebrate your life!

All of our love always,
Mom and Dad

After her graduation, Iana was quickly hired within the school district near her home. There were classes for the emotionally troubled, programs for the physically handicapped, instructions for the behaviorally disordered, courses for those with learning disabilities and then there was Iana's class, which was referred to as the "trash class." Consisting of a handful of students who defied categorization, her class was the final stopover before entering an institution.

In the spring of her first year, Iana also met David Holmes. He was good-hearted, and although he and Iana didn't see eye-to-eye all of the time, she could tell he was a man of integrity and deep religious faith. A whirlwind courtship ensued, followed by their marriage merely a few months after they met. Then, less than a year after their marriage, Iana and David became the proud parents of a little baby girl, Cilla Menheit Hamilton Holmes.

In considering the matter of baby names, Iana and David sought after a name symbolizing family ancestry. Both agreed on Cilla as their daughter's given name, because it had belonged to David's maternal grandmother, the only grandmother he had ever known and the woman who practically raised him.

Unfortunately for Iana, she had little knowledge of her birth parents. It was common for children born to parents of lost tribes not to have their births recorded in the District Register, and there were no schools or churches nearby her original home which would have provided the information pertaining to her birth and the names of her parents.

When Iana arrived in Philadelphia, all she had to her name was a new dress and a new pair of shoes (both of which had been purchased by the men who had rescued her) and her prized possession: her notepad. Based on her childlike appearance and tiny frame, the orphanage estimated her age at around eight or nine years old. Without any documentation to confirm her true age, the orphanage then assigned a "Gotcha Day" to Iana. This date usually represented the day a child was officially adopted, but in her case, her "Gotcha Day" was the day she arrived at the orphanage and served as the day used in place of her birthday throughout her life. Not only was she missing a past life; Iana was also missing her true age.

Like so many other times throughout her life, Iana refused to lie down and accept what was facing her. She began researching Egyptian girls' names, hoping to find a name that would be fitting for her mother, who by now Iana only had vague memories of. Resolving the issue did not turn out to be simple; Iana had read Egyptian names from A to Z in a book one afternoon, just to end up being frustrated and unable to put a name to the face that was fading in her mind. Her mood was grim, and she decided to use the name Hamilton since it *did* represent her adoptive parents. As she stood up to leave, her arm brushed against the book, knocking it to the floor. The book fell open to the section with names beginning with the letter M. Her eyes were immediately drawn to the name Menheit, and she took a moment to read the Egyptian meaning of this name.

"Menheit, a female Egyptian name meaning the power of light." Tears streamed over Iana's cheeks as she read the words aloud and slowly picked up the book.

In each portrayal of her mother, she always remembered a fireball or streak of light.

"This is perfect!" She sat back in the chair, her heart aching with thoughts of her mother. Iana had been taught always to believe in the spirit of a person which could, and did, have influence and impact for generations.

She closed her eyes and whispered softly, "Mama, are you with me now?"

There was no answer, nor did she expect one. She raised her eyebrows. "All right, then." She simply smiled and then eagerly headed home to share the news with David.

On April 25, 1917, Cilla Menheit Hamilton Holmes was given her name during a baptismal ceremony in the same church where Iana and David had been married. A legitimate birth certificate declared her date of birth as well as the city and hospital in which she'd been born. It acknowledged her mother's name and her father's name, both present and accounted for.

With Cilla fast asleep in Iana's arms, the pastor, using Holy water, traced out the symbol of the cross upon Cilla's forehead.

"In the name of the Father, Son and Holy Ghost, I baptize thee Cilla Menheit Hamilton Holmes."

David leaned over and whispered in Iana's ear. "God knows the things that give us great joy and delight. God knows the people who we need to come into our path who will help form us and shape us." Then he pressed his lips first onto Iana's cheek and then onto his daughter's.

The timing of David's words was exquisite after all of the questions that had been floating throughout Iana's mind over the past few days.

"Have I been baptized?" she asked herself silently.

She looked around the church and wondered if any part of her childhood had been celebrated in the way her daughter's life was being celebrated today. Had she ever received a hug so tight that it took her breath away? Would she ever learn the truth about her biological mother? She didn't know the answer to any of her questions, but she had no regrets. Her childhood was over now, and she had not lived her life wishing she could have changed her past.

One thing Iana *did* know for certain was that, on this glorious day, she was thankful to be alive and thankful to have an incredibly strong man in her life who loved and adored her. And, most importantly, she was thankful to have learned that genes do not make a family.

When all the guests had gone home, Iana began to sense an overwhelming sadness brewing within her. An intense longing was rising up in her mind, body and soul for a woman from almost thirty years ago. She felt ill at ease and began to question where her feelings were stemming from. Knowing better than to try and sleep with so much on her mind, instead she poured herself a cup of tea and reached for the only resource that could provide her with memories of her childhood and her biological mother. Notepad in hand, she walked out onto the front porch and sat down on the swing.

"This is the perfect end to a perfect day," she managed to say, taking a deep breath, unable to stop herself from shuddering as thoughts of her mother tiptoed back into her mind.

Powerless to her thoughts, Iana opened the tattered and torn notepad to an illustration that was unfamiliar: a child nestled in a woman's arms, the woman with one hand on the child's head, as they sat together on a swing tied to a tree branch in front of a night sky filled with twinkling stars. Both were smiling or laughing, and the whole scene warmed her heart while simultaneously intensifying her yearning for her mother.

She stared at the picture, racking her brain for even the smallest hint of a memory, and then let out a disappointed huff of breath. "I don't remember anything related to a drawing like this."

She took a sip of tea to warm her chilled insides and then gently placed her fingers on the face of whom she believed to be her mother. Without warning, a violent force pulsated up her arm and then throughout her entire body, and she quickly grabbed onto the swing to steady herself. Her next instinct was to call out for David to help her, but as she opened her mouth to scream, she unmistakably sensed the calming stroke of a hand on top of her head, followed by the whispering of a woman's voice.

"You're the core of this family, my child. It begins with you."

Iana felt as though she'd had the wind knocked out of her. Even as she struggled to stand, she was aware of a force greater than her own strength holding her captive. Using her last bit of strength, she managed to whip her head around, frantically searching for a face to place with the voice she had just heard.

"What begins with me?" she shouted into the night.

"Iana, who are you talking to?" David burst through the screen door and stopped dead in his tracks to find Iana's face drained of color, her complexion white and horrified. He reached out and laid his hand over hers.

"Are you feeling alright?"

She looked into her husband's eyes, still unable to speak. Giving a little shrug, she lowered herself back down onto the swing.

She was silent for a long moment. "You know, David, I'm probably just exhausted." She gave herself a little shake. "I probably just need a good night's sleep."

"Sure. Come on." David put his arm around her and helped her inside, promising to take Cilla's three o'clock feeding so she could rest.

After one last glance at the swing, she walked inside and headed up to bed.

As she lay beneath her sheets, she was more determined than ever to uncover whatever her past life held. What secrets were trapped in those notepads, in those drawings? What was buried so deep within her mind that she ordinarily kept it locked inside? Whatever she had experienced, she resolved she would know. And, after she knew, accept.

The next day, Iana spent the afternoon rummaging through boxes of her old notepads. There were sixteen of them in all, and as far as she could tell, nine of them were following her rescue from Egypt, from while she was in the orphanage and during her early days in the United States. The remaining seven were done throughout her adolescent years. It made her feel warm to look at them.

With Cilla visiting her grandparents for the evening, this was the ideal opportunity to launch an investigation into her past and hopefully discover the motive behind the spine-chilling happening from the night before.

"These have to be over twenty years old," she said, brushing off the dust from the well-worn covers.

For the next hour, she paged through drawing after drawing, observing that the majority of her illustrations were quite detailed and outwardly profound while others were a trouble-free child's drawings, stick figures almost.

She pressed her fingers to the center of her forehead and rubbed hard. "Why didn't I study art? These drawings are incredible."

Then she noticed more than a few of her illustrations incorporated Bible verses, which provoked the question: who had taught her the Bible and at what point? She had absolutely no recollection of attending a church or even of a pastor living in or around her home village.

"I-I don't know." She paused, touching her forehead again.

Iana became aware of tiny numbers scribbled in the lower right hand corner of some pages. She tilted her head for a closer look.

"What's this?" she murmured, surprised to hear the sound of her own voice. "Looks like I dated the work, but only with a day and a month. Why not a year?"

She was quiet, alternately glancing out the window and then back to the numbers.

"This doesn't make any sense, but then again, these entire notepads don't seem to make much sense."

Now dog-tired and discouraged, she rubbed her eyes with her hands and decided to call it a day. "I probably will never know if the scenes these pictures portray actually happened in my life."

Tension slowly gathered at the base of her neck as she moved to gather up the stack of notepads.

"Most likely they are just the product of an overactive imagination." She shook her head and then placed the notepads back into the box.

Just then, her eyes caught a glimpse of a withered and worn notepad tucked under one of the flaps at the bottom of the box. At first she waved it off, fully intending to look at it another time. But soon, exactly as it happened the night before, she became fully aware of being led by some strange force, and she found herself reaching her hand into the box and pulling out the old notepad.

"Is this the notepad I had with me when I was rescued?" She felt her emotions surging. "It is, isn't it?" She pulled the quilt from off the back of her chair and settled in.

"This might be a huge mistake, but here goes!"

Iana stretched out her legs and flipped open the notepad, then squirmed around in her chair, trying to get comfortable again. So far, most of the entries were more of the same; there were some very detailed drawings of a mother, a child and a little black dog, and then there were other, more childlike drawings.

"This is a wild goose chase." She frowned. "I might have to put this aside."

But despite her feelings, Iana wasn't ready to throw in the towel just yet. She turned over the next few pages and then abruptly stopped, her eyes wide open.

"Floating...afraid...floating...afraid...floating...afraid." The bizarre phrase filled the entire page. After that, the words filled another page and then another. Unexpectedly her heart began to race, and she was shivering as if she had fallen into a frozen lake. She clenched her fists tightly into balls and realized they were drenched with cold sweat.

"What's happening to me? God help me... Am I having a heart attack?"

Gasping for air, she fumbled to the next page, hoping to uncover the answer to the puzzling phrase. She turned the page to find nothing but a change in the wording.

"Floating...afraid" became "safe...not safe...safe...not safe." She clapped her hands over her ears, desperately trying to put a wedge between the chilling phrases that kept repeating in her head.

For a brief period of time the words ceased, and little by little she began to relax her hands as she felt warmth being restored all through her body.

She desperately wanted to slam the notepad shut and forget what had just happened, but now she was determined to find answers to what had gone unanswered for too long. She stared at the words for a few minutes then tentatively placed her fingertips on the pages and rotated them slowly back and forth. For a brief moment she felt strangely peaceful.

Then, gradually, she began to feel a slight quiver—but then it wasn't a quiver. She cringed in pain as she sat in stillness, trying to relax her aching arms and shoulders from the relentless surges that pulsated throughout her body, simultaneously wanting and not wanting to know about her past. She tried to say something, but her voice got trapped in her throat.

Her eyes locked on the written words again, and suddenly she was forced back, way back, somewhere in her mind. A feeling of peace and painlessness, but not a feeling of being dead, surrounded her; she sensed herself moving up or through a narrow passageway, a tunnel experience. She was a spectator, without any control over her own body.

As if she was moving about in slow motion, Iana watched silently as her own hand stretched across the desk and then picked up a pencil; to her amazement she began to draw a crude picture on the pad. Within a few moments, the instantly-recognizable image took shape right before her eyes: a little girl, completely naked, with huge black oval eyes and an indisputable expression of grief on her face. Without interruption she moved the pencil slightly right of the little girl and hurriedly began sketching the woman—the same portrayal she had drawn so many times in the past. Her dark eyes and mouth were wide open, and a straight line of huge teardrops ran down her face. Not missing a beat, Iana flipped to the next page and once again began to sketch an illustration. She began with layers of thick black clouds covering the top section of the page and then added a narrow, cone-shaped beam that projected from within the dark clouds straight down to the ground. Within the cone-shaped projection and just above her mother's outstretched arms, she drew the little girl floating, spread eagle and in midair. She wrote the word "NO" inside a circle and added a straight line connecting the circle to the woman's wide open mouth. Finally she scribbled the date 1781 at the bottom right corner of the page.

Then her body and mind were still.

Fear blew through Iana. Stunned and shaken to her core, she slid off the chair and rounded her body into the fetal position, beginning to sob so hard she could barely breathe.

A gust of wind rattled the windows, jolting her back to reality.

She sat quietly until her heart rate slowed to normal, until her twisted nerves and faintness eased a little more. The light had gone out of the day before she could muster enough strength to pull herself up from the floor. Briskly rubbing her arms for warmth, she was very grateful David had offered to pick Cilla up from her play date at her grandparents' house. Despite her trembling legs, Iana managed to walk into the bathroom to splash some water on her face. She rinsed out the washcloth and hung it up; when she finished massaging in her night cream, she caught a glance of her face in the mirror over the sink.

"What the hell happened to me?"

She felt her muscles tighten and quickly she looked away, bewildered. Then, from somewhere deep inside, a subtle thought planted itself within her mind.

"There is more for you to learn."

Over the next six weeks, Iana's mind shuffled between wanting and not wanting to know about what had happened to her as a child. Her degree in psychology supplied her with sufficient knowledge regarding the power of the mind. She was aware of the mind's innate ability to shield itself from harm by burying a traumatic event so deep that it is possible not to remember the ordeal for years and years.

Iana had observed this on a daily basis in her work with the children from her "trash class." Something horrific had happened to each them, an incident they either had observed or were actually involved in, one so terrible they couldn't bear to be reminded of it. And now it was conceivable for her to think that something horrific might have happened to her as well. Iana was also well aware of the fact that the longer she chose not to deal with the alleged traumatic events of her past, the more she would dissociate with them in order to protect herself from being horrified again.

She stood at the cross-roads of wanting and not wanting. Did she have the strength and courage to dig deep into her past? She hadn't asked for any of this, nor did she have a clue as to where to begin this journey. Wouldn't it be easier just to dissociate and move forward with the only life she knew to be real?

It was a typical Sunday morning church service. After shaking hands with the pastor and having a brief conversation with the choir director, Iana went straight home and made a beeline into the nursery to check on Cilla. She stood quietly in the doorway to Cilla's nursery, listening to the sound of David's voice reading from Cilla's favorite children's book, *Piggly Wiggly*. Every so often Cilla's little voice giggled with appreciation, melting the worry from Iana's face and calming the deep gnawing from her unidentified and mysterious past, replacing her unease with a smile.

"All is as it should be," she thought.

Iana turned, walked back into the living room and peeled out of her jacket, and then she sat down on the couch. Sunday afternoon was her favorite part of the day, her quiet time with the Lord, a time for her to reflect and give thanks for all that He had done in her life. She leaned back on the couch, intending to relax and listen to the rain that had started beating against the windows, but instead her mind drifted back to Pastor Chambers's sermon and to the Scripture reading for the day. *Isaiah 41:10: "Fear thou not; for I am with thee, be not dismayed; for I am thy God: I will strengthen you, I will help thee, I will uphold thee with the right hand of my righteousness."*

Pastor Chambers had spoken of God having each and every person in the palm of His hand—that He had designed everyone specifically for the race he or she was in and promised that He would never leave nor forsake them. And no matter people's trials and tribulations in this life, God had them right where they were supposed to be. *Do not fear! No weapon formed against us shall prosper.*

Iana closed her eyes. She didn't expect to sleep, but she drifted into a half-state caught between sleep and wakefulness, which she often found more comforting. Out of the blue, the words "*Father's right hand*" floated like incense into her mind. She sensed being loved, but this kind of love went far beyond what any human had the capacity to feel. She felt safe and unafraid; she felt alive with an overwhelming sense of peace and joy. Deep within her spirit, a distinct knowing was rising up; God was speaking to her, passing on to her that not only her daughter's life was as it should be, but that Iana could now find peace in knowing that all was as it should be within her life as well.

For an instant, and only an instant, Iana thought she had seen her mother in an elegant white dress standing at the foot of the couch.

She bolted upright and stared directly at the coffee table and then at the Bible her parents had given her for graduation. She nervously held a hand to it, as if even now it threatened to rebel against her. Iana hesitated, afraid of what would come next, but then she opened her Bible and scanned the pages, not sure what book or verse she should turn to. Unexpectedly, she stopped at the book of Jeremiah and thought for a moment. Cautiously, she turned page after page, finally ending her search with the twenty-ninth chapter, verse eleven: *"For I know the thoughts that I think toward you, says the Lord, thoughts of peace, and not of evil, to give you a future and a hope."*

Next to the page with the scripture verse was one of the pages that her parents had purposely inserted for her illustrations. And there on the page was a heartwarming picture of a father and mother, each holding the hand of their tiny daughter. She had depicted the scene in every detail; their faces were highlighted with joyful smiles, all beaming from ear to ear, as several tiny birds flew among the white puffy clouds, and a huge, bright yellow sun shone in the upper right hand corner.

She looked away, waving a hand in front of her face as she sat on the side of the couch.

"I'd like to think this was simply the heart's desire of every little girl, to be married and have children..." she trailed off. But she had a strange feeling this drawing may have represented something different.

Once more her eyes fixated on the scripture and a date clearly written in the bottom right hand corner: *Jeremiah 29:11... May 25, 1916.*

"Oh my God," she said, placing her hand on her chest. "Are you kidding me?"

It didn't scare her, but she definitely thought it was weird.

"May 25, 1916... That is the day David and I got married!"

This set in motion an unsettling and recurring thought, and chills raced up her spine. She snapped the Bible shut.

"The day this picture was drawn, was I foretelling my own future, right down to my wedding day?"

She took one long breath, then another.

"I'm not crazy, but this *is* crazy!" She sprang up from the couch and paced the room. "I'm not a crazy person, I know it!"

Iana didn't respond any further. She didn't have to. There was a heavy silence in the room while she dwelled in her own thoughts.

She admitted to herself that something bad and definitely unexplainable may have happened to her, and yes, maybe her brain didn't work like most other people's.

"I've been forcing myself to figure this out, and it's not working," she said, shaking her head.

Being in the world of the unknown scared her; she hated what it was doing to her, and she felt helpless to do anything about it. Now more than ever she knew that she didn't want to try to dig up her past or be connected to the meaning behind her drawings. Iana scolded herself, trying to believe that just because she uncovered some ancient notepads with dubious drawings in them didn't mean she should uproot her entire life or her family's. Her life was good and, despite all else, it went on, with its duties and obligations, its irritations and its pleasures. Her everyday reality didn't need to change.

"The mirror," she gasped as the memory of the words telling her she had "*more to learn*" snapped into her mind. Immediately she felt her body tense up. "Stop," she told herself. "It's okay."

Iana took a deep breath and let it out gradually. Then, glancing into the next room at David and Cilla, she decided to join them to clear her mind and calm her nerves. She sat down in the recliner, shifted her body to get comfortable, put her feet up on the ottoman and then let her head sink into the feathery pillow. A tiny smile crossed her lips and her heartbeat slowed to its normal pace as she tucked a warm comforter under her chin.

Thankfully David and Cilla remained totally engrossed in *Piggly Wiggly,* leaving her free to carry on with her self-help psychoanalysis.

"Okay Iana, the person you saw in the mirror was you," she scolded herself under her breath. For some odd reason that made her smile. Her thoughts then reminded her that she was all grown up, and whatever happened to her, those things had gone deep inside her mind—and while they were locked away, a lot of time had gone by. "*This* Iana got married and *this* Iana lives with David. *This* Iana has a daughter, and *this* Iana doesn't live back there anymore; she lives here. Nothing bad is going to happen to you here. *This* Iana is all grown up."

Iana shook her head. To some extent sitting and quietly talking to herself embarrassed her, but she had to confess this modus operandi was comforting, lifting her spirits and dispelling the anxiety of wanting to know.

"Iana is all grown up," she said softly and closed her eyes.

"Y-yeah, Iana is all grown up." Having overheard her last statement, David leaned over and gently kissed her lips.

Iana opened her eyes and smiled, and as she did, her shoulders relaxed and her tears came freely.

Puzzled by her reaction for a moment, David put the book down and began to search for the right words. Unable to find them, he comforted her by just staying by her side in silence, keeping a reassuring arm around their daughter.

After a few minutes, Iana began to calm down. She leaned over and gently touched David's face. She softly caressed his hair and then held out her hand, and, looking at him with a gentle smile, said brightly, "Would you two like some peanut butter and jelly sandwiches and some juice?"

David scooped Cilla up and lifted her onto his shoulders. Then he made a mad dash out of the bedroom, down the hall and towards the kitchen.

Iana lingered behind for a moment and then, with her head tilted to one side, she nodded slightly.

"My past doesn't get to weigh in on all of this. I know it'll take some time, but it's gonna be okay."

On her way to the kitchen she stopped in the hallway to look at her reflection in the mirror.

"*This* is what Iana looks like now!" she declared.

Getting back to business as usual made it easier for Iana to be in control of her thoughts and the images that played like a silent movie in her mind. She continued to remain focused and fought against the subtle beckoning to set aside her obligations as a wife and mother for her notepad and pen, although the urges, especially at first, were always unsolicited and several times even took her by force.

As the years went on, Iana didn't object to a certain amount of this mind game; it simply indicated to her that she had a lot in her head. The option to sit and illustrate her thoughts was now of her own choosing rather than the result of a supernatural compulsion to do so.

Today was a day to put everything else aside. There were things to be done. In only a few hours, her home would be filled with the chatter and giggles of six little girls anxiously awaiting the arrival of the last guest so the celebration of Cilla's sixth birthday party could begin. Iana had spared no expense; each little girl was given a goody-bag filled with candies and party favors, and she had planned party games such as Pin the Tail on the Donkey and Duck-Duck Goose. A dozen or so Happy Birthday pink streamers and balloons floated from side to side throughout her living room.

With her hands on her hips, she eased back, her eyes open and direct. "Well, that should do it!"

Then she turned her attention to the task of story selection. Anyone who knew Iana Hamilton was well aware of the fact that a children's event at her house wouldn't be complete until all had gathered on the front porch to hear her recite a story. Whether reading from a book or making it up as she went along, she had the neighborhood children mesmerized by her every word. She was affectionately referred to as the "Story Teller."

Today Iana had chosen to read from the popular Dick and Jane series of books.

Once the rest of the festivities were over, Cilla and her guests patiently sat on the front porch, waiting and wondering what story Cilla's mother had selected to tell today. Finally Iana walked out and sat down in the rocker directly across from her audience; she adjusted her glasses and then glanced down at the little girls, who were sitting all in a row and decked out in their Sunday best with their little hands joined together.

"How lovely," she thought.

After she had finished reading the story, the girls ran out into the yard to play until their parents arrived to take them home. Iana thought it pleasant to sit out like this on a warm spring afternoon. Pleasant, too, was listening to Cilla play with her friends. The sounds turned back her memory clock, and she wondered if those same sounds were a part of her childhood.

"Mama, look what I picked for you!" Cilla shoved a small bouquet of yellow dandelions and white clover practically smack-dab in her face.

"Sweetie, they are beautiful!" She leaned back to get a better look then gave Cilla a kiss on her cheek. Smiling, Iana squeezed her eyes shut, inhaled two deep breaths and lifted her head high. She then opened her eyes to find herself face-to-face with a pair of jet-black almond-shaped eyes staring directly into hers. Almost instinctively she began swatting her hands in the air, as if to keep away an unrelenting insect, and consequently her movements knocked the flowers from Cilla's hands, scattering them onto the ground. Her breathing immediately became erratic and deep, and she experienced the sensation of being trapped; something was pressing on her chest. She turned away, and the more she ignored the haunting eyes, the worse things got. She sprang out of her chair and paced the front porch.

"*What do you want...? Help me... Come and get me!*" launched into her mind.

Totally unaware of her startled and now frightened daughter, Iana covered her face with her hands and whispered, "Oh God, I'm not watching this. Please, God, help me!"

The sound of her child weeping off in the distance unleashed within her a force more powerful than the one that was holding her captive in this moment. Little by little, she was able to sever her mind and then her body from the unrelenting torment that had taken control. She shuddered once, and she was back.

Instantly she ran over and knelt down beside Cilla, scooping her trembling little body up into her arms. She held on as tight as she could and gently rocked back and forth until Cilla settled down.

"Honey, I'm so sorry. Please don't cry!"

"Mama, didn't you like my flowers?" she asked, choking on each of her words.

"I love your flowers." She kissed Cilla's tear-stained cheek and gave her a big squeeze until Cilla began to giggle.

"Mama, are you okay?"

Iana set Cilla back onto the porch, stood up, and smiled brilliantly. "I'm fine." She held out her hand for Cilla's, saying, "Ya know what? I thought I saw a bee sitting on those beautiful flowers, and it scared me. Mama got kind of confused. That's all."

But, in reality, that was the straw that broke the camel's back. This vicious curse that had overwhelmed her for months now was responsible for distress within her child. Rage spewed through her, burning and vile, and in this moment she had another vision, only this vision was initiated completely of her own doing.

"I don't care if the Praying Mantis is one of the most beloved insects," she spoke very softly.

Cilla, noticing the insect just moments after her mother, piped up, "Mama look! It wasn't a bee. It looks like a stick!"

It took all Iana could muster not to carry out the vision of beating this insect senseless and then tossing it into the trash.

But for fear of upsetting Cilla again, Iana anxiously leaned in to examine the Mantis. Her hands clasped together, and she fought valiantly not to wince as this cleverly-disguised beast hid among the leaves and then swiveled its head to scan the surroundings.

"Ya know, Honey, it *does* look like a stick." She lifted a finger and wagged it before Cilla's face before she could speak. "Mama was silly… Now run along and play with Maggie before she has to go home."

Apparently calm, Iana picked up the flowers, ever-watchful for the clever beast, and then arranged them into a bouquet. However, before she went inside to put them in water, she took a few moments to watch Cilla playing tag with Maggie. In that moment a line was drawn in the sand. She silently vowed to her daughter that she would never be the innocent recipient of her mother's baffling outbursts of lunacy, which by now, Iana linked to the haunting events of many years gone by.

Over the summer months, everything inside her calmed—even when she looked at the old notepads with the destructive images she had conjured up in the past. These days Iana took great pride in knowing she had honored her promise to Cilla.

In spite of everything, there had been several occasions when Iana mulled over the possibility of flying to Egypt and personally interviewing every living soul in and around her village. And with every thought of returning to Egypt also came the heartbreaking question: Just where would that village be? Sadly, the answer was always the same; she hadn't a clue as to the actual date, time or place of her birth. Yes, Greenwich Orphanage would surely be able to provide her with some information, including the location where archaeologists had rescued her, and just maybe, the village of her birth was in close proximity to that. But at the end of the day, she had to confess that there were too many *maybes* and that she had no business flying to Egypt. Besides, the airfare alone would have eaten a large hole in her family's budget, and she doubted that even a few men or women would still be alive or have any recollection of whom or what she was talking about.

In her heart, Iana believed she had fixed the problem, and she continued to live her life finding great comfort and strength in her faith. Praying the Serenity Prayer every day, she asked God to grant her the serenity to accept the things she could not change, the courage to change the things she could, and the wisdom to know the difference.

No one knew better than Iana that life never stayed stationary. Cycles were essential, for without them there was no bloom.

"Speaking of blooms," she said aloud, interrupting her thoughts as her eyes scanned the flood of red carnations, white daisies and blue asters that had sprung up in her yard. With World War I underway, Iana chose this design in support of the past war effort taking place in her neighborhood. The fragrance of roses that climbed up the arbor at the end of the front porch lingered in the air while a brilliant beam of golden sun illuminated the white roses she'd planted herself, as a personal acknowledgment to those men who had made the highest sacrifice during the war.

With crystal blue skies and a balmy breeze, it was the perfect day for gardening, she thought.

She adjusted her old straw gardening hat, yanked at the waist of the men's pants that she always wore while doing this type of work and then glanced down at her drooping flowers, currently overrun with wild flowers and weeds of all kinds.

"I have no idea what this is," she said, brushing a hand absently over her cheek, transferring a smudge of soil. "Looks like a feather duster!"

Despite the heat and humidity of the summer afternoon, her garden was in desperate need of attention. Thankfully, she enjoyed working in her garden and had done so since she was a little girl. Fondly remembering her childhood, she thought about sitting alongside her mother, Margaret Hamilton, who instructed her in the art of planting and caring for flowers. And Margaret Hamilton definitely considered it an art, particularly since her blooms won First in Show three years in a row and were featured from time to time in *Flower Garden News*.

So now, today, Iana took great pleasure in paying attention to detail as she worked in her garden. Carefully, she raised a brilliant yellow bunch of marigolds out of the plastic pack and then gently lowered the flowers into the soil, which she had prepared earlier. Keeping her eyes on her hands, she spread the soil and packed it snugly around the plant, and then smiled and thought, *"This is just as Mama taught me."*

Iana sat back on her heels and heaved a heavy sigh.

"I miss you, Mama," she whispered, placing a hand over her heart.

At that moment Iana's mind was flooded with more thoughts of how her mother had taught her how to press the soil around each plant by placing her own hands on top of Iana's.

Just remembering that, Iana took another breath, this time a stronger one as tears spilled from her eyes and trickled down her cheeks.

"Mama, you not only taught me how to tend a garden; you taught me how to be a mother myself."

She gave a nod and then took the bandanna from her forehead and wiped the tears from her eyes. At that same moment, she dredged up something more Margaret Hamilton had taught her. Laughing out loud, Iana fell back onto the grass and recited those infamous words her mother had articulated each and every autumn when she disposed of all the dead and dying foliage in her gardens.

"2 Corinthians 5:17: Old things pass away and all things become new."

"Iana, fall is the season of dying, but Honey, don't you worry. Spring will always come and all will be new. Just like in life!"

She laughed again and then became intensely aware of the fact that three years ago her adoptive mother had passed away, on a day quite similar to this one. Her mother had been working in her garden all morning on a hot July day, so she decided to sit down in her glider to rest; it was a longer rest than anyone had expected, though, because her mother fell asleep and never woke up.

"How 'bout that." Iana shuddered at the memory and decided it was time to call it a day. Instead of resting in her glider as her mother had done on that fateful day, Iana chose to unwind by sitting with Cilla and Maggie beneath a large oak tree, a safe distance from any porch swings.

"No point in tempting the fates." She tipped her head back and studied the sky.

As she sat enjoying the splendor of God's heavenly creation, afternoon faded to evening, and the first star became visible in the east. To her surprise, a radiant beam of white light materialized just slightly off to the right of the star. As Iana concentrated on this strange phenomenon, all at once she experienced the hair-raising sensation of being watched.

Iana sat motionless, her face showing her intense concentration.

"I am in the present!" She paused, turning away from Cilla and Maggie as not to disturb them, then sucked in air, gasping it bit by bit. Quietly, she reminded herself, "Focus your eyes on what's in front of you."

A few minutes later, Iana turned back to Cilla and Maggie, who were sitting cross-legged on the blanket, giggling and serving tea to their baby dolls and other invited guests.

"There is no one watching you!" Iana said firmly. "Focus your eyes on what's in front of you," she reminded herself again.

"Go ahead, reach out and touch them!" she inwardly commanded herself.

Iana decided to go with her thoughts and reached out her arms, grabbing Cilla in one and Maggie in the other.

"Oh you girls!" She then kissed both girls' cheeks in a couple of quick pecks. "Who gives a darn anyway? Just because you think something, that doesn't mean it's true!"

With a laugh, Iana shook her head, released her girls, and joined them for a cup of tea and a chocolate chip cookie.

The remaining summer months went on without incident. Iana and her family, along with Maggie, enjoyed a summer vacation at the beach, a trip to the Philadelphia Zoo and countless picnics in the park.

All was as it should be.

2

Twenty-eight years later...

Iana Hamilton Holmes
1896 – 1946
Beloved Wife and Mother

The insignificant life of an orphaned little girl
led to a story of greatness in the life of
Iana Hamilton Holmes.

The memorial service was exactly as Iana would have wanted it to be: small and intimate. Gorgeous sprays of white roses, lilies and carnations stood at each end of her dark, mahogany coffin. White roses together with angelic pink blooms in white wicker baskets that spilled over with gladioli and carnations decorated the base of the altar and lined the center aisle. As a final point, a beautiful silver picture frame held the photograph of Cilla's parents that was taken on their wedding day. Both were smiling, and their happiness was easy to see, as the photo was placed at eye-level, front and center before Iana's coffin. Cilla smiled through her tears, knowing her beautiful mother had a consummate passion for life, love and people.

A number of Iana's dear friends offered beautiful, heartfelt tributes to the strong woman, which only reinforced to Cilla the depth of their devotion and affection towards her mother. She could feel her mother all around her, and a peaceful knowing that her mother knew what was happening and that she, too, was at peace permeated her mind. Even in death, Iana was a source of continuous reassurance. It only made Cilla cry more.

James Woodrow, one of her mother's oldest and dearest friends, hurried over to her, put his hand on her shoulder, then took her hand in his and leaned down.

"Come on now, my sweet Cilla, please don't cry. You'll break this old man's heart. Come on now." He reached into his back pocket and pulled out a perfectly folded white handkerchief and handed it to her.

Mr. Woodrow was filled with sorrow as well. "She was a fine woman," he said over and over.

"God, I miss them," she said, wiping her eyes. "They still seem so alive, even on paper."

Cilla wept as she silently struggled to sort out the emotions that came with losing both parents.

The unanticipated sickness and death of her father, David, followed a year later by the sickness and death of her mother and best friend had left Cilla emotionally in limbo, in the ashes of lost love, lost lives and possibly her own shattered identity. The only family she knew was gone; she had no brothers or sisters. Her childhood friend, Maggie, was the closest she had to having a sister, but it had been years since she had seen or heard from her.

Her cheeks burned with the remembrance of the last time she had seen Maggie. Folding her arms across her chest, she couldn't shake the images of that day out of her head. She smiled as she remembered Maggie joyfully skipping across the yard, shouting to her that she would be right back; she was only going home to get another book for Iana to read. The next day rumors began to surface about little Maggie opening the front door to her home and finding her father sprawled out on the living room floor, his head forcefully turning from one side to the other, muscle spasms shaking his entire body and froth foaming from his mouth. After that he had lost consciousness, the shaking had stopped, and his skin turned the color of concrete, leaving his body lifeless and his eyes glazed. Alongside his body were a bottle of pills and an empty bottle of vodka.

Later, Cilla occasionally would hear her mother quietly talking with the neighbors about that day. Some said Maggie darted from room to room in absolute horror while others spoke of Maggie's spine-chilling behavior, of her walking over to her father and then sitting for almost an hour at the side of his motionless body, mimicking a mother caring for her child, softly humming a childlike tune while lovingly caressing his hair and carefully dabbing the drool from his chin.

She had also heard that Maggie's mother was terribly grief-stricken, and some said that Maggie herself never really recovered. Not long after her father's death, Maggie and her mother unexpectedly moved to northern New Jersey and were never heard from again.

Cilla stiffened, momentarily taken aback by her thoughts.

Just then, all eyes turned to the back of the church, several people gasped and voices murmured, whispering about the shadowy woman now standing in the doorway. Cilla assessed the woman with a critical squint, and after what seemed like an eternity, the mysterious character leisurely made her way down the center aisle to stop and stand alongside the pew where Cilla was seated.

Cilla studied her face for a few minutes, presuming the woman to be around her own age. She came across as scared and angry, wisps of wavy hair falling casually on her forehead and only accentuating the deep crease between her eyebrows. The tall, thin woman with dark brown eyes and long, black, wavy hair remained motionless before Cilla, gripping a ratty-looking handbag.

"Could this be Maggie?" she thought.

The woman nodded bashfully. "You don't recognize me?"

After a few minutes, a tear began to roll down Cilla's cheek. "Maggie?" Then she asked a second time, "Maggie, is that you?"

"It's me." Her emotions overtook her and she began to sob.

Cilla quickly stepped forward and pulled her close, comforting her and offering the support she needed while facing a few of the guests who were still eyeing her with disregard. All the while, Maggie didn't weaken.

"You'll sit with me." Cilla gestured for her to take a seat. "Where have you been all these years? Maggie, nobody knew if you were dead or alive. To tell the truth, people didn't know what to think after you left."

Maggie nodded in understanding. "I called your mom a few times but hung up whenever she answered the phone."

"Why would you do that?" Cilla asked.

"I don't know. Just scared I suppose."

After the vocalist finished singing Amazing Grace, Maggie looked at Cilla and smiled.

"When I was little, when I had trouble in my life, Mama Iana would tell me to hand that trouble over to her. She told me that my shoulders weren't big enough to carry so much trouble. She always made me feel better."

"I know she loved you."

"I loved her too, and I really have missed her."

Maggie's eyes were bloodshot, her shoulders were slumped, and everything about her suggested a deep sadness.

"Maggie, I'd be more than happy if you would join us for the luncheon after the service."

"I'd like that. I really would."

"We can talk more then." Cilla took one of Maggie's hands in hers and gave a tight squeeze. "I'm so glad you're here."

Cilla didn't know how or why Maggie had suddenly appeared in the church. But she *did* know that she didn't want to deny her the chance to say good-bye to a woman she had loved as deeply, if not more deeply, than her own mother.

"The service was beautiful," Mr. Woodrow stated, coming up beside Cilla once again. "Honey, you did a wonderful job. Now get something to eat; you're eating for two now, after all!"

Maggie looked her up and down. "You're pregnant!" she exclaimed.

Cilla smiled. "Yes I am. I'm going to be a mom in about three months. Mark and I have been trying to get pregnant for about three years."

"You look beautiful; you're going to be a wonderful mother."

"I was taught by the best!" Cilla's eyes got watery. "I wish Mama would have lived long enough to meet her first grandchild." Cilla wiped a tear from her cheek and then rubbed a hand over her bulging belly. She took a tissue from her purse, blew her nose, and returned the tissue to its place.

"I know, Honey. So do I." Mark, who had approached while she wasn't looking, placed his arm around her shoulders and then gently kissed her cheek. "I think it's time we get you something to eat and then get you home."

Throughout the luncheon, Cilla and Maggie talked about their childhoods. Maggie seemed overjoyed to hear the story of Cilla's life. Cilla, on the other hand, wanted to yell. Maggie told her that shortly after she and her mother moved to New Jersey, Maggie's mother met a man named Don, and they moved in with him. He was into all kinds of drugs and alcohol, but he looked after them. Her mother didn't have to work; instead, Don had her selling drugs to bring in money.

"Not exactly what I pictured for my life. Ranks right up there with seeing my father dead on the floor." She thought about her words for a moment, then added, "Except worse somehow."

"I'm so sorry for your loss; I never got to tell you that."

"After Mom got arrested, I lived on the streets, stayed in some shelters whenever I could. I did get a job in a bookstore; the owner took pity on me and let me stay in his back room until I saved up enough money for my own apartment."

"Praise God you're safe! Praise God." After only a momentary pause, she asked, "Maggie, why didn't you come to us?"

"I was too ashamed." Her eyes watered.

"Well, now you know Mark and I will do whatever we can, give you any help you need. Don't worry." Tears fell from her eyes. It broke her heart knowing her friend was in so much pain. "Hey, I have an idea." Cilla slid close to Maggie and looped her arm through hers. "Why don't you come home with Mark and me tonight? You can sleep in our guest room."

"Thanks, but I had planned on taking the eight o'clock bus back to New Jersey."

"Oh no, Maggie... oh no, you don't get to walk back into my life after all this time and leave now!"

Maggie hesitated a moment before saying, "I want you to know, I never did drugs or sold my body for money."

Cilla reached down and took Maggie by the hand. "The thought never entered my mind."

"I'd really like to spend the night with you and Mark. If you'll have me." She glanced up at Cilla. "Thank you for your kindness."

"Now, that's a good sister!" Cilla patted Maggie's hand and smiled.

Maggie was glad to be home.

It was late in the day by the time they returned to Cilla's house from the service. After Maggie was settled in her room, Mark and Cilla left her alone to rest. She tried reading a book, but she fell asleep after only a couple of pages. Almost two hours later, though, just a little past midnight, she woke up. Her tossing and turning for nearly thirty minutes proved to be fruitless, and she resigned herself to the fact that sleep wasn't going to come anytime soon. Maggie lay in bed thinking about her mother and the succession of men that had been in and out of their lives. A large part of the memories she had of her father had been shaped and twisted over the years until she had created her own truth, a truth she could find peace with. Her perception had become her reality.

The life-changing shock and grief of discovering her father's dead body was only compounded by her mother's recklessness and total disregard for Maggie's emotional well-being during the years that followed.

"I was just a kid!" She pounded her hand against the bed.

The memories infuriated her as though the events they contained had happened just a day or so ago rather than decades in the past.

She sat up in bed and instantaneously felt a jab of pain inside her head. After that she began hearing the recurring clatter of voices, communicating their unreserved and forceful opinions to her.

"Kiss my ass," she whispered.

Maggie was quiet for a few seconds, then she slowly and watchfully scooted back against the headboard and curled up into a ball, tugging anxiously at the sheet until it was snug under her chin. Next she raised her eyes and fretfully scanned the bedroom. Longing to relax her mind, she then closed her eyes and sighed so deeply that every muscle in her body tightened and then released into a state of euphoria. Her eyes still closed, she became aware of her breathing, relaxed and even.

Confident now that the clatter in her head had come to a standstill, she allowed herself to dig deep into her mind. Instantly her mind drifted to the image of her father. With her breathing becoming more erratic, Maggie inched her way to the edge of the bed and sat for a moment. Then, struggling to her feet, she unsteadily made her way into the bathroom. Once there, she supported herself with her hands on either side of the sink, and anticipation slowly began to creep up her spine. She leaned forward and looked into the mirror.

Without warning, the words, "*Give Maggie the message... The message... Your father... A message,*" vehemently returned to her energized mind.

She could feel the tension mounting once again inside of her. Breathing more heavily, she could *see* the emptiness she felt at that moment. Right then Maggie made up her mind; she nervously looked around the bathroom and then back to her reflection in the mirror. With a nod of agreement, she said out loud, "My message is here."

The streetlight cast a glow like twilight around the living room; it was just enough for Maggie to see several boxes piled up in the corner with the word "Mom" written on their sides. In some otherworldliness, she glided across the living room floor to the boxes, then reached for the top box and set it on the floor. She quickly ripped off the masking tape and, with the words, *"Give Maggie the message,"* repeating loudly in her head, she groped and slashed through one box after another. When the last box was empty and Iana's notepads were scattered about on the floor, Maggie began gasping for air and sobbing hysterically, realizing any hope of locating the source of her endless torment was as empty as the boxes that surrounded her.

Then, suddenly, she stopped crying. Sitting back and combing her fingers nervously through her hair, she summoned up her memories of *that* day. She closed her eyes and focused; in her mind's eye she saw herself running across the lawn back to Iana's house, up the front steps and across the porch, yanking open the front door and running inside. She remembered standing inside, knowing Mama Iana promised to take Cilla and her to the park. Screaming for Mama Iana, she ran down the hall into the kitchen and then back into the living room. She was shouting, her eyes darting all around as if Iana might hop out from a hiding place and shout "Boo!" But finally, she recalled that Mama Iana had a few errands to run and, thus, was nowhere to be found. Feeling dejected and alone, she dragged herself back to her house.

On the verge of tears again, Maggie opened her eyes, shrugged her shoulders and took one last look around the room. A momentary look at the Crucifix hanging above the doorway to the kitchen sparked in her a memory of Iana's vast collection of her own Crucifixes.

"The Bible... I saw the picture of my father in a Bible," she said softly.

With fear and suspense rising in her belly, in her mind she saw a child looking down at Iana's Bible, which was lying open on the floor. The outline of a man's body had been penciled in on the page, stretched out on the ground, with black circles for eyes and a mouth wide open. From his mouth a straight line was attached to a small circle above his head, devoid of any words. Sprinkled alongside his body were little round specks and an empty bottle. The date on the page indicated the illustration had been drawn a week prior to her father's actual death. At the bottom of the page, written in Iana's handwriting, were an asterisk and the words, "*Message for Maggie.*"

With her heart beating wildly and the eerie words droning on and on, she closed her eyes and silently prayed that somehow this would all go away—that she wouldn't have to deal with it anymore and that she'd get her life back.

Maggie dabbed her eyes with her sleeve, and as she was hoisting herself up from the floor, her eyes were instantly drawn to the Bible sitting on Cilla's coffee table, only a few feet away from her.

Her eyes narrowed, refocusing. "Could this be Iana's Bible?"

Idly, she tapped her fingers on the table, closed her eyes in amazement, and curved her lips as she let the tension drain away. Was this an answer to her prayer or a gift from her father, or both, wrapped up with a pretty bow and sitting right in front of her? At long last could her tortuous journey be over?

After a minute, she opened the Bible and began turning page after page, anxiously searching for an explanation to the words that had haunted her for years.

She leaned into the Bible and asked in a loud whisper, "Where's my message?"

Suddenly the rustling sounds coming from Mark and Cilla's bedroom gave her a tingling feeling, followed by a slap of fear. The room was suddenly filled with tension; she sensed danger all around her. Maggie glanced out the window and saw that the sun was starting to rise. Her time was up.

Without hesitation or remorse, she shoved Iana's Bible into her bag, rose from the table and, without a second glance, walked out the front door.

Mark and Cilla spent the next hour as people usually spent it when this kind of horrific disbelief and shock occurred. They were trying to make sense of something that made no sense at all.

3

Brooklyn, New York
2005

"This is the day the Lord has made!" Angela Roberts said with a smile.

It was her profound and unwavering belief that all she had to do was love the Lord and remain faithful and obedient to His word, and He would direct her steps each and every day. The Lord's faithfulness was too real to deny for Angela nowadays; God had demonstrated His love and His promise to her for over forty years.

Angela was born in 1956, ten years after her mother, Cilla Holmes, had a miscarriage during her first pregnancy. Despite Cilla's many, and often failed, attempts at having a child, though, she did not get to see her one and only daughter grow up. When Angela was eight years old, Cilla was killed in a car accident. Thus, Angela grew up not knowing her mother and living in extreme poverty. Jobs were in short supply, and for the better part of a year, Mark Holmes was forced to travel to where he could find suitable employment. On rare occasions he was able to find employment near their hometown, which allowed him to spend time with Angela in the evenings and on weekends. However, for the most part, her father's employment took him outside the city limits and, on rare occasions, even outside the state of New York, which meant he had to leave Angela behind to be cared for by other families in their neighborhood.

Like her great-grandfather, Reginald Hamilton, Angela Roberts was also respected and recognized within the business community as successful and abounding in God's blessings for her life. And like her grandfather, she achieved her station in life through hard work, perseverance and a steadfast belief in the Golden Rule: *Do unto others as you would have them do unto you.*

After ten years of Angela cutting, coloring, and styling hair, while simultaneously providing an occasional counseling session and always being a faithful keeper of secrets, her salon had been voted "*Simply the Best*" for the last five years running. Her clientele ranged from the weekly country club set to the stay-at-home moms who could only manage to pay for a shampoo and style once or twice a year. Her business was thriving, as was her life in general.

Angela and her husband, Nathan, had just celebrated their twenty-sixth wedding anniversary, with Nathan making senior partner at one of the most prestigious law firms in New York City the same year. She and Nathan had been blessed with two sons as well. Their youngest, Robby, had chosen to follow in his father's footsteps and was now in his second year of law school. Kenny, their eldest son, on the other hand, had been Angela's greatest challenge most of his life. As a child, when Kenny was loud and rebellious, Angela chalked his behavior up to him being a spirited little boy. But as he grew older, Kenny's strong, forceful and intense behavior had become apparent in many not-so-childish ways. He had been arrested for underage drinking in high school and again for drunk and disorderly conduct in his early twenties. The latest rumor floating in the community was that Kenny had been seen hanging out with a local gang that was under suspicion for a shooting that happened several months earlier. Needless to say, Kenny was in his mother's prayers more than once throughout her day.

The most significant part in the life of Angela Roberts was her deep and abiding faith and trust in Jesus Christ. Her husband, Nathan, wanted to truly share in that part of her life; she had the kind of connection that he desired to have with the Lord, and if truth be told, he was a little jealous.

Her life was good, and she was grateful for God's faithfulness. She couldn't ask for more.

Angela had just walked into the salon when Kate McGowan jumped out of her styling chair and practically knocked Angela off her feet.

"Kate, you finally cut your hair! Let me look at you." Angela brushed her fingertips over the much-abbreviated ends of Kate's hair.

"It's too short, but it only takes two seconds to deal with in the morning." Kate gave her head a quick shake. "I practically had to be blindfolded and smoke a few cigarettes to get it done."

"It's fabulous! Did Stephen cut it this time?"

"He sure did and will be cutting it from now on," Kate told her. "Angela, you have the best stylists in the city. I'll never go anywhere else."

Angela laughed. "That's what I want to hear." She rubbed her hand over Kate's arm, adding, "Stephen snarls and sends customers burning stares, but when it comes to hair, that boy knows how to handle a pair of scissors."

"I'll definitely be back," she said again. Then, with the words, "Thanks again Stephen," and a wave, she was out the door.

Stephen chuckled and then plopped a stack of mail on Angela's desk. "I just want to remind you that Rowena Fitzgerald will be here shortly."

Angela lifted a finger and wagged it before Stephen. "She's not as bad as you think—and don't believe everything you hear. Be nice to her."

"I'll be on my best behavior… and in the back room, if you need me." Grinning, he used his index finger to draw a heart in the air.

Just as Stephen made his exit and Angela was about to delve into the stack of mail on her desk, Rowena walked through the front doors.

"Wow… This is a first, arriving half an hour before your appointment," Angela said with a chuckle.

"I've just been driving around and thought I'd take a chance and see if you'd be ready for me."

Rowena was Angela's first client and hadn't allowed another stylist to touch her highlighted tresses in ten years. They enjoyed each other's company and had long since developed a comfortable friendship inside the salon and out. They complemented each other, although their lifestyles were completely different. Angela couldn't help noticing that Rowena's hands were trembling anxiously as she held tightly to a tissue that had been shredded into tiny pieces.

"This stack of mail can wait. Are we doing the usual today?" A slow smile spread on Angela's face.

Rowena remained unusually quiet during the shampoo; her eyebrows drew together with a faint vertical line between them. Falling silent and waiting a few seconds, she then asked, "Angela, have you heard anything about another shooting in the city last night?"

"No, but then I haven't had a chance to read the morning paper or listen to the news." She wrapped a towel around Rowena's head. "Did something happen again?"

Rowena tightened her arms across her chest.

"This violence is getting out of control. It's not safe to walk to the corner anymore," Angela continued.

"I don't mean to pry, but didn't you tell me you were afraid Kenny was hanging out with the wrong crowd?" Rowena asked calmly, but as she looked at Angela, she could see the concern on her friend's face.

Just as Angela was about to answer Rowena's question, Stephen walked up beside her and put his arm around her shoulder. "Angela, there is a phone call for you." Stephen words had an ominous sound to them, which she didn't like.

"Please take a message for me, will you?"

"The call is from Mercy Hospital. I think you need to take it."

Rowena sat frozen in her chair, staring at Angela in the mirror and trembling on the inside. She already knew the nature of Angela's phone call, and it wasn't good.

Angela looked at Rowena and then back at Stephen. Then she placed the brush back down on the counter and walked over to her desk, feeling less confident with each step that her shaking legs would support her. She took a deep breath and exhaled slowly, trying to regain her self-control.

"Hello, this is Angela Roberts."

The caller said she was a nurse at Mercy Hospital and that Angela's son had been seriously injured. The police had given the hospital Angela's phone number and asked them to call her.

"Wait a minute!" Angela responded with worried eyes. "My son?" She wondered if the call was some sort of practical joke. It wasn't making any sense. "Was my son in a car accident?" she asked, worry taking over her face.

"Mrs. Roberts, I don't want to mislead you and would prefer not to discuss this over the phone."

As Angela listened to the nurse, she felt a wave of panic wash over her, and she suddenly stared at Rowena, who had been listening to Angela's every word.

"Mrs. Roberts, are you there?"

Angela nodded. "Ah yes... Yes, I'm here."

"I'm sorry. I know this is a shock, but you and Mr. Roberts need to come to the hospital as soon as possible."

"What happened?" she asked, too frightened to even absorb what was happening, let alone understand it.

"When you get to the hospital, come to the fourth floor nurses station. Dr. Bennett will meet you there to discuss Kenny's condition."

Angela didn't even know what to say. How did this happen, and what was she supposed to do now? She needed to call Nathan.

She could feel herself sliding into blackness. Fighting to keep control, Angela asked hoarsely, "Is my son dead?" Tears poured down her cheeks at just the thought of it.

"No ma'am, he's not dead." The nurse reassured her.

"Thank God," she said in a whisper and closed her eyes. "I'll get there as quickly as I can."

"Please drive carefully."

Angela thanked the nurse for calling and then walked back over to Stephen and Rowena.

"I need to get to the hospital; Kenny's been in some sort of accident." Angela looked at Stephen blankly as he and Rowena exchanged a glance.

"Stephen, you won't mind shampooing and styling Rowena's hair, will you?"

Rowena looked horrified as she glanced from Angela to Stephen. Taking a few moments to think about Angela's suggestion, she then shook her head and quietly said, "I don't think so."

"I heard that! Thanks for the vote of confidence, Roe," Stephen said clearly, and then he turned back to Angela. "Oh Honey, her hair can wait 'til you're able to do it." Letting out a huff, he walked towards the rear of the salon.

"You're all nuts!" Angela said as she grabbed her keys and headed for the door, just as her cell phone started ringing. "You two can work this out; I need to get to the hospital."

Glancing at her cell phone and seeing it was Nathan calling, she put her purse and keys down on her desk and answered the call.

"Nathan, I just got a call from Mercy Hospital—"

Nathan cut her off, saying, "I know." He paused a moment before adding, "It's Kenny... He's been shot."

"Excuse me?" she asked, sounding slightly irritated. "Nathan, did you just tell me that my son has been shot?" At that moment, she felt as if she was having an out-of-body experience. "What the hell happened?"

"Angela, calm down. Kenny is alive, but he's in very serious condition."

Angela didn't say a word. She just listened.

"I'll explain everything to you when you get here."

Shaking her head, Angela responded, "Kenny's been shot?"

"Promise me that you will calm down before you get in the car. But Honey, please get here as fast as you can. Our son needs us right now."

"Nathan, tell Kenny I love him and that I'm coming."

As soon as she got into her car, Angela folded her arms across her chest, declaring, "I'm not going to give up hope." She immediately began praying, "Please, God, let my son be okay."

Twenty minutes later, Angela arrived in the hospital's parking lot. Remembering she was to go up to the fourth floor, she hurriedly walked through the emergency room towards the elevators. Once on the fourth floor, and looking confused and upset, she quickly found the nurses station and, in the calmest voice she could muster, said, "Kenny Roberts. Where is my son?"

Following the nurse's directions, and without a word, Angela turned and slowly walked down the hallway, sensing her life was about to change forever.

"Nathan," she whispered. He turned to look at his wife and then shook his head with a look of sadness. "He's not gone... Please tell me our son is not gone!" Angela's tears wouldn't stop flowing. "Please say something."

Nathan didn't even know what to answer. As he tried to make sense of and explain what was happening, one of the doctors walked up behind them.

"Mr. and Mrs. Roberts, I am Jason Bennett, Kenny's doctor."

"Dr. Bennett, this is my wife, Angela." Nathan cleared his throat and then wiped a tear from his cheek. "How's Kenny?"

Dr. Bennett paused for a moment. "I wish I had better news for you." Then, realizing he needed to take control of the conversation, he began explaining the extent of Kenny's injuries.

"Your son is very sick. Although the bullet entered into his brain so cleanly that I'm sure he didn't feel a thing, the damage done is considerable and irreversible. Kenny's brain function has ceased, as evidenced, for instance, by the cessation of him breathing on his own. The machines are breathing now for him. He is unresponsive to stimuli and has displayed the absence of any muscle activity."

Nathan could barely breathe but managed to squeeze out the words, "Are you saying our son is brain dead?"

Dr. Bennett waited a moment before answering Nathan's question. "The machines are breathing for Kenny."

There was one moment of silence, then another.

"We are doing and have done everything we can for your son. We couldn't stop the bleeding, and his blood pressure dropped uncontrollably several times. He's stable, but the machines are keeping him alive."

Angela shook her head. "Nathan, this can't be happening." Tears streamed down her face. "I don't want this to be happening."

Angela's emotions overtook her and she began to sob.

Nathan held her close, trying to comfort her despite his own despair.

Dr. Bennett could feel their heartache and decided to leave them alone. "I'll be here all night. If there is anything I can do for you, please have me paged."

"Thank you," Nathan said in a whisper and then closed his eyes. "God... Let him be okay... Please let him be okay."

Nathan and Angela stood at the foot of Kenny's bed, staring at their son's lifeless body, unable to believe what Dr. Bennett had just told them.

Angela slowly made her way to Kenny's bedside. An oxygen mask was hissing and her son's head was heavily bandaged and blood-stained. He had an IV in his arm and was the color of concrete with his eyes closed.

Unbeknownst to Angela, a nurse had come into the room and was standing beside Nathan. "I'm very sorry about your son. Is there someone I can call for you, your pastor or family member, anyone you want to come and sit with you?"

The gentle hums of the life-giving machines were pleasant-sounding and soothing to Nathan. He exchanged a momentary look with the nurse, staring blankly into her eyes.

"I don't know where he is." Nathan's eyes settled briefly on Kenny and then moved to the nurse. "Where is my son?"

"Mr. Roberts, I can't answer that, but I do believe that, although Kenny may not be physically responsive, that he can still hear you." She wrapped an arm around him. "Go and talk with your son."

Angela turned around to face them, and in a weakened state, she asked, "Where is the chapel?"

In his grief, Nathan couldn't bear to leave Kenny alone and suggested Angela go to the chapel by herself.

An hour later she returned to find Nathan curled up into a ball, crying with his arms over his head as though to shelter himself from the shock of his reality and the anguish of the thought that another human being had carried out such a brutal act upon his son.

"Nathan, Honey, what are you doing?"

He immediately looked up at Angela with a cold blank stare, initially wondering why she was making so much noise. He struggled to identify the low sounds of voices mumbling and whispering on all sides of the room. He looked like a wild man as he rocked back and forth, and his untamed eyes darted first to his wife and then quickly to the clock on the wall above Kenny's bed. The slow and methodical tick... tock... tick... tock grew in intensity, ultimately flooding his mind with paralyzing fear and anxiety. A wave of panic washed over him as he sensed his son's life was counting down to its final seconds on this earth.

"No! That's not true," he yelled and then ran over to Kenny, pulling his son close to him. "I don't believe you!"

Angela was overwhelmed with tears as she stared at her grief-stricken husband and lifeless son.

"Why is that clock so loud?" he yelled out again. "Open up the blinds; let the light into this room!"

Walking over to Nathan, Angela placed her trembling hands on his shoulders, pulled him free and then slowly backed away with him from their son.

"He's not gone," Nathan said, his voice breaking. "He's not gone."

"Come and sit down," she said to him as tenderly as she could. They huddled close together as tears began to slide down Angela's cheeks, regardless of her efforts to stop them and remain strong for her husband, who was now in far worse shape than he was an hour ago.

"It's so weird," Nathan confessed to Angela. "I feel like everything is going to be different, like our lives will never be the same."

Nathan no longer looked shell-shocked; now he looked tired and very sad. With time to consider what Kenny would have wanted for his life, he knew a decision needed to be made for his son. Slowly Nathan walked over to stand beside Kenny's bed. The truth was, his son wasn't coming back. He nearly burst into tears, trying to cope with the reality that it was time to let him go.

He looked up from Kenny. "Angela, we need to make a decision and then make arrangements."

"Decision... Arrangements?" All Angela could do was repeat Nathan's words. "No! My baby is going to come back; God isn't going to take my son!"

Nathan pulled her close and whispered, "No, Baby, he can't come back. He's gone, and now he needs to rest."

Angela looked into Nathan's eyes and then nodded her head. Her mind was, to some extent, willing to accept all that had been explained to her, but her heart was unwilling and unable to prompt her to say the words herself.

For the next few minutes, they held one another while Angela prayed.

"Lord, there's nothing we can do. This is all in Your hands now."

And then, with great difficulty, Nathan and Angela gave permission for Dr. Bennett to disconnect Kenny's life-sustaining machines.

Dr. Bennett placed a hand on both of their shoulders and, with a downhearted look on his face, said, "I need to prepare you for what is going to take place next."

Angela gave a quick, involuntary shudder and nodded her head.

"The process of dying is unpredictable, but due to the extent of Kenny's brain injuries, I don't think he will be able to hang on for too long."

Until the end of time, they would have to live with this moment. There were no words they could say to each other that would make it all right, so they didn't even try. They just sat and held one another, crying, watching and waiting.

For a long time there was only the sound of sobbing, and then finally the alarm from Kenny's heart monitor resonated throughout the room. Angela stood on one side of the bed while Nathan stood on the other, each holding one of their son's hands. Kenny drew in one long breath and then slowly exhaled for the last time.

"He's in God's hands now," Nathan whispered and then leaned over to softly kiss his son on the forehead.

"Dear Lord," Angela whispered, "why did You take my baby?" She leaned across the bed and collapsed against Nathan, sobbing.

"He's gone," Nathan responded slowly.

An hour later, Angela was still sitting beside Kenny on his bed, holding his hand, when all of a sudden she was aware of a life force so powerful, so huge, that it was physical. Her sense of it had no limits, and the force washed over her with such intensity that she grabbed the rail of Kenny's bed to steady herself. She couldn't believe this was happening, but it was, and there was nothing she could do to interrupt it.

An instant later, it was over.

"That was strange," she said flatly, her gaze still focused on Kenny. "Nathan, did you feel that?"

Her husband looked up. "Did I feel what?"

"I'm not sure how to describe it." A few seconds went by, and then she sat down in a chair beside the hospital bed. "Maybe an earthquake?"

Nathan walked around the bed to Angela and gently stroked her back. "Honey, it was probably just a rush of nerves."

"I-I suppose. You're probably right." She shook her head and then leaned over to place a kiss on her son's cheek.

"Rest in peace now. I'll see you again, my son."

The following morning, Robby arrived home from college and insisted he go along with his parents to the Harper Funeral Home, primarily to support them while they selected Kenny's casket and arranged the details for Kenny's funeral service.

It was a somber and heartbreaking day for all of them, and to make matters worse, Angela read an article on the front page of the morning paper depicting her son as a common street thug. *"Kenny Roberts, shot execution style, died last night as a result of gang violence in the city. The Blood Brothers, a local gang which is currently under investigation for an unrelated recent homicide, is also suspected in several of the area's latest shootings."*

The article also reported that Kenny Roberts had suspected ties to this "Blood Brothers" gang and was not a stranger to the police department, as he had a lengthy criminal record extending as far back as his high school days.

Despite how the media had portrayed Kenny, Angela wanted her son to be buried with dignity. She and Nathan agreed on a mahogany casket with brass handles and white velvet lining. In addition, the casket was to remain closed throughout the viewing and memorial service. Angela couldn't bear the thought of hearing all the well-meaning condolences while guests looked at her son as a gang member with a troubled past. What her son needed now was a peaceful rest, and she intended to provide that for him.

The next morning Angela went back to the funeral home alone to approve all the final preparations. Meanwhile, Nathan and Robby stayed home to organize the insurance forms and assist out-of-town guests with their reservations and transportation to and from Kenny's service, which was scheduled for the following day.

With everything in order, Angela stood up, ready to leave the funeral home. But as she did, Brian Harper, a dear, old friend who happened to be the Funeral Director, asked if she would like to spend a few minutes alone with her son before his casket was closed. Angela thought for a moment but then declined Brian's offer, explaining that she loved her son with her entire heart, but now that he was gone, what she needed was some time alone with herself and God before his burial.

Angela could see from the look in Brian's eyes what he was thinking.

"I can't even imagine what you must be going through." His fingers were trembling as he touched her hand. "I get sick thinking about it."

"We aren't supposed to bury our children," she said calmly. Brian nodded in agreement.

Wiping her eyes, Angela thanked him and then walked out of his office. She was unaware, however, that she had taken a wrong turn and was headed straight towards the Preparation Room in the rear of the Funeral Home. Suddenly realizing she wasn't where she needed to be, Angela quickly turned around—and at the same time, in a small room adjacent to the Preparation Room, she noticed a mahogany casket with the top wide open. She stopped dead in her tracks and wondered if it might be Kenny's casket. Just then, she became aware of an eerie feeling practically beckoning her to enter the room, almost as if she was being drawn there against her will.

"No, I am not going against my own wishes." She began to cry as she spoke the words.

She quickly turned, deciding not to enter, and moved like a robot towards the front door. But soon she felt as though entering the room was something she needed to do.

Angela stopped at the front doors and thought for a moment. Then, little by little, she turned around and walked slowly back down the hall towards the small room. Standing in the doorway, her body trembling and her eyes fixated on the open casket, Angela took the first step, then stopped and said a quick prayer, hoping she had made a mistake and that the casket held someone other than Kenny. She moved on autopilot, alternating between numb and hysterical the closer she got to the casket. At this moment there was no turning back, and with only inches separating her from the casket's mahogany exterior, Angela took one last step and stood alongside it.

Fearful of what she might find inside, Angela carefully turned her head and looked down. Sorrow struck her as she gazed upon her son. At once her mind was inundated with thoughts of the first time she had laid eyes on him, when he was a perfect little 7lb. 8oz. baby boy, complete with ten tiny fingers and toes, big brown eyes and pouty lips. Right now, as she stood alongside him, it was difficult for her to imagine feeling that happy ever again in her life. With tears streaming down her cheeks, Angela reached out and caressed the side of Kenny's face as gently as she had done when the nurse placed her minutes-old baby boy in her arms for the first time, which was nearly twenty-two years ago.

As she held her hand against Kenny's cheek, Angela was suddenly taken by surprise again, this time not with loving and fond memories but with a merciless force that nearly knocked her off balance. Quickly she grabbed the side of Kenny's casket to steady herself and then scanned the room for something shaking or out of place. But all was still and silent throughout the room.

Angela took a few minutes to regain her composure, and then she walked over to a chair in the corner of the room and sat down. Her thoughts instantly went to what had happened the previous day, just moments after Kenny died, and somehow the memory queerly summoned the legend of her grandmother, Iana, to the forefront of her mind.

According to the legend, Iana Hamilton Holmes intermingled with the dearly departed. In some versions of the legend, her gentle touch to the deceased prompted an undeniable vibration flowing directly into her body, followed by a simple message transferring into her mind. The messages were instantly recognizable to Iana; they were not frightening, nor did they suggest any sort of evil spirits. The messages were full of faith and assurance to the family that all was well and that they should not mourn the deceased's death for too long. Their loved one was standing on the edge of a space unlike anything here on earth, a place of spectacular beauty that was overflowing with peace, love and contentment. The deceased was ready for this new journey and desired to go. As soon as the vibrations ceased, Iana would find the family, deliver the message she had received, offer her condolences and be on her way.

Angela shuddered, haven't having thought about the legend of her grandmother until now. She had never bought into the theories of dead people sandwiched between their lives here on earth and their everlasting life in heaven or the premise that the dead could relay messages to the living as an explanation for them still to be hanging on. She was raised in the church and was a woman of strong faith; that line of conjecture would have most assuredly been frowned upon and bordered on being sacrilegious.

"Where did all of that come from?" Angela wiped a lone tear from her cheek. "I just lost my son, and I am exhausted. It won't happen again," she reassured herself.

She rose and walked back over to the casket to look at her son one last time.

"Okay," she said softly as she touched his hair and bent down to kiss him.

"I will see you again, and that I do believe. Rest in peace, my sweet son."

Less than twenty-four hours later, the service was beautiful, the church was full, and there were flowers everywhere. For most of the day, familiar faces came and went. The neighbors brought more food than everyone could possibly eat, and at the end of the day, Angela and Nathan just sat quietly, holding one another and crying together.

Monday morning dawned with brilliant sunshine and clear blue skies. It had been eight weeks since Kenny's death and had turned out to be one of the coldest winters on record for Brooklyn. Like most, Angela had never outgrown the anticipation of the arrival of spring. The crisp clean air and warm days offered a time of rebirth, which by now Angela was desperate to have in her life. She was starting to feel better and was ready to replace the dark and desolate days of the past eight weeks with hope for the future.

As she had done since Kenny passed away, she set aside time every Monday morning to visit with him. This Monday morning, rather than arriving with the customary single red rose to place on Kenny's grave, Angela opted for a stunning bouquet of yellow daffodils, symbolizing not only the rebirth of the season but also a rebirth within her spirit.

After visiting Kenny's grave, Angela decided to give herself a day off from the salon and to spend the day on the couch, sipping a cup of tea and browsing through old photo albums. She turned over one picture of Kenny, Robby and Nathan to read, *Kenny age four, Robby age two and Nathan, summer vacation, July,1987... My three boys all digging to China on Long Island Beach.* Smiling at the memory of happier times, she settled back on the couch and spent the next few hours sifting through photo albums, all of which celebrated the triumph of birthday merriment, high school proms and every sport the boys had played over the years. Not to be overlooked were the endless holiday pictures dating back to Kenny's first Christmas and including each and every holiday since then, ending with Christmas of last year.

"Kenny's last Christmas," she thought, looking at his face and then wiping a tear from her eye.

She could remember the family members and friends who had been there the day the picture was taken and all of the festivities that had occurred before and after the picture had been snapped. As she was sorting through the last pile of photos, she came across one picture of a woman holding a small child on her lap. The photo had yellowed over time, and the edges were torn and badly wrinkled; she was finding it difficult to recognize both the woman and the little girl. She checked for a date on the back, hoping for a clue.

Only the month was written on the back; the year had been torn away. *"Is this my grandmother?"* she thought as she reached for her glasses to get a closer look. Then she slowly ran her finger across the image of the woman sitting in the picture.

They locked eyes.

Angela stopped for breath, the way one does after running up a steep hill. All of a sudden, static and muffled words were darting back and forth in her mind, but she was unable to comprehend any of what she was hearing. Then, unexpectedly, the static and chaos gradually disappeared, revealing a clear and intense voice, which articulated the words, *"They could speak through* you."

Angela inhaled sharply and bolted upright to a standing position. Shaking and almost immediately drenched in sweat, she released her grip on the picture and watched it gently float onto the floor.

Suddenly an image of Kenny lying in his casket flashed into her mind, accompanied by thoughts of her grandmother, Iana Hamilton Holmes.

"Just who were you, Iana?" Angela wondered to herself as she walked into the kitchen to pour herself another cup of tea. Sitting down at the table, she began to analyze what had taken place in her life in the past few minutes, both physically and mentally.

Now she had a terrible urge to laugh at the whole thing, and she knew that posing her questions to anyone would undoubtedly give them the impression that she was a true neurotic. Other than the legend of her grandmother, to which she gave very little credence, and her two peculiar experiences with Kenny, Angela had practically no knowledge on the subject of paranormal activity or ESP.

"I *will* be a true neurotic if I don't find some peace about this, and there is only one way to settle it once and for all. I need to pay my son another visit."

Angela finished her tea and then grabbed her keys.

When Angela saw the sign for Rolling Green Cemetery, she slowed. It was on the outskirts of town, and by the time she arrived, the late afternoon sky had turned dark as low, thick clouds were gathering on the horizon. She took a few slow breaths as she entered through the front gates and headed for the section of the cemetery where Kenny was buried. She had planned out what she would say on her way there, but she kept changing her mind. Parking the car, she looked around with a sigh, then contemplated sitting alongside her son's headstone even as severe thunderstorms were looming off in the distance.

"Of course this is a crazy idea," she laughed to herself. "I can see the headline now... 'Grieving Mother of Kenny Roberts Struck by Lightning as She Lay Alongside Her Son's Grave.'"

A fine drizzle started falling down from the gray sky. A clammy dampness covered her skin, but Angela was bound and determined to make sense of what had been taking place since the death of her son.

She climbed out of the car, grabbed a blanket out of the trunk, hooked her purse over her shoulder then started to walk down the gravel path. A rumble of thunder triggered a slight pause in her step, but in spite of this, the scent of fresh flowers nearby stirred a sense of peacefulness within her, calming her nerves and granting her the courage to press on towards her goal.

A few steps from Kenny's grave, Angela noticed that the arrangement of daffodils she had placed earlier were now knocked over with several of their stems torn in half and thrown across the lawn.

"Darn animals!" She immediately gathered up what was salvageable and placed the flowers back into their container. Then she spread out the blanket and sat down with her legs folded underneath her.

Angela cleared her mind. She remained very still and quiet for the next few minutes then reached out and placed her hand over the place where her son's name had been engraved on the marble headstone.

"Well, here I am. Kenny, Honey, do you have something you want to say to me?" she asked, smiling to herself and feeling downright ridiculous.

At that moment a rustling in the nearby bushes shifted her focus from the task at hand to the wooded area that crowded right up to Kenny's tombstone. She wasn't afraid by the noise and was pleased to have selected this new wooded section of the cemetery, due to its serenity and her son's love of nature; it was the perfect final resting place for Kenny. Angela smiled as she recalled Kenny spending hours exploring the uncharted territory of the woods behind Nathan's parents' home. A miniature shovel held tightly in his hand, he would dig with passion and eagerness, dreaming of the day he would unearth the long lost buried treasure he had read about in his adventure books. Undeniably, the favorite part of his day in the wild was communicating with his feathered friends, chirping and whistling a tune that was without a doubt some form of communication between nature and him. And, of course, Saturday afternoon would not be complete without him bringing home a new addition to the ever-increasing collection of creepy-crawlies or feathery friends.

In truth, she'd never given Kenny's ability to communicate with nature much thought.

"Could it be possible that my son had a gift?" Angela cleared her throat. "Kenny, I'm here."

She wrapped both arms around the sides of Kenny's marker and then laid her face against the smooth marble finish. Attempting to assemble some sense out of what she was doing, she closed her eyes and focused on her breathing. Angela retained only a vague sense of the approaching thunderstorm and of the people walking past her. She became attentive to nothing but a deep concentration of hearing a word or feeling a vibration from her son—behavior she would have never expected herself to have, even though it was coming so naturally.

All at once an arrow-thin shaft of bright white light darted across the blackened sky. And, just as an earsplitting crack of thunder crashed above her, Angela felt a hand grab her forearm with startling force. Then she heard the words, "I need my message!"

It suddenly had become completely dark, but Angela could feel somebody breathing beside her. The next flash of lightening illuminated the sky with an adequate amount of light for Angela to discern the silhouette of a woman kneeling beside her with a penetrating, unwavering stare. Her long, dark, disheveled hair did not hide from view the wild, untamed expression on her face.

"Get away from me!" Angela screamed. Pulling her arm free and then shooting to her feet, she stood face-to-face with the woman.

The thunder was deafening, but Angela was able to hear the whisper that came out of the darkness. "I need my message."

"I don't have any messages." Angela took a step backward. "Get the hell away from me!" she shouted.

"You shouldn't be afraid of them. It's normal for you."

Angela stared at the woman, and then she hastily snatched up her blanket and ran across the lawn towards her car. Once there, she jumped in and immediately locked the doors.

"No!" she screamed and then huddled down in the seat, putting her hands over her face. Her heart began to race and sweat trickled down her forehead. She told herself to start the car, but she was frozen.

She tried to speak, and having failed, sucked in another short breath and tried again.

"Please stop this," she managed to whisper to no one but herself.

She closed her eyes and willed herself to open her fingers a crack to look back toward Kenny's grave. The woman was nowhere in sight, which left her wondering if the encounter truly had taken place.

The rational part of her mind knew that things like this could happen in the midst of grief and tension. However, at this point she contemplated the real possibility of Kenny or someone else attempting to contact her. The door was swinging both ways now; did her son need her, or were these events merely her grief-stricken mind playing tricks on her?

She put her palms together and moved them back and forth. "Maybe I need to see a doctor."

It took her ten minutes of slowly breathing in and out to finally stop shaking, to calm down enough to start the car and drive home. She turned onto her quiet, tree-lined street, and with her house in sight, she felt safer. She would be secure in her house until she could speak to her doctor about all that had happened. Pulling into the driveway, she then got out of the car, keeping her eyes on the front door. She promised herself that the time had also come for her to sit down with Nathan to get his opinion on what had been happening to her.

The next morning Angela dressed and waited in the kitchen for Nathan to come downstairs. As she'd promised herself, it was time to confide in her husband the entire ordeal that had taken place over the past few weeks.

Nathan appeared in the threshold of the kitchen, clean-shaven and already dressed in his new three-piece dark suit, briefcase in hand.

"Have you seen my keys?"

"No, I haven't. It's barely seven o'clock; why are you leaving this early?"

"Angela, this is the first day of jury selection. I told you yesterday that I would need to leave early this morning. Remember? I needed to tie up a few loose ends before heading over to the courthouse."

"Oh, I'm sorry. I guess I forgot."

"Are you okay?" He poured himself a cup of coffee and continued, "You look like you didn't get much sleep last night."

"There's something I need to talk with you about, and I don't think it can wait much longer."

"You mean right now? Come on Angela, you know how big this case is for me and for the firm." Nathan put on his coat and picked up his briefcase. "I hate to do this, Honey, but it is going to have to wait."

"But I need to talk about this with you now."

He waited for her to explain more, but she was taking too long.

"Look, I should be home at the usual time. Who knows, since this is the first day, I may get out of court early."

"You're right, all of this can wait. I'm just exhausted."

"You look it; Honey, you need to slow down a bit. Get some rest today. I'll be home later tonight and we can sit down and discuss whatever is on your mind."

He kissed her forehead and walked out the door.

Standing in the hallway where Nathan had just stood, Angela was overcome with an alarming sense of abandonment. She was left with no one to deny or affirm her peculiar experiences of late. She poured herself a cup of coffee and then walked over to her desk and sat down. All the while she rolled over in her mind the bizarre encounter at the cemetery, with the woman demanding a message from her, plus the two incidences with Kenny, first at the hospital and then again at his casket.

The death of her son had left a huge void in her life—more like a black hole some days—and she admitted to having trouble moving on with her life. Without any prompting of her own, thoughts of her grandmother Iana began floating into her mind once more, and again she recalled the urban legend of her having a so-called gift of receiving and then delivering messages of the deceased.

"Do I have those same abilities?" she wondered out loud.

At first she thought it weird and yet, in an odd way, wonderful. Just the thought of having an opportunity to interact with her son again sent her mind, body and spirit souring. And for a crazy moment, she wondered if all that was required of her was to accept and educate herself, to develop this theoretical gift that may have been passed down to her from her grandmother.

She sipped her coffee and wondered what the next step would be.

"Note to self: just to make sure I'm not losing my mind, I'd better make an appointment for a complete physical," she said, then turned on her laptop and typed in the words "Mediums, Psychic Medium and Spiritualism" in a search engine.

She was amazed at the full page of definitions and explanations that appeared on the screen.

> ***Mediums:*** Mediums are people who have a special gift that allows spirit-people to give messages from the afterlife. The objective of a medium's work is to prove survival of the human personality after one's demise and to help the bereaved come to terms with their loss. Sittings with mediums are not for fortune telling but are experimental sessions to provide evidence of survival. Any attempt to communicate with spirit is, by its very nature, purely experimental, and therefore results can never be guaranteed.

Angela leaned back in her chair after reading the definition and raked her fingers through her hair.

"That was a lot to digest," she said, closing the laptop. "It *does* give some clarification, though, to the legend tied to my grandmother."

Once she'd said the words, she took a shaky breath.

"Grandma Iana just might have been the real deal. But am I?"

For twenty-two years, Dr. Elizabeth Mansfield had been Angela's primary care physician. She had only ever seen her for preventative care checkups, gynecological exams and her yearly flu shots. Thus, Angela considered herself to be in good health, considering she was almost fifty.

Angela understood that depression following the death of a loved one was perfectly normal, and she thought that maybe all she needed was a prescription for Prozac and some therapy. However, she knew enough about depression to understand that what she'd been experiencing was not one of its symptoms. Her symptoms were right on target with schizophrenia, though: a complex mental disorder that makes it difficult to tell the difference between real and unreal experiences. That description hit a little too close to home for her. And if that wasn't enough for her to process while she waited to see Dr. Mansfield, she added her fear of the possibility that she had suffered a mild stroke after Kenny died into the mix.

She fought the impulses growing louder inside of her, begging her to either get to the bottom of this mystery or get the hell out of the waiting room.

Just as she was about to leave, a nurse opened the waiting room door and called Angela's name. In a few minutes, Dr. Mansfield would go over her tests results with her and the diagnosis would be handed down.

She took a deep breath and smiled. Whether she was ready or not, Angela was going to get to the bottom of this torment that had plagued her life over the past months. Now she was ready and willing to make the necessary adjustments in her life, whatever they might be.

Dr. Mansfield sat quietly, flipping page after page of Angela's chart.

"So what's wrong with me?"

"Angela, the symptoms of memory disturbances and disorientation concerned me, and that is why I ordered the MRI of your brain. Good news: Your MRI report is negative; no tumor, stroke or psychotic episodes."

"Then I'm not losing my mind?"

"No you're not!" her doctor laughed. "The EKG and labs are all within normal ranges as well."

"Dr. Mansfield, I know I didn't imagine these feelings I had or the woman in the cemetery. If there is nothing medically wrong with me, what could be the explanation for what I told you I experienced after Kenny died or at the cemetery?"

"From a medical standpoint, you just lost your son a few months ago, and the mind is a very powerful organ. Our minds can play tricks on us after a traumatic event happens in our lives. With that being said, we can do one of two things: We can wait and see how things go over the next few months, or maybe you'd like to set up an appointment with a psychologist."

"You just told me that I wasn't losing my mind." Angela stared back and waited fearfully, sensing that something could be terribly wrong.

"Calm down, calm down. All I'm saying is that some help might be nice as you go through the different stages of grief. That's all."

Dr. Mansfield scheduled another appointment for Angela in three months, and she prescribed her a mild sedative to help her sleep at night.

Angela left Dr. Mansfield's office weak-kneed but greatly relieved. She decided to forego her grocery shopping for now and chose instead to surprise Stephen with a quick visit to the salon.

Since Kenny's death, she was not emotionally or physically able to handle the day-to-day responsibilities of running a business, let alone being surrounded by people with their "what to say to her?" expressions and fleeting looks. Immediately following Kenny's death, Stephen insisted she take some time off and Angela agreed to allow him to handle things at the salon for a few months.

"Angela!" Stephen shouted from across the room as she walked through the door.

Kate McGowan leaped out of Stephen's chair and ran across the room, throwing her arms around Angela, practically knocking her off balance and through the plate glass window behind her.

"Oh Angela, I've missed you so much. Are you doing okay?" she asked, looking concerned.

"I'm doing fine, Kate, and thank you for the lovely flowers." Angela freed herself from Kate's unyielding embrace and then stepped back. "Glad to see you kept the haircut!"

"Ah, Stephen's the best."

"That he is!" Angela agreed.

"So what brings you downtown?" Stephen asked, readjusting Kate's plastic cape as she returned to her seat.

"I just came from an appointment with my doctor and wasn't in the mood for grocery shopping, so here I am."

"Is everything alright?" Kate asked.

"Clean bill of health!" Angela grinned over at her. "So how are things around here?" She directed her question at Stephen.

"Business has been good," Stephen answered without hesitation.

Angela reached out and touched Stephen on the shoulder. "I can't thank you enough for everything you've done for me."

"I'm just so sorry about your son." He nodded and then met her eyes.

Angela patted his arm and her eyes began tearing up as she thanked him again.

"I'm okay," Angela reassured him, but she wasn't very convincing.

Angela poured herself a cup of coffee and sat down at her desk. Then she flipped through the pages of the appointment book. Stephen had either cancelled all of her upcoming appointments or rescheduled them with another stylist. That was perfect for now, but Angela knew she needed to find the time to figure out what she was going to do about her clients in the weeks to come. After Kate left, Angela sat and watched Stephen create miracles on a new client with a pair of scissors and a blow dryer. Despite what she had told herself, she was beginning to wonder if she could do all of this anymore.

A few minutes later, Rowena walked into the salon. As usual, she was spouting off a laundry list of apologies—this time for being late rather than early for her weekly appointment.

There was a long pause as Rowena looked at Angela, and then she leaned over, wrapping her arms tightly around her dear friend.

“It is so good to see you.” Looking into Angela’s eyes, Rowena could see she’d been through a lot; she was sure of it. “What can I do to help you?” she asked gently. “You have a lot on your plate right now, don’t you?”

Lately, when people were sympathetic to her, more often than not Angela lost control and begin to cry. And the way Rowena had just spoken to her again made Angela’s eyes fill with tears. She quickly looked away to compose herself before answering.

“I’m sorry, I’ll be alright.” She wiped the tears from her face. “Thank you,” she responded, feeling moved by what Rowena had said to her. Still, she wasn’t sure if she should admit to Rowena the mysterious events that had been taking place over the past weeks. But Angela knew that if anyone would understand, Rowena would be that person. She was well-read on the topics of psychics and the paranormal, and she wasn’t timid by any means about having a conversation about either.

“Come on, let’s go and get something to eat or sit down with a coffee,” Rowena suggested.

“No, I’ll be fine. Besides, you have an appointment with Stephen.”

“Don’t be ridiculous, I’ll be here first thing in the morning and Stephen will fit me in.” She smiled and waved her checkbook in the air. “Be a good boy, won’t you?”

Stephen clenched his teeth and tightened his lips, then he managed a smiled and waved a hand in the air. “Go on you two. Rowena can fill you in on all the latest Country Club comings and goings!” he told them.

4

A warm spring afternoon always brought out crowds of people, and downtown was alive with shoppers, people riding bikes and tourists enjoying a carefree afternoon of sightseeing. Groups of people formed on the sidewalk corners waiting for signals to cross the street, couples and families waited outside restaurants to get a table, and others simply enjoyed an afternoon stroll while window-shopping.

Angela was glad she had accepted Rowena's invitation, and she found herself looking forward to spending time with an old friend. The happiness forming inside her was, admittedly, a bit surprising, considering how difficult her past weeks had been.

They arrived at O'Brien's, a trendy restaurant in Brooklyn, and sat down outside on the patio. Once their waiter came, they ordered two glasses of wine. In no time, both glasses were on their table.

"So, how are you, really?" Rowena began.

"I'm managing." Angela swirled her wine and took a sip.

As Rowena looked into Angela's pained eyes, she couldn't help but wonder if something more was going on in her life.

"Managing is good." Rowena nodded her head.

The waiter appeared again, and each of them ordered an appetizer along with another glass of wine. Angela hoped the alcohol would take the edge off of the unexpected uneasiness she noticed creeping up her spine. She reached down and clenched the sides of her chair as she pressed her lips together.

"Rowena, do you believe in life after death?" As she asked the question, the effects of the wine kicked in, and she continued, "Not as in a heavenly existence, but here on earth."

Having taken a drink herself, Rowena choked out the words, "Do I believe in *what*?"

Angela had felt so brave and bold in her mind, but after hearing the words come out of her own mouth, everything sounded outrageous.

"I know... I know." Angela shook her head.

"I can't believe what I am hearing!" Rowena laughed. "Angela Roberts, I've known you a long time, and never in all those years have you entertained notions of an afterlife here on earth."

"I don't know what's gotten into me." Angela wiped her mouth with the corner of her napkin. "But I need to tell someone what's been going on, or I think I'm going to lose my mind."

"Well, for God's sake, don't stop now!" Rowena's eyes widened with curiosity.

"Strange things have been happening to me since Kenny died." Angela took a gulp of her wine and continued, "Sort of extrasensory, paranormal-type things." After a moment, Angela sighed, adding, "You think I'm crazy, don't you?"

Wincing at Angela's words, Rowena responded, "Crazy—are you kidding me? I just read *Psychic Readings* by John Edwards and renewed my quarterly subscription to the *Quantum Physics Newsletter*."

The food came, but neither of them picked up a fork.

Angela dabbed her eyes with her napkin.

"Angela." Rowena looked her directly in the eyes. "Just start at the beginning."

Angela paused, trying to comprehend how and where she would find the words. She thought about making her mind up not to care about the whole mess anymore, but a voice was now resonating deep inside her, haunting her day and night with the words, *"I want my message."* And those words were penetrating her brain, no matter how hard she fought against them.

Rowena didn't say a word; she waited, suspended on the thrill of discussing a topic that, for most of her adult life, had utterly fascinated her. She took another sip of her wine and nodded, hoping it would reassure Angela that her story would be safe with her.

"Alright... Here I go."

"I'm all ears!" Rowena turned off her cell phone and pulled her chair closer to the table.

"Trust me, at first I thought I was hallucinating or that maybe I was dealing with some post-traumatic stress after Kenny's death. But now I'm not so sure."

Rowena reached over and held Angela's hand.

Angela took a deep breath and began describing the strange vibrations that coursed through her body when she placed her hand on Kenny, once at his bedside and then again at the funeral home. She compared them to an electric shock—like what happened as soon as a metal utensil came in contact with the red-hot coils in a toaster.

An unexpected, reassuring expression came over Rowena's face.

"Yeah, a little zap runs up your arm."

"I couldn't move." She stopped for a breath and took a sip of wine. Edging forward, she began describing in exact detail the encounter at the cemetery—and specifically the woman who demanded a message from her.

When she had finished, Angela downed the last drop of her wine, inhaled a long, deep breath, and sat back in her chair as she exhaled. She felt light and peaceful, as if a spring breeze had just blown over her.

"That's quite a story!" Rowena said quickly.

"I'm not making any of it up; this *really* happened."

Rowena found it fascinating talk. She was particularly intrigued by the vibrations Angela sensed and surprised to hear her say that now, in some odd way, she found them to be wonderful.

"You know what a 'medium' is, don't you?" Rowena asked, but she didn't pause for Angela to answer. Instead, she continued, "It's someone who communicates with and even relays messages from deceased persons." She enjoyed sharing what she knew on the subject, and being so fascinated by Angela, she questioned her extensively about each experience.

"I have researched 'mediums' and 'schizophrenia'... anything that could cause me not to be able to tell the difference between real and unreal experiences."

"You aren't schizophrenic," Rowena reassured her, a bit surprised that Angela had invested time on researching the subject matter.

"Well then... What am I?"

"I've known you and your family for many years, and just like you, I grew up listening to the tales of your grandmother, Iana. Unlike you, I believed them to be authentic." Rowena tipped her head forward and smiled.

"I must say that Grandma Iana has come to mind more than once over the past weeks." Angela shivered, feeling a chill from within.

"Well then... And I'm just putting this out on the table—"

Angela stopped Rowena in mid-sentence. "Oh believe me, I have thought of nothing else lately."

"If eye and hair color are passed down through the generational line, who's to say that gifts and abilities, such as what your grandmother possessed, can't be as well?"

"But how will I know for sure?"

"Well, my friend," Rowena gave her a tiny smile. "This is your lucky day!"

Over the years, Angela had become well acquainted with Rowena's scheming smile. She knew her friend very well and was quite sure that Rowena possessed the kind of dogged determination and stamina it would take to unravel the mystery unfolding in Angela's life.

Angela immediately flagged down their waiter and ordered another glass of wine. Then she braced herself for what was to come next.

"Dr. Matthew Howard, a tenured professor who is the Head of the Physics Department and Space Science Laboratory at New York University, just so happens to also be a friend of mine." Rowena checked her watch then pulled out her cell phone. "I can call him now if you'd like."

Angela shook her head in disbelief. "No, I'm not ready."

"You can't live like this forever. At some point, you're going to have to find some answers."

Suddenly the sound of screeching tires and smell of burnt rubber, followed by a loud bang, pulled their attention away from their conversation and to the flurry of activity a few yards away. Angela jumped from her seat and started walking towards the mass of people that had begun assembling both on the sidewalk and out in the street.

"What happened?" she asked a woman standing nearby.

"Witnesses to the accident claim to have seen the van flying down the street and then a man flying over the top. Then the van crashed into that parked car over there. Luckily, no one was sitting in the driver's seat of the car."

"Has anyone called 911?" Angela responded.

"Does anyone know how to do CPR?" a man shouted into the crowd.

Unexpectedly, the people, cars and all kinds of agonizing noises rushed and zigzagged around her; Angela closed her eyes, now very aware of her pounding heart, and willed herself to step off the curb. Taking one step and then another, and then without even thinking, she pushed some people aside and was suddenly looking down at a young man lying on the street. There was blood everywhere, mixed together with tiny shards of glass that twinkled in the sunlight. Angela noticed the boy's breathing was shallow and labored. Looking over beside him, she noticed a young woman sobbing uncontrollably, rocking back and forth with her arms wrapped tightly around her torso, pleading for the young man to open his eyes and begging him not to leave her.

Instantly Angela dropped to her knees beside him and, as though he knew she was there, the man's eyes fluttered open.

"I'm sorry," he whispered, and then his eyes rolled back into his head.

Angela could see him lose consciousness and was suddenly aware she needed to start CPR. She interlaced her fingers, placed them on his chest and pressed down hard while praying to herself, "Please, dear God, help me."

Suddenly, with one of the compressions to his chest, blood gushed everywhere. And, instantaneously, Angela experienced a concentrated vibration so powerful she struggled for air. She immediately put a hand over her mouth and the words, *"Sugar and spice and everything nice,"* floated into her mind.

And, with that, somebody grabbed her forcefully by the arm and pulled her out of the way. The team of paramedics continued the CPR as they hurriedly lifted the boy's near-lifeless body onto the gurney and into the ambulance.

Angela's panic-stricken state of mind was teetering on the edge of uncontrollable. Scared to death, she was finding it difficult to take in any air, let alone wrap her brain around what she had just witnessed and heard. She bent down, gulped in a huge breath of air and collapsed onto the curb while the limerick, *"Sugar and spice and everything nice,"* repeated over and over within her.

Struggling to remain calm amidst the flurry of horror and panic, she feared she was on the verge of passing out. Instinctively she cupped her hands over her face and began doing deep breathing exercises. Between the inhaling and exhaling, she frantically scanned the crowd for Rowena, but instead of seeing her friend, Angela began to see a distinct change in the breathing space around her. Bit by bit a green fog-like cloud was appearing right before her eyes, inch by inch creeping slowly towards her until finally her entire body was enveloped within it. And as far as she could tell, she was its only chosen victim. In a desperate attempt to ground herself, Angela quickly focused her eyes on the injured young man just as the doors of the ambulance were slamming shut. Without a moment to take another breath, her entire body began to quiver, and an earsplitting reverberation went off in her ears.

She was gasping and reaching up for her throat, attempting to drag herself out of this horrifying dream, when she noticed the green haze, which held her captive, was gradually fading to reveal an illuminating, fine white mist.

No other people, no thoughts or worries accompanied the images of a suffering and dying man; she could see no yesterday and no tomorrow, yet she felt no danger or sadness. Her world had just stopped, and it was a beautiful place.

"This is what beauty feels like," she thought.

As the white light increased in power, Angela became aware of an intense love and acceptance for her. Her heart slowed and the uncontrollable trembling, the nervousness, and the ear-piercing sounds disappeared. She was feeling better.

"None of this makes any sense," she whispered. "I don't know what's happening." Angela's eyes rose in surprise. "But I'm not afraid."

In next to no time at all, Angela experienced the sensation of feeling heavy and slow, and she had an eerie feeling of being stretched. The more she resisted, the more her energy drained from her body. In an attempt to relax, she took in a deep, cleansing breath, which seemed to increase the elevation of her entire body and then catapult her through the upper air in the direction of a perfectly spherical hole. In the blink of an eye, she was standing dead center in a tornado or tunnel-like structure. Terror and panic rushed into her mind when she thought of living through an out-of-body experience. Was it possible? Or, worse yet, had she died without knowing it and was now on her way towards heaven?

As she began to take in her surroundings, Angela's fears were quickly diverted when she observed a dazzling and radiant white light off in the distance. It was an illumination more magnificent than she had ever witnessed, and it radiated with unconditional love and a peace that passed all understanding. At a certain point, Angela swore she could hear trumpets and a choir of angels singing praises to God all around her.

Just as she began to settle down, soaking up the overwhelming ambiance of love and peacefulness, Angela's travels came to a screeching halt.

"What's going to happen now?" she questioned. "Is this the calm before the storm?"

She remained very still, waited a few minutes, and then watchfully turned her head to the right and then to the left. In that moment Angela realized her journey had reached its final destination. She was now standing completely surrounded by the brilliant and spectacular white light. Immediately she detected a jolt of excitement surging through her veins, which brought a smile to her face. Inside, her heart beat a little faster, but soon her mind prompted her to consider that this situation might suggest danger and doubt.

And with that worry, Angela's thought of the Biblical teaching of Peter walking on water. Recalling the parable, she remembered that as long as Peter hung onto his faith and did not doubt, he was safe. Peter's doubt would cause him to fall away and sink beneath the surface.

Angela quickly identified with the parable and anxiously began nodding her head in agreement. In addition, she confessed the words, "I will not doubt... I will not doubt" over and over.

It wasn't long until she sensed an undeniable stirring from within. A still, small voice assured her that all was well and that she had nothing to fear. The love she was experiencing was greater than any love she had ever given or received, and now it was hers for the taking. More significantly, Angela knew deep in her spirit and without a shadow of a doubt that the light was within her. Instinctively she tilted her head upwards toward the heavens, arched her back and opened her arms wide. Her spirit was soaring with thanksgiving and praise, and her heart desired to be bathed in this gracious love until the end of time.

"Well done, Angela." The words floated like incense into her mind.

Immediately her eyes opened wide, and for a brief moment Angela locked eyes with the light that had just spoken to her. Gulping in a huge breath of air, she then fell to her knees. She knew this voice, she could trust this voice and it was the voice that held her when she couldn't stand on her own.

Without taking her eyes away from the light, she smiled, then closed her eyes and bowed her head.

Her next sensation was that of her body shuddering, a jolt that awakened her entire system all at once—and she was back. Right away her pulse jumped, and she rubbed hard at the back of her neck where the tension settled. A fresh headache was brewing, making it difficult to raise her head, and her eyes fluttered against the bright afternoon sun as she tried to focus on her surroundings. And then, for an instant, the brief image of a brilliant white light flashed into her mind before it tucked itself away.

Angela sat quietly on the curb, her head cocked, and she nearly smiled at the familiar clatter of people enjoying the warm afternoon. She studied the cars and bicycles as they carefully maneuvered their way around a policeman who hurriedly swept up pieces of broken glass and a fireman who washed debris and blood from the street. She knew what happened here and knew too that she would deal with it. She was strong and able. Those things she knew about herself; deep inside she had always known them, and she would go on knowing and believing them now.

"It's a small and crowded world," she thought.

Just then, the squeal of sirens off in the distance directed her focus, almost in a straight line, to a group of people gathered on the opposite side of the street: in particular, a stylishly-dressed woman standing slightly off to the side of the group. Angela assumed the woman to be about the same age as she was, and she instantly began admiring her tasteful choice in hair color and style.

"Wonder who does her hair," she thought.

Then, for reasons she couldn't explain, Angela found herself not focused on the woman's choice in hair color but, instead, her smile. She thought it very pleasant, though she kept biting her lip and obviously seemed to be stressed out about something.

Angela shook her head, and as she looked at her watch, she instantly stiffened.

"This can't be right!" She tapped the face of her watch just as the next minute rolled into place.

She considered it for a moment. *"I feel like I have been sitting here for hours. But really... It was only thirty minutes ago that Rowena and I sat down for lunch."*

Out of the corner of her eye, Angela spotted the tastefully-dressed woman walking across the street. In fact, she seemed to be heading right towards her.

Still washed-out from her ordeal earlier, Angela was not in the mood to discuss the events of either the accident or her role in it. The only way to wrap her mind around what happened was to do something familiar and reliable: to keep to herself. The seclusion soothed her.

"Oh no, what if she's a reporter?" she thought. *"That is the* last *thing I need right now."*

Adrenalin forced her to an upright position. Her legs were shaking like Jell-O, her feet felt heavy, and she was tired and spent. Quickly, she looked through the crowd of people that had gathered behind her to the table where Rowena and she were having lunch. It was only a few feet away, but right now it seemed like a hike across the Mohave Desert.

Just as Angela stepped up onto the curb, a young man sped past her on a skateboard and accidently knocked her purse from her hand. Quickly, she leaned down to pick up her purse, but she was stopped and startled by the feeling of someone's hand lightly touching her on the shoulder.

"Excuse me, I don't want to bother you, but I-I had to let you know that what you did earlier... Well, I just wanted to say that it took a lot of courage."

Saying nothing for a moment, Angela smiled and then thanked the woman who was speaking to her.

"I normally don't do things like this." The woman laughed, waving an arm in the air.

"Things like what?" Angela bent down and picked up her purse then snapped it shut.

The woman took one long breath, then another. "Never mind. Please forgive me if I've bothered you."

"No, really it's all right. You go ahead." Angela nodded her encouragement.

"It's probably crazy and all in my mind." Biting her lip, she was now obviously torn between saying what she was thinking and just forgetting about it and walking away.

"Don't you worry about it." Angela's smile was sincere as she stepped further out of the street, inviting the woman to do the same. "Let's get out of traffic so you can tell me what's on your mind."

"I'm sorry, I haven't even introduced myself." She smiled. "I'm Patricia."

"Patricia, I'm Angela."

"There is no logical explanation for what I am about to say, other than I have this very strong feeling, very deep inside."

"And it has to do with me?" Angela asked.

After one last glance at where the accident had happened, Patricia reached out her hand and gently placed it on Angela's arm. Looking directly into her eyes, she smiled and then spoke. "Angela, I believe I have a message for you."

"A message... For me?"

"At first I wasn't entirely sure, but the more I tried to dismiss it, the stronger it became." She gave herself a little shake. "I know how this may all sound, but I think I am supposed to give you this Bible verse."

Angela saw something flicker in Patricia's eyes, and then she nodded her head in agreement and took a deep breath.

"A Bible verse?"

"It's Jeremiah 29:11. Are you familiar with it?"

Angela lifted her head, and her eyes met Patricia's. "For I know the thoughts that I think toward you, says the Lord, thoughts of peace and not of evil, to give you a future and a hope," she recited aloud.

Angela paused. With her knees about to give out, she eased her way back against the building to steady herself. Suddenly the shadows of angels floated like incense into her mind, and the same tenderness that floated over her when she had heard the words "*well done*" filled her spirit.

"Are you alright?" Patricia reached out to balance her.

"I think I'm going to have to sit here and cry for a few minutes."

"Oh, I hope I haven't upset you."

"On the contrary." Angela reached out and laid her hand on Patricia's. "Trust me; I'm fine—great, really—and thank you for coming over to me."

And with that, Patricia said good-bye and turned to walk into the crowd of people still gathered around where the accident had happened.

Angela took one last glance at where a young man had apologized, bleeding. Her heart sank momentarily as she thought about the young woman, the young mother-to-be. Her pain was familiar to Angela; she knew what it was like to cry huge, long, wracking sobs of pain. What frightened Angela now was speculating on what lied ahead for her and her unborn child.

"I'll probably never see her again," she said to herself.

"Angela," Rowena said angrily as she approached, fighting to stay calm, "where the hell have you been?"

"What's that?" Angela asked, feeling half dead. She felt as though she were hanging somewhere in outer space. Everything about her life was again suddenly unreal.

"I've been looking everywhere for you," Rowena blurted out, and Angela was shocked again.

"And what about you?" Angela said, and then she turned with a serious expression to look at Rowena. "Given the circumstances," she pointed to where the accident occurred, "seems to me all you had to do was follow the crowd."

Rowena didn't answer her; she only nodded.

"Okay, the truth is I ran into an old friend." Smiling at Angela, she held up her hand to shade her eyes, trying to hide her pleasure in seeing him.

"Of course you did," Angela said, trying to sound calmer than she felt, not giving a damn about Rowena's explanation at this point.

Without saying anything further, Rowena helped Angela to her feet, hooked her arm through hers and then asked, "You want to tell me who it is that you'll never see again?"

"You... I was hoping never to see *you* again!"

"Very funny. Remind me again why I am friends with you!" Rowena shot her a look and they both laughed.

"Come on, let's go home. I need a drink." Rowena smiled.

"I need a nap!" Angela said after a moment.

As the two women made their way through the crowd of people, Angela began hearing the words of the limerick again in her mind. Over and over, like a broken record, *"Sugar and spice, and everything nice."* She finally had to press her hands over her ears and then stopped dead in her tracks, turning to face Rowena.

"Angela, I'm right here." She put her arm around Angela's shoulders. "Just breathe deep and relax."

"Yes," she said as she nodded, relaxing again.

Then with full and clear-cut lucidity, she completed the limerick out loud.

"Sugar and spice and everything nice... that's what little *girls* are made of," Angela said hoarsely.

"What in the world *are* you talking about?" Rowena grabbed Angela's wrists.

For a long moment, they stared at each other. Angela's eyes were dark and glazed with tears; she reached up to brush the hair from her face.

"Now do you want to tell me what this is all about?" Rowena handed her a bottle of water she happened to have in her purse.

Angela took a sip to ease her dry throat. "Maybe it's time to enter into this new phase of my life." After another breath, she declared, "I want to see the professor."

5

Angela had been awake and alone for hours. In the early morning quiet, she drank her first cup of coffee, meditated and read her Bible. Tracing her fingers over the cover of the antique book, she found the carvings deep and smooth; she then reread a quote that the deacon at her church had hand-written on the first page.

"The most auspicious moment of your life is when you make the commitment to know the Truth, a commitment so firm there is no turning back." -Gurumayi Chidvilasananda

After her morning ritual with the Lord, she dressed in her running suit and sneakers for the second half of her morning routine. Along with being strongly committed to her faith, Angela was just as committed to health and fitness. She knew that regular exercise would increase her mental stability and slow age-related complications in the future. For a woman approaching fifty, she was in the best physical shape of her life.

She stepped outside and onto the sidewalk, rubbed her eyes, combed her fingers through her hair, and then filled her lungs with a deep, cleansing breath. Posed in a downward position, she was at ease with the painful pleasure of stretching her hamstrings and lower back, even at this ungodly hour of the morning. Physical exercise always restored to her a clear head and relaxed body; she delighted in this time of quiet focus, which muted the cluttered noise and uneasiness in her head. Zipping up her jacket, she set out walking at first, giving her muscles time to warm up and enjoying the sight of the early morning mist as it covered her gardens. Out of habit, she turned at the end of the driveway and increased her pace into a jog.

To divert her mind from the irritation of exercising, she started reviewing the latest round of events in her life. Even though she had a heart-knowledge that what she was experiencing was nothing to be afraid of or anxious about, her head-knowledge hadn't caught up yet.

"I'm not going to change my mind, and I'm not going to bother thinking about changing my mind."

Truth be told, these days she felt like she was physically in pursuit of answers to the never-ending questions that continued to stream through her mind. And no matter how hard she tried, she could never find them.

At the mile mark, she turned around and started back towards her house. The fog had dampened her hair and her jacket, but her muscles felt warm and loose. As she sprinted up the front steps and onto the porch, she heard her cell phone ringing inside the house.

"Cell phone... Where is my cell phone...?" she chanted aloud as she roamed the house trying to locate it.

Angela frantically followed the ringing sound into the kitchen to find Nathan sitting at the kitchen table with his head hidden by the morning paper, waving her cell phone impatiently in the air.

She gritted her teeth and grabbed the phone like an Olympic runner taking a baton in a race. Then she headed for the living room.

"Hello," she said, catching her breath.

"Angela, are you alright?"

"Oh, Rowena, I'm fine. I was outside and ran in to answer my phone."

"I won't keep you then, but I wanted to let you know about the lecture Dr. Howard is giving. You're still interested, aren't you?"

She held the phone, thinking about trying to get out of going.

"If you don't want to, you can just say it," Rowena replied to her silence.

"No, I do. But..."

"But what?"

"Some days I can barely breathe when I think about the feelings I have felt over dead bodies." She paused for a moment, then said, "Maybe I'm making too much of all of this and should just forget about it. I could go back to the shop; at least *there* I know who I am and what I'm supposed to do."

"Do you think what has happened lately to you is an accident?" Rowena asked her. "I most certainly do not. Just what if all of this is part of a bigger plan for your life?"

"If it's a plan for my life, then *please* tell me what I am supposed to be doing with all of it."

"Well, first of all, you can start by educating yourself on the subject by attending Dr. Howard's lecture."

Angela sighed. "I'm sorry, it's just that I feel so alone. I wish there was someone still alive in my family who could explain more of my grandmother's life to me."

"I take that as Nathan not knowing what has been going on."

Rowena's assumption made Angela sad—and feel sort of guilty—as she considered choosing to keep this part of her life a secret from her husband. She thought back to the day they were married, when Nathan and she had vowed never to keep secrets from one another. As they stood before God, they promised to make Him the head of their household, believing that His love for each of them and their love and respect for one another would enable them to find the solution to whatever they were facing.

"Only the day when Kenny died did I mention anything to him." Her eyes welled up with tears. "I'm not ready to talk with him about any of this just yet."

"Well, then for now we can do this together. You are not alone," Rowena responded.

"Thanks Rowe," Angela managed to say before her voice died. After a moment, she continued, "When did you say Dr. Howard's lecture was?"

"Tuesday morning at ten o'clock. Shall I pick you up?" Rowena asked.

"Pick me up, and let's do this."

"Great! Then I'll see you bright and early tomorrow."

After finishing the phone call with Rowena, for the rest of the morning Angela tried to do something that would keep her mind busy. She could only stomach bits and pieces of her memories, so she tried to clean, to work in her flower garden and to read, but in actuality, all she managed to do was dredge up the gruesome images of a young man's mangled and bleeding body as he lay suffering in the street before her eyes. The childhood limerick, *"Sugar and spice and everything nice,"* repeated over and over in her mind like a broken record.

By the end of the day, Angela was again physically and emotionally exhausted. However, she was finally prepared to accept whatever was required to restore peace to her life and family. Tuesday morning at ten o'clock couldn't come quickly enough.

Angela awoke before dawn... yet again. Over the past months, she had been having a lot of trouble staying asleep through the night. Even though she had been on a dizzying ride since Kenny's death, she didn't want to form a habit of relying on the sleeping pills her doctor prescribed. She was already on one ride that she didn't know how to step off of, and she didn't need to add another to the list.

Yawning, she rolled over and pulled the covers over her head, determined to stay in bed until sunrise. No point in cursing herself for waking up early again, she thought. She huffed out a breath and then began wondering what the day would bring. Unexpectedly, she sensed feelings of hope and expectation creeping into her psyche. Although she was startled by these unfamiliar sensations, they sent her spirit soaring. With half a laugh, she sat up and drew in a deep breath.

"Nothing like the smell of freshly brewed coffee," she thought, smiling to herself and very thankful she had programmed the coffee maker to brew an hour earlier than usual. For an instant longer, she fought the urge to get up, but then she succumbed to it and carefully, in silence, edged her way out of bed. After snuggling into her fluffy bathrobe, she tip-toed out of the bedroom and staggered towards the kitchen.

She paused at the doorway. "Today I'll take the first step on my journey," she said as a look of panic spread across her face. Her heart gave a little tug, but at the same time she sensed that all would be well with her. With a calming breath, she smiled shyly and allowed her emotions to rule her for a moment. Angela wiped a tear with the lapel of her bathrobe, shook her head and walked over to the counter. There, she poured her first cup of coffee, took her Bible from the drawer and sat down at the table. She bowed her head, closed her eyes and started her morning in prayer.

Later that morning, Angela and Rowena arrived at New York University, an hour before Dr. Howard's lecture was set to begin. As they strolled through Washington Square Park in the heart of Greenwich Village, it was impossible for them to miss the hundreds of bright-eyed, energetic college students headed to their classes. The impressive buildings and the amount of activity on the campus did not obstruct the view of the fabulous Fifth Avenue, and both agreed lunch and a little shopping after the lecture was definitely a good plan.

Fifteen minutes before ten o'clock, they settled into their seats, which were in the center of the second row. The Kimmel Theatre was an intimate venue, with only a hundred seats and a stage floor just a few feet from the first row. Some students trickled in through the doors at the back of the room, but for the most part the room was full and ready to hear Dr. Howard speak.

Angela opened the program, which read, "Tuesday, June 28, Effects of Electromagnetics on the Human Body."

Dr. Howard walked across the stage and up to the podium. The lights dimmed, signaling that his lecture was about to begin. Looking out upon the group, he immediately noticed Rowena sitting in the second row. He smiled and nodded his head, then mouthed the words, "*Nice to see you.*" Rowena smiled and nodded back.

"I saw that!" Angela jabbed her elbow into Rowena's arm. "I'm beginning to wonder what the real reason is that I am sitting here at a Dr. Matthew Howard lecture."

"So shoot me!" She smiled back at her friend. "There is a method to my madness, and it's two-fold. I'm helping you—and I truly mean that—and I'm also helping myself to a little eye candy first thing in the morning."

"Remind me again why I'm friends with you!" Angela grinned and shook her head.

"Good morning! For those of you taking my class, consider this an extension of our classroom study; in other words, it would be to your advantage to take notes during my lecture. You have been given fair warning... There *will* be a pop quiz!"

The students stirred, opening notebooks or booting up laptops to begin recording what their professor had to say.

"For all others in attendance, just sit back and relax as we begin to understand, step by step, what electromagnetic energy is and what effects electromagnetics have on the human body.

"Have you ever given a thought to the microwave that cooks your food with ease in only a couple of minutes? If not the microwave oven, then what about the light bulb over your head, or the X-ray machine which gave you the good news that your hand is not broken?

"All these wonders of modern life run on the basis of an amazing phenomenon called electromagnetic energy. We are surrounded by this energy, and our lives would have been completely different if this phenomenon had not been discovered or understood by mankind. This energy is said to be in the form of waves, but according to Einstein and Max Plank, electromagnetic radiation exists in the form of particles called photons. Each particle or photon is an extremely small grain of energy—an energy packet, so to speak. Is it possible for electromagnetic energy to be both waves *and* energy packets? Well, the answer has been found to be yes, they *can* be both, which further deepens the mystery behind electromagnetism."

The energy in the room went from enthusiastic to an obvious and uncomfortable difference of opinion. Angela looked around, noticing the majority of the students totally captivated and hanging on every word Dr. Howard spoke. On the other hand, Angela spotted a few students towards the back of the room who were slumped down in their seats with their eyes closed. Every now and then she witnessed students leaning over to consult with the people next to them, only to be answered with raised eyebrows and shrugged shoulders. The whispering and giggling of two female students seated in the front row resulted in an abrupt halt to Dr. Howard's lecture.

Dr. Howard paused and fixed his eyes with a penetrating, unwavering stare on the two female students. Following the brief visual reprimand, he continued.

"As I was saying, research has already established that all things have a resonating frequency or an energy packet. Recent studies have shown that when the frequency is elevated, the vibrations or waves pulsate at a higher level, which may possibly facilitate humans to see and hear them, perhaps even in other dimensions. One hypothesis is the ability of what some refer to as 'time travel.'

"We have documented information about people who became masters of both meditation and out-of-body experiences or body travels, which seems to defy all laws known in physics. For years the government has referred to this process as Remote Viewing and has actually employed people to work and study in this area. During war times, Remote Viewing was proven to be a dependable source for locating the opposition, enemy missile sites, documents and so forth in an effort to gain an edge in the battle.

"America's greatest psychic, Edgar Cayce, spelled C-A-Y-C-E, pronounced Casey, claimed to be able to see and read auras, but this power was never tested under controlled conditions.

"However, Edgar Cayce is best known for being a psychic medical diagnostician and psychic reader of past lives. One of the most common reasons people give for believing in the psychic abilities of people such as Cayce is the claim that there's no way he could have known this stuff by ordinary means. He must have been told this by a god or spirits or have been astrally projected back or forward in time, et cetera. His followers maintain that Cayce was able to tap into some sort of higher consciousness in order to get his psychic knowledge.

"Cayce, also referred to as 'The Sleeping Profit,' was known to go into a deep sleep and travel to places where he could heal people remotely. Some theories say that he would awaken from his deep sleep filled with knowledge on how to build things and even cure diseases.

"In short, the definition of electromagnetic energy is that it is the energy source required to transmit information, in the form of waves, from one place or material to another. This radiation travels with the speed of light and can be in the form of light, heat or practically anything else. The sun, the earth and the ionosphere are main sources of electromagnetic energy in nature.

"This concludes my lecture for today. Students, I will see you in class tomorrow morning, and all others, I thank you for attending. Have a good afternoon."

The lights came up, and with that, Dr. Howard closed his notebook and walked over to where Rowena and Angela were standing.

"Really now, what are two lovely ladies, such as yourselves, doing at a lecture on electromagnetic energy?"

They looked at each other and smiled.

"So, did you enjoy it?" Dr. Howard grinned as he asked.

"We did," they answered in unison.

"By the way, Rowena, you look spectacular, as always." He leaned over and kissed her on the cheek.

Rowena giggled and put Angela's teeth on edge.

"Where are my manners? Matthew, this is Angela Roberts, the friend I spoke to you about."

"Ah yes, I've been dying to sit down with you. It's nice to finally meet you, Mrs. Roberts."

"And you, Dr. Howard. Please, call me Angela."

"I'm so glad you decided to come. Rowena has filled me in on some of what you've been experiencing. Perhaps, if you have some time, you'd be willing to grab a quick bite to eat so we can discuss what's been going on? I have some free time before my next class."

"We're free for the afternoon," Rowena gushed and then smiled.

"Wonderful! Let me grab my briefcase and we can be on our way."

Angela gave her friend a sidelong glance of utter disbelief. Shaking her head, she uttered, "I can't believe you sometimes... You should see your face!"

"Whatever," Rowena muttered under her breath.

Ten minutes later, they were seated at a table in the cafeteria. During lunch, Angela told Dr. Howard the events that had taken place, twice following her son's death and another time one afternoon while looking at an old picture of her grandmother. Halfway through their conversation, Angela started to tear up. She hesitated for a moment and then went on to share the so-called legend of her grandmother, Iana Hamilton Holmes.

Immediately Dr. Howard noticed Angela and her grandmother had a couple of things in common, but he wasn't about to rush to any conclusions during their first meeting.

"Angela, I just spoke about this in my lecture. Vibrations or waves at a higher level may make it possible for humans to see and hear something, even in other dimensions. Based on this theory, I suspect your grandmother was able to tap into other human beings' 'Energy Packets.'"

"Honestly, Dr. Howard, my ears *did* perk up when I heard you say that." She took a long sip of her iced tea and pressed both hands on top of the table.

"The last time something happened," she began as she looked across the table to Rowena, "it was the day you and I had lunch."

"You never told me about any vibrations or episodes the day we had lunch," Rowena said in a spiteful tone. "You mean something more than the car accident happened?"

Dr. Howard looked surprised and glanced at Rowena before turning to Angela.

"Let me finish," Angela said. Dr. Howard could see there were tears in her eyes.

"Did you have another episode while you were tending to that young man from the accident?" Rowena asked.

Angela took a slow breath and then described a dazzling white light, going on to give a picture of her being transported through the atmosphere and into something she could only describe as a tunnel. Then a flash of apprehension coursed through her, gnawing away at her confidence.

"Dr. Howard, do you believe in God?" she muttered uneasily.

Rowena was caught off guard by her friend's question and cut her off. "Isn't that a little personal?"

"No, it's okay," Dr. Howard said. "Yes, I have a relationship with the Lord."

Angela stared across the table at Rowena, her heart pounding. She worried what she was about to say wouldn't come out correctly.

"Please, go on," Dr. Howard quietly urged.

Angela took her time responding.

"It was right after the accident. One minute my world was chaos and confusion and then I was standing in this beautiful place, completely surrounded by a brilliant and spectacular white light. I know that I heard... Yes, it was trumpets and a choir of angels singing. I felt peaceful and safe, and my desire to stay was overwhelming. I really didn't want to leave."

Angela became increasingly uneasy under Rowena's intense gaze.

"You think I'm crazy, don't you?" Angela asked.

Dr. Howard reached over and gently placed his hand on hers. "It's your testimony, Angela, and I don't think it's crazy," he reassured her.

Rowena didn't say anything or move right away. She sat studying her friend for a moment and then leaned in closer. "Honey, I don't think anything like that either! Honestly, you're absolutely glowing."

Dr. Howard nodded in agreement. He now had a good sense of her. Just from their short conversation over lunch, he had learned a lot about her life, and by the end of her story, he only wanted to know more.

Leaning back in his chair, he thought for a moment and then reached down to his briefcase and pulled out a folder with "RMTS10" on the front. Placing the folder on top of the table, he smiled.

"Angela, I have only discussed what I'm about to share with you with a handful of people. All of them believe that everything you—so courageously, I might add—just shared with me describes a bona fide example of what the psychic Edgar Cayce claimed to demonstrate. However, like I mentioned, his abilities never were tested under controlled conditions."

Stiffening, Angela responded, "You want me to be your guinea pig?"

He shook his head no and continued, "Over the years, researchers have gathered countless numbers of recorded documentation about people claiming to have experienced what we now describe as out-of-body experiences or body travels events. In my opinion, and based on my research, what you have experienced is just the tip of the iceberg for you. If I may be so bold, you have a gift."

Angela laughed. "A gift?" She reached over and picked up the folder.

"I believe you do, and I also believe your grandmother possessed this same gift. It seems to have skipped a generation with your mother." Dr. Howard paused for a moment before adding, "On the other hand, your mother may have possessed this gift as well; she may have been a 'carrier.' As you said, you were a child when she passed away, so there's no way to say for sure."

"This is all very interesting and sounds like a good science fiction movie," Angela said with a laugh. "But I came to your lecture with the hope of understanding what had happened to me, not really with a desire to take this any further."

Dr. Howard smiled and nodded in understanding.

"Just out of curiosity, what does this RMTS10 do?" she couldn't help but ask.

"Consider this for a moment: Thoughts are energy. Energy is vital to the transmission of information—in wave form, mind you —from one place or material to another. The RMTS10 monitors these vibrations. At a certain point, the RMTS10 is turned up to intensify the frequency to a level that is necessary for information to be received or communicated."

"Are you saying that these vibrations I feel could have messages behind them?"

"It's very possible. Didn't you say that your grandmother received messages and then delivered them?"

Without warning, Angela jumped up from her chair.

"Honey, for goodness sake, what's the matter?" Rowena chuckled to cover her annoyance. Angela stood frozen and stared at both of them, her mind flooding with the terrifying memory of being at Kenny's grave while a crazed, wide-eyed woman demanded a message from her.

"She wanted her message," she mumbled and then sat back down with her arms folded across her chest.

Dr. Howard watched Angela for a few moments and then determined this all was too much, too fast. He gathered his papers and rose to his feet.

"I hate to end our discussion, but I need to get back to class."

"So what do you think, Angela?" Rowena asked as Dr. Howard gathered his belongings.

"I would like Angela to take some time and digest all of this. Also, I suggest she keep a journal to jot down dates, times and places, along with the strength and length, of any future events."

"I can do that." Angela nodded.

Dr. Howard straightened his glasses. "We can discuss this more when I return."

"Vacation?" Rowena raised her eyebrows and smiled at him.

"A working one," he replied. "I'm about to head off on a three month sabbatical. I leave on the Fourth of July for London, England, where a colleague of mine lives. We are taking the next three months to work out any kinks with the RMTS10 and finish writing our notes."

"Humph... I was just about to invite you to our Fourth of July cookout," Rowena complained as she shifted in her seat.

"I'll take a rain check if you're offering."

"I'll hold you to it!" she perked up and said with a wink.

Dr. Howard leaned in and gave Rowena another kiss on the check. "You look gorgeous, kid! See you when I get back. And Angela, I would consider it an honor to work with you further. I'll be in touch, and it was very nice meeting you."

6

Even though Rowena had fabricated the idea of a Fourth of July celebration out of thin air, Angela found the idea appealing and decided to run with it—although she didn't make this last-minute decision until a few months later at the beginning of July. It had been months since she had entertained anyone in her home, and at this point in time, she was in desperate need of a diversion from what her life had become.

She knew that, with only two days left before the Fourth of July, hiring a caterer was going to be next to impossible. Therefore, if she was going to offer food at her cookout, she would have to step up and cook it all herself. And for Angela Roberts, that was going to be a huge undertaking; cooking was *not* her forte. Although she wasn't fond of making weekly menus and then preparing those same humdrum meals week after week, she was proud of the fact that the majority of meals that she served during the early years of her children's lives were well-balanced and prepared by her own hands. Take-out and pizzas were limited to weekends only.

Now that it was just her husband and she, Angela was very grateful that Nathan wasn't the type of man who insisted upon a home-cooked, meat-and-potatoes meal every night. These days they ate for survival, unless it was dinner out—then it was all pleasure.

Knowing too that Nathan wasn't fond of entertaining, Angela called him at work to check with him about her Fourth of July shindig ideas before she made any definite plans.

After getting the green light from Nathan, Angela realized that she had a lot to do and not a lot of time to do it. One dish Angela always received rave reviews about was her potato salad, so with a cup of coffee in hand, she sat down at her desk and listed those ingredients at the top of her shopping list.

She also made a mental note to carve out some time, if not today then soon, to plant a few flowers in the backyard and to find the American flag that was hiding somewhere inside her house.

"You can't have a Fourth of July celebration without the stars and stripes!" Angela smiled with pleasure.

With her list complete, she grabbed her purse and keys and headed for the grocery store. She couldn't remember the last time grocery shopping had brought a smile to her face. God knew she had too much time on her hands lately, too much quiet, too much space, and this get-together was exactly what the doctor ordered.

"You'd think this was the first party I'd ever given!" she thought, smiling, as she reached for a shopping cart.

Before she knew it, her cart was half loaded with hot dogs, ground beef, chips, pretzels and everything else she could think of for a backyard barbecue. She knew it was in the vicinity of four o'clock, and she still needed to stop by Party City for the backyard decorations.

"Cake... I need to order a cake!" She whipped her cart around and sailed into the next aisle, running head on into another shopper.

"Oh, I'm terribly sorry!" Angela pushed her hand through her hair and then pressed her palm to her forehead. "I need to slow down."

The young woman behind the other cart immediately straightened up. Her hands fell from the cart and to her sides. "It's you... You're the woman from the accident!"

Angela frowned, shuddering at the thought of it. Then she cupped her elbows with her hands and looked at the young woman's ever-expanding belly.

"Well..." Angela began, "well, aren't you just blooming!" Her brows lifted and her smile spread leisurely. "I'm so glad to see you again!"

"I'm glad to see you too." The young woman let out a long breath. "Though I thought I would be embarrassed if I ever did."

Angela's mouth dropped open. "My goodness, why would you be embarrassed?"

"The last time, when I first saw you, it was so horrible." Her eyes met Angela's. "I realized later that I didn't even thank you for everything you did for Nicky."

"Who could blame you?" Angela said reassuringly as she patted her hand. "I think you had a bit more on your mind that day than thanking me! You were scared and upset for good reason. Please dear, don't give any more energy to those thoughts."

Angela squinted and turned her head slightly at hearing herself use the word "energy" in conjunction with a thought.

Shaking her head, she asked, "So now, Nicky, is that your husband's name?"

"Yes ma'am, that was his name. But Nicky wasn't my husband, he was my boyfriend; we were planning on getting married, but..." The relaxed expression on her face settled into a cold stare.

Angela leaned against her cart. "You're not anymore?"

"No. No, ma'am; Nicky died."

The breath left Angela's body so fast that she felt dizzy.

"Oh, Honey, I'm so sorry." She grabbed the young woman by the arm, saying, "Come on, let's move out of this aisle. We can talk better in the health food aisle... it's always less crowded there!"

The girl smiled and wiped a tear from her cheek as she pushed her cart, following Angela until they found a good place to stop.

"Before we go any further, I don't know your name. I'm Angela Roberts."

With a small laugh, she tipped her head back. "I'm Rebecca Hale."

For thirty minutes, then for an hour, the two women stood talking about Rebecca's life after Nicky's death. Angela listened and watched as her frame of mind went from agitated energy to seemingly completely worn out, from joy to despair. It didn't take Angela long to figure out that after Nicky's death, Rebecca's life took a rapid spiral downward, and now she quite possibly sat on the edge of hopelessness and failure. Suddenly Angela remembered her own life spiraling out of control after Kenny's death; once the spiral began, she couldn't seem to control the fall.

Immediately Angela began to worry if something could be physically wrong with Rebecca. She looked so pale and drawn that Angela began wondering if she had been eating enough. Was she seeing an obstetrician and getting her prenatal checkups? Was she taking vitamins? Did she have a warm bed to sleep in at night, and if so, where?

Out of the blue Angela felt both panic and nausea, and a dose of dry understanding gushed into her mind. It continued to rise as she did some rapid scheming in her head.

"What are we going to do?" The entire burst came out in a disorganized bunch, and she could barely comprehend her own words.

"Ma'am, what do you mean, what are *we* going to do?"

Angela shook her head and then grabbed Rebecca's hand. "Well, the first thing we are going to do, my dear, is you and your baby are going to come to my Fourth of July cookout!"

"I can't... I just can't! It's not necessary, but it's awfully sweet of you to invite me—er, us."

"Just think about it," Angela told her as she pulled one of her business cards out of her purse and handed it to Rebecca. "My home number is at the bottom; you think about it and give me a call."

Tears welled up in Rebecca's eyes again as she reached out and took the card. "Mrs. Roberts, I don't know what to say."

"Say you will be there on the Fourth!" Angela said with a big smile. "Oh, I almost forgot: do you know what you are having yet?"

"A little girl." Rebecca smiled and laid her hand on her belly. "Sugar and spice and everything nice..."

Angela shifted back, and with a quiver in her heart, she completed the limerick, "That's what little girls are made of."

Rebecca laughed. "I didn't think anyone else knew that poem."

Angela's heart was beating a mile a minute. "Oh, it just came to me one day and has refused to leave." She let out a sigh and then smiled. "I need to get going. Please think about the Fourth and let me know."

"I will, ma'am. Thank you." After a slight pause, she added, "Mrs. Roberts, I'm glad we ran into each other!"

They both laughed and then pushed their carts in opposite directions.

When Nathan found her, Angela was knee-deep in mulch as she shoved pansies and marigolds into the flower beds that lined the slate patio in the backyard. He leaned against the door frame and thought that, even in her dirty cut off jeans, a baseball cap and thick gardening gloves, his wife of over twenty-five years was still incredibly beautiful to him.

With his hands in his front pockets, he moved into her line of vision. She glanced up from under the brim of the ball cap and then sat back on her heels.

"Nathan, you're home early." She reached over, scooped up a handful of mulch and tossed it under the flowers.

"I haven't been sleeping much lately. I decided to call it a day and come home to relax with my beautiful wife and a glass of wine."

She hadn't heard that tone in Nathan's voice in a long time.

"Really...? Beautiful?" She wiped a smudge of dirt from her cheek. "In that case, I could use a beer." She angled her head and smiled.

Because he was watching her face, Nathan caught the flash of surprise that traveled over it. "Let me change and I'll be back in a minute. I might even fire up the grill tonight!" He picked up his jacket, flung it over his shoulder, and began to whistle as he walked towards the house.

While she waited for Nathan, Angela strolled around the backyard, taking her time, mainly just to see if she could talk herself out of telling him everything that had been happening since Kenny died. But the seed had been planted and she couldn't find a good enough reason to uproot it now.

Maybe he'd be shocked, stunned or even worse *uncertain* of her mental stability. But any of that was better than keeping this secret from her husband. It was time.

As she came around the side of the house, Nathan was already sitting at the patio table, dressed in his comfy pants and leisurely sipping his glass of wine.

Angela sat down and reached for her beer.

"I like you coming home early."

"This was one of my better ideas." He reached over and took her hand.

The sun was behind him, but it filtered through the leaved branches. Angela smiled at how tender and attractive he looked sitting in the flecks of summer shade.

They both had forgotten how therapeutic it was to sit as long as they liked, to do nothing and to talk about whatever came into their minds.

"We should do this more often," he said as he smiled at her. "I forgot what this was like."

Angela lounged back in her chair. "It's been a long time, hasn't it?"

Although it wasn't completely dark yet, the patio lights began to flicker and glow softly, lighting the edges of the patio. A few early lightning bugs blinked on and off over the bushes and flowers, reminding Nathan of happier times.

"It doesn't seem that long ago when we'd sit out here and watch the boys chase after fireflies."

"Kenny would take Robby's fireflies out his jar when he wasn't looking and put them in his."

Nathan smiled, leaned forward and tapped his glass to Angela's bottle. "Good times. Where did the time go?"

"I can't believe Robby is in his second year of law school."

"And then there was Kenny." Nathan opened his eyes wide and shook his head.

"Don't say it like that!" Angela picked up her bottle of beer, tipped it forward and then finished it with one huge gulp. "I like to think of Kenny as a spirited child." She let out a gut-wrenching belch that would have awakened the dead.

Nathan only smiled. "That's my girl!"

Without saying a word, he stood up and sauntered toward her just the way he had when they were first dating. She waited for him and then smiled the moment he extended his hand to her. Nathan stood looking at his wife for a long moment. A smile flickered at the corners of his mouth, and then that mouth was on hers. The kiss was slow; a shivering of the senses rushed through Nathan's body, and he shuddered as his lips moved silkily over hers. Angela hugged him close to her. His fingers gripped at her lower back as he remembered what she felt like, the softness of her hair against his cheek. It was like a homecoming for both of them. They were each the best friend of the other, and even after twenty-five years of marriage, their relationship was still comfortable and sure.

When he eased back, her eyes blurred and her lips parted. "Who says we ain't still got it?"

"Well, in that case, shall we do it again?" His mouth slid from hers to just below her ear.

"Oh." She let her head fall back and turned it enough for him to get better access.

"Ya know, we really need to stop this." She couldn't resist nipping that sexy bottom lip of his. "Maybe just a little more... sometime after the holiday!"

Nathan laughed and gave her a quick pat on the backside. "I'm going to hold you to it!"

She grabbed his hands, pulled him close and kissed him once more. She breathed deep and looked into his eyes. "Nathan, I need to talk to you about something." The tone in her voice suddenly took a turn from playful to profound.

He didn't say anything for a moment. "Sure, Honey. Let me get another drink."

"You'd better make it a double."

The night air was close and heavy, the kind that summer storms are made of. The thought of an old-fashioned thunderous storm suited Angela's frame of mind right now.

Nathan returned and sat down across from her, and instead of his relaxing glass of wine, he now sipped a scotch and water.

"It's a double, by the way," he said and then handed her another bottle of beer.

"Thanks." Angela took a long, deep gulp.

Blowing out a breath, she leaned back in her chair. "Okay, let me start at the beginning."

For the next hour, Angela explained everything. Nathan nodded his head, recalling her asking him if he had felt something happening in the room immediately after Kenny died. "I remember saying that it was probably just your nerves."

Angela continued and described, in detail, the intense vibrations that flowed through her body when she held Kenny's hand. In addition, she told Nathan about the incident that had taken place at the funeral home and then about the one that had happened in their home one afternoon.

Nathan was careful not to send Angela any wrong signals; as she spoke, he remained completely silent and still. He made a mental note not to display any facial mannerisms, such as rolling his eyes or making any comments, until she had finished speaking.

Sweat trickled down the back of Angela's neck in the thick, drowsy heat, and she paused for a moment. This was harder than she had thought it would be. Nathan was so quiet; his quality of listening was more intense than she had ever known it to be.

As soon as she told Nathan about the white light and how she felt like she'd been floating through the atmosphere and into a tunnel, his eyes finally rose in surprise. "Angela, how can you be so sure of all this?"

She stared down at her hands for a moment. When she looked up, she had tears in her eyes.

"I have been trying to make sense of this myself," she explained. "It started out as research and wanting to feel better... I really don't expect you to understand. I just know that it's not all in my head and that I am not going crazy."

"Honey, I never thought that for a minute. You're not crazy!"

She wiped her eyes with the back of her hands.

"Angela, listen to me: I trust you." Nathan took her hand in his. "I see how much this means to you. I believe you; you are *not* alone in this."

There was a seemingly endless pause.

"You have me, and more importantly, you have God. Didn't you say that He has a plan for your life, and that He will never leave you?"

"I did say that. I believe that." She wiped a lone tear from her face.

"What do you want to do?" he asked.

"Well, I've already done something... On impulse," she admitted. "I realize now it may have opened a can of worms that didn't need to be opened."

He nodded. "Okay. What was it?"

"After my conversation with the young woman from the accident—her name is Rebecca Hale, by the way—I got the impression that her life was hard right now. As far as I could tell, she's got no relatives on either side."

Nathan's mouth dropped open in anticipation of what she would say. "You took pity on her, and..."

Angela lowered her voice to a whisper. "I invited her to the cookout."

"Of course you did!" Nathan chuckled. "Stay calm. That's not such a big deal. We'll figure it out."

"There's not much to figure out. Rebecca already called this afternoon to say she would be coming."

"Well then, the more the merrier!" Nathan said, throwing his arms into the air.

Angela leaned over and kissed him, putting a halt to any further conversation. Without saying a word, she then led Nathan into the house and upstairs to their bedroom. She didn't want to think about anything; instead, she wanted to show her husband how much she loved him.

Angela enjoyed having her morning coffee on the patio. It was pleasant to sit out there in the early hours of the day, and pleasant too were the thoughts of having company for the afternoon. The weather was perfect for the day's plans; a quick morning shower cleared away any humidity that lingered from the night before, leaving a soft blue sky and a balmy breeze freshening the air with the delicate scent of plant life. She sipped her coffee and thought her gardens had turned out to be lovely, consisting of a beautiful array of flowers in different shapes, sizes and colors.

There were white chairs and tables set up on the lawn, draped in the traditional colors of red, white and blue. Adorning each table was a patriotic flower arrangement, each spilling over with red roses, white lilies, blue carnations and a small American flag. Long folding tables lined the patio where the time-honored barbecue menu would be presented.

She turned her head when she heard the sliding glass door open. Nathan stepped out holding two flutes of champagne and orange juice.

"Good morning. Can I interest you in a Mimosa?"

"You certainly can."

Nathan walked over, kissed her good morning and then handed her a drink. Looking around at all her preparations, he tapped his glass to hers. "You've outdone yourself, my dear." Then he grinned and added, "Last night, and now all of this."

She knew that expression on his face. "Well, sir, if you play your cards right, there might be an encore performance in the offering." She touched his knee and then ran her fingers up his inner thigh and began to rub in a way that had every muscle in his body quivering with delight.

With a shake of his head and a quick shiver, he playfully asked, "Who are you and what have you done with my wife?"

Angela laughed and patted his leg.

"That's not fair. You know my weaknesses." He pressed a kiss to her forehead.

"Nathan, I'm so nervous." Her expression quickly changing, she let out a sigh and then took a sip of her drink.

"You're nervous because you're excited and happy."

"I just want everything to be special. It has to be perfect."

"And because you are the type to worry about every little detail." He reached out and took Angela's hand for a moment. "You've got everything under control, and everything already looks perfect."

"It's been a while since I've done anything this large without caterers doing most of the cooking."

"Its hamburgers and hot dogs... And I'm cooking them on the grill!"

"And it's a good thing, since only two people said they wouldn't be able to make it."

He cocked his head and nearly smiled. "Now *I'm* nervous. How very tricky of you!"

"This place is going to be packed!" She pushed herself up to her feet. "A beautiful day, good food, family and friends, laughter and music. I'm ready for a party!"

She walked past Nathan and then stopped to press her lips to his cheek. "In my book, that counts for a hell of a lot!"

Yes, it was good to have her house open again. Angela was always entertained watching people gather in small groups at tables and around a bar. She leisurely walked around the tables, listening to snippets of gossip, political debates, and discussions on sports and the latest movies.

She paused by the table where Rowena was seated and then deliberately leaned down to air-kiss her cheek. “Hello, ladies.” As she expected, fashion was the topic of conversation, and Angela was thankful she knew the styles and colors that flattered her. The choice of a black and white embroidered sundress that fell just below her knees produced a bevy of compliments.

“Angela, everything is wonderful!” Rowena scanned the area. “That’s some hotdog stand Nathan’s got going over there.”

Angela angled herself around to see Nathan decked out in a “Kiss the Cook” apron, dripping in sweat while flipping burgers and swaying right along to “Get Down On It” by Kool and The Gang.

“I think he’s having the time of his life,” Angela said with a laugh. “Excuse me; I just saw the Goodmans come in.”

Midway through the party, Angela needed to relax and found a quiet spot away from the festivities. As she sipped her wine, she took a moment to focus on Nathan; a tender feeling came over her as she watched him slaving over his hot grill. She took in the beauty of the day and was thankful to have a house full of friends and family. She thanked God for blessing her with the energy it had taken to get it all done.

Letting out a long breath, she then turned her focus to two women huddled together off in a corner. One appeared awestruck by what the other was saying to her. Angela grinned and squinted her eyes with the hope of making out what they were saying.

“Oh, I can’t believe it!” one said.

The other woman enthusiastically nodded her head, saying, “And it’s *true*.”

Smiling to herself, Angela thought, *“I’d like to be a fly on* that *table.”*

Suddenly Dr. Howard’s words *“thoughts are energy”* rang out in her mind. Angela was beginning to feel comfortable with the phenomenon that was occurring more and more often in her life, and she was starting to accept Dr. Howard’s explanation about it to her. Thus, she decided to dip her toe into the world of science and do some experimentation of her own.

“There’s got to be some energy going on over there,” she mumbled to herself.

Nonchalantly, she strolled towards the corner of the patio where the two women were seated. Still heavily engaged in their deep gossipmonger, neither noticed Angela standing slightly off to the side.

"Oh my goodness, Sheila Davenport and Denise Chanceford, I didn't see you girls come in." Angela leaned down to air-kiss Sheila's cheek, but instead of leaving it at that, she pulled Sheila up from her seat and embraced her, remaining in the moment longer than what would have been considered normal. "I'm just so happy you could make it!"

With her eyes closed, Angela waited a moment longer and then thought, *"Nothing. No vibrations."*

Upon releasing the visibly-shaken Sheila from her grip, Angela stepped back.

"Alright..." she thought as she switched her focus to Denise. Then she quickly walked over to her and repeated the same routine. Once again, she came up empty handed.

Angela quickly straightened up and smiled. "So nice to see you both! Can I get you anything?"

Sheila responded, "No, no, we're fine." Denise vigorously nodded her head in agreement.

"All right then," Angela said with a smile. Then she grabbed her glass of wine and, without delay, quickly turned and headed towards Rowena's table.

Stiffening in her seat and rubbing her shoulders, Sheila rolled her eyes and puckered her lips in annoyance. "I'd heard she was terribly grief-stricken for months; maybe she's on Prozac or something."

Denise shook her head. "I've never known Angela to be so touchy-feely."

For the next thirty minutes, Angela mingled with her guests. As she did so, she cleverly gripped their hands, laid a hand on top of their shoulders and, on occasion, bear hugged them in a way that would suggest she was finding a long lost member of her family.

Unbeknownst to Angela, Rowena stood nearby, watching her antics from beginning to end.

"That girl may have been able to fool everyone here, but she can't fool me. I know exactly what she's up to!" Rowena waited patiently for her, and the moment Angela released her grip from her last unsuspecting victim, Rowena walked up beside her and hooked her arm through hers. "So how did it go?"

"Great! I think everyone is enjoying themselves."

"Not more than you are." Rowena eyed her friend.

Angela did a double take. "What's *that* supposed to mean?"

Rowena leaned over and whispered in her ear, "Trying to tap into some of those 'Energy Packets,' are we?"

Rowena knew that what Angela was doing was harmless, but she couldn't resist giving her a hard time about it.

"It's not that I don't support you, Honey. I just want you to be mindful of how ridiculous you've looked for the past thirty minutes!" Laughing so hard she nearly lost her balance, Rowena set off that hideous snorting sound which only made her laugh harder. "Girl, I bet half of these people think you're nuts!" she said, holding her stomach and trying to catch her breath.

Angela narrowed her eyes, and then she joined in her friend's laughter. "Have I mentioned lately that I hate you?"

Still laughing and wiping tears from her eyes, Rowena managed to ask, "Angela, what were you thinking?"

Angela rolled her eyes and then caught sight of Rebecca walking through the sliding glass patio doors. She responded, "Tell me again *why* I am friends with you!"

Adjusting her smile, then taking a deep breath, she turned to greet Rebecca. "I didn't think you were going to make it!" she called.

Rowena responded dryly, "Who the heck is she?"

Angela shot back with a smile, "My new best friend!"

Angela walked over and greeted Rebecca with a hug. "I'm going to pour myself another glass of wine," she told her. "Can I get you something to drink?"

"Sure; a glass of water, please."

Angela reached into the cooler and pulled out a bottle of water. She poured it into a glass then added a slice of lemon before offering it to Rebecca.

"Thank you. This heat is really getting to me today."

Angela shook her head. "I'm glad I wasn't pregnant over the summer months; both my boys were winter babies."

Nathan stepped forward when he saw Angela talking with a young woman he didn't recognize.

"Sorry to interrupt," he said. "You must be Rebecca." After shaking her hand, he pulled out a chair and offered it to her. "I've heard a lot about you," Nathan said, smiling at her.

"Thanks." Rebecca sat down and looked around the back lawn. "Your home is beautiful," she said to them both.

"I'd be more than happy to show you around later," Angela told her.

"It's the most beautiful house I've ever seen."

"Oh Nathan, Becky and Eric Mitchell are leaving. Rebecca, please excuse us for just a minute."

Rebecca took in a deep breath and allowed herself to ease back into her chair. Though her insides were quivering, she did her best to take a relaxed sip of her water while she watched the other guests. Here she was, Rebecca Hale from the lower East Side, an invited guest. Not only was she sitting in one of the most prominent neighborhoods in Brooklyn, she was sitting in the company of the powerful and well-to-do.

"This is definitely a first for me," she said to herself, her voice trembling.

She glanced over her shoulder, and the beauty of Angela's home took her breath away. It was complete with cathedral ceilings and crown moldings, elegant couches with deep rich cushions and high back chairs. A massive crystal chandelier, consisting of clear crystal balls, spiraled down from the ceiling above a high-gloss dining room table. Generous floor-to-ceiling windows along the back of the house exposed a carpet of plush green grass and trees—*lots* of trees—behind the house. Rebecca liked the smell of trees.

"So what do you think?" Angela asked when she returned, sitting down beside her.

"I'm sorry; about what?" Rebecca let out a shaky breath.

Angela held out a hand and smiled. "Are you up to meeting some of my friends?"

Rebecca rose to her feet. "Ah, yes... Yes, that would be nice."

Angela led her over to the table where Stephen, Kate and Rowena were still sitting and proceeded to make all the necessary introductions. Then the two sat down to join them.

"Darling, you look fabulous. When are you due?" Kate squinted against the sun as she studied her.

"In three months." Rebecca flushed deep and rosy.

"Do you know what you're having yet?" Stephen chimed in.

"Yes, a little girl."

"Do you have a name picked out?" Rowena asked, continuing the round of questions.

"I do." Rebecca smiled.

"Geez guys, give the poor girl a chance to catch her breath!" Angela said, looking directly at Rowena.

Ten seconds of silence followed. Then Rowena asked, "Well, what is it then, or is it a secret?"

"No ma'am, it's not a secret. Her name is India."

"India... You mean, like the country?" Kate deliberately bumped up the southern accent in her voice.

"That's it, she's cut off!" Stephen laughed and then gave her a squeeze. "When she kicks up the southern accent, she's had too much booze."

Rowena shook her head and then narrowed her eyes.

Angela stared at Kate and then let out a huff of breath. "The name is different." She stroked Rebecca's arm up and down. "And furthermore, I like it!"

Rebecca found everyone extremely friendly and easy to talk with; they were almost like family, she thought.

When the party was over and the guests were on their way home, Rebecca lingered behind, insisting on helping Angela and Nathan with the after-party clean up.

"Well, that's it." Angela turned out the patio lights and pulled the sliding doors shut. "Thanks for staying to help with the mess."

"It's the least I could do," Rebecca said.

"You'd better think about going soon, though; I don't like the idea of a pregnant woman out on the roads at night, especially on a holiday."

"There's sure to be DUI's tonight," Nathan said as he patted Rebecca on the shoulder.

"May I use your phone?" Rebecca asked. "I need to call my friend to pick me up."

"Of course." Angela nodded. "Use the phone in the living room."

Rebecca walked out of the kitchen and into the next room. She paused for a moment, then took a quick scan over her shoulder to see Angela still in the kitchen wiping off the counter. After hesitating for a split second, she slowly made her way across the room to one of the high-back leather chairs, perfectly placed in front of the window. She assumed it to be Nathan's; she giggled, feeling like Goldilocks as she sat down and leaned back in the luxurious chair. Slowly she turned her head from side to side while she inhaled, drawing in its rich perfume. Deciding to wait a few more minutes before calling for her ride home, she jumped up and hurriedly walked over to a bookcase that covered the entire wall. From floor to ceiling were pictures of Nathan, Angela and their boys. A slow, lazy smile spread across her face as she looked at one picture after another.

Unexpectedly she stopped, her breath caught, but she didn't shake. She simply stood as she was, her eyes linked to a photograph of Angela's eldest son, Kenny. Tiny beads of sweat formed on her forehead, and she wrapped her arms around her body, trying to fight against the pain rising up inside her; it was shocking, sharp and horrid. Tears instantly formed in her eyes and fell down her cheeks. She hadn't wanted to hurt him, and she'd believed they'd be together and happy forever. Now, without him, she was broken in every way. Rebecca lifted her hands to remove the picture from the shelf. She trembled as she pressed it to her chest.

Beginning to sob, she fell to the floor. Rough, violent sounds gushed out of her and into the room; the misery of grief coursed through her stomach. She was alone and again feeling as if a part of her was missing. Once more the devastation and despair of her life were at the forefront of her mind.

Angela rushed into the living room and then stopped dead in her tracks. Rebecca was as white as a ghost and down on her knees, ferociously rocking back and forth, sobbing uncontrollably and clutching a picture in her arms.

She rushed over to Rebecca, fell down beside her, then slid her arm around the girl's shoulder, pulling her close. "Rebecca, what is it?"

Nathan followed on Angela's heels. "Should I call 911?" He braced a hand on his wife's shoulder.

"Rebecca, tell me what's going on. Is it the baby?" She pressed her hand to Rebecca's belly.

Rebecca's eyes widened and she set the picture—which Angela could now see was of Kenny—on her lap. She studied his picture, taken when he was still vital and alive. With tears running down her cheeks, she looked up at Angela and Nathan.

"Roberts... Your last name," she choked out. The little color that had come back into her cheeks faded. "Kenny Roberts. He's your son?"

"Yes. You knew him?" Angela nearly managed a smile.

Tears spilled down her cheeks again, and she spoke in a nearly normal tone, murmuring his name over and over.

Nathan grabbed a blanket from the closet and bundled it around Rebecca. Then he went to get her a glass of water. Fighting off a shiver, Rebecca took a sip then handed the water back to him. A myriad of emotions pulsated inside of her; she couldn't separate the shock from the fear, the fear from the shame.

After a few minutes, Nathan bent down, picked her up off the floor and, without a word, carried her to the couch and lowered her onto its cushions. "Come on now Rebecca, you need to calm down and tell us what is going on."

"Whatever it is, maybe we can help," Angela reassured her.

For the next five minutes they sat quietly in the dimly lit room, Nathan on one side of Rebecca and Angela on the other.

Folding her arms across her chest, Rebecca took a deep, cleansing breath. She was calm again. Her eyes traveled the room once more, this time landing on the Roberts's family photograph.

"Yes, I knew Kenny."

Angela glanced over at Nathan, not believing what she had just heard.

"How? When?" Angela and Nathan asked in unison.

"I guess for a little over a year."

Rebecca stood up. Her knees wanted to buckle, but she kept her balance and walked slowly across the room.

"I'm not proud of what my life has become," she admitted immediately. She was afraid for her unborn child and never gave a single thought anymore to her own health. Rebecca tried to push away the fear she felt, and taking a deep breath, she continued, "Kenny wasn't either, and he was trying to leave the gang he was in."

"The gang he was in?" Angela looked over at Nathan.

"So the rumors were true." Nathan sighed.

"Mrs. Roberts, you just don't up and quit a gang. Once you're in, there is no easy way to get away from it."

Angela was upset at first, but she settled down once Nathan reminded her that what Rebecca said was true. Over the years, he had prosecuted cases of gang violence, and he had learned that when people violated their oath of loyalty to a gang, they usually felt the consequences of their decisions physically and, in extreme cases, paid with their lives.

Rebecca lowered her voice to a whisper. "The guy you saw me with, Nicky... He wasn't in the same gang as Kenny."

"So," Angela began, elongating the word, "Nicky didn't like Kenny?"

"They were enemies," Rebecca answered.

"What did he have against our son?" Nathan asked.

"It's hard to talk about."

"Rebecca, take your time." Smiling, Angela handed her the glass of water Nathan had gotten for her not too long ago.

After a long pause, Rebecca said quietly, "Kenny and I were in love." She felt a warm glow spread through her. "We were planning on coming to you the day after Kenny was shot." Rebecca pressed a hand to her swollen belly.

The room settled into uneasy silence.

With her head down Angela asked, "Rebecca, is Kenny the father of your baby?"

Wiping her eyes, Rebecca nodded her head.

Angela's eyes traveled to Nathan, who said, "Don't you tell me that Kenny, my son, was shot and killed because you were pregnant with his child."

Angela suddenly rose from the couch and shot back, "Please, oh dear Lord, no!"

Rebecca cast a look in Angela's direction. "I'm sorry Mrs. Roberts!" Drawing in air and looking into Angela's eyes, Rebecca shook her head sadly. "Nicky found out and went crazy."

Angela flinched at her words, then her eyes narrowed and hardened. "You shut up. Just shut up!" Quickly, she put her fist to her mouth to keep from screaming. Her heart started to race, her chest got tight and she felt as if her breathing was cut off. She felt like a volcano on the verge of erupting.

Rebecca could feel the heat of Angela's gaze on her and refused to face her or Nathan.

"I tried to stop him..." Her voice remained steady, but her eyes reflected her grief.

"What do you mean, you tried to *stop* him?" Nathan asked.

"Were you there when Kenny was shot?" Angela whirled around to glance over at Nathan. "I just can't believe this!"

Nathan shook his head in disbelief. "Honey, let Rebecca finish."

Rebecca's eyes watered. Blinking rapidly, she responded, "It was late." She could barely remember that night, even though it hadn't happened very long ago. "I heard yelling out in the alley, and it woke me up. I got out of bed and looked out the window, but it was so dark; the street light had burnt out."

"Did you see Kenny?" Angela asked.

"No, not at first... Only the silhouette of a man. But then I recognized Nicky's voice. He was yelling for the other guy to get down on his knees." Her cheeks burned in remembrance.

"Why didn't you call the police?" Nathan asked.

Rebecca shrugged. "I was scared." She sat down and began sobbing until no more tears would come. And then, with a profound sadness, she continued on. "I remember running out the back door and into the alley. All at once, I saw Kenny, and he was down on his knees with his hands tied behind his back. In an instant, the gun went off. I saw the flash, and then Kenny fell over onto his side."

Angela jumped up, gasping for air, fighting for her every breath. She felt her head start to spin and braced herself against the back of a chair. Doubled over and raw with emotion, she held one hand to her stomach while she raised the other and pointed her finger directly at Rebecca. "There will be payment for you, for the blood that is on your hands. I swear to you, there will be payment!"

"Angela, please." She looked over at her husband when she heard the tremble in his voice, and she saw from his face was plagued with sadness and anger.

Angela crouched down on the floor and spoke calmly this time. "You tell me... I want to know how you could live with yourself all this time knowing a crime—a felony—had been committed right before your eyes." All at once, Angela reached over and grabbed Rebecca's water glass off the table and heaved it against the fireplace. "And you did *nothing*!"

Through the storm that rushed through her mind, Angela suddenly had a mental picture of herself standing directly over Nicky's dying body. Her face sobered and her eyes opened wide; she could see her face an inch from Nicky's. As he opened his eyes and stared back into hers, he immediately said, "*I'm sorry,*" and then he was gone.

"I was face to face with my son's killer." Her hands shook and she cried harder. "Oh my God, I tried to save that bastard's life!"

Nathan raced over to her and pulled her close. "Honey, you didn't know who he was or what he had done."

She felt dead inside, like somebody had reached inside of her and scooped out her soul. In an instant her eyes went hot, exposing her own vicious thoughts. "My son died a brutal death. Your Nicky's death... It doesn't seem to be enough."

"No, it's not. It wasn't." Nathan shook his head. "Kenny and Nicky lived the lives they wanted to live and have paid a terrible price for it." He got up, walked over to the window and looked up to the night sky. "Evil does exist, and justice was not served for our son. Nicky didn't pay for his crimes here on this earth, but God is a God of justice. That young man's judgment will come; his sinful actions will be dealt with. Not by our hands, but by the hand of God."

Angela dismissed his words with a wave of her hand. "I want to *see* justice for our son!" she snapped back.

"Angela, we have to believe that. For our own peace of mind and sanity... We *need* to believe that. For us, there is nothing we can do now but heal and move on."

She opened her mouth to speak but instead just shook her head. All of that seemed unimportant to her now.

Nathan didn't know how much more Angela or Rebecca could bear in one night. "We are all in shock right now; we need some time to... To think." He held out his hand in silence. "Rebecca, let me drive you home."

Unconsciously, Rebecca rubbed a hand over her throat, remembering the sensation of Nicky's hands tightening against it.

"Mrs. Roberts, I did try."

Angela gave her a long, measuring look.

"I remember turning around to run away, to go and get help, but Nicky grabbed my arm and then he threw me to the ground." She fought against the panic. "I felt his hands around my neck; he kept squeezing tighter and tighter. I clawed at his face, but that only made it worse. When he let go of my neck, he yanked me up to his face. He swore he'd come back for me if I breathed a word of this to anyone. That the same would happen to me and my bastard baby."

Rebecca's eyes were wide with madness. "He threw me back on the ground and then he... He raped me."

Even after hearing Rebecca had been raped, the resentment and pain remained with Angela.

For a moment she just stood staring at Rebecca. "I appreciate your honesty," she said flatly.

Angela's judgment had been harsh and quick for Rebecca. Without saying another word to her, she stood tight-lipped and dry-eyed. Slowly, she turned and walked out of the living room and up the stairs.

Angela sat on the edge of her bed, and for a split second she considered Nicky's dying apology to her. Her face somber, she thought, *"Is it possible that somehow Nicky knew who I was?"*

She shivered at the memory of clasping her hands together and then placing them on Nicky's chest to administer CPR while a powerful surge of vibrations coursed through her body. Intermixed with her grandmother's legendary telepathic abilities, Angela wondered whether or not she had tapped into another human's Energy Packet. Was Nicky's apology possibly her first encounter of receiving a *"OneWay"* message from a deceased person?

She stopped for a moment to suck back the fresh rage.

Had this bizarre experience tipped the iceberg that Dr. Howard referred to?

It was difficult for her to rationalize and then absorb something as bizarre as human Energy Packets. But she had felt and she had seen. And there was no denying the facts.

Angela let out a long sigh as she laid her head back onto the pillow, and soon she drifted off to sleep.

7

Nathan picked up his keys, cast a sorrowful look up the stairs, and then held out his hand to Rebecca. "It's late. Let's get you home."

He guided Rebecca out the front door and down the driveway to his car. A flash of heat lightning lit up the night sky while a thick, drowsy heat, so close it was hard to breathe, saturated the air.

"Don't worry, I'll turn the air on," Nathan said with a smile. "I remember Angela having a rough time breathing when she was expecting the boys, and she wasn't even pregnant in the mid-summer heat."

"Oh, I'm used to this heat." Her hands trembled as she wiped her forehead.

"Are you okay?"

"Oh, sure. I'm just a little tired, that's all."

"I don't mean to pry," he began but then hesitated before going on to ask, "but have you been getting regular checkups throughout your pregnancy?"

"Mr. Roberts, you're not prying. You have every right to question if your granddaughter is healthy and being taken care of." She gave a nervous laugh. "I go to the clinic once a month; I'm going to give her the best I've got."

Nathan quickly turned his head and shot Rebecca a nervous look. He had never imagined that, on this day, he would hear himself referred to as a grandfather.

He nodded as a grin slowly crept over his face.

While waiting for a traffic light to change, Nathan sat quietly and listened as Rebecca talked about the plans she and Kenny had for their future as a family. Nathan glanced over at her; her heart was breaking, but she refused to let it show. She shared with Nathan her belief in God and that, although she didn't go to church, she was a Christian. She'd prayed for so long and worried even longer, but her heart always told her to hold on, not to give up on Kenny. They had so much in common, and she knew Kenny was a truly good man; he was everything she had ever wanted in a partner. And in the end, Kenny was trying to right the wrong choices he had made early on in his life through his own relationship with the Lord. In fact, Kenny had come to know and love the Lord just as much as she did.

Rebecca truly believed that if God ordained it, they would find their way out of the darkness and into a life filled with all the blessings God wanted for them.

But life wasn't always fair. Now it was time to let Kenny and all of their dreams go. Now she desired God's best for her life and for India's life, believing His will was better than anything she could ever imagine.

She ran her hand across her belly. "I've put you through so much already, little one. I'm sorry. But I promise you, when you're born, I'll make it up to you. I'll find a way."

The aching sadness in her eyes was undeniable. Nathan lifted his glasses to wipe a tear from his eye.

Now he was finding himself sympathetic towards and also able to identify with Rebecca. He and Angela weren't the only ones who had lost Kenny. Rebecca had lost someone she deeply loved, and right before her eyes, all her hopes and dreams for their future had vanished.

"Mr. Roberts, the light is green." She pointed up at the stoplight.

"Oh!" he said. Nathan sat quietly a moment longer, looking into her eyes while his own filled with emotion.

This young woman, he thought, is the one who Kenny fell in love with—who he wanted to spend the rest of his life with. After all these years, he now could believe that his son had a true and genuine desire to clean up his act and change his life. Rebecca's baby was a part of Kenny, the son who originally gave him the title of "father." Not a day had passed since his death that Nathan hadn't thought of him or missed him; he would *always* love him. Not only did this new life carry a part of Kenny, she carried a part of all of them. In a few months, Rebecca would give birth to their daughter and bestow upon his son, whether dead or alive, the title of "father."

Nathan choked back the tears as he became fully aware of the impact Rebecca had on Kenny's life. In their short time together, she had managed to affect his life in such a way that neither he nor Angela had been able to do over the span of Kenny's life.

He spread his hands over the steering wheel and took a breath. "You know," Nathan said, his voice full of emotion. "I want you to know that what you did for Kenny and your daughter is what any loving mother would have done."

"I sure did need to hear that from you," Rebecca said, her smile sincere.

Then she felt Nathan's hand slip over hers. It reminded her of Kenny's.

It didn't take long to arrive in the neighborhood where Rebecca lived. It was on the outer, rougher edges of Brooklyn. The row houses looked old and tired; the ones on either side of Rebecca's were nearly falling down. Summer flowers had been planted in the window boxes, but they had simply given up for lack of care and now stood wilted among the tangles of weeds. A bike was chained to the post outside of Rebecca's front door, which was stripped of everything that was portable.

Rebecca's home was three stories high and narrow, with the front door barely five steps from the curb. Two of the front windows on the second floor had been boarded up, and most of the shutters tilted to one side. The brick was old and faded except for where someone had spray painted graffiti.

Nathan got out of the car, leaned on the hood, and tried not to believe what he was looking at.

"Something, isn't it?" Rebecca said as more of a statement than a question.

"It's something alright. Half of the windows have holes in them."

"I don't have one of those."

"How lucky for you!" Nathan said. "Seriously though, Rebecca, you can't bring a baby home to live in this." Nathan, still shocked by the neighborhood's condition, stood beside her on the sidewalk.

They stayed there for a moment in silence, looking up at the house.

"Come on, I can at least see you to your apartment."

As they walked up to the front door, something small and furry darted out from one of the bushes and bolted across the front step, barely missing Nathan's feet.

"Just a field mouse," Rebecca told him with a smile.

Nathan smiled back and then pushed open the front door. As he did so, the smell of grease from decades of cooking just about knocked him off his feet. He cupped his hands over his face. "I wish I would have grabbed the hand sanitizer from the glove compartment."

"Oh, trust me... You're going to need plenty of that."

Nathan immediately fixed his eyes on the stairway inside the front door. The carpet was torn and filthy, decorated with what appeared to be droppings from assorted visitors throughout the day and night.

"Are there rats inside?" he asked, looking from one side to the other.

"Well, I never saw any, but other people living here say there may be some in the basement."

"I wouldn't say maybe; I'd count on it!"

Cautiously, Nathan walked up three broken steps and then stopped.

"What floor do you live on?"

"The third."

"Of course you do!" he said looking down at her.

Gripping the wobbly railing and pulling himself up the steep stairway, while fighting for each breath he took, Nathan finally reached the top of the first flight of stairs.

"I feel like I deserve to do the Rocky Balboa dance after that!" He took in two deep breaths, lifted his head and then took a quick look down the hallway and rolled his eyes, thinking twice about taking another step. Flanked on either side of him were cobwebs hanging from the ceiling, peeling and faded wallpaper, beer cans, cigarette butts and an array of assorted trash lining the edges of the hallway.

"The higher we go, the worse it gets."

"Welcome to my world," Rebecca said as a man's voice rose from nearby, cursing out another person from behind one of the apartment doors.

Taking a quick glance over his shoulder, Nathan gave her a strong, steady look and then shook his head.

As they made their trek up the third floor stairway, the sounds of blaring music, laughter and foul words seemed to surround them. The sound of a baby wailing brought Nathan to a complete standstill.

"No!" He whirled around to face Rebecca. "You need police protection just to get to your front door!"

"Really, it's not that bad..." her voice trailed off.

"Are you kidding me? How can this get any worse?" There was silence as he dragged his breath in and out again.

"I know what this must look like, but it's all I have."

"Rebecca, I wouldn't wish this on my worst enemy, and I know this is not what Kenny would want for his family."

Deciding against making the obvious comment, Rebecca merely smiled and walked on to her apartment door.

"I know what you're thinking Rebecca... Kenny isn't here."

They were both quiet while Nathan let those words sink in. In that moment, God planted a seed, and Nathan allowed God to move upon him.

He then stepped forward, up to the door to what he assumed to be to Rebecca's apartment.

He looked at her and then smiled.

"But I am," Nathan said. "I'm here."

Rebecca swallowed hard and then carefully spoke. "What are you saying?"

"Well." Nathan took the key from Rebecca, then unlocked and pushed open her apartment door. Stepping inside, he continued, "I guess I'm saying that the first thing you are going to do is gather up some of your things and put them in a suitcase."

Rebecca quickly lifted her hand. "Oh no, I've already done the whole shelter thing—"

Nathan cut her off in mid-sentence, grabbing her hand and giving it a squeeze. He spoke from his heart. "Did I say anything about a shelter?"

Nathan went on to explain his plan of action, hoping to convince her of what he felt Kenny would want him to do. "I know this sounds crazy, but for now, you and my granddaughter are going to stay with Angela and me."

Rebecca stepped back and drew in a deep breath. "I don't know about this."

"I have never believed in coincidences, Rebecca. It isn't a coincidence our paths have crossed; there is a reason. Running into Angela one afternoon at the grocery store just opened the door that was meant to be opened."

Their lives had been incredibly separate, but now these three people had so much to give one another. Rebecca had lost so much in her life already—as had Nathan and Angela—but now, out of tragedy, their lives were connected. If given the chance, they could come together, resulting in something beautiful and precious for all of them. Suddenly the Bible verse Isaiah 61:3 came to Nathan's mind, and he said aloud, "To give them beauty for ashes, the oil of joy for mourning, the garment of praise for the spirit of heaviness." This was their moment, he thought, their "beauty for ashes." And both of them felt its power.

"What about Mrs. Roberts? Doesn't seem to me that she would be thrilled with me living in her home," Rebecca said, looking down at her hands.

"You let me worry about Mrs. Roberts." He smiled at her. "She was in shock. I know my wife, and I assure you that once she settles down, she'll see things in a different light." In all honesty, however, although Nathan's spirit was telling him to do what was right for Rebecca, and although he was determined that his granddaughter was not going to live in this hell hole, he wasn't sure of what Angela's reaction would be when she learned of his decision.

"If you're sure about this," Rebecca said quietly, feeling her heart tremble a bit.

"Good. Now let's get your things and get the heck out of here!"

"Mr. Roberts," she said gently, sounding almost like a daughter to him. He felt tears fill his eyes as she finished, in an incredibly genuine tone, "Thank you."

It was late when they returned home. After parking, Nathan showed Rebecca to the guest room and let her alone to settle in.

Once he had showered and finished his nighttime routine, he sat down on the bed next to Angela. He silently debated for a moment whether he should wake her or wait until morning to let her know the decision he had made. He glanced over at her nightstand and saw her prescription sleeping pills. As he sighed and looked across the room, he met his own eyes in the mirror over the dresser, and he immediately knew the answer to his quandary. He silently agreed with Angela's decision that a sleeping pill was definitely in order after the events from earlier in the evening, and he knew that trying to wake her from this drug-induced sleep would be next to impossible.

He smiled, then leaned over and gently pressed his lips to her cheek.

"This can wait 'til morning, my love."

The next morning, Nathan smelled coffee and bacon the minute he opened his eyes. It should have put him in a better mood, but it did little to lift the spirits of a man who had tossed and turned most of the night, worrying over the possible ramifications of the life-changing decision he had made. And, because he'd made this decision without first consulting his wife, it was going to take more than the smell of coffee and bacon to put him at ease.

In the immortal words of Ricky Ricardo, he had a lot of "splainin' to do."

After pulling on his sweat pants and sweatshirt, and feeling a little more confident, Nathan casually strolled into the kitchen.

Catching the movement out of the corner of her eye, Angela turned to the doorway and smiled.

"Good morning. I felt like a traditional breakfast for a change. Coffee's ready; just sit down and I'll get it."

"Thanks," Nathan said as he grabbed a piece of bacon and sat down at the table. "You're in a good mood."

"Oh, I've been up for hours, and trust me; I didn't start out my morning in a good mood." She heaved a heavy sigh and then poured Nathan a cup of coffee. "So, did you get Rebecca home okay?"

There it was... She had given him the opening. However, Nathan chose to wait a little longer before dropping the bomb on how their lives had changed even more since last night.

"I did." He sipped his coffee.

"I conked out. What time did you come in?" She scooped a spoonful of scrambled eggs onto his plate.

"Oh, about midnight, I guess."

"Midnight? I thought she lived just on the other side of town. It took you two hours to drive her home?"

"Yeah, I guess about that long."

"Did you stop for a drink?" Angela asked. "Well, after what happened last night, I can see why you would have."

"No, I didn't stop for a drink."

Puzzled, she put a plate of toast and bacon on the table and sat down. Tilting her head, she asked, "Nathan, did something happen when you drove Rebecca home?"

Nathan settled back in his chair with his second cup of coffee.

"I couldn't believe the filth, the disgusting conditions this girl was living in; it made me sick to my stomach. Bullet holes in some windows, other windows boarded up, stinking and rotting trash dumped in the backyard and in the halls... Probably rats, and I'm *certain* there were mice."

"That bad, huh?"

"Bad is an understatement!" His eyes stayed level with hers. "We talked for almost an hour. Angela, I'm telling you, something happened inside of me. It hit me hard and made me stop, and I saw Rebecca differently."

Angela set her toast down and picked up her coffee. "What do you mean, you saw her?"

He covered his face with his hands, pressing his fingers against his eyes.

No matter how hard it was or what Angela's reaction would be, he couldn't keep pushing it aside. He had to tell her. In his heart he knew that he had done the right thing, the thing that Kenny would have wanted his father to do for his little family.

"Our son loved her. Because of Rebecca, Kenny was ready and willing to change his life—something you and I weren't able to get him to do."

Saying nothing for a moment, Angela rubbed her hands over her face.

"All morning, I've been thinking about last night." She let out a long breath and blinked at the tears. "Maybe I was too hard on Rebecca."

"She referred to me as the baby's grandfather." Before she could respond, he leaned forward with a smile on his face. "I'm going to be a grandfather! And that, my dear, makes you a grandmother!"

She inclined her head royally and then burst into tears.

"Angela, why are you crying?" he asked, letting out a nervous laugh.

"I'm allowed to cry when my son makes me a grandmother!" Nathan quickly picked up his napkin and handed it to her.

It sounded so simple; the thoughts of shopping for a little girl, and all of the light pink and adorable ruffles that came along with it, started a smile on her face. She didn't resist the onslaught of images: her sitting in a rocking chair while holding a tiny baby in her arms again, the same rocking chair she sat in when she rocked Kenny and Robby, and the leisurely stroller-walks she'd have with her granddaughter on warm, sunny afternoons. A glimmer of hope glided into her heart, reminding her they could survive whatever life brought into their path. The love she and Nathan had for one another had brought them through many rounds of trials in the past, and it would continue to do so now, with whatever was about to come in the future.

"Angela, when I allowed that to sink in and then heard a baby crying in that hell hole, I couldn't do it!"

"You couldn't do what?" Angela deliberately widened her eyes.

"Okay, okay. I just couldn't walk away... I couldn't leave them there." He got up and walked over to the counter. "I just felt Kenny wouldn't have wanted it."

"Alright. So where did you take her?

"Honey, just hear me out." His voice broke, and though he turned away quickly, Angela saw the tears spring to his eyes.

"Please, just tell me where she is."

Nathan abruptly turned back around to face Angela, but instead of meeting her eyes, his attention was instantly drawn to just behind where Angela was sitting.

The look on Nathan's face had Angela turn in her seat.

"I think you just found her." He cocked his head and then timidly flashed a quick smirk.

Gasping, she lifted her hands to her mouth and then slowly emerged from her chair, asking, "Nathan, what on earth?"

He cut her off, saying, "I told you I couldn't do it!"

Angela held up her hand to interrupt. "It's fine." She turned back to face Rebecca and then stepped forward. "I was afraid you'd never want to see me again after my dreadful behavior last night."

Rebecca met her eyes. "No," she responded. "It was just as much of a shock for me as it was for you. I never imagined I'd meet Kenny's family after he died. No one even knew that I existed." A lone tear rolled down her cheek.

"Rebecca, I'm so sorry." Angela held out her arms. "Can you ever forgive me?"

Rebecca smiled at Angela, who gave a slight nod and then walked over to Rebecca and pulled her into an embrace.

"It's going to be fine, dear." Angela squeezed a little tighter.

Rebecca nodded. "I know. Don't worry about me." She wiped her eyes.

"I'm sorry," Angela said a second time. "You're a very special young woman. I want you to know that Nathan and I care deeply for you already."

With tears flowing, the two women held tightly to one another. As soon as Nathan saw the look on Angela's face, he knew another word from him wouldn't be necessary. Taking another place setting from the cabinet, he set it on the table and then took his seat.

"Come on now; let's eat before all this food gets cold. Remember, she's eating for two!" he announced.

For the next hour, they ate breakfast and discussed what was going to happen next. Even though this all seemed like a dream come true for Rebecca, the thought of her and her baby turning out to be a financial burden dampened her spirits. Prior to getting pregnant, Rebecca had a part-time waitress position and had managed to set aside a modest savings account, but now, after months of being unemployed, it was nearly exhausted.

After sharing her concerns with Nathan and Angela, and despite the fact that both repeatedly reassured her that neither she nor the baby would put any strains on their finances, she still was unrelenting on her position of finding a part-time job to help out with expenses.

Recognizing Rebecca's anxiety and concern, Angela smiled and then, having just thought of it, offered her the receptionist position in the salon. She went on to explain that she was slowly fading herself out of the day-to-day responsibilities, turning more over to Stephen. Furthermore, Rebecca already had met and got along well with the other employees and several of her clients at the Fourth of July celebration. As far as Angela was concerned, this was a perfect fit.

Angela's eyes became bright with excitement. "And after you have the baby, if you want to, you can go back to the salon full-time, and I'll stay home and watch India... No charge!"

"Ah... There is a method to your madness!" Nathan laughed. "You have been duly warned, Rebecca."

"Don't listen to him!" Angela reached over and slapped Nathan on the shoulder. Then she got up from the table and started clearing the dishes, smiling to herself. "Would you like to go upstairs and lie down for a bit?"

"No, I'm fine," Rebecca said and then began to chew on her bottom lip. "But there is something I would like to do this afternoon, if you don't mind."

Nathan shrugged and looked at Angela. "We don't have any plans, do we?" Then he turned to Rebecca. "What is it?"

"I would like to visit Kenny's grave... But I don't know where he's buried."

Nathan and Angela looked at one another and smiled. "Of course we'll take you to Kenny. It would be our pleasure," Angela said and then smiled.

"Maybe get some flowers to put on his grave, from India and me?"

"That would be lovely," Angela told her. "Kenny would like that."

When they arrived at Kenny's grave, Nathan and Angela lingered behind so that Rebecca could have some quiet time with him. They smiled at one another as she carefully knelt down in front of Kenny's tombstone, holding her swollen belly. Timidly, she placed her hand on his name and then quickly withdrew it. With tears streaming from her eyes, she pressed her hand to his name once more and this time held it in place.

Nathan quickly grabbed onto Angela's arm before she could take another step. "She's okay; let her be."

When Rebecca calmed down, they noticed she was talking to Kenny, just as if he was sitting right there in front of her. A few minutes later, she turned and looked over at Nathan and Angela, smiling as she placed the flowers in the vase. Then she bowed her head in prayer.

Nathan put his arm around Angela and pulled her close, "I don't know what verse it is, but the Bible tells us that God will restore double for what the enemy has stolen away."

"Zechariah 9:12, a double recompense." Angela smiled and looked at Rebecca. "God was faithful, Nathan. There stands our double recompense: Rebecca and a brand new granddaughter."

Nathan snuggled up to her. "I love you."

On the way back to the car, Angela suddenly stopped and whispered, "Kenny is at peace now." Nathan smiled and nodded his head.

Rebecca reached over and took Angela's hand. "I never told you India's middle name."

Angela shrugged and shook her head. "No, I guess you didn't."

"Kenny loved you both so much. And if our baby was a boy, he wanted to honor his father by naming him Nathan. But since the baby turned out to be a girl, Kenny wanted to honor you by giving India your middle name, Cleopatra."

Suddenly Rebecca jumped and bent forward.

"What's wrong?" Angela asked, concern in her voice.

Placing a hand on her stomach, Rebecca replied, "The baby... She just kicked. She's been so active today!"

Without delay Angela placed her hand on Rebecca's stomach. "Hello there, Miss India Cleopatra. Your grammy can't wait to get her hands on you!" Smiling, Angela said, "She's moving again. Little India Cleopatra has one strong kick, but then again, her strength comes from a long line of strong women!"

8

Angela and Nathan made up their minds from the get-go to spare no expense when it came to their first grandchild. It seemed only fitting and proper that Kenny's bedroom be converted into a nursery for his baby girl, so from sunrise to sunset, Angela worked tirelessly cleaning out the old to make way for the new. Some of Kenny's belongings—those cherished possessions she wasn't ready to part with just yet—she put in boxes and stored in the basement. As for those she *was* willing to part with, she donated to the Salvation Army.

To show her appreciation for everything Nathan and Angela had done for her and the baby over the past month, Rebecca relinquished the entire decorating process of India's nursery over to Angela. What's more, Rebecca knew the room would bear a strong resemblance to rooms she had seen in *Better Homes and Gardens* magazine: tastefully decorated and perfect for her little girl.

After having two boys, Angela immediately decided there should be pink in the room, and lots of it. She chose a soft dusty rose color for the walls and white for the trim. Next she hired an artist friend of hers to stencil India's name in lime green on the wall above her crib, with tiny butterflies accenting her name and taking flight to the ceiling.

There was no denying that shopping for little girls was much more exciting than shopping for little boys, and when Angela caught sight of the "Dreams Come True" bedding and comforter set, she snatched it up in a New York minute. That set wasn't the only thing she bought, though; by the end of her shopping spree, she had purchased the coordinating bumper pads, dust ruffle, sheets, receiving blankets and mobile which played Brahms's Lullaby. From pink pacifiers to pink Huggies, her granddaughter would be a living, breathing vision of pink.

Dreams had come true for all of them. *"This is perfect,"* she thought.

With the shopping and decorating complete, Angela stepped back to take in the nursery she had created for her granddaughter. All was ready and waiting for the arrival of Miss India Cleopatra. She looked at the white crib, decked out with the "Dreams Come True" bedding, and pictured her tiny, precious granddaughter sleeping soundly. Then she looked over to the matching dresser, changing table and rocking chair. Suddenly her heart ached as she vividly remembered holding Kenny's tiny hand when he was only minutes old.

"Oh." Angela lifted a hand to her throat as it filled with emotion.

Nathan walked up behind her and embraced his wife. "Looks like we're having a baby!"

She pressed a hand to her heart. "I know."

"Then why do you look so sad?" Nathan smiled. "We always wanted a little girl, and this baby... We felt her kick and watched her move in Rebecca's belly. I didn't realize how much I loved her until all of that."

"I love her too—and I love Rebecca, like she was my own."

Angela laid her head against Nathan's shoulder and glanced over at the bassinet. Both Nathan and she believed now that everything over the course of the past year had been leading up to this moment—all the good and all the bad.

Tears spilled down her cheeks. "Kenny will never hold his baby's hand."

"Dear, is that what's got you all upset?" Nathan kissed her forehead. "We will hold her hand for Kenny."

Their eyes met. "There's nothing I'd like better," Angela said after a moment. Comforted by his words, she inhaled and exhaled deeply. "Only a couple more weeks and she'll be here."

"We're certainly going to have our hands full." Nathan wiped a tear from her cheek. "Soon there will be a baby in this house. Are you ready for that?"

"We can handle it," she assured him. "We're a family. With God's help, we can do anything."

Angela had realized a new purpose for her life. It all seemed so normal, eating together at the end of the day, talking about their jobs, rehearsing the plans for when Rebecca went into labor, making sure they knew the best route to the hospital and had the phone numbers to call when India arrived.

Although Angela welcomed this new chapter in her life, however, every so often the memory of the distraught woman with madness in her eyes had begun to unnerve her a bit.

Arriving at Bloomingdale's one afternoon, Angela noticed an elderly woman curled up on the sidewalk just outside the revolving door. At first glance, she thought her to be just another homeless person, and quickly dismissing the image, she pushed on through the revolving door. Soon after entering the store, Angela became aware of the peculiar sensation of having met the old woman once before.

"Oh, this is just crazy!" Angela rubbed the back of her neck and intentionally let her body relax for a moment.

Annoyed, she glanced at her watch, blinked, then realized there was just enough time to pick up a few things and then make it to the café for her lunch date with Rowena.

Although she had promised Nathan a diaper bag would be her only purchase, Angela departed Bloomingdale's loaded down with not only a new diaper bag for India slung over her shoulder but also at least three bags of goodies in her hands. Remembering she had to hit the ATM before meeting Rowena, Angela abruptly whirled around, blindsiding the person walking close behind her and knocking her own shopping bags to the ground.

"I'm so sorry," Angela exclaimed as she quickly bent over to gather up her bags. Slowly she stood up to find herself face-to-face with a wild-eyed woman with unkempt salt-and-pepper hair. Her mouth was moving, but she wasn't articulating any words.

Shaking her head in disbelief, Angela attempted more than once to cross out any ideas brewing in the back of her mind that she had met this woman previously. But she felt the heat of the odd woman's gaze upon her, and it shook her to her core. Angela pretended not to notice her gesturing mouth or her arms that were outstretched towards her. Without delay, she adjusted the diaper bag on her shoulder and hurriedly walked past the woman, heading in the direction of the café where she had arranged to meet Rowena.

As soon as Angela arrived, she saw Rowena's hand in the air, and she quickly made her way over to the table. She sat down and immediately ordered a vodka tonic.

Looking over the rims of her sunglasses to meet Angela's eyes, Rowena laughed. "Good Lord Angela, you look like you just saw a ghost!"

Frowning in exasperation, Angela replied, "I don't see her now," looking from one person to the next.

Chuckling, Rowena asked, "You actually *did* see a ghost?"

"No," Angela snapped back, "I didn't see a ghost!" Calming down just slightly, she explained, "This woman, I've seen her sitting on the sidewalk outside of Bloomingdale's the past few times I went shopping."

"Girl, she was probably homeless."

"I don't know... But there was something about her." Angela lowered her voice to a whisper. "Like I had met her before."

Rowena cracked up. "Seriously; you've seen one, you've seen them all."

"Will you lower your voice? And that's an awful thing to say!"

Rowena rolled her eyes. "You know what I mean; all worn out, that downtrodden look. I'm just sayin'... the way they look at you sometimes, it's downright scary."

Angela looked around to see if anyone had overheard Rowena's remark.

"It was creepy," Angela said, shivering and shaking her head. "I turned around and there she was, standing right behind me."

"Duh. Does the term 'snatch and grab' mean anything to you?"

Angela glanced over at her. "Don't *you* sound all Cagney and Lacey!"

"Look, I saw it all the time when I was growing up," Rowena responded. "Picture this: A well-dressed woman, just coming out of Bloomingdale's, loaded down with packages in both arms, with this homeless woman right on her heels," Rowena said and examined her fingernails. "She probably needed money for food, drugs or alcohol."

"Well, she wouldn't have gotten very far," Angela said as she gave a quick glance over her shoulder. "She wasn't any spring chicken."

"She probably wasn't as old you think. Living on the streets, alcohol and drugs... That stuff ages people real fast."

"I suppose you're right."

Angela sat back and relaxed in her chair, realizing that her emotions had gotten the best of her and that considering there might be any other significance to meeting this woman was totally bizarre.

Folding her arms across her chest, Rowena said, "Mark my words: Never make eye contact with a homeless person!"

"Oh for goodness sake, that's just awful." Angela rolled her eyes and then said, "Tell me again..."

Holding up her hand, Rowena cut Angela off. Then, in unison, they finished, "Why we are friends!" and topped it off with laughter.

Angela was the first to arrive home, and she needed to relax. She went upstairs and undressed, slipped into her silk pajamas and sat down on the edge of the bed. Pausing for a moment, she then sighed as contentment began to settle over her. Calm and tranquil, she leaned back against her pillow and closed her eyes. Drowsy now, and soothed by the warmth of the late afternoon sun on her face, she was asleep in only a few minutes.

Deep in her mind, where secrets laid in wait and whispered, a dream came and took her to an enormous mountain. Angela saw herself standing alone on an embankment at the edge of a thick wooded area. She felt like running away but couldn't unbury her feet from the tangle of weeds that had twisted and tightened about her ankles.

There were colors; warm and vivid reds, greens and yellows burst up from the ground and through the trees, leading up to the heavy black clouds above her.

Soon Angela found herself enclosed by the brilliant colors swirling all around her; they immediately prompted the emotions of love, peace and joy to rise up within her spirit.

Then, in a flash, she felt a chill in the air as the aura became chilling and dark.

Off in the distance, Angela watched as a woman emerged from a thick fog and then slowly walked across the field. She was silent and had her arms outstretched, her fingers pleading for help that didn't come. Her flowing gown was torn and dirty, as were her naked feet, and her hair was a web of black and gray that covered a face marked with madness.

"*I know more than you... I want my message!*" Crazed screams echoed through the thick fog.

Angela put her hands to her ears and tried to shout, but she could barely get out the words, "I don't have any messages."

The screams stopped as abruptly as they began.

Then, unexpectedly, Angela focused her attention on the faint sounds of rustling in the high grass nearby, and she heard a child's voice softly singing a lullaby. As it mysteriously inched closer, Angela didn't sense fear but instead had a peculiar longing in her heart to know this child.

"Don't be afraid. I won't hurt you," Angela whispered.

Sad and pale in her gray dress, the child appeared to levitate from the grass and then float like incense in Angela's direction. She hovered momentarily and then settled on the ground directly in front of Angela. Her gaze was deep and penetrating, and she slowly raised a hand.

At that moment, as if she had been struck by lightning, the young girl exploded into hundreds of tiny pieces, shooting up towards the heavens and then gently falling back to earth. Little by little, the pieces merged to form the same image, and once more the girl stood before Angela.

Her words gently tiptoed into Angela's ears. "*You're mine.*"

Fear raged through Angela like a sudden, violent storm. Instantly she stiffened. "I am *not* yours!"

The young girl smiled and held out her hand again. "*My blood... It is within you.*"

Nathan's muted words, "Angela, wake up. You're having a bad dream," jerked her back into reality.

Angela opened her eyes wide and tried to speak, but she found she couldn't. She nodded and then choked out, "Thank you."

Nathan smiled. "You're welcome."

He pulled her close and kissed her on the cheek. "My God, Angela, you're shaking and as pale as a sheet. What were you dreaming about?"

She still had trouble speaking. The images were fluid in her mind, but when she tried to get the words out to describe them, she hit the same stumbling block over and over again.

"I want my message. My blood is within you," Angela finally said without looking up.

"Just relax. Everything is fine now."

"You always say everything is fine," Angela lashed out angrily. "How is everything fine? How am I supposed to relax when I am *petrified*?"

"Angela, it was just a dream." He rubbed her arms.

"It doesn't help when I seem to be running into the woman who was in my dream everywhere lately."

"What woman? What's going on?" Nathan demanded.

Angela got up and walked around the room, swinging her arms while breathing in through her nose and out through her mouth. She described to Nathan the encounter with the woman she'd seen earlier that day and now had seen in her dream.

"Well, that explains why you might have had a dream about her," Nathan reassured her.

Angela abruptly stopped and whirled around to face Nathan. "In my dream, she wanted that darn message from me."

Out of the corner of his eye, Nathan saw her open her mouth as if she was about to say something, but then she quickly closed it again.

"What is it?" Nathan stood up. "Honey, talk to me."

"Wow," Angela said after she managed to close her mouth again. Now she remembered. She knew exactly where she'd seen the woman before, and she knew who she was.

"All of it happened at Kenny's grave. Nathan, I know who she is."

Saying nothing for a moment, Angela laid her hands on her thighs and rubbed them. After having seen the woman once at Kenny's grave, Angela was sure the visions would not return. If she closed her eyes, she could imagine the woman, and she shivered at the remembrance of that day, accompanied with the words, "*I want my message*!" To this day, she still couldn't explain it, but whatever it meant, it was not gone or over.

"Are you sure?" Nathan asked. "That was almost a year ago."

Angela paused for a moment, closing her eyes and leaning back against the wall. "I knew there was something I was missing."

The look on Nathan's face was utter shock. "We should call the police—or perhaps Dr. Howard—about this."

"What?" she asked, placing her hand on her chest. "Are you kidding me?" She looked into Nathan's eyes. "You're not kidding, are you? And tell them *what*?"

"If this is the same woman from a few months ago, for whatever reason it seems to me that she really believes what she's saying." Nathan looked up sharply. "Honey, I don't mean to upset you, but if this woman really believes you hold some sort of message for her, we may need some help with this."

"I'm okay. I'm okay," she said, taking a long breath.

"A couple of months ago, the firm handled a case similar to what you've told me. The psychologist explained the behavior as part of the mind essentially removing itself from the present, while another part of the mind comes to the forefront, holding back the memory and pain about something that happened in the past."

"Dr. Howard hasn't returned from London yet." Angela stepped back and wiped her face. "Besides, I don't want to say anything about this right now."

"Honey, I don't know if we can wait." Nathan offered her a box of tissues; she took one and dabbed her eyes. "Usually there's a lot going on with people like this. Who knows what's going on in her mind? She could be dangerous!"

Angela looked deeply into Nathan's eyes. "I don't want to go wild here," she said seriously. "I want things as normal as possible, for Rebecca's sake."

Nathan raised his eyebrows. "Oh, I'm supposed to just fall back, put all of this on the back burner until this woman assaults you? That makes a lot of sense, Angela."

They stared at each other across an abrupt silence.

Nathan's gaze burned through her. "And if I refuse? What then?"

Shrugging, Angela responded, "I honestly don't know." She hesitated, torn by conflicting emotions. "I don't want to psychoanalyze this woman or get all hysterical over this."

"Hysterical, no; concerned, yes. And my concern is that this woman could have some serious mental problems or be some sort of stalker. "

There was distress in his voice, something she rarely saw from him.

"I'm all right. Don't worry. I'm just..."

"You're not all right, and don't tell me not to be concerned."

She leaned against him and let him rock her for a moment until his warmth seeped into her own chilled bones. She drew in a breath. "Maybe a little traumatized, I guess. But the more we make of it, the more upset I will be. We need to step back for now."

Because there was still so much tension in her voice, Nathan squeezed her hand and smiled. Then he quickly added, "As much as I can, I hope sooner or later she'll either find someone else to bother or she'll go too far and hang herself."

Angela took another breath, a stronger one. "She's coming back," she told Nathan with a nod. "Even though she scared me to death and there was nothing I could do, that day at Kenny's grave my heart broke for her. She got inside my head. You'll think I'm crazy, but I suppose you could say I have a soft spot for her." And she did. She just felt it.

"Excuse me?"

"Oh, don't get me wrong. Clearly, around the edges, I'm nervous." She stepped back, pressing her hand on her heart, then running it up to her throat and to the back of her neck.

"The thought of her coming back only makes all of this worse, if you ask me. Quite frankly, I thought someone with your education would be more sensible about this."

Angela walked up to him and brushed her lips over his. "Why don't we go downstairs and see about a Brandy and some hot tea for now?"

"For now." His voice softened as he tipped up her chin. "Don't expect me to feel sorry for her."

Shaken more than she cared to admit, she reached up and laid a hand on his.

"I'll be down in a minute; I want to grab the diaper bag I bought to show Rebecca."

That gave her a little more time to calm down before joining Nathan and Rebecca downstairs. Angela stared into the mirror for a moment. Then, with her head tilted slightly to one side, she nodded and felt, to some extent, peaceful with the woman who invaded not only her conscious world but now her unconscious world as well.

The next morning Angela was up and out of the house before Rebecca awoke. With Rebecca's due date only weeks away, Angela had cut her hours back to only four per day. This morning Rebecca would arrive at the salon around noon, which gave Angela plenty of time to put the finishing touches on the surprise baby shower.

Angela placed the pink diaper cake in the center of the table. The guests would be arriving soon, and she was a bit nervous.

"The place looks beautiful," Rowena exclaimed the minute she walked in the front door. "Angela, you did all of this yourself? If I ever have a baby, I want my shower to be just like this."

"What? What... Oh my God, you're crazy!"

Smiling, Rowena responded, "Rebecca is going to love it! You've done a marvelous job."

As Angela put the last minute touches on the diaper cake, the first guests started to arrive.

"Rowena, will you watch the door for me and flip the sign over to 'Closed'?"

"Sure." Rowena strode elegantly across the room, smiling from ear to ear.

"She's a born hostess," Angela said under her breath, then grabbed a trash bag and walked out the back door of the salon.

The sight of an overturned trash can immediately set her mind in motion, and she internally questioned if someone had been lurking outside her salon in the middle of the night.

"Get a grip Angela," she said and then picked up the trash can, put the bag inside, and secured the lid tightly. "It was probably an animal."

Although she reassured herself with a rational explanation, Angela couldn't shake the strange sensation that someone had been there—especially when she combined the knocked-over trash can with the sight she had seen earlier of a grocery cart parked in the flowerbeds outside the front window, crushing some of the flowers she had planted. At once the question re-emerged: had someone been outside of her salon? And, furthermore, was that someone still lurking around?

With more guests arriving, including the guest of honor, Angela dismissed the thought and joined in welcoming Rebecca to her baby shower.

"Surprise!"

Rebecca opened her eyes wide and then did a double take. There were presents all over the counters and chairs.

"What's all this?" Her mouth dropped open when she realized that a couple of the large pink bags were stuffed with baby items.

Rebecca stared wordlessly at Angela, her heart pounding. "Baby gifts? What's going on?" she asked after finding her voice. Then, after a brief pause, she added, "Mrs. Roberts, this is so nice." She glanced around the room in excitement and shock. "You didn't have to go to so much trouble for me."

"Nothing is too much trouble for my first grandchild—and her mother, of course." Angela smiled as she held out a large white box. Setting it down on the table in front of Rebecca, she opened it. Angela then gently reached both hands under a white blanket trimmed with white satin ribbon and placed it before Rebecca.

"My great-grandmother, Margaret Hamilton, had this blanket made for my grandmother, Iana Hamilton Holmes. It was passed on to my mother, Cilla Hamilton Rogers, who I don't remember much of, but this blanket has remained in our family for several generations."

Rebecca held it against her cheek. "I'm going to start crying again," she said as she waved a hand in front of her face.

"And now I would like to pass it on to my granddaughter, India Cleopatra," Angela finished.

"I don't know what to say. It's all so beautiful."

Angela kissed Rebecca's cheek and thought she looked lovelier than ever.

"So from here on out, no more talk like, 'You didn't have to go to so much trouble for me,'" Angela said. "Got it?" she added with a wink.

As the afternoon wore on, Angela was shocked to see Rowena actually participating in the typical baby shower games. In fact, Rowena took first place in the "Pin the Sperm on the Egg" contest.

Another first was that, for the first time since Rebecca and Angela met, Rebecca seemed to let her guard down, actually appearing to be a bit on the giddy side.

"I'm so glad you had a good time." Angela grinned. "I wanted everything to be perfect for you."

"I've never had anything like this in my life!" Rebecca sat beside Angela. "Being a part of your family is very important to me." A tear spilled from her eye, and Rebecca rubbed it away. "You're all so close. I never had that. Being an only child and with parents like mine... Most of the time it was very lonely."

"You're not alone anymore." Angela took her hand. "So, fresh start. And that's a promise."

Angela was on cloud nine. The baby shower was a huge success, and by the time Nathan arrived most of the guests had gone home. Finding Angela and Rebecca in the back room, he decided not to disturb their conversation. Instead, he quietly turned around and walked to the front of the salon to begin packing up the gifts.

After a few minutes, Angela joined Nathan out front.

He waited until Rebecca was out of ear shot then turned to Angela. "You're worried about her, aren't you?"

"Not worried," she said, taking his hand. "Let's start with just keeping an eye on her."

"We can do that," Nathan replied.

"Now, let me help you." Angela glanced around the room. "Rowena drove her SUV so that she could take the gifts back to the house. But by the looks of it, you'll probably have to take some of them in your car as well."

"Not a problem; I'll get my car," Nathan said.

"No, it'll be quicker if I do it," Angela offered. "I'll be back in a few minutes."

"I'm parked just around the corner." Nathan reached into his pocket and pulled out his keys. "I'll start carrying some of these to the door."

"You're a good man!" Angela laughed.

"And don't you forget it!" Nathan smiled and gave her a swat on the rear.

Angela's lifted her head. She smiled back at Nathan and then turned, and at the same time, her eyes met squarely with the eyes of the woman from her dream. She was standing outside the front window.

Shaken right down to the soles of her feet, Angela managed two steps with an effort that sucked the breath out of her. Pushing forward, she leaned against the front counter, gasping for air; she then screamed a single high-pitched shriek of terror.

Nathan whirled around, dropping a handful of gifts onto the floor. Taking a quick scan around the room, he immediately noticed Angela, collapsed onto the floor.

What he saw next shocked him: The madwoman with crazed eyes was standing dead center outside the window. Statuesque and clutching a large leather-bound Bible in her hands, with her gaze centered directly on Angela, the woman let a slow, steady smile move over her face. Then her mouth gestured the words, *"I want what is mine!"*

The room was suddenly filled with tension, and Nathan's rage spewed up inside of him.

"Angela." He ran over and dropped to the floor beside her.

As terror spread through her, she curled into a ball until she could find her breath.

"Nathan, it's her!" Angela blinked her eyes rapidly, looking up at the window, and then scooted across the floor, out of the woman's line of vision. "She's come back."

"You son of a bitch!" With fury set in his eyes, Nathan bolted towards the door. "Call the police!" he shouted to Rowena.

"Nathan, don't!" Angela pleaded. "Don't go out there!"

"You and Rebecca get out of here. Go back to the house, now!"

Nathan ran outside, but before he could get to the woman, she was gone.

"Where the hell are you?" he asked the empty air, shaking his head as he continued to pace up and down the street.

Reluctant to leave, he took one last look up and down the sidewalk, then leaned back against the wall and adjusted his glasses. With an absent glance to the right, Nathan noticed a photograph wedged in the bush beneath the front window, where the woman had been standing only a few minutes earlier.

He waited a moment before wandering over. Then, with the utmost gentleness and care, fearful it would disintegrate at his touch, Nathan leaned into the shrub and pulled out the photograph.

He looked carefully at what appeared to be an elementary grade class picture. He suspected it was from the early 1900s based on the woman standing off to the side of the class, who appeared to be their teacher and in her twenties. At first glance he thought her appearance was neat as a pin; she was conservatively dressed in an ankle-length black skirt and low-heeled shoes along with a stiffly starched white blouse, which in all probability was right in line with her disposition. She wore her brown hair in what he assumed women called a "bun" in those days. Smiling, he thought the style did not compliment her attractive, thin face; instead, it made her look harsh and extremely unhappy.

His eyes were then drawn to a little girl he gauged to be in the vicinity of eight or nine years old, sitting in the center of the front row, with a circle drawn around her. As he studied her smiling, angelic face, bright green eyes, and brown curly hair, Nathan sensed that there was something out of the ordinary about her. But he couldn't explain it to himself, let alone to anyone else, and chose not to pay any attention to it. Soon it was gone. He shoved the photograph into his shirt pocket and walked back towards the salon to check on Angela. As he started to pull open the front door, the sensation he'd felt a few moments earlier struck him again. There was something abnormal about the child. He shot a quick glance over his shoulder to where he had discovered the photograph and, pausing momentarily, wondered if he had just stumbled across a clue of some sort.

He fixed a smile on his face and shook his head. "Nah... Too much like a 'whodunit' crime novel."

Out of the corner of his eye he saw Angela standing at the window, and he went back inside.

"I'm sorry. I wasn't able to find her."

She gave a nod. "No, she didn't hang around too long."

"Perhaps we should give it a little time," he suggested.

Although it was late September, the haze and humidity had hung in the air since morning. The sky was dark now, and a storm was on the horizon. There was an ominous, threatening aspect to everything around them, but it agreed with Angela's mood as she stood and dwelled on the very real possibility of her next encounter. The mere suggestion of this woman's human presence in Angela's life, even for a moment or two, had taken its toll and now weighed heavily on her mind.

Nathan had become very aware of his wife's emotional state lately; she looked overwhelmed and distraught. He glanced over as Rowena came out of the back room carrying a cup of hot tea.

"The cops are on their way," Rowena said. "Stephen called them on his cell on the way out the back door."

As Nathan reached out to take Angela's hand, he saw her eyes dart over to Rowena. Obviously worried, she took the tea.

"Well, we are going to press charges, no matter what!" Rowena shook her head.

"I'm alright. I'm fine." Angela felt her head spinning, and she staggered back on her rubbery legs as Nathan flew around to grab her from behind.

"She might need to see a doctor." Struggling with her temper, Rowena drew in a breath. "I wish you would have found that worthless piece of trash!"

"No," Angela said, running her hand through her hair. "Today was a day for joy and new beginnings, not for misery and chaos."

"Wait!" Nathan reached into his shirt pocket and pulled out the photograph. "I found something while I was outside, in a bush where she had been standing."

He wiped it off and handed it to Angela. "Honey, do any of these people mean anything to you?"

Since her faintness had passed, she set down her tea and took the photograph from Nathan. Her hands shook as she touched the photograph, and she felt strangely breathless. A weak smile formed as she looked at the little girl with big green eyes and curly hair.

She didn't turn when she heard Nathan's voice behind her asking, "Are you okay?"

Angela slowly turned the picture over and immediately felt a shiver creep up her spine as she saw a name in small, elegant writing. The ink had been dry for decades, and in the corner was written, "Iana Hamilton, Greenwich Orphanage, 1902."

"My grandmother." Angela lifted her head, turned, and met Nathan's eyes.

Just seeing the writing and reading her grandmother's name filled Angela with yearning. The picture had been taken so long ago... What had she been like back then? If she closed her eyes, she could imagine her grandmother, all grown up and sitting in a chair with her arms open wide, smiling down at her.

She needed air, and she told Nathan so. He could see something in her eyes that tugged at his heart, so he cupped her chin with his hand and kissed her softly.

"All right, some air would do you good. I'll be just inside the door if you need me."

With the photograph in her hand, Angela stepped outside and stood on the sidewalk, breathing in the crisp, clean air the autumn rainstorm had left behind. She first thought it weird, then wonderful, to finally acknowledge her secret desire to be more acquainted with her grandmother, if only through a childhood photograph. As she ran her fingers over her grandmother's face, she thought about how, over the years, she hadn't looked for it or pursued the legitimacy behind the myths attached to her name. Now almost a year after Kenny's death, and after all that had taken place, Angela was finding it more and more difficult to casually dismiss this photograph as simply being in the wrong place at the wrong time.

"Coincidence is God's way of remaining anonymous, Albert Einstein once said." She managed a smile.

Then she focused on the picture once more. "I come from you," she whispered.

That was all it took. The wind came up fast, cold, and furious. Like a flash she spun around and felt a rumble, like the booming crash of thunder, flinging her back against the front wall of her salon. At once Angela remembered that there were two persons that had invaded her dreams—not just the one woman. She slowly slid down the wall and collapsed onto the sidewalk, her face showing her intense concentration. Suddenly the words, "*Your blood is within me,*" slammed into her mind and jerked her head back against the wall.

Her eyes shot straight up to the sky. Gasping for breath as if someone was choking the life out of her, she struggled to get up. Again, though this time more sharply, the words came into her mind: "*You are mine... My blood is within you.*"

"What is happening to me?" she asked quickly as the memory of a small child with sad eyes and a gray dress flashed into her mind. She sat very still as the full implication hit her.

Shaking her head twice, she leaned forward and forced her eyes wide open, her lids heavy with exhaustion. She slowly began to relax and her breathing began to even. She struggled to remain calm, convinced that she hadn't experienced a seizure and that she wasn't choking on anything, since her airway was clear.

Almost immediately Nathan burst through the front door and crouched down in front of her. "Easy, Angela, easy. Just breathe, nice and slow."

She pushed at Nathan's hands a few moments later, realizing she was on the ground, cradled in his lap.

"What happened?" he asked.

"She was in my dream!" Angela instantly stiffened. "The little girl in this picture and the little girl in my dream, Nathan... It's the same person."

She went on to recount the dream, careful with every detail.

"This is a part of the first dream you mentioned?"

"Yes. There was only one dream, a few days ago."

"Angela, come on. The little girl in this picture—your grandmother—came to you as a child in your dream?" It was his tone that scared her, not his words.

She took a long breath. "I know how that sounds."

"I just don't know how to answer that."

She gave herself a little shake. "She said her blood was within me."

"Well of course it is... You *are* her granddaughter!"

"Nathan, you know the legend. My grandmother is said to have received and then passed on messages from beyond the grave."

"Then do you think, if you give this crazy woman the 'legendary' message she keeps asking for, that she finally will have peace in her life? That she'll stop bothering you?" His voice was full of weight and aggravation.

"Right now, I think there is some kind of connection between that crazy woman, as you call her, and my grandmother."

Nathan stood up. Taking Angela's hands, he pulled her up into his arms and managed a smile. "Just how the hell do we go about finding what that connection is?"

"We need to find her, Nathan."

"I don't like that idea. Even if it's all true—and I'm not entirely sure it all is—you can't trust a crazy woman to have all her facts straight."

"She wanted a message from me." Angela took a deep breath. "Whether it's true or not, she believes it."

"And what do you believe?" Nathan asked.

He probably wouldn't take it well, she thought. But it had to be said. She'd promised honesty and no more secrets, so she finally forced herself to glance up at him and answered his question. "After the shock wore off and I started to relax, I started to consider the talk I've heard about dreams—the bits of information that have been passed along to me about my grandmother's so-called telepathic abilities. Combined with my own vibrations and messages when Kenny died, and then during Nicky's accident and death, it's too much for me to ignore anymore."

"Honey, maybe you need to focus more on your grandmother as a living, breathing woman. She lived a good life; she got married and had a child, not unlike you. Why not give all this science-fiction mumbo jumbo a rest for a while?"

"The details of Dr. Howard's research, along with his understanding about electromagnetic transport, entail the theory that our thoughts are energy. His natural assumption when I met him was that whatever enabled my grandmother to hear messages from people that have passed on may very well be within me as well."

"Honey." Nathan stopped in front of her and rubbed his hands over hers. "I understand how you feel about all of this."

"I believe it, too."

"But we're not talking about some backyard bully here; we're talking about someone who could be seriously mentally disturbed. Right now I'm more concerned with your safety and your life than with your grandmother's past. I don't want to lose you!"

"Nathan, I refuse to give in to her," Angela interrupted. "Yes, it was disturbing and shocking. I don't like having anyone command my thoughts. And the way she looked at me... You think I'm not angry, not anxious? You're mistaken."

He considered what she said for a moment and then draped his arm around her shoulders as they walked back towards the door of the salon.

"I have no idea what we're doing here, but then again, that's never stopped us before," Angela pointed out.

Nathan wrapped his arms around her, holding her close to him. "So, Nancy Drew... Where do we start?"

Grinning, Angela nodded. "We have this picture. In all probability, it fell out of the Bible the woman was holding up at the window. Now we have the name of the orphanage in Philadelphia where my grandmother lived and went to school, so we can start with that."

All of a sudden there were flashing lights and two squad cars, and then police were walking through the front door of her salon.

Rubbing her arms, Angela stopped and looked at her husband, already having made the decision not to file a complaint. She didn't want an argument with him—not tonight, not after the wonderful day it had been for Rebecca. She wanted the day to end on a high note.

"So, are we in agreement here?" she asked. "No complaint; we handle this and get in touch with Dr. Howard when he returns."

Nathan nodded his head and smiled. Then he opened the front door, and together they stepped inside.

"Nathan, Angela, this is Officer Logan," Rowena explained. "He wants to ask you both a couple of questions."

"I appreciate you coming down here, Officer Logan," Angela said as she took a seat in front of the window. "But I'm afraid the 911 call earlier was made on impulse. We don't want to press any charges or file a complaint."

"Ma'am, that's entirely up to you. Are you completely sure about this?"

She caught herself looking towards the front window, her pulse pounding. There were two policemen outside on the sidewalk and one standing directly in front of her. *"This is ridiculous,"* she internally reminded herself.

"I am. I'm sure, Officer."

"Just so you know, we've briefly dusted for prints and checked the perimeter. Your door and locks haven't been tampered with, so it doesn't look like anyone tried to break into your salon."

"Thank you," Angela said with a small sigh of relief. "That's reassuring."

"But that's not to say whoever was here earlier won't try at another time," Officer Logan warned.

At first Angela was upset, but she settled down once she reminded herself that the officer was only doing his job.

"Any chance, ma'am, you'll change your mind?"

"No. I'm sure," Angela insisted. "I'm just glad it's over."

"Well, if you're sure, I guess we're done here." Officer Logan handed Nathan his card. "Call us if she comes around again."

Nathan laughed in response. "I certainly will, Officer."

"Mrs. Roberts, for the next week or so, we'll have a cruiser go by your salon several times during the day and night to make sure there's not any suspicious activity. Have a good evening."

Angela smiled and nodded.

Nathan sat down beside her. "We're a team. You and I will get through this chapter of our lives together."

Laughing, Angela covered his hand with hers. "How are we ever going to explain any of this to Robby?"

"With much prayer!" Nathan replied.

9

Two weeks had passed since Rebecca's baby shower, and no surprise return visits from the wild-eyed woman had burst into Angela's and Nathan's lives. They enjoyed the calm days, and for the most part, life seemed to be back to normal. The only nervousness or anxiety they harbored was solely reserved for Rebecca and the arrival of their first grandchild.

They had plenty of work to do. Between finishing up the final preparations for the baby, Nathan and Angela stopped by the local soup kitchens and shelters on a regular basis, hoping to find this woman or at least some information about her identity. With only a police artist sketch to show, their attempts were proving unproductive day after day.

A little distance, Nathan decided, was in order. The woman was a mystery, and since there were no finite answers to her identity or location, he decided to funnel his energies into the second half of the puzzle: the increasingly mysterious life of Iana Hamilton. He'd already generated a letter to the Greenwich Orphanage in Philadelphia requesting any information they could offer on her. Using the computer and his courthouse connections, Nathan was also able to generate a chart of Angela's family ancestry, and now he could verify the births, deaths and marriages in her family line.

While Nathan was putting together his charts, Angela spent an afternoon up in the attic, rummaging through boxes of Kenny's old baby things. Searching through at least a dozen cardboard boxes filled with baby clothes, blankets, toys and books, she hoped to find a keepsake from Kenny's childhood that she could pass along to India.

"There's nothing up here that Rebecca would want for her," she said, feeling a bit defeated.

She eased back and then reached around for blankets and toys. Stuffing them all back into their box, she closed the lid.

After putting the box back in its place, she decided to go downstairs and to join Nathan in the living room.

She studied the mountain of papers and files in front of him. "You've been busy."

"I thought you'd like to see this." Nathan pulled out an old sketchpad and turned it around for Angela to see.

"Oh." A slow smile spread across her face. "I forgot about my grandmother's notepads."

"This last section has page after page of your grandmother, depicted with two little girls."

She sat back in her chair and smiled. "Unless it was one of those ill-kept family secrets, my mother didn't have a sister."

Nathan agreed with that, but he would have liked to know more about the unidentified little girl in the drawings.

"Look at this one. Your grandmother's sitting under a tree, again with the two little girls. Now read the caption at the bottom: 'Cilla's and Maggie's Tea Party, June 1935.'"

"It's probably just one of my mother's childhood friends."

"As far as I can tell, your father's side doesn't include anyone with the name Maggie or anything close to it."

Angela nodded but then admitted, "Anyway, there is no one alive now to say."

"I also have some e-mail correspondence from the Greenwich Orphanage," Nathan said and then stared at her.

"Is there anything that will help us?" Angela inquired.

He was silent for a long moment. "Most of it is just standard; the date she arrived and graduated, that she was an excellent student who excelled in art and mathematics. One teacher wrote that Iana had a reputation for keeping to herself, spending the majority of her free time huddled off in a corner drawing in her sketchbooks and notepads."

"That's sad." Angela sighed.

"Doesn't seem anyone really got to know her." Nathan sat back in his chair. "You know what I *do* find interesting? The intake form from the orphanage—it doesn't show a date of birth for her, just an asterisk."

"Which means?" Angela got up from her chair and walked around behind Nathan to look at the email.

"This is intriguing. They have estimated her date of birth between 1894 and 1896."

After one last glance at the email, Angela walked back to her chair and sat down.

"Estimated, huh? She was alive; she definitely existed." Angela gestured with her hands up and down her body.

"You know there were a lot of myths and legends about your grandmother," Nathan said cautiously, then pushed his glasses up the bridge of his nose. "Did you know, for instance, that your great-grandparents on your father's side were on the Titanic when it sank in 1912?"

"You're kidding!" She opened her mouth to speak but didn't say a word. Her heart began to beat faster; she was suddenly filled with a powerful sense of direction. "Maybe this is a sign for me to keep going; there is so much about my family I don't know."

All the information so far had confirmed what had been passed down over the years. Iana had been found by a group of archaeologists, alone and in the vicinity of a deserted village. The government's account in her file ranged from vague to absurd; one account told of a terrible tragedy within her village, when many had died during vicious fighting for the land against the rebels and the settlers, while another agency alleged Iana had been traded by her parents for food and the land they lived on.

Nathan cringed just thinking about it. She was barely more than a toddler, wide-eyed and terrified, yet she had already lived through a plethora of pain and still was willing to endure more. He thought about her trip to America, how it must have terrified her and how little she must have known of what was to come. She had traded one life of insecurity and uncertainty for another packed with *more* insecurity and uncertainty. Lost in thought, Nathan reflected that he had never faced anything quite like it and was sure he never would have survived it. As he read the last line of that particular entry sent from Greenwich Orphanage, he sat and thought about how brave she must have been that day in the desert.

He was surprised how much he had come to care about her, despite the little he actually knew of her. It was more than a little unusual to realize that he was captivated with a child from so long ago. *"She was absolutely amazing,"* he thought.

Nathan got up from his desk and stared out the window; he could see from the light that it was late afternoon. He felt disoriented, having just come back from a moment in time so far away.

Angela walked up behind him and whispered in his ear, "I think you two are bonding."

After a moment, Nathan responded, "Your grandmother must have been a very interesting person."

Angela wrapped her arms around his waist. "Wanna go for a ride?" she asked and then gave him a tiny smile. "Why don't we drive to Brooklyn Heights? We have the address of my grandmother's home from the 1940 Census Report."

Nathan checked his watch. "Traffic won't be too heavy now."

"It's twenty minutes from here," Angela said, waving the directions she'd printed out in the air. "Who knows, maybe the house or an old neighbor will help us track down some clues into my grandmother's past."

Nathan laughed. "I feel like we're Mulder and Scully in a scene from The X-Files!"

"Ooooh yeah... The skeptical Dana Scully and the alien theorist Fox Mulder." Angela laughed.

"Laugh if you will, but Mulder made a believer out of Scully!"

Nathan picked up his notebook, set his cell phone to "Record" and pulled out his dark glasses. He adjusted his shades on his face and then looked at her over the rims. "Let's hit the pavement!"

Amused, Angela grabbed her purse. "I'll assume that's your way of saying we're going to Brooklyn Heights."

A few minutes later, they were backing out of the driveway.

She was shaky as they entered the outskirts of Brooklyn Heights—which was silly, she told herself, as they drove in silence up one street and down another. Both were lost in their own thoughts. Eventually, Nathan pulled over to the curb and stopped the car in front of 486 Canal Street.

The white Cape Cod house was decorated with bright blue shutters and had a front porch. Upon seeing it, Angela instantly felt her soul being restored, and she remembered the nickname of "Story Teller" her grandmother had acquired over her years in that house. Then she imagined Iana sitting on that front porch with the neighborhood children gathered at her feet as she recited one of her infamous stories on a hot summer night.

Angela slowly stepped out of the car and quietly stood on the sidewalk, admiring the home where both Iana and her mother had lived.

Nathan walked up beside her and smiled. As he looked down at her, he noticed she seemed distant, but he had no idea what she could have been thinking.

"My life is here," she said simply. "This is something I should have done a long time ago. I should have known about this place."

It was clear that she didn't want to talk, so Nathan nodded in understanding while he stayed by her side.

Angela took a step forward. "Family history, times and people who came before us... All of that matters. But, until everything that happened this past year, I hadn't given them much thought or value."

"Well, you're here now." Nathan managed a smile. "Take as much time as you need."

Angela had a sense of belonging. There were tears in her eyes as she and Nathan stood on the sidewalk watching two men next door lift a tree, with a huge burlapped ball covering its roots, out of the back of a truck. They proceeded to set it into a hole in the ground. Then a woman wheeled out a red wagon that was spilling over with brightly colored pansies and marigolds, followed closely by an elderly gentleman loaded down with a bag of mulch in his arms. Nathan looked over at them as he continued to walk down the driveway, and then he crossed the yard with Angela by his side.

"Hi there." He smiled broadly as he walked towards the old man. "Need some help?"

Angela turned to face the gentleman and studied his face.

The old man shook his head. "Nah. You people looking for something or someone?" he asked with a smile, and then, after putting down the bag of mulch, he took a white handkerchief from his back pocket and wiped the beads of sweat from his brow.

"We are, as a matter of fact. My grandmother." Angela waved her hands saying, "Well, actually, just some information about her."

Nathan looked around and slipped his hands into his pockets. "This is quite a place you have here."

"Keeps me busy. Lived here over fifty years with my wife," he said, tilting his head toward the old woman who was making her way back to the house, "and pretty much know everyone that's come and gone on this street. Now does your grandmother have a name?"

"Yes... Aah yes, her name was Iana Hamilton Holmes."

"Iana Holmes," he repeated. He looked at Angela for a long moment then bowed his head. "Oh yes, Miss Iana. She was quite remarkable."

"Thank you. That's wonderful to hear," Angela said, beaming. "Well, sir, I'm her granddaughter, Angela Roberts, and this is my husband, Nathan."

"Good evening, and pleased to meet you. I'm James Woodrow." He continued, "And if you don't mind me sayin'," sliding his glasses down his nose to get a better look at her, “you’ve got your grandmother’s eyes.”

“Really?” Angela looked up at him, and neither of them spoke for a moment.

“The house has hardly changed since Iana and her husband, David—a good and God fearing man, by the way—built it years ago.” He felt wistful thinking about the children. “This house was always full of kids. What a full life they had.”

Angela smiled. She felt warm and at ease with him, so much so that it amazed her. She hadn’t expected to feel this way about her grandmother’s house or anyone who lived near it, but denying her feelings was easier said than done at this point.

“There’s an old legend about your grandmother, ya know,” Mr. Woodrow told her.

“That’s what I remember about her most. I’ve heard bits and pieces over the years, and I was hoping to find someone who could tell me more about her life. I was so young when my mother, Cilla, died, that I don’t really know much about either of them.”

“I’m so sorry,” he said softly, imagining the grief she must have gone through as a child. “Miss Iana was a beacon of light.” He looked up at the sky. “She helped people find their way in the darkness.”

“That’s a lovely thing to say,” Angela replied, glancing at him with a shy smile.

“Many years ago, my father would tell me ancient Native American legends. One was about a woman who traded her life for her child and who now lives among the stars, a beacon for all to find their way in the darkness. That was Miss Iana to me.”

For the next hour, Mr. Woodrow shared his memories of Angela’s grandmother, revealing that there were times over the years that he had thought he would mourn her lost life forever. He considered himself lucky and blessed to have crossed paths with her in his lifetime. It didn’t take Angela long to recognize the obvious respect between her grandmother and Mr. Woodrow; it seemed like they had been well acquainted with each other.

Angela suddenly felt the hair on her arms and on the back of her neck rise as Mr. Woodrow explained something he believed as well as felt: From the moment he had met her, Iana seemed like a spirit from a different world, a kind of woman he had never met before. He would take to his grave the belief that she had a special bond with all things in the universe; Iana had taught him that everything around them had its own spirit and was to be respected because it was sacred.

Angela nodded silently, moved by every word that he said.

His voice was quieter when he spoke again. "Some were frightened by the legend of your grandmother, but for me, I found peace in knowing when people were standing on the threshold between their last breaths and the hereafter, your grandmother eased their souls. Then they could depart this life in peace and with no regrets."

Angela could see there were tears in his eyes now.

"Mr. Woodrow, it was a pleasure speaking with you." But Angela's connection with him was more than mere appreciation of a speaking partner, and she knew it.

"Now, is there anything else I can help you with?" Mr. Woodrow asked.

"You're probably busy. We shouldn't take up any more of your time," Angela said as she thanked him.

"Are you sure there isn't anything we can help *you* with?" Nathan asked. "Maybe give you a hand planting that tree?" he said, rolling up his sleeves.

"Heavens, no! My daughter and her husband will take care of that." Mr. Woodrow spoke softly as he looked over at them. "They pretty much do all the work around here now." He rubbed the back of his neck thoughtfully. "I'm grateful they are with me."

Mr. Woodrow looked at Angela and asked again, "Now, you're *sure* young lady, that there's nothing more you need to ask me? I'm 95 years old; you never know when the good Lord will call me home," he said with a wink.

Nathan immediately opened a notepad he had brought along to the page with the illustration of Iana sitting under the tree. "I... Uh... Yes sir, there is, actually. We are curious about the identity of this little girl named Maggie." He pointed to the illustration of Iana with two children that had the names at the bottom of the page.

"There were several families with young girls Cilla's age, but little Maggie Deveraux was like a second daughter to your grandmother. That little girl loved to read and spent so much time with Miss Iana and your mother."

"That's her name, Maggie Deveraux?" Nathan asked as he wrote it on a piece of paper.

"Yep, that sure does look like Maggie. Sweet little girl, too." He smiled as he remembered her, and then he frowned. "That terrible day... I think it broke the child's spirit."

"What happened to her?" Angela asked.

"An accident. Terrible... Terrible thing that child saw. Found her father dead on the living room floor. Her parents were simple, uneducated people; her father drank too much and treated her mother terribly. Suppose it was all too much for the child; some neighbors said she went insane, others said her mother killed her father and that's why they left the area. Rumors flew around here for a long time about the horror the child saw. That's pretty much all I know of it. I don't know if she's dead or alive after all these years," he said, shrugging his old shoulders with a downward glance.

Angela paused. "It sounds awful, so awful. That poor little girl."

"I just thought of something... Something I want to show you. No one else knows about it," he said. Angela looked perplexed as he stood smiling at her.

Mr. Woodrow went inside his house. When he returned a few minutes later, he held out a small leather book to her. Angela took it from him and looked at it. There were no words on the outside cover, and it was obviously very old. She handled it carefully and then opened it to see Iana's name on the first page.

"What is this, Mr. Woodrow?" Angela, looking confused, turned the first few pages, and then realized what she was holding. "My goodness, it's her cookbook, isn't it?"

"It is," he confirmed. He nodded happily and then went on to explain how he had come to acquire it.

"A year before Miss Iana passed away, she promised her dining room table and chairs, along with the matching hutch, to my daughter, Stella." Mr. Woodrow said that Stella had always admired the furniture and that Angela's grandmother, being the woman that she was, just ending up giving it to her.

"Miss Iana didn't ask a red cent for it." Mr. Woodrow's face beamed, and he continued, "She only asked that Stella feed lots of babies at the table and enjoy it as much as she had."

Angela smiled, thinking about what her grandmother had done.

"It was almost six months after Miss Iana passed that we asked about the set; I felt that was the appropriate amount of time," Mr. Woodrow said matter-of-factly.

"I think so too," Angela responded with a smile.

Mr. Woodrow blew out a breath and looked off towards where Iana once lived.

"When I was cleaning out the drawers, I found that." He smiled slowly as he gestured to the cookbook. "Something strange about that little book."

"What could be strange about a cookbook?" she asked with obvious interest.

"From the moment I found it, I had the oddest feeling, deep in my gut, not to give it away."

Angela looked surprised as she acknowledged what Mr. Woodrow was saying.

"I sensed I was to put it away and just let it be." He smiled at her. "And that is exactly what I did all those years ago. Until today."

"That's incredible," Angela said and shook her head. "It's hard to believe it's been as long as it has."

Mr. Woodrow placed his hand on her arm, nodded his head and smiled a slow smile that lit up his face in a way she had never seen before. "Perhaps, my new friend, you were meant to be here. It was meant for this time."

Angela opened the book and turned a few pages, seeing her grandmother's familiar handwriting in the notes scribbled alongside the different recipes, specifying ones to try again or ones not to. It felt like a celebration.

"I don't cook!" Angela said with a laugh.

She turned to Nathan and looked up at him, first with amazement and then with pure happiness.

"Maybe after all these years, I will learn." Tears welled up in her eyes. "My grandmother can teach me."

"I really appreciate how nice you've been to us," she said, turning and smiling wholeheartedly at Mr. Woodrow.

"Thank you," he said softly. "Something tells me that you and your grandmother have something in common." Having finished the sentence, he nodded and slowly walked away.

Angela remembered that Dr. Howard had told her the same thing; she knew what Mr. Woodrow meant.

He waved and was still smiling as they drove away, and on the car ride home, Angela thought about the things he'd told them... Especially about Maggie Deveraux. It must have been hard for her—no, worse than that: heartbreaking. *"People can be incredibly nasty to one another sometimes,"* she thought. It was hard for her to comprehend living the life Maggie had.

As Nathan unlocked the front door to their house, he also thought about Maggie and the pain she had endured because of her parents. He wondered how one life linked the two lives; how did this little girl go from a life of intolerable pain, behind closed doors, to being filled with joy and feeling whole again while in the presence of Iana? He didn't have the answer yet; he knew that much as he walked in the front door of their home and turned on the light.

And that night, as they lay in bed, both thought of Maggie instead of Iana. Nathan decided not to spend any more time with emails or notepads for a few days. He needed to work out the questions trickling into his mind since talking with Mr. Woodrow. Maggie Deveraux... Who was she? Now that he had a name, he needed to research her life.

10

It was another rainy day as Angela looked out the window. She had been worried most of the afternoon and had lavished her attention on Rebecca. Watching her like a hawk, she jumped at each flinch of discomfort on her face. She imagined her reactions to be strictly maternal, since India's due date had come and gone several days ago.

Now, as she stood in front of the window with her grandmother's cookbook in her hand, she again wondered what Iana's life had been like. And then, putting it her out of her mind, she sat down in her recliner, picked up the white baby blanket she'd given to Rebecca, and held it to her cheek. In less than a minute, she had forgotten everything but India.

Nathan, on the other hand, kept his mind off of Rebecca by keeping himself busy with researching Maggie Deveraux. The day after meeting Mr. Woodrow, he was able to locate three Maggie Deverauxes, one living in northern New Jersey and the other two living in California. Except for that bit of information, his hunt for information had come to a screeching halt.

Angela was still curled up in her recliner in the family room, lost in her thoughts, when she heard the bathroom door open and then close.

"Rebecca," she called out.

"In here," Rebecca responded.

"Are you feeling alright?" Angela asked as she got up and walked towards the bathroom.

"My stomach's been cramping something terrible; I think it's a bout of food poisoning."

"You think it's food poisoning?" Angela broke into a grin.

Rebecca felt a sharp pain in her abdomen. "Ooooh," she moaned and pressed both hands to her belly.

"You okay?" Nathan asked, looking up from the computer.

"She could be in labor," Angela said with a smile.

"Is she?" Nathan asked Angela. Then he directed his words toward Rebecca. "Are you?"

"I don't know. I've never been in labor before." Rebecca felt another sharp pain—or was it a contraction? She really didn't know.

"I think we'd better call Dr. Peterson," Angela said.

Rebecca tried to push away the fear she felt. "Maybe it's false labor," she said, although she was well aware of the fact that India was a few days late. She bent forward as another contraction hit. "Ooooh man, that hurts."

"Nathan is getting the car; just sit back and relax," Angela advised her. "And you can toss your theory of food poisoning out the window. This isn't an angry digestive system; more like an angry uterus!"

Five minutes later, Angela heard the car horn, followed by, "Come on, Honey, let's get you to the hospital."

She helped Rebecca out of the chair, and they had only taken four or five steps when Rebecca slowed noticeably and then stopped walking altogether. Thinking another contraction was coming, Angela stopped and stood alongside of Rebecca, grasping her arm.

"Okay, here we go again. Take a deep breath." Angela sucked in a big gulp of air and blew it out slowly.

"No, I'm alright." Her voice weakened. "I need to ask you something before we leave."

"Sweetie, what is it?" Angela asked.

"Mrs. Roberts, would it be alright if we took the picture of Kenny with us?" she requested with a look of terror as the pains ripped through her again.

Angela leaned over and kissed her on the cheek. "How could we leave him behind? He's about to become a father!"

Rebecca had never felt such pain in her life, and she could barely catch her breath as they walked, with Kenny's picture, outside and down the driveway towards the car.

"Don't!" she screamed out in pain as Angela continued to help her move forward. "I don't want to move."

"Rebecca," she said, feeling helpless, "you can't stay here. Relax; the baby isn't coming as quickly as you think." But suddenly feeling suspicious, she asked, "When did this start?"

"I don't know." She started to cry. "I had a backache all day today, and my stomach hurt for a while, but I thought it was something I ate."

"Oh my God," Angela said with a look of panic. "It's been all day."

Rebecca looked like a child all at once, and Angela felt sorry for her, but she knew she had to start moving towards the car right away, no matter how much she said it hurt to do so.

"I'm scared," she whimpered.

Angela slid into the back seat beside Rebecca and reached over, taking her hand. "I'll be right by your side. I promise."

Rebecca was suddenly gasping in agony, and Angela could see that she was almost screaming with pain.

"Start driving unless you want to deliver this baby in the backseat of your Mercedes!"

"Angela," Nathan said as he looked in the rearview mirror to see that his wife had a peaceful smile on her face. "You're going to kill me! I'm too old for all of this."

She leaned over the front seat and whispered in his ear, "Love you, Grandpa... Now drive!"

After being admitted to Labor and Delivery, Rebecca was totally focused on her work. She made little noises as she fought through each painful contraction. Suddenly her entire face was clenched, and she began to push. She was delivering her baby, and there was nothing anyone could do to stop her.

Angela watched and was grateful to have never gone through anything like this; she delivered both of her boys by C-section on their due dates. In thanks, she bowed her head, praying that God would guide the hands of the doctors and nurses surrounding Rebecca.

Next she heard a tiny moan, and she instantly opened her eyes.

All of a sudden, realizing Rebecca needed her to help, Angela held her shoulders and lifted her up with each contraction. At the same time, she coached her in the Lamaze method of breathing. For a second time Rebecca let out a gut-wrenching scream, as though a terrible force was tearing through her. Angela reached down and lifted the sheet; the baby was coming into the waiting hands of the doctor, with her little face screaming at the world in outrage. And within an instant, the doctor was holding India Cleopatra.

On October 24th at precisely 8:05 in the evening, Rebecca and Kenny's daughter made her entrance into the world. It was love at first sight.

Angela was still sitting beside Rebecca when the nurse handed her this tiny, only-minutes-big baby.

"This baby is a miracle. Our miracle." Angela leaned over and hugged Rebecca, then bent down and softly kissed her brand new granddaughter's forehead. "You are loved, my precious little India."

Rebecca looked over at Angela. Tears filling her eyes, she whispered, "Mrs. Roberts, what if I am a failure at being a mother, just like my mother was?"

"That's nonsense, and you know it. You're exhausted, and your hormones are raging right now," Angela said with a laugh. "You have never been a failure, nor will you be a failure as a mother. Remember, God doesn't make mistakes or failures," she said with a wink at Rebecca as they admired the baby.

"I hurt," Rebecca moaned and then eased her body back against the pillows to get more comfortable.

"Try not to move too much; you had an epidural. The doctor said you might get a headache," Angela said as she rose to her feet. "I'll let the nurse know you need something for pain."

"Thanks," Rebecca said, wiping a tear away while trying to absorb what had just taken place and thinking about the future. "Maybe our meeting was supposed to happen."

It was impossible for Rebecca not to think that now.

"Maybe," Angela said honestly. "Maybe our meeting happened for a reason, or maybe not. I can't say for sure, but I like believing that it did."

"Nobody ever really gave me a chance before, except for you and Mr. Roberts." After a pause, and thinking about Kenny, she suddenly asked, "Are you happy about it?"

"I am happy," Angela replied. "I'm very happy."

Almost on cue, the nurse walked through the door with Rebecca's pain medication. "How you feeling, Hon?"

"I hurt!" She smiled.

"Well, of course you do... You just had a baby tear right through you!" The nurse checked her vital signs and administered a shot of pain medication. It didn't take long for the medication to work, enabling Rebecca to doze off.

Angela couldn't wait to cuddle with her new granddaughter. She glanced over at Nathan and asked, "How much have you thought of Kenny today?"

Nathan shook his head. "What do you think?"

"I know. Me too." She wiped a tear from her cheek.

Angela watched the nurse gently clean the baby, dress her and then swaddle her in a blanket. She felt a warm glow spread through her and exhaled a long sigh of contentment, realizing the tragedy of losing her son hadn't been a curse on her life. His death had been turned around; it was truly God's blessing in their lives.

"Would you like to hold your granddaughter?" the nurse asked.

Angela's mouth came apart into a grin. "I can't wait," she responded.

With her granddaughter tucked safely in her arms, she walked back over to the rocking chair and sat down. She desperately wanted Kenny to be there with them.

"Hello, little baby," Angela whispered. "Your daddy is so proud today."

Nathan nodded in agreement. "You are so beautiful... You look like your daddy."

"I'm not changing my mind about staying home with her. I'm still going to do that."

"Honey, I wouldn't have it any other way." He leaned down and kissed her on the cheek.

Angela still had trouble believing how blessed she was. Nathan was a doting and loving husband, and she loved him completely. Still, she always felt like a part of her was missing whenever she thought about Kenny, and she knew that, most likely, she would always feel that way. But finally, after all this time, the light of truth was shining brightly, melting away the darkness and anxiety that surrounded losing her son. Her family was intact; her family had life in it. She was a wife, mother and now grandmother; her relationship with Nathan had deepened, and so had her relationship with God.

"Thank you, Jesus," she said softly.

Angela and Nathan had dozed off while the baby was in the nursery with the doctor. When Angela opened her eyes, she found Rebecca stirring.

"The b-baby," she murmured. "Where's India?"

Angela sat up in her chair. "The doctor is checking her out."

"Is she okay?"

"She's fine."

Just then the nurse walked into the room, carrying India in her arms. "This little girl is starving," she said with a smile and then gently laid the baby in the crook of Rebecca's arm. "A nurse will be in shortly to help you with the breast feeding."

After a few minutes of Rebecca talking in baby jibber-jabber while counting India's ten tiny fingers and toes, Angela and Nathan sensed it was time for them to leave.

"Alright you two, you're going to be busy with the nurse. So, Rebecca, we'll give you some alone time with your precious daughter," Nathan announced.

Angela wiped her eyes. "Wow, I need to sit back down for a minute."

Nathan put his hand on her shoulder. "Don't cry. Please don't cry."

"I'm allowed to cry when my firstborn son makes me a grandmother. I'm damn well allowed to shed a few tears." She sat down and blew her nose.

Nathan pulled out another tissue and handed it to her.

"I always knew this day would come. From the moment you hold your child in your arms, you think about the day when that child will have a child of their own. You don't think about it every day, but you know that someday you will hold your grandchild in your arms. Life cycles." She opened her arms to Nathan. "You're a grandfather!"

He looked back into her eyes. "Yep. The way I see it, I hit the jackpot! We've got the daughter we always hoped for and now we've got a granddaughter, too."

Tears flowed again. "I'm going to need more than just one tissue now."

"Look at you." Nathan smiled and brushed Angela's hair from her damp cheeks. "Sitting here crying happy tears."

Rebecca smiled and nodded. She had enormous respect for Nathan and Angela and was grateful for everything in her life. She was overjoyed to see Angela so ecstatic. "I still can't believe all you've done for me," she said solemnly.

There was an endless pause as Angela looked at Rebecca and then the baby, and then she got up and held out her arms to her. "We don't want anything to change," Angela said sincerely, and she could feel Rebecca shaking in her arms.

With Angela's emotions in turmoil, Nathan stepped over, held out his hand and suggested they go home to allow Rebecca some quiet time with India.

"Very well." Angela took a deep breath and straightened to her feet, reaching for Nathan's hand as he reached for hers. "I need one more look before we go." She sat back down beside Rebecca and gazed at India with adoration. "There's my baby girl. Grammy will be back bright and early tomorrow morning."

"Yes. Now step away from the baby," Nathan said with a grin as he reached down and took Angela by the hand. "We will, my dear."

Nathan and Rebecca exchanged amused looks before Angela reached over and patted India's little head again.

"Your grandpa thinks he's being funny."

Angela fought back more happy tears and waved her hand in the air. "As soon as I get home, I need to call Robby."

"He's an uncle," Nathan reminded her.

"On second thought, I don't think I can wait 'til we get home; I'll call from the car."

Angela leaned over again and whispered in Rebecca's ear, "We love you."

"Me, too," she sniffled.

"Okay, we'll see you in the morning." She crouched down to kiss India's head. "You be a good little girl for Mommy tonight."

"Rebecca." Nathan drew a breath as he stopped at the door. "Kenny... He'd be proud of you." The best Nathan could do after that was a nod, and then he walked out the door.

Angela kept her eyes on India and crossed her hands over her heart.

"Hallelujah," she proclaimed.

Angela and Nathan stepped off the elevator, walking hand-in-hand, laughing and talking as they made their way to the front door of the hospital.

"Maybe a glass of champagne is in order when we get home," Nathan said with a wink.

"That would be very nice—and definitely in order." Angela smiled back at him.

Suddenly the lights flickered off and then back on, and Angela looked around nervously. "The rain's started; it's pouring outside."

Nathan nodded. "I'll get the car and bring it around."

Angela agreed. Just then, a flash of white lightening lit up the night sky, immediately discharging a ground-shaking explosion. The hospital lobby went pitch black.

"That must have knocked out the power," Nathan said.

"Y-yeeaah," Angela groaned as her whole body stiffened.

"It's okay," Nathan said, leaning in next to her. "They have emergency generators when the power goes out."

A few moments later the lights flickered on. Angela took a breath and looked up, and when her eyes instantly locked on what was in front of her, she froze, shocked. Someone heading the other direction passed her and nearly knocked her into the wall.

"Angela, what's the matter?"

She timidly took Nathan's hand. "Nathan, you see her, don't you?" Her eyes were deep and sharp as she looked at him.

"See who?" He looked vague.

Not more than twenty feet away was an elderly woman, soaked to the skin and huddled up in one of the chairs by the front doors. Right away Angela recognized her unkempt dark, wiry hair. She sat perfectly still with her eyes wide open, staring blankly at the ceiling.

"What are you talking about?" Nathan asked.

Angela pointed towards the front doors of the hospital. There was a long, terrifying moment of silence when neither of them moved; Angela considered turning and running back to Rebecca's room as quickly as she could.

Suddenly, something strange clicked into her mind. The name "*Maggie Deveraux"* floated into her consciousness, and then it was gone.

Angela shook her head in disbelief. "This doesn't make any sense at all!"

"What doesn't make sense?" Nathan asked.

All of a sudden, something broke through her anger and anxiety, prompting her to take the woman a cup of water.

At this point, Angela had a myriad of emotions coursing through her body, none of which were loving and kind. There was no way she felt like honoring this woman with a cup of water right now. But she couldn't shake the overwhelming sense that she needed to extend grace to the person who was hurting her and doing everything possible to destroy her comfort, her security and her joy.

"She probably won't even want any water if I offer it to her," she thought, trying to reason her way out of it. However, she found no argument or solution acceptable, and it became apparent that she would have to follow through with her inclination.

She put her hand gently on Nathan's arm and spoke cautiously. "Nathan, don't ask me to explain this, but I think that Maggie Deveraux is sitting in that chair."

Nathan remained relaxed. "Maggie Deveraux? Where did that come from?"

"I don't know; call it a divine intervention or something. I heard her name very clearly, so real and right here with me. This is too close for me to deny."

"I see the woman, but I... I'm not sure, exactly." He strode after her.

"I know all of this sounds bizarre, but I have a complete and very unexpected peace about it... like something in my soul is giving me God's perspective, along with the certainty of His presence. The woman who's been following me, the woman who was at the salon... I think that's her. I think she's Maggie."

"What exactly are you up to, God?" Nathan asked, looked up, and then took Angela's hand. "You're right when you say it sounds bizarre." With a sigh of resignation, Nathan concluded, "Well, we've had one miracle tonight; maybe we're in for another."

"All I know is that the longer I walk with God, the more easily I hear His voice and His instructions."

"You were given instructions, too?" Nathan asked.

"I'm supposed to offer her a cup of water."

"A cup of water... Are you sure about this?"

"I know it seems pointless, but maybe God has a plan for us and a plan for her."

"Angela, come on. A cup of *water*?" Nathan said, smiling.

He started to walk away but then stopped and shook his head. "But then again, it was a grocery store that led you to Rebecca, and look how that all turned out." He hesitated for a second. "I give up... I'm not going to question any of this! As far as I'm concerned, the next step is to obey."

"Yep," Angela said and then shrugged. "I don't think I can stand to wait another minute. It's driving me crazy."

A moment passed while they both looked around the lobby, a little uncomfortable with the task that was suddenly placed before them. Nathan turned to Angela and broke the silence.

"If this is what you believe, and giving her a cup of water is what we're to do, we'll do it together."

Nathan got a bottle of water from the vending machine and then extended his hand to Angela. Together, the two of them slowly made their way towards the woman. Angela had to stop for a moment to will her feet to walk the next step on this path of obedience, and then suddenly and quietly, she clearly felt God's impression on her heart. *"Today it will be natural water, but this will guide her to the living water."*

Soon, Angela and Nathan were standing alongside of her. As Angela reached out her arm to give her the water, the heaviness lifted from her heart and she smiled.

"Maggie?" she asked softly.

This woman didn't seem quite as daunting anymore. Her frailty was growing more visible, and even her meanness seemed to have less force behind it.

"How do you know my name?" Staring angrily into Angela's eyes, she grabbed the bottle of water from her hand.

Angela looked at Nathan and then took a step forward. Instantly, Nathan took hold of her arm and pulled her back.

"Be careful," he quietly warned. "Don't do anything silly!"

He had very little to say, but it was obvious from the tone of his voice and his word choice how concerned he was for his wife.

"This could be our only chance to find out who she is," she whispered back.

Nathan tugged her closer. "You've got five minutes."

Angela took a deep breath and smiled. "Maggie, by any chance is your last name Deveraux?"

Instantly, the sound of her name seemed to bring a sense of peace to her. Angela detected a faint smile come to her lips as she continued to stare out the window.

"Maggie Deveraux... Maggie Deveraux," the woman whispered to herself. She looked up through her wet, spiky lashes, then smiled and fixed her eyes on Angela's.

"You have your grandmother's eyes." Her mouth tightened. "Your grandmother," Maggie said as she lifted an unsteady hand to rub at her temple. "Mama Iana."

For whatever reason, the shock of her statement wasn't as jarring as Angela had expected it would be. It was almost as though she had expected Maggie to say just those words. Cautiously, she moved closer and slowly knelt down beside her. Reaching over to take Maggie's hand, she quietly asked, "You know my grandmother, Iana Hamilton?"

Immediately Maggie pulled her hand free, and with a little huff she twisted her body tight against the back of the chair, sending Angela back on her heels. Glancing over her shoulder, she shot Angela a narrow look.

"I don't know what you're talking about."

In a gesture of peace, Angela held up a hand as she sucked in her breath and smiled, but she kept her eyes strictly on Maggie's face.

"Mama Iana," she murmured, running a finger along the dusty windowsill.

"Yes, Mama Iana. She had a little girl, Cilla. You were friends with her, weren't you?"

"Cilla." Maggie moved her shoulders gently and then bowed her head.

Angela caught a wistful look in her eyes before she turned to stare out the window again. A new flash of lightning made her tremble; instinctively she closed her eyes and huddled against the back of the chair. Maggie could see it perfectly, the way it once had been.

"Mama Iana, she used to tell us stories, ya know. I can see her sitting on the front porch with a book in her hand. When it was real hot, she'd make us fresh squeezed lemonade." She frowned a little and then looked at Nathan.

"He has mean eyes," she told Angela.

Angela laughed and stood up, slipping her arm through his. "No, he's not mean. Maggie, this is my husband, Nathan."

Nathan smiled and nodded his head. "It's a pleasure to meet you."

Maggie looked solemnly at Angela, who nodded. "Is there anything we can get you? Something to eat, maybe?"

"I'm sure the hospital cafeteria is still open, or maybe you'd like something from the vending machine," Nathan said.

"I like crackers," Maggie told them as she opened her eyes wide. "The ones shaped like little animals."

"Great. Animal crackers it is!" Nathan took Angela by the hand. "Maggie, you wait here and we'll be back in a few minutes."

"Nathan," Angela said, "maybe I should sit with Maggie while you get the crackers." She turned to study him.

Air hissed out between his clenched teeth. "I think we should give Maggie a few minutes to catch her breath."

"You're looking very serious," Angela whispered in his ear. "Are you okay?'

He nodded and smiled at Maggie. "This will only take a couple of minutes, and we'll be right back."

Nathan walked with force, seeming irritated as he hurried down the hall. "I think you really have to figure out what you want before you get any more involved in this woman's life."

"I have to figure out... what I want?"

"Angela, that was weird!" His heated eyes narrowed. "The woman is obviously unbalanced and could present a threat to you or to our family. It's crazy that she's Maggie—the little girl in your grandmother's drawings. Is that even possible? I want you to stay away from her."

The statement took her so off guard that she walked up the hall another three feet before it finally registered. "You what?"

"Honey, I know how much you want to make sense of all of this—Maggie, your grandmother and the connection you feel to her life—but I'm feeling it may be unsafe."

"Where is all of this coming from?"

He placed his hands on her shoulders and said, "I've given this some thought—"

"Oh, have you?" she interrupted with a gleam in her eyes.

Nathan immediately recognized the hint of temper in her dull tone.

"And exactly how did you come to that assumption?" she asked.

"There, you see?" He lifted his hands from her shoulders and then put them back down again. "Your reaction is sheer emotion, without any logic or thought."

"I see." She nodded slowly. "So you think I haven't given any thought to Maggie possibly becoming aggressive towards me, or considered the chance that she may be a bit off balance? Nathan, the woman has had three opportunities to hurt me, and she didn't. Yes, I was afraid, but I'm not anymore. I've come too far to stop now, and you know it."

It occurred to him this conversation was coming a little too late and that he was now on very shaky ground.

"I'm concerned that you may be too emotionally involved to act cautiously."

The exasperation on his face took the edge off her temper. "Besides being a pretty face, my dear, I do have a certain amount of street smarts." She brushed by him to continue looking in the vending machines for Maggie's animal crackers.

"Angela." He stopped in front of her and took her hand. "I hope you believe me. I know how you feel about all of this, but..."

"You're going to tell me again to stop. And your concerns are justified, and I love you for trying to protect me. But I won't be chased away from what's mine; I have a right to know my heritage, and I'll never find the answer to my questions about my grandmother if I give up now."

"That's a tough way for me to look at this." Nathan was shaken by what she'd said, but he couldn't disagree. "Okay," he said, reaching out his hand for hers, "we'll keep things as they are for now."

"I'll be less afraid if you're right here with me," she said as she squeezed his hand.

"You going it alone isn't even an option." The frustration was obvious in his voice and on his face, but she smiled reassuringly at him.

"When Robby hears about this..." she began, then exclaimed, "oh my gosh, *Robby*! I haven't called him about the baby yet."

"We'll call him as soon as we get home. Or as soon as we get in the car." Nathan leaned over to press his lips to her cheek. "We support each other; we always have and always will."

"Thank you." She cuddled up next to him. He nourished a deep inner part of her, and she felt safe just being with him. As they walked back to Maggie with two bags of animal crackers in tow, Angela had a sense of peace toward her marriage that she hadn't felt in years.

"When I married you, I meant what I said: For better or worse. I just hope all of this gets easier," Nathan said and gave her another hug as she beamed. The day had been everything she had wanted it to be.

Meanwhile, the storm was rolling closer, gathering force. Maggie glanced back toward the window. She felt a driving need to be outside to meet it. So, moving away from the window, she walked towards the front doors.

And then she was gone.

11

Angela awoke early the next morning, ready and anxious to begin her day. India would be coming home tomorrow, Robby would be coming home in a week, and with only three weeks until Thanksgiving, her mind was buzzing with her "to do" list. As she lay quietly, close to Nathan, feeling his heart beat next to her, she smiled and looked up at him, full of contentment and joy. "I never thought I'd be this happy again," she whispered.

"Nor did I," he said just as softly and then rolled over onto his side.

She leaned over and kissed his shoulder. The aroma of freshly brewed coffee lured her out of bed and into her soft, oversized robe and plush slippers. She tip-toed out of the bedroom and made a bee-line towards the kitchen to collect her prize.

She always enjoyed her first cup of coffee on the patio. But this morning as she stepped outside, the nippiness in the air hit her with a surprising, harsh little slap, which had her heading right back into the kitchen.

"It's the end of October already, and the holidays are right around the corner," she thought to herself. Suddenly she was filled with the anticipation and excitement for upcoming festivities. Sitting down at the kitchen table, she imagined herself taking India to see Santa, and oh, all of the decorating she would do this year.

"I am definitely going to buy a 'Baby's First Christmas' ornament this year for the tree," she mused to herself.

Angela took the holidays very seriously. Thoughts of those Christmas mornings years ago when Kenny and Robby were both still young enough to believe in Santa brought a smile to her face. As she poured another cup of coffee, she remembered how hard it had been some years financially. In the beginning, she'd had to put off her shopping for those big ticket items for the boys until the week before Christmas, just to take advantage of the sixty and seventy percent off sale prices.

Christmas morning was always frantic and bordered on hysterical. *"Good God, how many Christmas Eves did Nathan struggle to assemble a bike or two?"* she thought as she buttered a piece of toast.

But when Christmas Day was over, it was always worth every minute.

She smiled again, thinking about Robby coming home for Thanksgiving break. She was now free of her obligations to the salon and could focus on her family and the holidays. The truth was, the way Stephen managed the salon over the past year proved it would carry on just as well without her. If she had an urge, she could go back for a customer or two, but she didn't have the desire even to do that.

Home was where she was the happiest, and she was determined to make this year's holidays magical for her family.

Despite her determination, she was feeling a bit troubled. She moved over to the window and stiffened with thoughts of Maggie; she didn't know why, but she sensed something ominous was about to take place in her life. Casually she looked around the room and then dismissed the thoughts. And with that, she decided to peruse cookbooks in preparation for her home-cooked Thanksgiving feast. For the first time in years, Angela was excited about cooking and baking; she was bound and determined to prepare every dish with her own two hands, come hell or high water. And she meant it, too.

Angela poured herself another cup of coffee and opened the first cookbook, turning page after page, hoping for a recipe to jump out at her. But nothing much did. She set one aside for another, and skimming the pages she found a recipe for peanut butter fudge. "Kenny loved this!" she said and immediately put it under the dessert category on her menu.

"Look at you, surrounded by cookbooks first thing in the morning." She didn't turn when she heard Nathan's voice behind her. "You're not wasting any time, are you, Martha Stewart?"

"Do you think I can handle fudge?" she asked as her face began to glow.

"I think you can handle just about anything you set your mind to." Nathan poured himself a cup of coffee and then sat down across from her.

"I've got a general idea of what I want to make for Thanksgiving Day—all the standard dishes—but I'll be darned if I can find a recipe in any of these cookbooks for green bean casserole." She struggled with temper and giddiness.

"Angela, relax. Just enjoy what you are doing and the rest will come," Nathan offered, unfazed.

She paused and then leaned forward to take a bite of toast Nathan was holding out to her.

"Okay. I don't see that it will matter much if we have green bean casserole or not."

"Wait!" Nathan sprang up and immediately walked over to the corner cabinet, opened the door and pulled out a small leather book.

"Voila!" Raising the book in the air, he smiled and then, proud as a peacock, strutted back to the table and set the book down in front of her. With a laugh, he leaned over to kiss her cheek. "Here, why don't you look through this? I'll bet there's a green bean casserole in these pages."

"My grandmother's cookbook! I can't believe I forgot all about this." She picked up the book and then tipped her head. Looking at Nathan, she exclaimed, "You're my hero!"

He fixed a smile on his face and nodded as if in agreement.

Angela stretched out her legs and began flipping through the pages. Most of the recipes were more of the same types of things she had found in her own cookbooks.

"Find any green bean casserole recipes?" Nathan asked after a little while.

Frustrated, she drew in a breath. "Nope. Just lots of soups and salads, a couple of her favorite main dishes, appetizers and desserts, and a few candy recipes." She smiled at a handwritten note. "Here, look at this." She turned the book around for Nathan to see what Iana had written alongside the Christmas Bread recipe: *"Make again, hubbie loved it!"*

It was sweet, Angela thought, and she lingered a moment in the mental picture of her grandmother preparing the bread for her grandfather.

"I'll take some of that on Christmas morning," Nathan said. He lifted his coffee mug, took a huge gulp and then pushed back from the table. "I'm going to leave you to your holiday preparations." He then rinsed out his mug and set it on the counter. "Think I'll give Robby a call."

"Ask him what his flight number is for when we pick him and Manny up at the airport next week."

Feeling somewhat downtrodden, Angela considered going online to look for recipes, but at the last minute she ordered herself to take one more look through Iana's cookbook.

She propped an elbow on the table, cupped her chin in her hand and began flipping through the pages once again.

"Nothing!" Now at her wits' end, Angela spread a hand over her face. "I can't believe how frustrating this is."

She closed the book, cleaned up the kitchen and decided to get dressed and head over to the hospital to visit her brand new grandbaby. As she started to walk out of the kitchen, Angela unexpectedly felt inspired to check her grandmother's recipe book for a third time. Baffled, she fought the idea, not imagining her thought could have any meaning. But then again, Angela was growing well acquainted with unusual thoughts and sensations that were revealing themselves more frequently in her life. Finally, she chose not to ignore the feeling and gave her grandmother's book another look.

This time, instead of starting at the beginning, Angela opened to the middle section of the book and slowly began turning page after page. And as she began reading the words on one particular page, her eyes grew wide and she felt strangely breathless.

Several aluminum sheets
Pistons, bolts, rivets, screws
Wires, bits of metal
Engines (4)
Electrical machinery
Lights (6 red, 2 white)
Cushioned seats
Wings (2) (sp-59.6m)
Tail (1) (ht-19.3m)

40.7772 position N, 73.8725 position W
EMP
7-4-7
11-25
458

Today I have a knowing!

While it may appear unsystematic and unintelligent, this is an intelligent system that we all are a part of. There is a force, a power, a consciousness that created and supports this knowledge.

Angela's hand trembled. She wished there was more to read, something that would bring more clarity to this bizarre list of items. She couldn't quite explain it to herself, but whatever this was, Angela knew it wasn't something she was supposed to put in the oven and bake for an hour at 350 degrees. She stood up and walked to the patio doors.

"What '*knowing*' did Iana receive?" Angela said semi-sarcastically. Her head was full of all kinds of wild ideas, and she needed to empty her mind. With the book in her hand, she walked outside, breathing in the crisp morning air that was just beginning to get a little warmer.

"Here you are," Nathan said, and she turned around to meet his eyes. "Angela, you look upset."

"I found something." She paused and looked down at the book. "I started looking through Iana's recipes again and found a strange, somewhat bordering on alarming, entry towards the back of the book."

"What could be so alarming in a recipe book? Unless it was the eye of newt, tongue of dog recipe?" Amused at himself, he started to leaf through the book.

"Very funny. But I'm serious, and it's disturbing. Read it for yourself." She turned to the page. "Take it inside; I need another minute here."

"Alright." He took the book and then saw something in her eyes that tugged at his heart. "It's really upset you, hasn't it?"

She hesitated. "It could just be meaningless, I suppose."

"I'll look over it. In the meantime, why don't you go shower so we can visit Rebecca later?"

Sliding her arm around his waist, she said, "All things considered, what's been running through my mind *does* seem a bit far-fetched. You're right; seeing Rebecca and the baby will take my mind off all of this."

"Oh, I almost forgot. I spoke with Robby, and he's pushed his flight back a week. He said something about an internship with a law firm out there, and he needs to check it out before Thanksgiving break."

She took one long breath, then another. "Uh-huh. He better get his butt home in time for Thanksgiving!" She shot a grin over her shoulder as she started back inside.

Angela walked straight to the bathroom and began undressing while she talked, in a no-nonsense sort of way. "Who and what *was* Iana Hamilton Holmes?" She picked up her clothes and put them in the hamper then leaned in to start the shower. "What exactly *was* her life all about?" She tested the water and stepped in.

"Whatever it was, I hope this doesn't open up a new can of worms for us."

For the past two weeks, Angela had spent her days dusting, cleaning, vacuuming, shopping for groceries and buying bottles of wine for Thanksgiving Day. All of this, along with helping Rebecca care for India—and those excruciating two o'clock feedings—didn't give Angela much time to think about the strange entries she had discovered in Iana's cookbook or the unexpected encounter with Maggie the night India was born. There were, however, a few occasions when the prospect of bumping into Maggie again did appeal to her; the woman fascinated her now. It was hard to guess what would happen in the months to come; some days she still couldn't believe what had happened in her life over the past year. But for the first time in a while, she wasn't reacting to what had been thrown at her. Angela had made a choice: she was going to do whatever she needed and wanted to do. It felt like a turning point for her.

She had just finished baking the last batch of Robby's favorite chocolate chip cookies for his homecoming in two days. A spiced apple and cinnamon candle burned in the living room and filled her home with the scents of fall and the upcoming holiday season.

She polished her mother's silver bowl and filled it with glossy red apples. As she placed it on the center island in her kitchen, she noticed it had started to snow outside. She was in remarkably good spirits and suddenly felt festive enough to begin humming Christmas carols.

"I think it's time to do some decorating." She went directly upstairs, first poking her head in the nursery to check on India and then heading to the closet in Rebecca's bedroom. She pulled out several boxes, carried them downstairs and dropped them onto the living room floor. Next she poured herself a glass of wine and drew back the living room curtains; she stood quietly staring out the window, thinking how beautiful the snow looked as it swirled in the air before gently falling to the ground. It had been too long since there were children in her home for the holidays, she thought as she sipped her wine. Having India in her home for this time of year made her feel like a kid again herself.

"Thank you, Lord. This is just what I wanted," she said before hurrying back upstairs for the remaining decorations.

Angela adorned her front door with a grape leaf wreath with berries. The array of green leaves mixed with brightly colored orange and red leaves symbolized the change in her life and also captured the richness of the holiday season. Her dining room table was decorated with a horn-shaped basket overflowing with sunflowers, two-tone orange roses and burgundy carnations nestled among eucalyptus and golden wheat stems. Tilting her head to the side and smiling, she said, "That will do, yes!" Then she made a mental note to buy candles for each side of the arrangement.

On the mantel above the living room fireplace stood Angela's prized collection of Lenox Pilgrim figurines, nestled among wicker baskets that were spilling over with pumpkins, gourds and Indian corn in a variety of colors and sizes.

"Two thumbs up!" Nathan's voice came from behind her.

"Thanks, Honey. Before I knew it, I had decorated the living room, dining room and kitchen for Thanksgiving."

"I can see that." Tucking his hands in his back pockets then narrowing his eyes, he gave her handiwork a serious and lengthy scrutiny. "It's beginning to feel very holidayish in here."

"I like to make it count. Only about four weeks till Christmas, after all!"

"I suppose it's too much to ask if we could honor my family's tradition of decorating on Christmas Eve rather than the day after Thanksgiving."

"I'm sorry, did you say something?" Despite herself, Angela chuckled all the way into the kitchen.

Now he laughed too. "Fine. I'll take that drink now."

When Nathan awoke the next morning, it was cold outside and snow was beginning to fall again.

"No point in going to the office today," he said simply. "The day before Thanksgiving... Yeah, I think I'll stay out of the office party arena." He went to the refrigerator for juice and then sat down at his desk to drink it.

All he wanted to do once he was up, had taken a shower and was dressed was grab a cup of coffee and research Iana's strange entries from her cookbook. Finally, after faxing some notes to the office and making a couple of calls to his top clients, he let himself sit down at his computer to begin his research. He was going to share all of his findings with Angela eventually, but not just yet.

The house was quiet as he picked up the book and started reading the peculiar entry again. He loved a challenge; it was exhilarating, like a spy thriller, and there was nothing like solving a mystery to divert his mind from his worries. Nathan chewed his lip and then typed, "40.7772 N, 73.8725 W" into the search engine on the computer in front of him. Instantly the website for LaGuardia Airport popped up.

"What?" Frowning, he pushed back from the computer, waited a few seconds and then entered it again. The same result appeared as before: *"LaGuardia Airport, 40.7772 degrees N, 73.8725 degrees W, an airport in the northern part of New York City, near the borough of Queens. The airport is on the waterfront of Flushing Bay and Bowery Bay, and it borders the neighborhoods of Astoria, Jackson Heights and East Elmhurst."*

A slow, lazy smile moved over his face as he realized what the numbers represented: longitude and latitude. Nathan felt excitement well up inside of him; quite frankly, he hadn't expected his search to be this easy. He took a quick look at the list in the cookbook again and then stepped away from his computer and stretched. He knew Iana's handwriting so well by now that, with that one clue, he could read and interpret the rest of the lines. *Electrical machinery; wings, tail, engines.* Putting it all together in his mind, he could see it.

"She's describing an airplane—a 747. She *wrote* it!" He stood at the window for a moment with the small leather book in his hand, thinking about Iana.

"How did I not see that?" Cursing to himself, he then leaned back against his desk and adjusted his glasses. "Iana's recipes... 1925."

Nathan paced the room. The trial lawyer in him suggested something wasn't right; he could feel it, and it urged him to walk back to his desk. After sitting down, he typed in "Boeing 747" and proceeded to read article after article about the plane.

"The 747 first flew on February 9, 1969," he said dryly, then scooped a hand through his hair and took off his glasses. "She died in 1946." By his quick calculations, that was *twenty-three years* before the 747.

As Nathan thought of it, he began to investigate when LaGuardia had been constructed. He blinked, and leaned in closer to read, "*The airport was dedicated on October 15, 1949.*"

"How is that possible?" he asked aloud. His eyes narrowed, and he took one long breath and then another. "That's quite a bomb you just dropped on me, Iana Hamilton Holmes."

But the thought made him pause. Nathan adjusted his glasses and looked more closely at the list.

"How could Iana have known to write the description of a jumbo jet, or even the longitude and latitude of an airport?" He shrugged and drummed his fingers on the desk. "Neither of those things existed in 1925!"

Nathan sat in total silence for a long time. Then he closed the book carefully, looking at it as the treasured thing it was.

With baby India in her arms, Angela walked into the living room to find Nathan sitting at his desk, staring out the window.

She cleared her throat. "Sorry to interrupt."

Startled, Nathan turned in his chair, and after a long pause, said quietly, "What? Oh, no; as a matter of fact, I need an interruption right about now."

"There's something I need to talk to you about," Angela told him.

"Good, I need to talk with you too." He swiveled away from his computer, took off his glasses and rubbed his face with his hands.

Angela could see him working his thoughts out in his head. "Okay, you go first." She put India in her baby swing and then sat down on the couch.

He vacantly stared and lifted both hands to the sides of his head. "My head is reeling."

"Nathan, what's going on?"

As he started to speak, the phone rang. When it hit the third ring, Angela assumed Nathan wasn't going to answer it, so she answered it herself.

"Hello."

"Hi Mom," came the words through the receiver.

She smiled at hearing her son's voice and then glared at Nathan from across the room, silently scolding him for not answering the phone himself. "It's Robby," she whispered.

"I only have a minute. Just wanted to remind you and Dad to pick us up at the airport later this afternoon."

"Is everything alright?" she asked. "You sound anxious."

After a moment, Robby responded, "Everything is fine, Mom. I still need to pack, and I couldn't find my suitcase, but then I remembered I gave it to a friend to use."

"You only have one suitcase?" Angela responded. "Your dad and I bought a set of luggage for you before you left for college," she reminded him.

"Yeah, I know, but the latch on the one bag snapped off."

"Wonderful!" Angela didn't bother to hide the disgust in her voice.

"Mom, calm down. I can rig something up; it's too late to run across town now."

"Just don't miss your flight." Angela placed a hand to her head.

"I won't. Flight number 458. Love you! See ya soon!"

"Got it, Flight 458. Love you too!"

Angela said good-bye and walked over to Nathan. She put her arms around his neck, and her eyes became bright with unshed tears. "I can't wait to see him! We have a lot to do."

Nathan held up a hand to silence her. "What did you say Robby's flight number was?"

She eyed him a moment before responding, "Flight 458."

Nathan's eyes nearly popped out of his head; surely his ears had deceived him. All at once, he spun around in his chair and began frantically leafing through the pages of Iana's cookbook.

"Nathan, what it is?" Angela sat down in the chair facing him. He looked as if he was struggling to find the right words to say to her.

"This is too much to deal with right now." He straightened his glasses.

"Something's wrong? What's too much to deal with?"

"Here... Right here." Nathan turned the list around for her to see. "The numbers 458. Iana wrote those on that weird list you found in her recipe book."

She smiled a little. "And?"

"Okay." He took a deep breath. "Okay." Getting up from his chair, he began walking back and forth as he talked. "I did a little research on the list this morning. First, consider the date of Iana's death: 1946. Now look: 'electrical machinery; wings, tail, engines...' Iana was describing an airplane, right down to the model: a 747." He pointed to the numbers on the list. "Then 40.7772 degrees N, 73.8725 degrees W. These numbers are the coordinates for LaGuardia Airport."

"Why would she do that?"

"I'm not entirely sure yet." He took a long breath. "Essentially what I'm telling you is that both the 747 and LaGuardia weren't in existence in your grandmother's lifetime."

His words ended as suddenly as they had begun, and Angela sat frozen, feeling her heart pound and listening to the clock tick in the stillness of the room. She stared at him in anger.

Nathan could feel the heat of her rage. He opened his mouth to speak, but she wouldn't let him get a word out.

After a bracing breath, Angela stood up and said, "This is crazy. It's insane, and I don't want to hear another word... Not today!"

Rebecca had just come down the stairs to see Angela storm off into the kitchen.

"Is everything okay?" she asked Nathan.

Nathan nodded, then took a sip of his coffee. "Too much information, too fast."

Angela marched into the kitchen, ranting and raving under her breath.

"What the hell was that?" She pressed a hand to her pounding head, mumbling to herself while she hunted for a clean bottle in the cabinet.

"I should be feeling relaxed and excited—my son is coming home and tomorrow is Thanksgiving—but instead I am tense, tight and irritable."

She filled the bottle with formula and put it in the microwave to warm.

Angela thought about her reaction, shook her head and smiled. "If I didn't know better, I'd say I was suffering from first trimester emotions!"

Feeling in better spirits, she took the bottle from the microwave and headed back into the living room, knowing full well that she wasn't going to be able to enjoy the day or think about anything else until she straightened things out with Nathan. Having come downstairs, Rebecca was sitting beside India. Handing her India's bottle, Angela then walked over to Nathan's desk and sat down in front of him.

"Sorry. I didn't mean to fly off the handle like that," she said as she leaned back in the chair.

"Are you okay?" Nathan sounded worried.

"More or less," she told him.

"I love you, Angela," he said as he reached over to take her hand. "Maybe you just need a breather from Iana."

"Maybe I'm losing it," she said with a smile.

"Okay, here's the deal. We enjoy Robby coming home today and Thanksgiving tomorrow."

When Angela agreed, he nodded.

"All of this can wait until after the holiday."

Picking up Iana's cookbook typically brought a smile to her face, but this afternoon as she looked at her grandmother's handwriting and the unexplained list, Angela felt a twinge of loneliness leap in her heart. Things had happened, pushing her in directions she had never expected to go, and there wasn't anyone remaining in her family line that could help her with any of it.

So here she was with a psychopathic woman, one who decided to show up in her life from time to time. And being the Christian woman that she was, and knowing Maggie's needs, she was finding it nearly impossible to walk away from that situation. If all of *that* wasn't enough, now there was a cryptic list found tucked away in her grandmother's favorite cookbook.

Without much hope, she set the book aside and rose.

"Who would have thought a year ago that we'd be entrenched in a spine-tingling thriller that just keeps unfurling in our lives on a daily basis?" With a shake of her head, Angela gave in. "Well if there is anyone who can make any sense of this, it's Dr. Howard." She shrugged nonchalantly.

"It's crossed my mind a couple of times." Nathan sat back in his chair and nodded in agreement. "I've been thinking that maybe we should give him a call."

"You're probably right." Angela stiffened. "But after the holiday, once Robby's gone back to school... Then we'll talk to him." She bit her lip as tears welled up in her eyes. "This is just very strange. I think in the end, Iana may have been a little bit crazy."

Nathan put down his glasses and focused his attention on her. "Don't go there, Angela." He rubbed the small of her back. "Don't worry about it. Not today. I have faith that all things are possible and that we'll find the answer."

Smiling, Angela agreed. "You're right."

Nathan checked his watch. "I should probably think about heading across town to the airport. It's still snowing and the traffic's sure to be heavy the day before Thanksgiving." He smiled at her as he grabbed the shovel and walked out the door. "I don't want to be late picking Robby up."

Angela pulled back the curtains. The snow lay in graceful drifts as her husband was outside shoveling the driveway.

"This is just who we are," she thought, *"what we are and what we'll be, regardless of the trials and tribulations in our life. Or maybe because of them."*

She was in no rush to do anything now, although if truth be told, she was looking forward to digging in her heels on the preparations for Thanksgiving dinner. The more she thought about it, Angela was finding it difficult to resist the urge to begin baking the traditional pumpkin and apple pies. And with that, she remembered her grandmother's Christmas Bread recipe, and she unexpectedly found herself with a newfound burst of energy.

"Sounds like a plan to me," she said to herself as she smiled. Then she grabbed Iana's cookbook from Nathan's desk and walked into her warm and welcoming kitchen. Stopping just inside the door, she folded her arms across her chest and smiled at the thought that in twenty-four hours her house would be full of family and friends. She laughed when she remembered, years ago, how she had longed for an ordered, quiet house. Now she stood reveling in the anticipation of the holiday season and all the activity it brought with it. Robby would be back at school soon enough, back to the life that he was building. So for the next few days, she would treasure every minute she had with him. Today Angela would put Maggie, family legends and odd lists of presumed airplane parts out of her mind. Her son was coming home, and her family would be under one roof again.

She propped the recipe up on the counter where she could see it. Humming busily as she opened one drawer after another, she practically made a production out of gathering the list of ingredients on her grandmother's recipe. She carefully went about measuring the flour and then the sugar. Setting that bowl aside, she moved on to whisking the egg whites and butter together and then added the remaining ingredients.

Angela laughed when she realized she had forgotten the most important thing. "Instructions!" she exclaimed. "I don't know how to operate this new-fangled invention." She rummaged through some papers and then found the instruction booklet for her food processor. After a quick scan of the pages, she flipped the switch and *presto!*... the blades began to twist and turn.

Realizing she had some time to spare, she picked up the television remote and turned on the local news. Then she poured herself another cup of coffee and began leisurely looking through her grandmother's cookbook once more. She sighed as contentment began to settle over her.

Slowly, and with what seemed a great effort, Angela dragged her eyes over the strange list Iana had tucked away in the back of the book. Rubbing the back of her neck, she sat down onto the bar stool, remaining very still until she had read every word. Trailing her fingers across the page, she emptied her mind and shut her eyes.

Her mental sight went completely dark; she could feel the darkness but nothing else. After a while she noticed the faint outlines of an unfamiliar location. Every so often a beam of light appeared out of thin air, crossed the wall like a ghostlike finger and then slid off into nothingness again. Then she heard a rumbling that seemed to consist of many voices, protesting and disagreeing in the distance. When the voices stopped, she could hear someone moaning.

A cool wind brushed by her, and without warning a fog rose up like a cloud, limiting her vision. Suddenly the room went ice cold, and, shivering, Angela instinctively clutched her arms and tried to move away from the coldness. The surprise of the frigid air forced her back down onto the stool, and she slammed her elbow against the side of the counter. At the collision, pain shot through her body. But then, to her surprise, the mist slowly began to thin, floating and swirling like cobwebs and touching her face with its softness. As she waited, a dim light filtered through the mist, and she shaded her eyes with one hand, as if that could help her make out the image through the thinning mist. Her flesh cringed, and when she opened her mouth no words came out. Eyes wide, she stared at the numerical image gliding towards her.

"458," she whispered. "That's Robby's flight number!"

Instantaneously she thought of Robby; in her vision he was in the dark and, like Kenny, with the dead. She fought not to panic, trying to let her body go loose and limp.

At the same moment, a mental picture of a jumbo jet sitting on the runway flashed erratically in her mind, followed by the image of a woman coming towards her with tears on her cheeks. Angela could smell thick, black smoke along with stagnant waters off in the distance.

With a gasp, Angela's popped her eyes open wide, straining her muscles. And, after several tries, she finally rocketed up from the stool. Gripping the edge of the counter as shudders racked her body, she leaned over until she could find her breath and then crouched down to the floor.

Just then the television crackled into her life. "We interrupt regular programming to bring you breaking news out of LaGuardia International Airport. American Airlines, Flight 458 from Los Angeles with more than two-hundred passengers and crew members aboard, made a hard landing. It lost the tail section and caught fire at LaGuardia Airport this afternoon." There was a brief silence. "More than one hundred people were taken to nine area hospitals, but the majority of them have relatively minor injuries. At this point in time, the number of fatalities stands at two, while at least five people were reported to be in critical condition."

At first Angela did nothing, felt nothing, but as the images and words began to register in her mind, suddenly everything came out in rapid succession. Soon she was loud, scared and crying, "Noooooooo!" Her despair crackled like a bolt of lightning as it seared through the atmosphere. "Not my son... Oh God, not again... What's happening? Lord, please help me!" Her eyes were wide with lunacy, her hands reaching out towards the television in a desperate attempt to reach her child.

Nathan had just come in from shoveling the driveway. The task had taken longer than he had expected, and since he now was running late for the airport, he was in a hurry. It took him a few seconds to realize what he was hearing, and when Angela didn't answer after he called her name a second time, he walked towards the kitchen to find her.

"Angela!" He made a leap, grabbed her arm and then wrapped his arms around her, holding her close even as her head whipped from side to side.

"Nathan," Angela began, her voice breaking. "Robby's gone!"

Nathan stared at her as if she was crazy. "Gone? What do you mean, he's gone?"

Tears ran down her face. "I s-saw it." Falling against her husband, she cried, "Lord, why did You take my baby?"

"You saw what? Honey, stop; tell me what you saw." He touched his hand to her cheek but didn't say a word. He just listened.

She eyed her little kitchen television. She couldn't take it in, couldn't believe it as she listened to the reporter give more details of the crash. Robby couldn't be dead. He was young and healthy. He was coming home, and they were going to celebrate India's birth and Thanksgiving as a family.

She then gripped Nathan's upper arms and her voice trembled. "I don't know if he's dead or alive."

"Try and calm down. Come on, Honey, take a deep breath."

Fighting back her tears, she took a breath and then exhaled it slowly.

"It was so real, Nathan. The numbers, the jet, LaGuardia... I saw them all in my mind." Angela looked around the room nervously and then gestured towards the television. "Flight 458 crashed on the runway."

They stood in silence. Nathan straightened his glasses as he watched the television, his hand softly touching Angela's shoulder while the strange concept trickled through his mind.

"Nathan, please say something." She wiped a tear from her cheek.

His eyes met hers. "I don't know what to say right now." Nathan shook his head, trying to shut out the reporter's words on the television.

While Angela walked across the room, sat in a chair and rocked back and forth with her hands tightly clasped together, Nathan stood by the window, looking out. Neither of them turned when Rebecca walked into the kitchen. "Mr. Roberts, your cell phone has been ringing."

Nathan was quiet for a moment then turned around, facing her. "Rebecca, I need some time to... think." He turned back to stare out the window, wondering if they could survive the loss of another child.

"Is everything alright?" she asked. The pulverizing sound from the food processor was insane, she thought. Pressing a hand to her pounding head, she asked Angela if it would be alright to turn it off.

Angela turned in her chair. "I'm sorry, what?"

"This food processor, I think it's finished doing whatever it was supposed to do."

"I don't want to go through this again." Angela said, and her tears started again. "I don't know what I'm going to do."

Puzzled by her response, Rebecca turned off the food processor and then gave Nathan a perplexed look. At the same time she heard the news bulletin announced on the television. As it filtered through her headache, she turned toward the set and saw the wreckage of Flight 458.

"Oh no, those poor people!" she exclaimed. "And the day before the holiday!"

"It's unbelievable," Nathan said.

Rebecca could see their pain, so she gave him a sympathetic look and then said, "I hope you don't mind, but when I saw it was Robby calling again, I answered it."

"You just spoke to Robby?" Nathan's voice trembled.

Angela's body went limp. She fell back against the chair, feeling exhausted both mentally and physically.

"Yes," Rebecca assured him. "He's been calling to tell you that he missed his flight."

"I'm not understanding this." There was a lump in his throat as he said it.

Rebecca didn't answer at first; she only nodded. "Robby will be home later tonight. Something about the latch on his suitcase breaking off... He said his clothes fell out all over the sidewalk and he missed the cab to the airport."

Nathan's eyes watered again. Blinking rapidly, he said, "Thank you, God," then raised his eyes and his hands towards the ceiling. "In Your holy name, I fall before You with thanksgiving."

A feeling of warmth enveloped Angela's body. Even in her worst moments, she had always relied on her faith, and now she knew without a doubt that God had heard her plea. He had heard her prayer.

"Robby is fine." And all she could do, as she looked at Nathan and then Rebecca, was cry. Then, with a feeling of panic, she realized that Manny would be coming home today as well, and on Flight 458. She had a somber look on her face as she thought of calling his mother. After running her hands up and down her arms, she picked up the phone, dialed the number, and then hung up before leaving a voicemail. She knew it was selfish, but she didn't want to put any more of a damper on her day.

Life was no longer as simple as it had seemed earlier in the day. Not thinking clearly, she wiped her face and then walked back to the counter. "Guess I should finish baking the Christmas Bread for breakfast tomorrow morning."

Nathan looked at her, confused. "Why don't you go upstairs and lie down for a little bit?"

Angela shook her head. Irritated, she said, "I don't need to lie down. What I need to do is bake this bread!" She reached in front of Nathan for her spatula. "If it turns out okay then I'll make it again for Christmas morning." Angela's lips trembled.

"Are you alright?" he asked, his forehead wrinkled in concern.

A door was opening that honestly worried her, and she felt very unsure of herself after everything that had happened in the past hour. She glanced down at her hands. "I don't know," she admitted. "I feel odd." And she sounded it, too; like she was confused and worn-out.

"What kind of odd?" He was suddenly worried she might be on the verge of collapse. "Are you having any chest pains or trouble breathing?"

"No, nothing like that. Just numb, sad... relief." She couldn't think of any other words, but those sufficed to reassure him.

Nathan embraced her. "I'm worried about you."

"I know what you're thinking." Angela ran her fingers through her hair. "But seriously, this isn't my first time at the rodeo with this stuff."

"Still, I think we need to talk about what happened."

"And we will, with Dr. Howard. Right now, I just want to call Robby and hear the sound of my son's voice."

Robby called her before she could call him. As soon as she heard his voice, she started crying again, and she couldn't even form her words. She just sobbed uncontrollably into the phone, and for a minute Robby didn't know what to say.

"Mom, I just heard on the radio that a plane crashed at La Guardia." Robby didn't say anything for a moment. "Is Manny okay?" She could hear the panic in his voice.

Tears filled her eyes again until they ran down her face. "Honey, I don't know."

She was scared—not for herself, but for her son.

"Let's not talk about it right now. Let's just get you home."

"I was in such a rush this morning; I didn't talk with Manny today. We made plans last night to meet each other at the airport." Robby paused for a moment before saying, "I forgot my phone and needed to go back inside to get it. On my way in, the latch on my suitcase broke. Then I missed my cab."

"It's fine, don't worry about this now." She wiped her eyes. "Everything will be alright. Most of the passengers walked away without a scratch."

"I'm trying to make sense of this." Robby's voice trembled. "I'm sorry."

"You're apologizing to me?" Angela clutched a fist to her chest. "Sorry? Oh Sweetie, I have never been more thankful for your forgetfulness and disorganization in all my life!"

"Maybe it's not such a bad thing," he replied, a hint of a smile in his voice. A few minutes later, he told Angela that he was on standby and had to leave for the airport or else he wouldn't get a seat on the flight to New York.

"My plane gets in at midnight; it's Flight 1125."

"That's perfect. We were thinking of going to St. Michaels tonight for the Thanksgiving Eve service. I'd say we have a lot to be thankful for tonight."

"I'll think about you tonight when you're at church. Will you light a candle for Manny?"

"Absolutely. And I'll be thinking about you too."

There was a warm bond between them that scarcely needed words.

"Have a safe flight. See you soon. Love you."

"You too, Mom," he said softly, and a moment later, they both hung up.

Pastor Stephens walked up to the pulpit to give his sermon. He began by saying, "Thanksgiving isn't only about sharing a wonderful meal with your loved ones; it's also a time to meditate on all you are grateful for."

"Amen," Angela whispered as she wiped a lone tear that was sliding down her face. It broke her heart to think about what Manny's parents might be facing tonight.

"Let us pray." Pastor Stephens proceeded to say a short prayer and then began his sermon.

After the service, Angela remained seated; she bowed her head and said a prayer. When she finished, she felt better, though her heart still ached for Manny and his family.

"Tonight was good, don't you think?" she asked Nathan.

Nathan agreed. "How do you feel about heading to the airport now?"

Placing her hand on her stomach, she said, "I just realized I haven't eaten much today."

"We can get a bite to eat while we wait for Robby's plane to come in."

Angela nodded then added, "Before we go, Robby asked me to light a candle for Manny."

"Light the candle," Nathan said. "I'll wait here for you."

Angela bent over to pick up her purse, along with the church bulletin. "*Thanksgiving Eve Service, November 25, 7:00 p.m.*"

Something in her eyes prompted Nathan to reach out to her. "Angela, you okay?"

"What did you say?" Her eyes rose in surprise. Recovering quickly, she sat down and offered the bulletin to Nathan.

"It's the date on the church bulletin."

"November 25th is today's date." Nathan gave his wife a puzzled look.

She glanced around the church. "It's more than that." After a moment, she continued, "I'm sure of it. Nathan, it can't be anything else."

He just looked at her, waiting for her to continue.

"Replace the word '*November*' with the number for the month of November," she instructed.

"Angela, what is going on with you?" Nathan blurted out.

Yanking the bulletin from Nathan's hands, she demanded, "Why do you keep asking me that? I'm fine."

Nathan patted her hand. "Okay. I'm sorry." Straightening his glasses, he asked her to go on.

Angela groaned. "November's the eleventh month, and today is the twenty-fifth. When you put them together, they make 1125, which is Robby's flight number and also one of the numbers Iana wrote on that stupid list of hers."

The color drained from Nathan's face, leaving it white and horrified. "If you're suggesting she somehow predicted that Robby..." He stopped short.

"I don't know what I'm suggesting." She reached out and laid her hand over his. "I've never experienced, or heard of anyone experiencing, anything like what happened to me today." Angela sat for a moment, tongue-tied and shaken. "You've got to see this, Nathan. Think back to the list... The numbers 747, 458 and now 1125."

"Of course I see it." He leaned back against the pew. "I just don't know what to *do* with it."

"I'm no expert in the mystical and clairvoyant, but we saw it today." She gave a little shrug. "Everything up to now has been fulfilled according to what Iana wrote and what I saw in my vision."

"You don't think something will happen to Flight 1125, do you?" he asked quietly as she leaned against him and took his hand.

"I don't know." Tears trickled down her cheeks. "Nathan, I'm scared."

"I know, Honey. So am I." He repeated, "So am I."

They said very little to each other on the way to the airport. It was nearly midnight when they arrived, and both were—and looked—exhausted by the activities and emotions of the day. It had been undeniably hellish.

As soon as Angela stepped off the escalator, she headed straight for the windows on the observation deck. She wanted to watch with her own eyes as Flight 1125 touched down on the runway, taxied on the tarmac and finally come to a complete stop at the terminal gate, safe and sound.

Although it had been nearly twelve hours since she had heard the devastating news of Flight 458, and regardless of the fact that she had spoken with Robby earlier, Angela couldn't help but be concerned. And until she could hold her beloved son in her arms, Angela knew she'd be unable to dwell in the peaceful haven she longed for.

With a heavy heart, she watched the flashing red lights of the emergency vehicles off in the distance, her mind consumed with thoughts of Manny and his family on this Thanksgiving Eve. She wiped a tear from her cheek but couldn't allow herself to feel any more emotions right now; she just prayed for God's grace and mercy on their lives.

Suddenly, and only for a split second, she felt something similar to fear; her vision of Flight 458's crash landing flashed before her eyes, but now it seemed more like a dream, even though she knew how real it had been for her. Then, just as abruptly, thoughts of her grandmother drifted into her mind. *"The stories about her are quite mysterious and somewhat romantic,"* she thought. And then, as mad as it seemed, she could feel Iana nearby. At that moment, she would have hated to have to explain the strange sensation to anyone, but she was absolutely certain it was Iana Hamilton. Angela whispered her name, but there was no answer, only the gentle feeling of her presence. As she stood and looked up at the night sky, something bright caught her eye; instantly she focused her attention on a brilliant star, just off to the right of the full moon. She smiled, sensing a welcoming and belonging, but then frowned, thinking it odd. *"But all of that's irrelevant now,"* she thought, walking slowly towards the other end of the window. Looking out at the night sky again, Angela could have sworn the star was moving right along with her.

Angela turned from the window as she remembered the beautiful words Mr. Woodrow had spoken about her grandmother. *"Miss Iana was a beacon of light. She helped people find their way in the darkness."*

She turned back to the view of the night sky, and with that, a melodious voice floated into her mind. *"All is well. All is as it should be. You are exactly where you are supposed to be, as is your son."*

Angela brought her hands up and pressed them to her face as she instantly felt a peaceful calm pervade her mind, body and spirit.

A few minutes later, the sound of a woman's voice rang out over the public address system, announcing the arrival of Flight 1125 from Los Angeles. Angela could hardly contain her excitement; she drew in a deep breath and then wiped her eyes. Staring out the window, she saw it: Robby's plane landed on the runway with a hard thump, startling her. She opened her mouth, closed it again, and then took a calming breath. It didn't take long for the passengers to disembark the plane and move through the passenger walkway, and all of them looked to be a mixture of exhausted and excited.

Finally, behind a crowd of people, Angela saw a young man moving towards her, smiling and waving his hand in the air.

"It's Robby," Nathan said quietly, meeting her eyes squarely as he watched them fill with tears.

"I know." Angela clutched a fist to her chest.

Nathan put his arms around her and gave her an enormous hug, lifting her off the floor the same way he had done when they were first married.

Then he looked at her for a moment before saying, "C'mon, our son is waiting for us."

Angela reached out a hand for his and squeezed. "Yes he is!"

12

Angela was surprised she'd slept so well. Maybe it was her mind's way of escaping, or maybe it was due to the security of having her son tucked safely away in his bedroom. Whatever it was, she awakened to the sunlight the and smell of coffee and bacon.

At first, she was embarrassed that she'd slept so long while members of her family fixed their own breakfasts. Then she remembered the Christmas Bread she had made specifically for Thanksgiving Day… and the horror she'd experienced in the midst of preparing it. She was tempted to roll over and force herself back into the escape of a deep sleep.

Instead, though, she got up, took a long hot shower and dressed for the day.

By the time Angela went downstairs, Rebecca and Robby were seated at the dining room table and had already eaten their breakfast. She stopped for a moment and stood in the doorway, watching as they talked and laughed at India reaching for the rattle Robby was dangling in front of her. It warmed her heart to see Robby fussing over India. She smiled; he looked so cute, and she thought Rebecca and he looked like proud new parents. For some reason, that thought felt right to her.

She shook her head and patted her face with both of her hands. *"Shame on me,"* she thought. *"Listen to yourself; Robby's not been home a full twenty-four hours and you've got him married off and parenting India,"* she scolded herself silently and then walked over to join them, smiling at Rebecca.

"And look at this." Angela flipped her fingers over Rebecca's hair. "You got your hair cut. I like it!" Her short, straight hair framed her face with a sort of classic, timeless look. "It looks so young and easy."

"I just did it this morning." Instinctively, Rebecca reached up and pulled her fingers through it.

"You did a good job." Angela looked down and smiled at India, asking, "Doesn't Mommy look pretty?" She gave India a quick hug and nuzzled her neck. Then, with a grin at Robby, she looked back at the baby and listened with amazement to her excited and unintelligible babbling.

"She's a happy little girl." Robby smiled at Rebecca. A flush glowed on her cheeks as she gave a weak laugh. *"He has such a great smile,"* Rebecca thought. It was sort of slow, so that it altered the angles of his face and lit up his deep, dark brown eyes.

Angela put one arm around Rebecca and the other around Robby then gave them both a squeeze. "Welcome home, son. I missed you."

"I like being missed." He gave her a quick peck on the cheek.

Angela laughed as she waved him away.

"Did anyone remember the Christmas Bread I made yesterday?"

"Christmas Bread?" Robby ran his tongue over his teeth. "Mom, it's only Thanksgiving."

"Never mind; I saw the recipe in grandma Iana's cookbook and thought it would be perfect for this morning." Angela lifted a brow, turned and walked into the kitchen. But as she looked over her shoulder at them, she smiled, thinking, *"Them being a couple... It's a pretty thought, anyway."*

"Come on up here, baby girl," Robby said, snuggling India in his arms. "Your grammy is one crazy lady."

"Feels a little like old times," Nathan commented as he walked into the kitchen to find Angela stuffing the Thanksgiving turkey.

"I should have had this turkey in the oven an hour ago." She closed her eyes for a moment. Abruptly changing the subject, she added, "I've been having these thoughts that something has happened to Manny."

"We were hoping you'd sleep a while longer." Nathan poured her a cup of coffee.

"I slept like a rock." She took the coffee Nathan offered. "Thanks."

"Has there been anything on the news this morning?" Nathan poured himself a cup of coffee and grabbed a sugared green grape from the platter Angela had put together.

"From what I've heard, the names of the two who died in the crash haven't been released yet," Angela replied.

"They're probably waiting to notify the next of kin before they release the names to the press."

"I just don't get it, Nathan. I just don't get it." Angela paced the kitchen once, then returned to the turkey, while Nathan sipped his coffee.

"What? Why are you so upset?" Nathan picked up the remote. "Did something happen that I don't know about?"

"No, nothing new." Rather than meet Nathan's eyes, Angela kept hers fixed on basting the turkey. "Nathan, Robby was supposed to be on that plane. Why was he spared and not Manny?"

"First of all, you don't know that Manny wasn't." Nathan raised his eyebrows and popped another grape into his mouth.

"Remember the woman in my vision?" Angela looked up at Nathan. "She had tears running down her face and she was coming towards me. What if that was Manny's mother?"

"Or one of the passengers?" Nathan looked at her over his glasses.

"Maybe." Angela gave a slight shrug. Then she felt a shudder run through her, and her breath backed up in her lungs. Chilled with sudden panic, she was more than half afraid she'd see the woman step out of the fog and become part of her life, flesh and blood.

"I don't know. All this stuff's been going on in my head lately." She sniffled and held a hand under her eye to rub away a tear. She couldn't hide the fear that had taken residence inside her.

"Something is wrong. I can feel it."

All the same, she decided not to say anything more about that vision or apparition—whatever it had been.

By afternoon the kitchen was abuzz with activity. Watching the Macy's Thanksgiving Day Parade had become a tradition over the years in the Roberts's household, and this Thanksgiving was no different. Angela, Rebecca and Rowena scurried about the kitchen, cooking the time-honored green bean casserole (which Rowena had a recipe for), mashed potatoes and sweet potatoes. Angela smiled as she prepared her traditional turkey stuffing, whereas Rowena had insisted on preparing the latest gourmet stuffing recipe. In the dining room, Kate McGowan, Angela's client and friend, finished folding the white linen napkins and then snapped a snowy white damask cloth in the air to settle over the table. After that, she placed crystal candelabras at each end of the table and lit the long, white tapers.

The sweet scent of hot apple cider and cinnamon that wafted from a pot on the stove, along with the aroma of pies baking in the oven, saturated every nook and cranny of their home, creating a warm, festive atmosphere. There was laughter and chitchat, and that was nice, Angela thought. She realized how much she had missed those sounds since Robby had gone off to school and Kenny had died. She poured herself a glass of wine and lingered a moment to listen. Nathan, Robby and Stephen were in the living room, which was the customary meeting place for their heated political debates. Today's topic of conversation was how the country was going to hell in a hand-basket under the current administration. Then, out of the blue, the prevailing winds shifted to forecasting the winner of the upcoming College National Championship football game on New Year's Day. It made Angela laugh and settled her down a little. Then she noticed Robby walk across the room and let out a long, low whistle that had India's face lighting up with delight.

Angela folded her arms across her chest and smiled. Her home had life again.

Then, unexpectedly, thoughts of Manny's family once again crept into her mind. Angela had already resigned herself to believe the worst had taken place. *"What does that family have to be grateful for today?"* she asked herself internally. Yes, it was disturbing, disorienting and shocking, but in addition to those emotions, guilt was popping, uninvited, into her psyche. Such guilty feelings prompted her to wonder if her own Thanksgiving celebration should have been more low key.

Angela knew only too well that when you lose someone—when you aren't able to save that person—the pain is incredibly deep. Time, as you know it, seems to stand still; it just stops. And when it starts up again, it's not the same. It's never what it was before that horrific moment. Never.

She sighed, looking down at her hands. "Okay, that's enough. I just have to do one thing, and that is to enjoy this day," she said as she walked into the dining room. *"I'm probably overreacting anyway,"* she thought.

Angela took her seat at the table. Her heart warmed as she took a quick look up and down its length; the whole Roberts family, along with its two newest members, were seated side by side and accompanied by friends. Because Angela had welcomed Rebecca into her home, she found comfort in knowing that India would grow up with a loving family. Then a fleeting look at Robby and Rebecca incited thoughts within her, once more, of a wedding day and babies of their own. It was romantic and exciting, she thought, but she had to take a breath, swallow hard and order herself to cease thinking about her happily-ever-after picture of her son and Rebecca.

When everyone had settled down, Nathan offered the blessing of the food and also prayed a few words for Manny and his family.

Angela was halfway through dinner when she felt a shudder run through her body, but she quickly straightened and eased back into her chair. While she sat, the odd sensation peaked and then ebbed several more times. In an attempt to divert her attention from the peculiar feelings she was experiencing, she struck up a conversation with Rowena, only to find herself very distracted and preoccupied.

She deliberately took a sip of her wine. *"The more I make of this, the more upset I'll be,"* she thought. Nevertheless, there was no doubt in her mind that it was going to be awfully hard for Robby, Manny's family and for her, too, should her intuitions prove to be correct. She wanted desperately for this sensation to end, but she couldn't let on to anyone.

"Lord, please help me make it through this evening," she silently prayed.

When everyone had finished the main course and the first piece of pumpkin pie was being served, the telephone rang. Instantly, a mushroom-cloud of silence blanketed the table, a silence so profound it was almost eerie. Then, after what seemed like an eternity, Angela gave a half laugh, brushed a hand over her face and got up to answer the telephone. Her vision wavered, and she felt as if she was looking towards the telephone through a rippling surge of heat.

"Hello." That little word had her heart trembling, but her voice remained steady. However, her eyes mirrored the grief she heard coming from the other end. A few minutes later, Angela said a few words and then slammed the telephone down in frustration and collapsed into a chair.

"What's going on?" Nathan asked from his position at the table.

"That was Mrs. Ramirez," she said, her eyes filled with tears. "Manny died a little while ago from his injuries in the plane crash."

Nathan instantly got up, walked over and wrapped his arms around her. "I'm so sorry, Honey."

Angela wiped her eyes and then looked over at Robby. His eyes flashed white-hot anger as he threw his napkin across the table then pushed back from it and kicked his chair. Before Angela realized what was happening, Robby crossed the room, snatched his coat from the hall closet and rushed out of the house.

"No! Robby, wait! Please, let me help you." Angela started to go after him.

Nathan grabbed her arm, keeping his eyes focused on hers. "Let him go. He needs to be alone right now."

"Yes." Though her hand trembled, she lifted it and placed it on his.

Clearing his throat, Nathan suggested a prayer. Holding out his hand to Angela, he led her back to the table to join the others. Everyone bowed their heads and joined their hands as Nathan led them in prayer once again for Manny and his family.

"Heavenly Father, Lord, be with Manny and with those who have so loved him in this world. Guide him to the light of Your eternal rest and peace, and console those of us who remain with Your strength and love. May all of us use this difficult time to become sources of support and comfort for one another. Amen."

After everyone had gone home, Angela kept herself distracted with India's needs until the little girl was asleep.

In the living room, a warm fire crackled and simmered in the stone fireplace. The house was quiet, settled and warm. Angela tried to read, then tried to watch TV, but she was too fidgety for either. She pulled herself up from her recliner with considerable effort, then slowly walked over to the front door and opened it. Immediately her eyes widened when she saw the headlights from an approaching car coming down the street, but when the car passed by, she shrugged her shoulders and stepped outside onto the porch. Shivering, Angela pulled her warm flannel robe snuggly up under her chin as she looked out onto the freshly fallen snow. For as bad as the situation was, the moonlight reflecting on the snow, combined with all the stars in the sky, filled her spirit with a quiet tranquility, if only for a brief moment. A minute or two later, though, her fretfulness returned. Angela dabbed her eyes and then made a concerted effort to calm her breathing. She took one last sweep of the street: up, then down. No one stirred.

Her muscles went limp; she leaned against the front door and yawned.

"I can hardly keep my eyes open," she said to herself but then decided that, under these circumstances, a sleeping pill was the only way she'd be able to get the sleep she needed. As she started to climb the stairs for bed, the front door suddenly opened, and Robby was standing in the doorway.

"Oh Robby, thank God you're alright!" Angela stepped over to him, ran a hand down his arm, and said, "I was beginning to worry. How are you?"

Shaking his head, he leaned against the doorframe and stared at her. His eyes were bloodshot, his shoulders were slumped and everything about him spelled sadness.

"Why, Mom...? Why did God let this happen to him?"

"It's awful, just so awful, I know." She opened her arms to him.

"It makes my stomach churn," he said and then broke off, cursing himself for not calling Manny the previous morning. "If Manny would have known I wasn't going to make the flight, maybe he could have changed flights too." Blowing out a breath, Robby walked into the living room and dropped into a chair.

"Robby, you can't blame yourself for Manny's death—or for not doing something you think may have somehow prevented it."

"How could God have let this happen?"

"God didn't let this happen. As for the 'why,' that's a question that I can't answer and that God never will."

"The whole thing just pisses me off!"

"When Kenny died, I was angry with the man who had shot him, and I was angry with God."

"I was angry when Kenny died, too," Robby said, as somber as could be.

"That was the biggest storm of my life," Angela admitted. "But it was God's grace that kept me going—that, and the love I have for you and for our family. You all needed me, and I wasn't going to abandon you."

"Mom, I don't want to be angry with God. Really, I don't." He sighed and put his head on her shoulder.

"It's alright if you're angry," she told him. "God isn't angry with you." She put one hand on his cheek and placed the other on top of his hand. "Your feelings aren't right or wrong... They just *are*. Pastor Stephens told me that anger was a normal response to loss; it's a natural human emotion. Recognizing, accepting and expressing our anger can be a very healing experience."

Robby glanced up at her. "Guess I did a lot of healing tonight." He smiled and laid his head back on Angela's shoulder.

"It's okay to accept your humanness and your feelings," she responded in a whisper.

The next hour was spent as it is usually spent when these kinds of horrific shocks and devastating losses occur; everyone was trying to make sense of something that made no sense at all. "Why?" Robby asked at least a hundred times, and all Angela could reply was, "I don't know. This never should have happened."

Robby's eyes filled with tears. Collapsing, he laid his head onto his mother's lap and cried the hardest he'd cried in a long time. What was left of Angela's composure shattered once again.

"He's gone." Robby closed his eyes and settled his mind while Angela gently brushed her fingers over his hair. After a few minutes, she felt the weight of his body relax, and his breathing became slow and steady. Angela leaned over to peek at his face, and there he lay, her precious son, peacefully asleep on her lap.

"I was so afraid I had lost you—that you wouldn't come back to me." She kissed him softly on his cheek. "You've got a life to live. For now, we'll wait and see what the morning brings."

Angela's plans for Black Friday shopping would have to be postponed. That afternoon, she found herself gripping the steering wheel of her car as she maneuvered through the snow-covered streets to meet with Brian Harper, an old friend and the director at the Harper Funeral Home.

After the horrors of the 9/11 terrorist attacks, the Harper Funeral Home was inundated with the deceased from that catastrophe, providing services for at least a dozen burials and cremations a week. Brian Harper and his staff did their best to keep up with the front end services, such as the selling of coffins and urns, working with the grieving families and clergy to organize viewings, and completing the endless amount of paperwork that was associated with an end-of-life tribute. However, the back end of his business—the body preparation, the embalming and dressing of the deceased—eventually required some outside assistance.

During lunch one afternoon, Rowena casually mentioned the situation that Brian Harper was in, with regards to his business. Then she recommended that Angela give him a call to offer her professional services as a make-up artist and hairdresser. It didn't take long until Angela's own heart urged her to make that call, and Brian accepted her offer without delay. Angela had become a great help to Brian. In her spare time, she'd taken over the responsibility of dressing the deceased until he could hire additional full-time help. And today Angela would do for Manny what she had done years ago for the innocent victims of the 9/11 terrorist attacks.

The cheery sound of chirping birds and the warmth of the afternoon sun seemed almost inappropriate as she stood in front of the Harper Funeral Home. As she approached the front door, her heart began to pound and her palms were sweating. "God, please help me. I can't do this alone," she said in a quick prayer, then took a deep breath and reached out her hand to open the front door. With confidence, she stepped inside.

"Angela, I'm so glad you could come." Brian smiled and leaned in to kiss her cheek. "It's good to see you again... I wish it was under better circumstances, though." Angela nodded in agreement. "I didn't mean to impose on your holiday, but Mrs. Ramirez requested you for Manny's final dressing."

"Not at all. I'd like to do what I can to help the Ramirez family. This is a very difficult time for all of them." Tears filled her eyes. "I remember how it feels."

Just being there brought back memories of Kenny's death. She took a deep breath and exhaled slowly.

Brian paused a moment before saying, "If this gets to be too much for you, please let me know."

She gave a slight shrug. "I'll be fine. Don't worry about me; with God's help, I'll get through this."

After a few minutes of casual conversation, Brian glanced at his watch and reminded Angela that time was of the essence. He suggested they walk back to the Preparation Room so she could get started.

The Preparation Room was small and contained a single metal table and two chairs. The floor was tiled institutional gray with green speckles and the walls were painted a cinderblock shade. What relieved her was that, after entering the room, she wasn't nearly as uncomfortable as she'd been prepared to be. Placing her make-up case on one of the chairs, she sat down in the other and realized she had no clear idea what she would do when Manny arrived.

However, she didn't have to wait long before the side door opened an inch. Frozen, she stared as the door opened a bit more and Manny's lifeless body was wheeled into the room on a gurney. She rose slowly from her chair, and then she saw him. Her knees trembled. Her breath caught. He was laying still, eyes closed with the barest hint of a smile on his face. She slowly walked over to stand beside Manny and thought he looked more peaceful than she'd ever seen him look during their short time together.

She stayed beside him for a moment. Moving slowly, she reached her hand over to touch his face and then quickly pulled away.

"The disinfect spray, razors and eye crème are in the cabinet." The young man's voice brought her back to the present.

"Sure," she responded and gave him an uncomfortable smile. Then she took a deep breath, knowing that since he'd walked back out the door, she was on her own now.

Angela walked over to the cabinet and took out the disinfectant spray and some cotton balls. It was all coming back to her; the eyes, mouth and other orifices had to be cleansed before anything else could be done. After she had finished shaving Manny's face, she placed a small amount of crème on each of Manny's eyelids to keep them from dehydrating and sinking back into his head. She noticed on the Embalming Log that his clothing had not yet arrived; now all that was required of her was doing his make-up and touching up his hair.

When she had finished, she filled her lungs with air and then let it out slowly.

"Rest in peace, Manny," she whispered, gently laying her hand on his shoulder.

At once her body shuddered; her head snapped back and her eyes widened with terror. Instinctively, she grabbed at her right wrist with her left hand in an attempt to twist it free from the merciless force that held her hostage, connected to Manny's corpse. Her whole body struggled to fight against it, and she screamed at the sensation of her body floating, drifting upwards where she couldn't see, hear, or find her way out.

Suddenly, an arc of a white light sizzled through the void. Right behind it came a horrifying sense of unbearable pain and frozen terror, and horrific images of the dead and dying trickled into her mind. In a millisecond, the trickle became a torrent and the torrent became a raging flood. Another intense jolt of electricity shot through her unsuspecting body and a low groan emitted from her throat; at the same time, her eyes locked onto a man who spoke with a deep, raspy voice. He came close, passed by her, then disappeared. In the midst of the whirlwind, she could vaguely hear someone scream from a distance, either in rage or in grief, and then her mind flashed to Manny. She shuddered once more and then her body and mind went still.

From somewhere inside, Angela peered out through Manny's eyes. She quickly turned away, confused. She felt nothing but the faint registering of a bizarre thought: *"EMP... Electromagnetic Pulse."*

Angela pulled back, shocked. Her mind raced. Suddenly another thought clicked in her mind: the list in Iana's book of recipes. And with that, another violent surge of vibrations sliced through her body. This time she tumbled towards the edge of the metal table and hit her chin as she slumped to the floor, her chest heaving and heart racing. The tile felt cold against her hands, neither of which was in contact with Manny any longer.

Then it was over, leaving Angela startled and drenched in sweat. She stayed on the floor, regaining her breath, while her eyes remained wide open, staring blankly at the ceiling. Angela didn't want to close them, not even to blink.

All of a sudden the door burst open, and in an instant Brian was at her side.

"Angela." Brian lifted her up. Feeling her body tense immediately, he gently put his arm around her waist and slowly guided her to a chair. "Take a deep breath and just let it out slowly." She did so, following his lead. "Now one more." Her body relaxed a little.

"What the hell happened in here?" Brian demanded. "I heard you scream and came in to find you collapsed on the floor. Are you alright?"

Angela looked around nervously and nodded. "Fine. I'm fine." She hadn't even realized that she'd screamed.

"Stay still, you're bleeding," Brian told her.

Angela's hands moved quickly to the cut on her chin; it felt raw when she touched it, and she saw the blood on her fingers when she pulled her hand away. After a couple of moments, she lifted herself to a standing position and walked over to the sink. Hunched over it, she supported herself with one hand while splashing water onto her face with the other. She kept her eyes tightly shut as she groped for some papers towels, and then she wiped off her face and tossed the wet towels into the trashcan. The sting between her shoulder blades made her stiff, so pushing a not-quite-steady hand to the back of her neck, she began massaging out the tightness. Steadier now, she opened her eyes, and her attention immediately shifted to a shape, a reflection, a shadow in the mirror that she caught out of the corner of her eye. Her eyes stung, and she took one very careful breath before quickly spinning around to see only Brian moving towards her.

"You sure you're okay? You look awfully pale."

Angela needed a minute to think it through. There would definitely be ramifications and complications if she decided to confide in Brian the truth of what had just taken place with Manny's body.

"This is out of hand!" She quickly turned away from him and then slammed her fists down on the counter.

"Wait a minute," he managed. "Wait, Angela, what is it?" He stopped himself when she sent him a questioning look.

"I saw—" she quickly corrected herself, "*thought* I saw..." She stepped back and glanced over at Brian. "All of this is so freaking out of hand!" She was tense and straight as she spoke to him, never taking her eyes off his, her whole body taut with frustration.

"This is my fault. I apologize." Her hands were trembling as he took them into his own. "It's too soon; you don't belong here."

"No," she said, looking straight ahead and then finally turning back to him. "No, this isn't your fault, not at all. I wanted to be here. Really, Brian, I did."

"Then talk to me!" Brian prodded.

Angela shook her head. "I don't know exactly. But something... It feels like the inside of my head is loud." She looked up, startled, and a tiny burst of fear jabbed her stomach. "In my mind... For a moment, I heard Manny's voice. He spoke to me."

Brian took a step back. "What do you mean, for a moment?" For the next few seconds, it was as if time was suspended. A dry silence hung in the room.

Angela's eyes locked on Brian's. Without a word, she clamped her mouth shut, spun on her heels, and walked away. Just the way he looked at her made Angela realize that she had to come up with an explanation for her comment. But knowing it would be impossible to describe the vastness of what had just happened to her, she also realized that time was not on her side. Manny's viewing would take place first thing in the morning, with his burial immediately following. She needed to see Dr. Howard. This event with the dearly departed was not the same as the others; this time she was capable of hearing sounds and voices.

Brian followed after her, grabbed her by the shoulder, and spun her around. "I know this is upsetting, but I want you to know that it's going to be alright." He swallowed hard and nodded. "Go ahead."

"Oh God, I'm sorry, Brian. I'm sorry; you must think I'm crazy!" Angela said, smiling. She gave his hand a slight tug and then looked away.

"It's okay," Brian said, hitching up the sleeves of his sweater. "I don't think you're crazy, but I *do* believe you may be suffering from mild PTSD."

"Post Traumatic Stress Disorder?" Angela asked, raising her eyebrows slightly.

"PTSD symptoms typically start within three months after a traumatic event, like the one you've experienced. In a small number of cases, though, PTSD symptoms may not appear until years after the event. The symptoms can come and go but tend to occur when you're in stressful situations or when you're reminded of what you went through. Flashbacks or reliving the traumatic events—even hearing and seeing things that aren't there—are not uncommon."

"I appreciate your concern."

"It's perfectly normal to have a wide range of feelings and emotions after a traumatic event, and that doesn't mean you have PTSD. But if you're experiencing fear and anxiety, a lack of focus, crying and disturbing thoughts... If you're having trouble getting your life back under control, Angela, you may need to speak with a therapist about it."

Angela shook her head. "Thanks, but I assure you that none of what you have described applies to me right now."

"How can you be so sure of that?"

"Trust me, I just am, and it's impossible to explain any of it right now." She fumbled in her purse for her cell phone but soon gave up on that mission for the present time.

Brian slumped back in his chair and smiled, "Do we need to have a discussion about denial?"

Angela held up her hand. "That won't be necessary," she said, and they both laughed, relieving the tension. "I'm gonna go clean up," she announced and then headed for the bathroom. In a few minutes she returned with her hair combed and a little make-up on the gash in her chin. Her face was still red, though, and her eyes still looked puffy. She sat down next to Brian, avoiding his eyes in an uncomfortable silence, and then spoke.

"I can't," she said in a choked voice. "I can't explain any of this to you right now." Angela looked at him blankly. "But Brian, please don't move Manny's body from the Preparation Room until I get back."

"No... Angela, you know I can't do that," Brian said firmly. "His viewing is in the morning. The body needs to be dressed and positioned in the casket as soon as possible—"

Angela interrupted, "I'm asking you to trust me with this." There was nothing Angela could say, no words she could offer that would help him understand what she was asking of him, so she didn't say anything further.

Even though he wasn't totally convinced he should agree with her request, and still somewhat shocked she had asked this of him in the first place, Brian reluctantly conceded. His smile was quick, but it was there. "One hour, Angela."

"Thank you, Brian. I'll be back in an hour," she told him. Grabbing her keys and purse, she headed out the front doors. And as soon as she got in her car and backed out of the driveway, she called Dr. Howard. After finishing that call, she quickly dialed Nathan's number and asked him to meet her at Dr. Howard's office.

Twenty minutes later, Angela was taking a seat in front of Dr. Howard's desk, and suddenly she had a quick—and not entirely comfortable—flashback of her phone conversation with him earlier.

"Why don't you tell me what's going on?" He pulled out a pad and wrote down the date and time, and his voice brought her back to the present.

"I appreciate you seeing me on such short notice." She leaned back in her chair and shut her eyes.

"It's my pleasure. And the timing couldn't be more perfect."

"You know, the more afraid I become, the more imperative it is for me to find answers." She turned to the window.

Dr. Howard settled comfortably in his chair with his hands resting across his chest. "How fortunate for you, Angela. I just happen to be in the business of finding answers." He looked at her, pleased that she seemed to be more at ease. "Would you like some tea?"

"No. But thank you, Dr. Howard."

"Since we're going to be working together, why don't you call me Matt?"

"Yes." She smiled, ordering herself to relax further. "That would make things easier, I suppose." The confession brought a self-deprecating smile as Angela ran her fingers over the top of Dr. Howard's desk. "My call earlier... I must have sounded like a crazy person."

He gave her a blank look. "Angela, crazy?" There was a pause before she caught the whisper of a weary sigh. "I certainly don't think you're crazy, or even that you're imagining what's happening to you."

"I'm glad to hear that." She drew in a long breath. "I wanted to help Manny. But in the dream—or whatever it was—when I was faced with him, I fell apart. I failed him, and I failed myself." She lifted one hand in a gesture that spoke of aggravation. "I'm not going to let that happen again."

"No, I don't think you will." Dr. Howard took his time as he carefully lifted a packing box from beneath his desk. "Meet the RMTS10," he announced and set the device in front of her. "My feeling is that Manny was drawn to you; somehow he was able to sense your compassion."

Angela paused and met Dr. Howard's quiet, patient gaze. Then she stared at what resembled a circuit board sitting on his desk.

"Hmmm." Puzzled, she tilted her head, studying the stems of copper wire as they twisted and turned to form some sort of geometric shape above the circuit board contraption. "Well, I recognize the copper wiring, but that's about all." She smiled over at Nathan, who was sitting beside her.

"Think of it as an antenna," Dr. Howard said with a grin.

As he walked around his desk, it was with a sense of pride and satisfaction. All of his work, the preparation, the planning, and the creating... Everything he wanted to accomplish had come to fruition and was sitting right in front of him. With a sigh, he switched on the device by turning a small black knob centered beneath a display window.

"These arrow buttons on each side of the display window enable us to increase or decrease the amount of frequency that is needed."

"Yeah, okay," Angela said. But then she immediately added, "Okay, wait." She shifted in her seat to turn towards Nathan. "Frequency? What does that have to do with hearing Manny's voice?"

Dr. Howard explained, "I believe the RMTS10 will raise the frequency level of your consciousness while you are in a trance-like state. If we are able to vibrate at a higher level, we become lighter in mass."

"Well." Angela shook her head. "And who doesn't want to be lighter in mass? To heck with Weight Watchers," she said with half a laugh. "Just get an RMTS10."

"So, the lighter mass," Dr. Howard continued, "will not only move you through time more efficiently; the RMTS10 will also enable you to reach that higher vibration level, thus allowing you to experience audio while in a trance-like state."

She gave a quick shudder and tried to offset it with a laugh. "Are you telling me I would have been able to hear what Manny was saying to me with this device? That his voice and the others would have become clearer, more real?"

"From what you described about your latest encounter, I believe Manny was trying to feed you information. Perhaps details of the crash... His message to you."

Exhausted and still a little raw on the inside, she sighed. Nathan comforted her by rubbing her shoulders.

"Scientists have been studying the effects of consciousness—how it works in the universe and on sub-atomic particles—for decades. As you know from high school, everything is made of atoms. The atoms are made of smaller particles called sub-atomic particles. Theory holds that the human consciousness has an effect on these sub-atomic particles. In fact, in experiments, these sub-atomic particles have been proven to act differently when a human is watching them in real time than when their reactions are simply recorded by a machine and viewed at a later date. Theory also has it that extra terrestrials may have used consciousness to fly their space crafts from one part of the galaxy to another by bending the fabric of space."

"Time travel?" Nathan asked.

"Some say that these beings break down their atomic structure and then transmit it to another part of the universe, using only their consciousness or thoughts. Once these particles reach their destination, they reassemble. This is Cross Dimensional Teleportation, which can even reach dimensions in different time periods," Dr. Howard finished, nodding toward Nathan.

"Okay," Angela said after a moment. "I'm going to try to understand all of this, like it's not insanity."

Nathan held up a hand. "Cross Dimensional Teleportation?" he asked, sending a sideways glance towards Dr. Howard. "Iana Hamilton?"

Dr. Howard grinned at Nathan.

"My theory is, Angela, that your grandmother possessed the ability to raise her consciousness to a higher level than normal, enabling her to move back and forth through time."

Leaning forward, Angela smiled at Dr. Howard. "Go on."

"I can't explain how she *obtained* this ability, but after looking through some of the notebooks you sent over that contain her drawings, and having read all of the legendary testimonies, I believe she did *possess* this ability. My dear, it seems that your grandmother has passed on to you, through her drawings and now through the mystery of the so-called recipe for Manny's plane crash, all her messages for our present time."

"I see." He could hear the smile in her voice. "So how will the RMTS10 help me help Manny?"

"This device is tuned using the natural scale of A432, just like the original Stradivarius violin. Whatever you were hearing will become clearer with this device, and it'll be collected on the USB drive as well."

Angela drew her eyebrows together. "Okay," she said, rubbing the back of her neck.

Dr. Howard smiled and then continued, "Inside the RMTS10 is a 144-faceted crystal 64-tetrahedron. This crystal is geometrically wrapped in a type of Torus coil. The 64-tetrahedron grid is a fractal structure that continues to grow to infinity; the vacuum's equilibrium is to time without end, to infinitely big and to infinitely small, also known as a Torsion Field, where the universe expands and contracts. The Torsion Field is not an empty space but is filled with energy. The RMTS10 literally pulls energy from space, from all around us."

"Matt," Angela said but then broke off when he looked up from the RMTS10. "I'm sure all of this is absolutely fascinating and quite possibly something I need to know—"

"Angela!" Nathan caught her arm as she started to stand up. "Let him finish."

"It's going to have to wait for another time." Her voice was strong and icy as she dug her keys out of her purse. "I have a dead body that is going to start decomposing soon, and I need to get on with this."

"Nathan, its okay. Angela is right. All of this can wait; she needs to get back to Manny before his body is moved."

Nathan lapsed into silence. Angela sat down beside him, her hand in his, waiting for Dr. Howard to go on.

"When you get back to the funeral home, place the RMTS10 adjacent to Manny's body. Before you do anything else, put on the headphones. The minute you begin to detect any type of background noise or static, turn the knob to zero in on that frequency. Once you have found the frequency that coordinates with the background noise, the RMTS10 will lock it in and slowly begin to raise the level."

"Do I need to touch Manny again?"

"Yes," Dr. Howard said. "The frequency won't begin to increase until you make contact with him. As the level increases, and if my calculations are correct, you will begin to vibrate at the identical natural harmonious frequency. Your mass will become lighter, allowing you to quickly pass through the Einstein-Rosen Bridge more efficiently."

"And whatever I hear will be gathered and collected on the USB drive?"

"That's right. I'll be able to play back the data that is collected on my computer in the lab."

"Matt, what effects on Angela's body will the RMTS10 have?" Nathan asked.

"Unfortunately, I don't have an answer to that question. This is the RMTS10's maiden voyage. I suspect she may experience some minor cellular changes, but most likely they'll only be temporary, without any side effects."

Nathan tensed. "You haven't given me a hell of a lot to go on." He looked down at his hands; then, hastily, he wiped them on his jeans. After a moment of consideration, he nodded. "Honey, I don't know about this."

"Nathan, I've... *We've* come too far to stop now." She didn't expect a response, but she made herself crouch down in front of him. She looked into his eyes; the comfort they once held for her was gone, and they were as dark as ever. It was so difficult to look at him, at that blank expression.

"Dr. Howard, I wish you were coming with us." Nathan continued to look at Angela. "I'd feel a lot better if we could have gone over this whole plan earlier, and not moments before it was to be executed."

There was no response. Dr. Howard rose from his desk and walked out of his office to give them some time alone.

Nathan continued to stare at the RMTS10, to stare and stare, even when a tear slipped out of his eye and ran slowly down the cheek that Angela had kissed.

Saying nothing, Angela reached into her purse and took out the picture of her grandmother, the same one Nathan had found in the bushes. Studying the picture, Angela weighed her options.

Nathan's lips curved slightly; he could think of nothing but the strength in the young woman's face. "She was a very brave and courageous lady."

Angela shifted beside him then put the picture back into her purse. "I read once that the past tends to send out ripples. Every finger dipped into the pool sends those ripples out, and they touch on those who come after. Generation after generation."

"Mr. Woodrow... He believed Iana was a beacon of light for us to follow," Nathan said.

"Nathan, I believe I have been touched by one of those ripples of my past."

"Ya know, there's no shame in walking away," he said quietly. "No shame in not going back to the funeral home today."

"I've got a job to do." She managed a small smile.

For some reason that made him smile, too. "Well then, we'd better get started." The grin he sent her was lovely and sure.

Satisfied with the outcome of their meeting with Dr. Howard, Angela and Nathan headed for the door. "Tell me," Angela said as she felt the last of the residual tension fade away while walking across the parking lot towards the car, "how do you feel about pizza later on tonight?"

“You’ve got such a way with words.” Nathan reached down and patted her on the buttocks.

13

It was raining hard when Angela and Nathan returned to the Harper Funeral Home. The weather gave Nathan little pangs of apprehension as he contemplated being in such a place on such a dreary afternoon. The sheets of rain and the traffic it created had put them slightly behind schedule, which only added to his increasing anxiety. Gripping the steering wheel, he assured himself that soon they would be home, safe and sound. He and Angela would pick up the threads of their lives, the old and the new.

When they stepped inside, into the cathedral-like splendor of the Harper Funeral Home, Nathan immediately noticed the eerie quiet all around them. This world was cold, *so* cold, he thought, with death ever-present. No one seemed to take any particular notice of them; Brian was seated at his desk, busily writing notes on a pad. There were voices whispering as a memorial service came to a close and quiet sobs of grief emanating from a smaller room adjacent to the sanctuary. A couple that Nathan estimated to be about the same age as Angela and himself sat side by side, holding hands as they browsed through documents in front of them, obviously making the final preparations for a loved one.

Nathan scooped a hand through his wet hair, scattering rainwater through the air.

"Are you ready?" Angela looked up, laying a hand on his arm.

"I'm here, aren't I?" Nathan held out his hand in front of her. "It's now, or not at all."

Angela nodded in agreement and then proceeded down a narrow hallway towards the Preparation Room. She opened the door, and just as she had asked of Brian, Manny's body had not been touched or dressed in his suit.

Nathan hesitated for a moment and then slowly followed Angela into the room, but he remained standing just inside the doorway. When he looked across the room and saw Manny, his legs buckled. On a metal table only a few feet away, Manny was white as death. One of his arms had fallen to the side of his body so that his hand dangled over the table's edge. Nathan's heart began to thud; he wanted all of this to be over, but there was nothing he could do.

"It's going to be alright." Angela took his hand and squeezed gently. "Trust me, this won't take long. I'm coming back."

"Yeah." He tried to swallow hard but couldn't. Worry had dried up every bit of saliva in his mouth. "Yeah. You're going to be all right."

He hesitated a moment and then slowly walked over to Manny's body, setting the box gently down on the floor at his feet. Nestled in the foam padding, the RMTS10 sat ready for its maiden voyage.

Angela took a piece of paper out of her purse, spread it out on the table in front of her and then read aloud the instructions Dr. Howard had given to them earlier, which she'd written down on the car ride.

She then reached for the headphones, and for a second time Nathan reminded her that it wasn't too late to walk away. Without saying a word, Angela placed the headphones on her head. She intended to do whatever was necessary to help Manny move on to the other side.

Lifting the device out of the its padding, Nathan carefully set it down on a small table alongside Manny's body. Then he stepped back and kept his eyes on Angela.

With fingers trembling, she placed her right hand on the side of the headphones and pressed slightly. "I think I'm hearing some sort of background static."

Nathan watched the readout as the first two numbers locked into place.

"Cross your fingers."

She did, on both hands, and then closed her eyes.

"Wait, not so fast!" He shifted, bracing himself beside her. "Give me your hand."

Giving Nathan a sharp look, instantly she tore her hand away. "It may not *work* if you're holding my hand."

Nathan looked at her for a moment before saying, "Angela, when all of this started, I made a promise to you that I would be right by your side, whatever you chose to do."

"Yes, I remember." Angela started to protest again and then took his hand, allowing her emotions to flow more freely. "What if I can't get back?" She leaned into him and then dropped her forehead on his chest.

"Honey." With his hand under her chin, he lifted her face. Tears filled her eyes. He brushed one from her cheek. "Then we go together!"

"Promise you won't let go?" Her breath hitched before she pressed her cheek to his.

"Never, not ever!" The smile died out of his eyes. "I wouldn't dream of running out on you, and there is *nothing* that could keep me from pulling you back to me." He put his arm around her, immersed in the simple pleasure of caring for her.

Suddenly Nathan pointed to the RMTS10. "Numbers are locked in," he told her. "Remember when you touch Manny, the vibrations should begin."

"Just give me a minute." She took a deep breath and blew it out.

"Take as long as you need."

"What's our time?"

"Four minutes, twenty seconds. We're moving right along, and we'll be eating that pizza before you know it."

"Nathan, if anything should happen..." Tears fell from her eyes.

Nathan held up his hand to silence her. "There's no need to say anything."

"No, let me finish." Angela shook her head, trying to shut out the words. "Nathan, I love you, and I will always love you."

Nathan nodded. "I know you love me. And I thank God every day for blessing my life with you." He pulled her close and hugged her. "Angela, I'm so proud of you." He took a deep breath and said, "What you're doing takes a lot of courage."

"I'm ready," she whispered. Then she began the process with a short prayer. "God, please show me what to do."

Nathan watched as she began tenderly stroking Manny's hair. His heart filled with an overwhelming love and admiration for his wife, even though his doubts were getting the best of him.

She then placed a hand on Manny's shoulder. Smiling, she began speaking to him as if he was still a part of her world. She continued to speak, and her words were coherent, but it seemed like there was no one to hear them. *"Has Manny already crossed over?"* she thought. *"Will he come back to me?"*

"Damn it, Manny, talk to me!" she demanded and then felt a jolt, the nauseous roll of it rumbling in her gut. She felt it once more, and then nothing.

Her eyes widened in surprise. "Please, Manny, come back," Angela said and then looked at Nathan. "Something happened. I felt it, and then it all just stopped."

"Stay put. Stay just where you are." Frowning, Nathan studied the RMTS10.

"All right." She nodded and did as he asked.

"The numbers aren't locked in anymore." He wiped a hand over his mouth.

"Should we call Dr. Howard?" Angela snapped out.

He rolled around the idea in his mind before he shook his head. "Not yet."

"Oh, good Lord, it's a man thing! Always wanting to fix things themselves," Angela declared.

Ignoring Angela's comment, Nathan began to joggle and rotate the copper antenna. After that, he detached the USB drive, waited a few seconds, and then inserted it back into the jack. Still, nothing happened. "I think it's time for more radical measures."

"Maybe you should call Dr. Howard," Angela suggested again.

Clearing his throat, Nathan replied, "When all else fails, just turn the darn thing off and back on again."

"Oh, my dear God, you're going to..." she said but trailed off when she heard the faint sounds of a man's voice.

"That's it! It worked. Angela, the numbers are locked in." Nathan took her hand in his. "Try it again."

"Quiet!" Angela tightened her grip on Manny's shoulder and waited.

Suddenly her world was white and cold. Soon there were shadows, jerky and retreating, and voices whispering under a deafening roar. Then his face, close to hers; dark eyes so blue they glowed.

"Manny?" Angela whispered.

Unexpectedly, another round of deafening sounds shrieked all the way through her mind, and at the same time a gut-wrenching pain slammed into her. Anguish was digging into her muscles and bones, and she tried to move away, tried to escape it. Her hands were wet with sweat, slippery enough that she almost lost her grip on Manny's shoulder.

Wincing in pain, she asked again, "Manny, is that you?"

In a flash, her white world exploded, becoming red and hot. *"Manny is not my name."* The words hissed into her mind, and then the man with the dark blue eyes pressed his hand to his lips and, in a deep raspy voice, whispered. "My name is Legion." He looked around and then grinned, his razor sharp fingernails stroking his left cheek. "And there are many with me."

Shaking her head to clear her mind and to rid herself of the stench of his foul, smoky breath, Angela finally looked up at him and asked, "Where is Manny?"

And then, just as quickly as the man had emerged, he drifted away, up into a swirling white vapor. A minute later, he returned to hover directly above her. Staring down with those dark eyes, he seemed oddly close again, as if she could reach up and touch his face.

Angela broke into tears. "Where is Manny?" she screamed.

After a few seconds, he reached out an evil finger and gently touched her lips. "Shhh. He did not lose his soul, but another did. Many demons were entered into him, and now he is with me."

Then it was done. He was gone, and she was alone.

A tear trickled down her cheek in pity, in sadness, and as she turned to brush it away, her gaze fell upon an opening, a dazzling white light, glimmering off in the distance. She took a step, then waited for her head to stop spinning. She felt a weak vibration that prickled her fingertips. It lasted only a moment, and then her body went limp. Angela quickly pushed her mind to snap back into focus, and for an instant her heart stopped.

"I'm floating!" she cried out desperately.

In a split second, she was moving rapidly through a narrow, cone-shaped tunnel, suspended in midair. She had no sense of time passing. It could've been five seconds or five minutes; she couldn't tell how long it had taken for her interstellar transport to come to a screeching halt.

"Where am I?" she thought hazily. Her pain was everywhere, but now it was dull, aching gently in her limbs. She managed to push herself up, and so she sat and smelled the air. Her mind drifted a little, but her calm state quickly evaporated when she heard a woman's voice off in the distance. Like a train's whistle, initially it was faint and far away, but soon it was blaring, and finally it was screeching. In that brief moment, Angela observed that the world she now was in was—or seemed to be—revolving in slow motion.

"Everyone, please remain in your seats. Stay calm. The captain has everything under control." The intensity of the woman's tone vibrated all through the atmosphere, and Angela instinctively covered her ears with her hands.

Briefly, she couldn't breathe, but squeezing her eyes shut for a moment, she forced air in and out until she was able to calm herself. She leaned forward slowly, carefully, and rested her forearms on her knees. And as she lifted her head, she caught sight of a man moving towards her. Inside, her heart beat faster, but she remained calm and quickly staggered to her feet. Adrenaline shot through her body, and shaking her head twice, she gritted her teeth and fought against the sick roll of panic that was seeking to control her mind and body. She watched intently as the man very slowly and deliberately inched his way closer to where she was standing. She blinked away a tear, and with that, he was standing directly in front of her.

"Everyone's here," hissed into her mind.

She opened her eyes wide and stared into this man's—Legion's —dark, cold eyes. Then, suddenly, everyone came out in rapid succession, loud and scared, crying, angry and confused.

"My watch has stopped." " So has mine!" " The engines stopped!" "It's dark!" "I'm bleeding!" I can't feel my legs! Help me!" "We're going to crash!" "Fasten your seat belts!" " God help us!" "I'm trying to get it under control!" "Allah Akbar... Allah Akbar!"

In the wild confusion of the moment, one thought pierced her mind like a javelin: *"EMP."*

Trembling, Angela forced herself to step back, barely noticing the rumble, then dismissing it as thunder. The ground seemed to tremble under her feet. Blank for a moment, she stared down; the roar filled her ears, and she knew. Above her head came the sound of a plane crashing to the ground.

Gasping for air, Angela fought to keep her balance. Her hands trembled as she brushed the hair from her cheeks. It lasted no more than five minutes, or so she estimated, and then all was still.

A heartbeat later, Angela's face went blank and then twisted with the kind of suffering that plagues the evening news when a woman's holding her dead child after an act of violence. She dropped to the ground, hugged her knees and began to rock from side to side, sobbing uncontrollably.

"Manny, where are you?" Angela asked, closing her eyes and taking a long, slow breath.

"I'm right here, Angela," he answered with a strained smile.

Angela looked up and watched with fascination as Manny responded without moving his mouth. Startled, a tiny burst of fear jabbed her stomach. "I can hear you, Manny."

"I want my mother to know it's going to be alright. And that I love her."

Angela's eyes were fixed rigidly on him. She smiled and said sweetly, "I will tell her."

A jolt of electricity shot through Angela's body, and her world went dark.

All Nathan could do was stare at Angela lying motionless on the floor. When he laid a hand on her shoulder, she reached back and gripped his arm tight. Her lips quivered at the corners and his frown deepened.

"How long was I out?" Angela asked after a long moment.

Nathan sat for a moment, his eyes stung. After taking one careful breath, he replied, "Not long. Honey, you gave me a terrible scare."

"Gave myself one too." Murmuring, she wrapped her arm around Nathan's neck.

"Maybe we should go to the hospital and get you checked out."

"No." Pulling herself up to a sitting position, she said, "I must have hit my head though." She pressed a hand to the back of her head.

"You've got a nasty bump," he said as he went in for a closer look. "Got some nicks on your hands, too." There was sadness in his voice when he added, "I tried to help you down the best I could, but I couldn't quite prevent all of this."

"Don't worry; it's nothing," she told him. "And I don't need a doctor," she answered with an impatient moan.

"You're shaking. You're injured and scared."

"Not scared." She drew in a breath. "Just a little traumatized, I guess."

"I'm taking you home. You can tell me about it there."

"I..." she began, but then obliged, saying, "you're right, that's probably best." She drew back a little and wiped her face as it creased with a wild smile. "It was quite an adventure."

"Yeah, well, try horseback riding the next time you want to be adventuresome." Leaning over, Nathan kissed her on the cheek. "My heart can't take any more of this."

He trailed off and turned to press his face into Angela's warm throat. "I thought you were dead," he said, his shoulders shuddering. "I eased you down to the ground, looked down at you lying there and thought 'She's dead.' I can't remember anything else until I was down on the floor and put my hand on your throat. Felt your pulse beating."

Nathan took a deep breath to try to calm himself down and wiped some sweat from his forehead with the back of his hand.

"Nathan, I'm sorry." Smiling, she lifted her hands to frame his face. "I'm just a little shaky, not seriously wounded."

He swept Angela into his arms. “I’m just so relieved you’re here and okay.”

With a laugh, Angela gave him a light cuff on the back of the head. “Don’t you owe me a pizza tonight?”

With a soft laugh, he said her name tenderly, then paused briefly to angle his head down and touch his lips to hers. “I guess I do.” He brushed a hand through her hair.

“I’m fine. Really. Just needed to calm myself down a little.”

“Then just relax,” he ordered. “You wait here. I’ll take the RMTS10 to the car and come back to get you.”

“I can do that.” She squeezed his hand.

Alone, she let out a long, cleansing breath, then sucked in another and let it out as she ordered her legs to carry her to the entryway of the funeral home.

She managed to take only a few steps before she simply lowered herself down to sit on the floor. “Dear Lord,” she managed, sitting down while everything inside of her jumped and jittered. She felt as though she’d fallen off the side of a cliff and was even now just barely hanging on by a thread.

What was she supposed to do with all of this? And how could she figure it out when she couldn’t think straight?

She decided she wouldn’t try to make any decisions about it tonight—not until she could talk with Dr. Howard. Struggling up to her feet, she wiped her damp palms on her pants and then walked out of the room without a second glance. For tonight, she’d return the RMTS10 and the data to Dr. Howard’s office, order pizza, and then go home to her family—go home to normal.

However, this evening Angela Roberts had done something more than just normal, and she knew it. She had a message to deliver.

14

A pretty day in early December, brilliant sunshine and above normal temperatures meant only one thing for Angela Roberts: It was time for one of her favorite holiday rituals.

She flashed a grin. "Today is perfect for stringing the lights outside." Resisting the temptation for a bit longer, Angela continued to sip her coffee. The house was still quiet and lovely; nevertheless, the memories of what happened a few days ago at the Harper Funeral Home still haunted her. It had been his voice, she remembered, that had been the most terrifying... The way it had shifted from a gentle whisper to a powerful tone in quiet, unwavering insanity.

"You'd think, for as involved as I am in all of this, I would have heard something by now." She sat back in her chair just as the phone rang.

Angela glanced at the caller ID to see Matthew Howard's name on the screen. "Wow, from my lips to God's ears!" She grabbed her cup of coffee, cleared her throat and then answered the telephone.

"Hello, Dr. Howard."

"Angela, how are you?"

"I was beginning to wonder if you had forgotten about me."

"I'm sorry it's taken me so long to get back to you."

"So how did I do?" she asked proudly.

"You did an excellent job," Dr. Howard complimented her. "The information that you collected proved to be quite valuable."

"Do I dare ask what you mean by 'valuable'?"

"It's a little too involved to discuss over the phone. Is there any chance you and Nathan could meet me in my office around two o'clock this afternoon?"

"I'll have to check with Nathan, but I'm sure he'll want to be there."

"Well, good then. I'm looking forward to seeing you both."

When Angela and Nathan arrived at Dr. Howard's office, right away they noticed a man and woman huddled together with him, everyone deep in conversation as they looked intently at a computer screen.

Angela slipped her hand into Nathan's. "What's all this about?"

"I guess we're about to find out." Giving her hand a squeeze, he entered the office by her side.

Every eye shifted to them, and after a moment of silence, Dr. Howard stood up. He motioned for them to come closer and began speaking enthusiastically to them, saying in an energetic tone, "Angela, Nathan, come on in!" Without saying a word, they sat down and looked at Dr. Howard for a long moment.

"I'm delighted to report that the RMTS10 performed impeccably. The data that was collected on the USB drive was not only clear and incredible," he said as he brushed a hand through his hair, "but, unfortunately, it contained some startling undercurrents as well."

"Nothing major, I hope?" Angela asked slowly. "You *did* get what you needed, didn't you?"

"I think we did. I've spent hours going over the data, but no matter how I twisted and turned the recording, my findings and concerns remained the same. And that is why I contacted my friend in the FBI."

"What concerns?" she asked.

"Well, besides the obvious, the sounds of sheer terror in the background from the passengers." Dr. Howard adjusted the volume and found the words and phrases that had him troubled. "Angela, all of this must have been a nightmare for you."

"It still is sometimes." Angela turned away with a look of sorrow in her eyes. "The nightmare of Manny's death isn't over yet, is it?" Just saying it reminded her of the grisly scene again, and she closed her eyes for a second as Dr. Howard's friend reached his hand over to Nathan and Angela to introduce himself.

"Mr. and Mrs. Roberts, I'm Federal Agent David Matthews with the FBI, and this is Federal Agent Olivia Beckett."

As Angela listened, she felt a wave of panic wash over her, and she suddenly stared at the RMTS10.

"Sometimes talking about it helps," Agent Matthews said quietly.

"Agent Matthews, I presume by your presence at this meeting, you are already aware of what I am able to experience and what I have already experienced."

"More or less." He touched her arm, smiled gently and then went on to say how impressed he was with what she had done that night, how hard it must have been for her, and how his heart ached as he listened to the horror and panic in the passengers' voices. When he had finished, he looked Nathan and then Angela square in the eyes, and said, "I believe what took place on Flight 458 was a terrorist attack."

He said it with such finality that it nearly took Angela's breath away. After several deep breaths, she rubbed a hand along her throat until she could swallow. With another shaky breath, she shook her head in disbelief. "That's ridiculous!"

For an instant Nathan was too shocked to speak—but only for an instant.

"Why do you feel it was a terrorist attack?" Nathan turned instinctively and looked into Dr. Howard's eyes.

"I couldn't confirm my findings until the NTSB retrieved the Black Box from the crash site," Dr. Howard replied. "NTSB stands for the National Transportation Safety Board—"

"I know who the NTSB is. What did they find in the Black Box?"

Angela's color faded, leaving her face pale and horrified. "If you're suggesting Manny somehow caused..."

"No." Agent Matthews reached out, laying his hand over hers. "Just the opposite, I believe Manny tried to stop Javeed. Please, let me finish."

Relaxing again, Angela nodded.

"We checked the passenger list for Flight 458. All the passengers check out except for one passenger, Omar Javeed. Middle Eastern decent; however, for the past ten years he was living in Los Angeles and working for Oak Ridge National Laboratories, studying the effects of a high-energy EMP."

"EMP?" Nathan asked, putting his arm around Angela and pulling her close. "That was on Iana's list."

"An electromagnetic pulse, also sometimes called a transient disturbance, occurs when a source emits a short-duration pulse of energy. It could possibly be used to create EMP weapons, both nuclear and non-nuclear," Agent Matthews explained.

Dr. Howard placed the NTSB Report in front of them. "Here, this word 'EMP' is the same word written on Iana's list and the one that you stated sounded clearly in your head during your vision. Now listen to the data that was collected."

Dr. Howard clicked the "Play" button, and instantly the words *Allah Akbar* and *EMP,* together with the shouting that watches were stopping and the lights were going out, filled the room. It all had been collected on the USB drive, understandable and unmistakable.

Angela said nothing for a moment, but a dozen varied images flashed into her mind.

"What does all of this mean?" she asked.

"The CIA has also confirmed Javeed's direct link to an operative of Al-Qaida in the country where he was living before he came to the United States," Agent Matthews replied.

"I can't believe this." Angela lowered her eyes. "This can't be real."

"I don't mean to upset you, but this is very real. The direct effect of a large EMP is to induce high currents and voltages in the victim, or in this case, in the aircraft. It would damage the electrical equipment or disrupt its function. That would explain the aircraft's instruments and engines cutting off and the lights going out. And here's the big one: The watches stopping. Mrs. Roberts, not all the watches had stopped." Agent Matthews glanced over to Nathan.

"And you're sure about that?" Angela demanded.

"Very sure. In Manny's personal affects we found his watch, intact and still ticking." Agent Matthews smiled.

"Manny's watch wasn't digital, was it?" Nathan asked.

"No, it wasn't. He still had to wind it up, so it was not affected —which is even more evidence that an EMP was involved."

"I feel a little queasy." Angela pressed a hand to her stomach.

"We believe what happened on Flight 458 was the result of an EMP's heating effects or the disruptive effects of the very large magnetic field generated by its current," Agent Matthews went on to explain. "An EMP typically contains energy at frequencies from DC, zero hertz, to some upper limits, depending on the source."

"Okay." She took a huge breath. "Okay, if this is all true, why haven't we ever heard of EMPs before?"

"Recently on Capitol Hill, the former Speaker of the House addressed members of the Electromagnetic Pulse Caucus," Agent Matthews said.

"Whoa… There's an Electromagnetic Pulse Caucus?" Nathan looked at Agent Matthews then Dr. Howard.

"I know what you're thinking, and I myself was a bit skeptical, too, until I read an article published in *Politico Magazine*. The Speaker was on Capitol Hill to point out that an electromagnetic pulse was equally as dangerous as a nuclear threat, comparing the fallout from an EMP to that of a high-altitude nuclear blast. The Speaker went on to state that an electromagnetic pulse has the potential to be the ultimate cyber security threat, because it can take our source of power completely away from us, destroying American power grids and electronics. That would be a deathblow to our society."

"So Flight 458 was a test run for bigger things to come?" Nathan asked.

"There is no concrete evidence as to whether Javeed was working alone or carrying out directives from Al-Qaida. Our investigation is still ongoing in that area."

Angela turned to Dr. Howard. "What do you think about all of this?"

"There is no denying any of this for me, based on the data collected and what you have stated. Angela, it all fits with the findings in the NTSB report."

She stroked her hand gently up and down her arm. "It certainly does seem to."

"Undoubtedly, my speculations about you were accurate." He smiled. "And I suspect that Agent Matthews is going to try and recruit you for the FBI."

Letting her head fall back, Angela laughed.

"Mrs. Roberts, I have to admit that when Matt first described to me these visions or paranormal occurrences—the vibrations, seeing images, and then the strange list you found in your grandmother's cookbook containing the numbers 747, 1125, 458 and the letters 'EMP'—to tell you the truth, I didn't give it much merit."

Angela nodded and smiled.

Agent Matthews paused for a moment. "Then the strangest thing happened. Just as Dr. Howard called me and our investigation started, my partner of ten years was unexpectedly pulled from the case, no explanation given, and transferred to another department."

Angela angled her head. "How is that strange?"

"The next day Agent Beckett was assigned to this case and now is my partner. The moment she saw your name in the file, she immediately recognized you as the granddaughter of Iana Hamilton."

"How would you know of my grandmother?" Angela asked, turning to Agent Beckett.

"Like gossip, the paranormal adds a little something to any story. I grew up with the legend of Iana Hamilton; that legend is quite common in this area. My own grandmother believed wholeheartedly in Iana's abilities and often told me stories of her speaking to the deceased and then conveying messages to the mourning families. As a matter of fact, she delivered a message to my grandmother the day that my grandfather passed away."

"That is so nice to hear. Thank you for sharing that with me."

"It goes further than that," she said. "When I was in college, I wrote my senior thesis on Iana Hamilton. And as soon as I saw your name, I told Agent Matthews that I was banking on you possessing the same abilities as your grandmother." Agent Beckett tossed the FBI file onto the desk. "And by the looks of it, you do."

"Made a believer out of me!" Agent Matthews nodded in understanding. "If it hadn't been for Matt's years of study in the field of electromagnetic energy, the RMTS10 and what you did, I venture to say that our investigation may have never taken on the direction that it did."

"That's true, Mrs. Roberts." Agent Beckett smiled. "We would have never known of this Javeed person, let alone what he had been doing."

"I doubt we would have ever even known to look into the EMP theory." Shaking his head, Agent Matthews added, "Looking back over the past week, it's as if something—or someone—was guiding all of us."

Smiling, Angela and Nathan looked at one another. "Almost like a beacon of light in the darkness." Tears squeezed out of Angela's eyes as she said it, and Nathan nodded, satisfied with her response. Then they quietly rose and headed for the door. Dr. Howard lightly touched Angela's shoulder as she turned but Angela didn't respond.

As Nathan drove them home, Angela wondered to herself why Dr. Howard hadn't mentioned anything about Legion... But part of her had cautioned her, for some reason, not to ask him about it. Was it possible that she was the only one who had heard Legion's voice? Could it be the case that he had been speaking directly to her in some way the RMTS10 couldn't detect? She didn't know the answer, but the thought sent a chill to her core. In the end, she decided to ignore Legion altogether. She had more important things to think about and do.

She quickly set aside her original thought of merely calling Mrs. Ramirez after learning more of what had taken place during the pandemonium on Flight 458; now, she decided, she needed to talk to her in person. The Black Box had not only confirmed what Angela had witnessed while in her clairvoyant episode; it had also revealed that, at some point during the chaos, Manny and another male passenger had made a full-on attempt to overpower and disarm the radical, Omar Javeed.

Agent Matthews assured her that any details of the crash wouldn't be released to the press until after she had spoken with Manny's mother. And now there was no question in her mind; she needed to speak face-to-face with Mrs. Ramirez as soon as possible.

Mrs. Ramirez agreed to meet with Angela and Nathan that evening. As Nathan drove their car towards the Ramirez home, Angela knew she would need all the courage and strength she could muster. And for Angela, that meant turning to and leaning on the Lord. She asked Nathan to make a stop along the way.

It was seven o'clock at night when Nathan and Angela pulled into the parking lot of St. Michaels Church, and there were still people milling around in the sanctuary after the evening service. She stepped inside and went straight to the altar to light a candle. Then she got on her knees, bowed her head, and prayed.

"Heavenly Father, I need help. Please show me how to help the Ramirez family through this storm. You were the One who helped me when I lost my son; You were with me every step of the way, even when I didn't acknowledge You or give You the glory. The Bible tells us in 2 Corinthians 1:4, God comforts, encourages and consoles me in every trouble. That You enable me to console others who need comfort. I pray for Your wisdom and guidance during this time in my life. Use my mouth and my hands to show comfort in this time of sorrow. In Jesus' name, Amen."

When she finished praying, Angela felt better, although her heart still ached for Manny and his family.

Twenty minutes later, Angela and Nathan were seated in the living room of the Ramirez home.

"How are you doing?" Angela asked.

Mrs. Ramirez pasted on a smile. "I'm okay. Just a little tired." Her emotions threatened to overcome her, so she rose to her feet and walked across the room to her bookshelf, idly perusing the books' titles and running her fingers over their spines.

Nathan removed his glasses and wiped his eyes. "Honey, let's not do this now."

Shaking her head no, Angela continued, "It's been a lot for you to deal with. I know that."

"Mrs. Roberts, I appreciate you coming," Mrs. Ramirez managed, turning back toward her.

Angela and Nathan exchanged looks. "Why don't you come and sit down?" Nathan asked and then rose to help Mrs. Ramirez back to the couch.

"I wish I could tell you more," Angela said as she reached over and took Mrs. Ramirez by the hand. "I want to tell you more."

Mrs. Ramirez looked at her. "What is it?"

"First of all, I want you to know that Manny is at peace and that he loves you very much." Angela's voice weakened.

Mrs. Ramirez nodded as a tear escaped her eye. "Thank you. That means a lot."

"There's more."

Angela nearly burst into tears as she went on to explain what she could about the plane crash, telling Mrs. Ramirez that the NTSB had officially identified the downing of Flight 458 as a terrorist attack. Her son, Manny, was considered a hero.

As Angela spoke, details of what happened buzzed in Mrs. Ramirez's mind, and she began shaking her head in confusion. Then, sobbing, she fell to the floor.

"Angela's right," Nathan said. "And in turn Manny will be awarded The Medal of Honor for his bravery, for distinguishing himself by his conduct, for risking of his own life above and beyond his call of duty in the presence of an enemy of the United States."

"You can be very proud of your son." When Angela saw Mrs. Ramirez start to shake, she carefully lifted her back onto the couch. There were tears on Angela's cheek as she reached out, touching Mrs. Ramirez on her shoulder. "Manny was a young man who lived his life, albeit short, with integrity and honor, even in the face of death. He and his actions will never be forgotten."

After several moments of silence, Mrs. Ramirez whispered, "I feel him here, with us."

They all knew who she was talking about, and Angela nodded, tears still in her eyes. "Me too," she said and then lowered her head and closed her eyes.

"Thank you for coming here tonight," Mrs. Ramirez smiled. "It's strange not having Manny here, even though we'd grown used to him being off at college."

"I know," Angela said softly. "We'll see you tomorrow. Try and get some rest tonight."

Angela suggested a sleeping pill, but Mrs. Ramirez refused. She didn't want to have a woozy head when she said good-bye to her son for the last time.

A few minutes later, Angela and Nathan said good-bye and walked out the front door.

"Now all we have to do is get through the next twenty-four hours," Angela said as they drove away.

"How could this happen?" Angela whispered to Nathan as she watched a member of the Honor Guard escort Mrs. Ramirez to her seat in the front row. As soon as Mrs. Ramirez and her family had taken their seats, Manny's casket was carefully lifted from the back of the hearse. A hush fell over the crowd of people, many of whom were crying and blowing their noses as they watched Manny's casket move slowly towards his final resting place.

Tears streamed down Mrs. Ramirez's cheeks as the Honor Guard gently placed and then positioned Manny's casket on the lowering cables for burial. There were flowers standing next to it, and the smell of them was heavy in the air. Mrs. Ramirez knelt on the grass and rested a hand on the smooth wood.

It was all so unbelievable, so agonizing, so much more than Angela had ever thought she could bear—except that now she had to. She had no choice. This was the hand that life had dealt her, and she had to live through it, if only for her husband and remaining son.

The American flag was beautifully draped over the lid of Manny's casket so that the blue field with stars was over Manny's head and left shoulder.

For a long time, there were only the sounds of sobbing. Then Pastor Stephens delivered a brief but beautiful eulogy and sermon, which was followed by the folding of the flag. In total silence, the Honor Guard carefully folded the flag into the symbolic tri-cornered shape, devoid of the red or white stripes; only the blue field with the stars was visible when he was finished. At that point, the Commander of the Honor Guard turned smartly, then he slowly but surely proceeded over to Mrs. Ramirez. He stood directly in front of her with the tightly-folded American flag resting on his palms, its straight edge facing her. He knelt down on one knee and presented it to Mrs. Ramirez.

"On behalf of the President of the United States, it is my high privilege to present to you this flag from a grateful nation as a token of appreciation of your son, Manny Ramirez, for the distinguished and courageous actions he rendered to our country and his fellow citizens."

He then rose, looking Mrs. Ramirez directly in the eyes; he brought his hand to the saluting position in one swift motion and then brought it back down to his side.

Taps being played indicated the conclusion of Manny's service. It was a moment of such blinding pain. Tears slid down Angela's cheeks, for she knew that Mrs. Ramirez never in her lifetime would forget this day.

"I'm so sorry," she whispered to her. They had both lost a son and there was nothing else to say. The two women stood and hugged each other for a long time.

Before leaving the cemetery, Mrs. Ramirez laid a single red rose on Manny's casket and then kissed the box. She walked away, gripping her husband's hand, her eldest son's arm wrapped tightly around her waist.

Angela shook her head and then turned to find Nathan deep in conversation with Pastor Stephens. Sitting back down, she felt as though she'd been hit by a freight train as she thought about the past few days. Letting her head fall back, she stared up at the bright blue sky. *"Not a cloud anywhere,"* she thought.

Unexpectedly, an icy shiver darted up her spine, and for a moment, Angela could have sworn she'd witnessed a dazzling white light streak across the noonday sky. Sitting straight up, she let out a little laugh, quickly dismissing it as a vapor trail from an airplane. After a few minutes she calmed down and let her head fall back once more.

"It's like déjà vu," she whispered. She took one very careful breath, narrowing her eyes as she searched for the memory this moment reminded her of.

Moments later, a bright white light flickered and floated, coming to rest directly above her.

"That's interesting." She cocked her head and nearly smiled. "It's one o'clock in the afternoon... That can't be a star." Angela continued to scrutinize the white light, nearly mesmerized by its brightness. She sat silently for a moment and then smiled at her own question. "If not a star, then what are you?"

From nowhere, a powerful and undeniable sense of strength and unity welled up within her. In her spirit she felt a strong sense of the importance of carrying on, along with a comforting reassurance.

Angela quickly sat straight up, totally focused, and then felt herself begin to tremble. She instantly remembered all the terrors of this new chapter in her life.

Then a thought clicked into her mind. *"But yet, no matter how daunting, you failed to be terrorized or defeated."* Angela pulled back, shocked. She had an impulse to call for Nathan, but she resisted it. *"You have been granted a glimpse into the past, and at the same time, my child, have faithfully kept a firm grip on the present."*

Angela puzzled over the thought for a moment, searching for an explanation as she settled back into her chair. Also, somewhat annoyed at her reaction, she took a tissue from her purse and dabbed her eyes.

She was confident now that she wasn't experiencing a past event and just as confident that she was very much in the present moment. But whoever or whatever was on the other side of that light was *not* in the present. It was from the past—*her* past.

Angela closed her eyes; she sat placidly and then, as if someone had placed a warm blanket across her shoulders, "*I will show you the way*," floated peacefully into her psyche.

Her eyes opened slowly, responding to the gesture and feathery voice. "Grandmother?" She tried to focus, to see who the lovely voice belonged to, but couldn't.

Almost immediately, Angela gasped. "I can feel you," she said, her own voice sounding very distant.

She waited a few moments and then heard, *"You're not alone, Angela."* When the voice spoke this time, it was sharper.

She pressed her fingers to her eyes, and in that quiet moment, Angela realized she was basking in the presence of her grandmother, Iana Hamilton. She had been watching her, guiding her and offering silent support from the other side, and that brought her comfort. A smile whisked over her mouth. "Out of the darkness, as a beacon of light."

15

It was the morning of Christmas Eve, and the Roberts's home was already overflowing with all of the excitement and anticipation that came along with the holiday season. Angela and her family's plans for Christmas were very traditional. For Christmas Eve, she planned an informal family dinner, which would also include her closest friends: Rowena, Stephen and Kate McGowan. And this year, much to Nathan's delight, Angela granted his request to hold off on decorating the family tree until Christmas Eve.

Rebecca sat staring out the living room window, deep in thought while taking in the view. Remembering her past Christmas mornings with a sigh, she turned away from the picturesque setting. Only a year before, she reminded herself, she'd been living in a rundown apartment with no job, broke, miserable and alone on Christmas Day. Turning back to look out the window again, she caught a glimpse of a deer walking across the lawn, and it brought a smile to her face. She thought, "*How beautiful, her coat thickened for winter, her eyes watchful and on alert for any disturbances,*" and then watched as the deer passed through the trees and out of sight.

Her eyes then caught sight of the bright red and white poinsettias grouped together and placed on each side of the stone fireplace in the living room. Another long survey of the room brought a nod of approval. A wreath adorned with a large red bow had been hung above the mantel and yet another with tiny white lights around it was on the front door; a small white pine Christmas tree stood in the corner of the entryway, decorated with little red and green ornaments.

Instantly something began to settle inside of her. It took her less than a moment to recognize it as contentment. She smiled to herself, and just as she started upstairs to shower and dress for the day, she saw Robby heading down, trying to comfort a screaming India. "She's hungry!"

"I'll get the bottle," Rebecca said.

"Thanks. I could use some help."

"She probably needs changing, too."

Robby met Rebecca at the bottom of the stairs and quickly handed India over to her. "On second thought, I'll get the bottle and you can take care of whatever needs taking care of down there."

Gathering India into her arms, Rebecca smiled at Robby and then nuzzled her little darling. "Come here, baby girl. Mommy is going to get you all cleaned up."

After she had changed India's diaper, Rebecca walked back into the kitchen where Robby was hurriedly preparing India's bottle. She handed India over to Robby and then smiled as she leaned on the doorjamb. *"Robby is absolutely amazing with India,"* she thought. He was patient, loving and gentle with her. She watched as he brushed his fingertips over India's hair. She wasn't quite sure how to read his face, though; he was definitely restless and confused—maybe even anxious. Her motherly instincts, however, sensed there was more on his mind than he was letting on. She had watched Robby interact with her daughter over the past few weeks and there was no denying the love and affection he held in his heart for India. Now Rebecca wondered if those same feelings had taken root in his heart for her.

To the best of her knowledge, Robby had never been truly in love... Possibly in lust a few times, but never in a loving, committed relationship.

Lost in her thoughts, she hadn't heard Robby speaking to her.

"Hey, you okay?" He squinted at her.

"I'm fine," she said with a wistful smile. "Just thinking how my life has changed over the past year."

"All of our lives have changed."

"Isn't that the truth?" Rebecca scooped her fingers through her hair.

"With all that has happened, I've been thinking that I should be here to help out more. Ya know, just be here for support." The rapid and shaky stirrings of his heart irritated him. "Yeah, I mean for Mom and Dad."

Rebecca blew out a breath. "This is awfully sudden."

"I've been thinking about transferring to NYU for the rest of the semester."

Rebecca didn't try to stop her smile. "Well, I think that would be wonderful."

"You do?" Robby asked.

"Well, yes." Her eyes sparkled when she heard his words, but she didn't want to pry into his personal life, so she didn't ask any questions. Sure, she had plenty, but she controlled her urge to ask them. “Ya know, for your mom and dad.”

“Oh.” He gave a nervous laugh.

Robby set the empty bottle aside and got up slowly from his seat. Moving towards the bassinette, he leaned over and gently placed India down on the mattress. Instantly her head popped up, and she began to cry.

“Shhh.” Robby quickly placed a blanket over her and then softly patted her back.

A slow smile spread across her face as Rebecca watched Robby continue to lovingly caress the top of India’s head. *“That’s the sort of thing a father might do,”* she thought.

Shoving his hands into his pockets, Robby wandered over to the refrigerator and pulled open the door.

“So, I’m supposed to go out and find a Christmas tree today.”

“Is that so?” she asked cheerfully. “I used to love getting the Christmas tree when I was a kid.”

“I was thinking, maybe you’d like to come with me?” Robby turned from the fridge and kept his eyes on hers.

“Okay.” She thought she had spoken calmly but couldn’t be sure with the blood rushing to her head. “I could do that.”

They smiled at each other, realizing they were in the midst of negotiating spending time together.

Just then, Angela walked into the kitchen, setting a bag of groceries on the counter. She stared at Robby, at the face she’d known so well. There had been a time when she would have known what he was thinking, and certainly what he was feeling, but those years had come and gone; her little boy was now a grown man, a man in love and scared to death.

“Am I interrupting?” When Angela laughed, Rebecca blushed.

“Yes,” Robby said, watching Rebecca. “You up to watching India for a few hours?” he asked, closing the fridge without having gotten anything out of it.

“Absolutely. You two going out?” This time Angela smiled wide.

“A little Christmas tree shopping. We shouldn’t be long,” Robby told her.

“Go on, then, and have a good time. India and I will be just fine.”

With her knees about to give out, Rebecca sat down on a stool and frowned at Robby when Angela strolled out of the room. “Well, that was awkward.”

“Not for me. As a matter of fact, I don’t think I’ve ever had so much Christmas spirit.” Robby laughed and then did his strut around the room.

The sky was heavy with clouds that would certainly bring about a covering of frosty winter white snow before it was all said and done.

"We're going to have quite a storm," Rebecca said, hesitating at the door and looking up at the clouds.

"Exactly. And just in time for Christmas Eve." Robby smiled at her.

"Be careful," Angela warned, handing Robby a thermos filled with hot chocolate as the two walked out the front door.

Robby looked over and smiled at Rebecca. "In case you've forgotten, we *are* in the midst of the Christmas season. Santa Claus is going to put coal in your stocking if you don't get into the spirit of things soon."

Rebecca shook her head, trying to hide her smile. "You must have been bitten by one of Santa's elves this morning. All this Christmas spirit... Next you'll be baking cookies."

"And so what if I do?" He laughed. "It's Christmas magic!"

"That I have to see!" Amused, she slapped Robby's shoulder.

There was a real holiday mood as they drove in the car, and tiny snowflakes swirled down and covered the ground around them. They sipped hot chocolate and sang along to a variety of holiday songs that played on the radio; it was a scene akin to a Thomas Kinkade Christmas print.

Half an hour later, Robby turned into the parking lot of the local fire station, parked the car and walked around to open the door for Rebecca. Extending his hand, he smiled. "Let the games begin!"

She smiled big and innocent. "You're on, mister."

They entered the large grouping of trees, all waiting to brighten someone's home. "I feel like Hansel and Gretel walking through a forest," Robby told her, and they both laughed.

"Hope we don't run into the big, bad witch," she said, turning her head side to side.

Robby held a firm grip on her hand so she wouldn't fall as they walked with their heads bowed against the snow that was swirling and falling around at their feet.

The air was crisp and clean. Robby took a deep breath, filling his head with the scent of pine from the freshly cut trees. Tiny white lights as luminous as fireflies twinkled amidst the falling snow and, every so often, they could hear the sound of children's voices shrieking with excitement, having found their perfect Christmas tree.

Rebecca stopped to take in the moment. Unexpectedly, a whack on her shoulder snapped her back into reality. Looking annoyed, she turned around and saw Robby hiding behind a six-foot Douglas fir, watching her. It was almost juvenile, a grown man darting from tree to tree, crouching down like a wild animal, watching and waiting, preparing to strike. Both hands weighed down with ammunition and ready to fire at a moment's notice, he threw a hail of snowballs upon his unsuspecting prey.

Laughing until it hurt, Rebecca lost her balance when Robby walked up and wrapped his arms around her like a defensive end tackling a quarterback. Falling to the ground in each other's arms, they laid in the snow, laughing and gazing up at the twinkling lights against the gray sky while snowflakes floated down to rest softly on their faces. Both now oblivious to the world around them, it was like a scene from one of those romantic comedies Rebecca loved and had watched over and over again.

Robby started to get up, then cursed under his breath and tossed Rebecca back down in the snow. "I might as well finish this out."

Rebecca heard herself make some sort of sound, and then his hand raked through her hair. She saw his eyes, then everything clouded, and his mouth was hard and hot on hers. Her hand lifted to his shoulder in a kind of confused opposition, then relaxed and dug in, sliding down to his elbow when his head lifted.

With his hand still caught in her hair, he said, "Damn."

He pulled her straight up and held an arm tightly around her waist so that her body was pressed against his. When his mouth swooped down a second time, any brains of hers that hadn't been fried the first time were now burnt to a crisp. When he deepened the kiss, she let out a tiny moan and Robby was in deep, all wound up in that hair, that alluring scent of hers, those soft lips.

When he managed to let go of her, to step back from her, he saw the flush rising in her cheeks. It made her eyes greener, larger. He wanted to whisk her off her feet and carry her somewhere—anywhere—to finish what their kiss had started. Instead, he took a deep breath and another step back.

"Are you exactly where you want to be?" Robby leaned in and kissed her cheek.

"I am," she said as she smiled.

The snow had really picked up and the wind had started to blow. Robby couldn't see anything but trees all around them and started to worry they might have trouble getting home. But as he tightened Rebecca's coat around her neck, he smiled. "As much as

I like hearing you say that, there is still the matter of a Christmas tree."

"Well then, I'd say it's time for some serious tree shopping," she said, holding onto him so she didn't stumble.

It didn't take long for them to decide on a six-foot Blue Spruce. Their festive mood continued, and they stopped to buy a bottle of champagne on the way home.

Pulling into the driveway, they immediately noticed the newly added outside holiday decorations. Angela's home looked as though it had been ripped from the pages of the *Home and Gardens* holiday edition. Fresh-cut evergreen boughs twinkled with white lights and had been draped around the front door and porch banister. Stepping inside, they were instantly transported into another world. Candles flickered in cut crystal votive holders, another evergreen garland had been draped across the fireplace mantel, and the doorways were each adorned with tiny white twinkling lights. The soft hum of Christmas music played in the background, and Rebecca just wanted to sit down and take in the splendor of Angela's home. It had a spirit of its own, and it was filled with the warmth and loveliness of the amazing woman who lived there.

"Wow, you guys picked a winner!" Angela said, bouncing India on her hip. "The tree will look fantastic in front of the living room windows."

For the next twenty minutes, the three of them fussed over the tree, first moving it to the right and then shifting it to the left. After that, they pushed the tree closer to the front window and then pulled it farther away, into the corner of the living room. Finally, after all their options had been exhausted, they positioned the tree centered in front of the living room window, exactly where it had started.

It was after nine o'clock when the last guest had gone home from their Christmas Eve dinner. Angela and Nathan usually attended midnight mass on the night before Christmas with the boys, if she could talk them into going, but tonight they were on their own, and Angela was fine with that. After India had fallen asleep, Robby and Rebecca settled in on the couch to enjoy another time-honored Christmas Eve family tradition: watching *It's a Wonderful Life* on television.

"Hope you don't mind that you're stuck with just me for mass tonight," Nathan said as he glanced over at Robby and Rebecca, then back at Angela.

"Not a bit," Angela told him as her lips spread into a wide smile. "It's the season of miracles—a time for peace, love and joy!" She chuckled as Nathan helped her put on her coat.

As they walked up the steps into St. Michaels, she could see a cluster of tall pine trees on either side of the main altar, banks of poinsettias adorning the place, and candle light emanating from inside. Angela walked to the altar and lit two candles, one for Kenny and another for Manny, and then knelt for a moment, thinking of her son and her family friend. She wasn't sure what prayers she should say or even how to say them, so all she did was think of the people in her heart. And this Christmas Eve, she was grateful that Rebecca and India were brought into her life.

Nathan and Angela sat in a pew toward the rear of the church and were impressed (as they always were) by the beauty, pomp and ceremony of the midnight mass. When they sang "Silent Night" toward the end, there were tears rolling down Angela's cheeks. She wasn't sure why, or whom they were for, or even what she was crying about. All she knew was that she was deeply moved. She had an odd sense of peace, joy and ease. She thought of Kenny, and for a peculiar moment, she felt as though he was sitting in the pew with them.

On Christmas morning, Angela, Nathan, Robby and Rebecca exchanged gifts. Angela had bought Robby a new leather briefcase for his first semester at NYU, and she gave Rebecca a long wool scarf, similar to the one she'd told Angela she admired. Nathan bought Angela a beautiful diamond and gold bracelet from Tiffany's, and she gave him a tie clip with a single round diamond attached to his three initials set in 14K gold.

"I can't believe Christmas is over." Kneeling, Angela jiggled a white stuffed kitten in front of India. She knew India didn't have a clue as to what was going on, and it was so much fun to watch her wiggle and smile at her toys, especially at the twinkling lights on the tree.

"Nothing like Christmas lights to keep a child entertained," she said as she sat back on her heels and sighed happily.

All their gifts to each other were a great success. And their Christmas dinner was peaceful and uneventful, although they all admitted to missing Kenny.

Angela and Nathan cleared the dining room table. Afterwards, while everyone retired to the den to relax and watch television, Angela wandered into the living room to take a last look at the tree while she sat alone with her coffee and her memories of the day. From watching Robby sit cross-legged on the floor, showing India her toys, to the candlelight and superb meal she had prepared and served on her mother Cillia's china, her new memories were certainly fond. She wanted to slow down time, just for one day, but before she knew it, the day had flown by and her house was quiet once more.

Placing another log on the fire, she looked over at Kenny's picture on the bookcase. Gently touching his face, she said, "I miss you, son."

Angela shook her head and smiled. Then she grabbed an afghan off the back of the chair, wrapped it snuggly around her shoulders and sat down on the couch. Exhaling slowly, she leaned her head back, closed her eyes and shifted her body to get comfortable. Then she put her feet up on the ottoman and descended into a deep, relaxing sleep.

In her dream Angela could see the pattern of blue stripes on a couch, and somewhere off in the distance a voice was repeating the words, "*Brassy and shiny... Brassy and shiny.*"

A few seconds later, the figure of a man materialized lying on the floor beside the couch, and she quietly observed his fist clenching and unclenching.

"Angela," he called to her. *"Look in front of you."* Her eyes rested blankly on the floor.

"*Help me; I don't want to die like this.*" He glanced over at her, a mannequin with a voice, his eyes black and deadly serious.

Everything was constantly shifting back and forth; one minute Angela knew what was happening and the next minute, she heard *"Brassy and shiny... Brassy and shiny,"* and watched the man's fist clench and unclench. Angela's body tensed up all of a sudden. She was in pain, and the density and closeness of the moment now frightened her.

Suddenly a little girl rushed into view and fell down on the floor, groaning in sorrow.

"Daddy... Daddy," she said with panic in her little voice. "Mommy, what's wrong with Daddy? Mommy, where are you?"

Immediately a woman emerged. Dressed in a faded bathrobe, with a bottle of gin in one hand and a half-empty glass in the other, she grinned at the little girl the way a coyote would grin. The woman leaned towards her and then said softly, dangerously, "*Dead. Your daddy is dead.*"

The little girl shrank in on herself, her face red, and a tear formed in the corner of each of her eyes. "*No,*" she said as she shook her head. "*Daddy is* not *dead!*"

The woman's head whipped around, then her gaze clamped down harder on the little girl. *"You did this, didn't you?"* the woman shouted before knocking back her drink in one gulp. *"You had some thoughts in your head again, didn't you?"*

The little girl thought for a moment and shook her head. *"No, Mama."*

The woman slapped her hand against her forehead. *"Stop fussing over him."* She took two deep breaths, lifted her head high and walked over to his body. *"Everyone knows he never loved you. Isn't that* right, *Daddy?"*

Angela's eyes focused on the woman.

With a puzzled look on her ugly face, the crazed mother nervously pointed a finger at the closet door in the hallway. *"Go home... Now!"*

Angela quickly shifted her eyes to the closet door, and for a half a second she wondered what the woman meant.

Then the little girl's eyes shut tightly, her face contorted in agony, and hot tears ran down her cheeks. Her hands hung lifelessly by her sides, and her tiny body shook as she cried. *"No, Mama,"* she sobbed and then screamed, *"I... don't... wanna... go... home!"*

The intensity of the woman's anger vibrated in the room. Her dark, angry eyes fixed rigidly on the little girl. Walking over to the closet door, she yanked it open. *"Get in!"*

Her threatening tone triggered something in the little girl, who promptly stood up and unconsciously gripped the arms of the chair. For a moment, she looked confused, and then she slowly started walking towards the open closet door. Angela noticed a change in her face as she looked over her shoulder at her father lying motionless on the floor. Then, without a word, she clamped her mouth shut, spun on her heels, and dashed back to his side. In that instant, she bent down and snatched a round, shiny object from his hand and then quickly stood up to face the woman.

Suddenly the look of rage returned to the woman's face. *"Go home!"* She raised her hand and made her index and middle fingers into the form of scissors. Grunting with effort, she ran towards the little girl.

Instantly the sounds dissipated, and Angela's gaze was locked on the little girl's huge, pleading eyes, which were in turn locked on hers. She watched as the little girl turned back towards her mother and slowly raised a hand to the left side of her face, rubbing at the raw and sore nasty cuts on her cheek. The sound of her little voice cut through the silence: *"No, Mama, don't. I will go home."*

The woman's eyes were blazing, her teeth were bared, and Angela could hear her growl with annoyance as she slammed the door shut.

Then whispers came from inside the closet. *"Dead Daddy, Daddy is dead."* Louder and louder, *"You're a dead Daddy, you're a dead man!"*

Angela sprang from the couch and screamed, "STOP IT!" clamping her hands over her ears to block the deafening sounds within.

"Angela! Angela, wake up!" Nathan shouted, frantically grabbing her by the shoulders and shaking her.

Suddenly Angela's body jerked, slamming her against the back of the couch, and she slid down sideways onto her back, feet still on the floor, hands balled in fists that she pressed tightly against her chest. Terrified, she opened her eyes and the room came into focus. She shook her head hard, trying to clear her mind. First looking at Nathan and then over at Robby, she said, "It was Maggie... Mr. Woodrow's description of the night her father died."

There was no response, just a terrified look on both Nathan and Robby's faces.

Angela shook her head slowly as a wave of unexpected emotions flooded her. "I saw it in my dream. She looked at me; her scared little face was two inches from mine."

"Honey?" Nathan said, trying to snap his fingers a couple of times. "You with me here? Are you okay?"

She took a deep breath and let it out slowly. "Huuuh," she gasped.

"Honey, listen to me. No one is going to hurt you," Nathan said firmly.

"Maggie... I watched as her little life crashed in a ball of flames, and there wasn't a damn thing I could do about it."

Nathan waited a few moments. "Okay. Can you sit up?" Wrapping his arms around his wife, he held her close. "Try and tell me about your dream."

They were quiet for a moment, then Angela unclasped her hands and shook her head. "Maggie suffered through a horrible childhood, and I feel so bad for her."

"Angela," Nathan said, handing her a tissue.

Angela took the tissue, crumpled it, and then smoothed it out. "I know. There wasn't anything I could have done. It was a dream, right?"

Her eyes settled on the delicate poinsettias in the vase next to her. *"What sins had been committed in that house?"* she asked herself. Gently she touched a velvety petal, felt it slide between her thumb and forefinger.

"Maggie was my mother's best friend; my grandmother loved her as a daughter." Shifting her gaze back to Nathan, she continued, "What am I supposed to do with this?"

"Honey," Nathan said, taking her free hand and giving it a squeeze. "I don't know if there is anything you need to do. It was a dream."

She sniffled and wiped her nose. "Darn it, Nathan. To *me* it was a dream, but I know it was real for Maggie; intellectually, I know it. I've heard the stories about Maggie, saw with my own eyes the after effects of her tortured, abused life... All that disgusting stuff." She took a deep breath and continued, "Right now that woman is out there somewhere, alone and tormented."

She paused. Tears trailed down her face and she wiped them away fiercely, annoyed at their persistence, not caring anymore about her makeup.

"I feel so scared and angry. Scared about what's going to happen to her and angry about what her demented, uncontrolled mother did to her." She bit her lip and cried a little more.

Nathan remained silent, sensing that Angela needed a few more minutes to cry it all out. He knew that she understood Maggie's pain. For over fifteen years, Angela had volunteered at the local women's shelter and had worked with adult survivors of child abuse and their families. Angela knew how devastating the effects were, not only for the survivors, but for the spouses and other children.

Angela's eyes were red and her face was puffy. She had worked her way through half a box of tissues before she was able to stop her tears and get her breathing under control.

"Whew," she said with an embarrassed laugh. "I guess I needed that." After a brief pause, she said, "And I now feel guilty for putting you through this on Christmas night." She blew her nose and glanced over at Robby. "I'm sorry I'm such a mess. If anyone can recommend a good therapist, now would be the time."

Nathan scratched the back of his neck casually. "I can't recommend a therapist, but I *can* recommend a slice of warm apple pie."

"I'm on it," Robby said. Getting right up, he headed straight to the kitchen.

"Yeah," Angela nodded, grinning to herself. "I'm okay, just feeling a little weirded out."

Several months previously, and upon hearing Iana Hamilton's friend, Mr. Woodrow, give his account of Maggie's painful childhood, Nathan had put in a call to a friend in Children and Youth Services requesting any information that might still be available on her. The file was decades old and thin, with only bits and pieces of a social worker's report, but it shed some light on Maggie Deveraux's life.

A family history form had shown that her family's house had no heat and that their electricity had been repeatedly disconnected due to nonpayment. The father had spent most of Maggie's early years in prison on assault and battery charges, including multiple arrests for drunken and disorderly conduct. When Maggie was around the age of four, her mother suddenly abandoned the family, but she returned a year later. Nathan also discovered that, around the same time, Maggie had been taken to a juvenile center. There it was revealed that she had suffered numerous abrasions and multiple fractures, all the results of suspected abuse and most likely the reason for her mother's sudden disappearance.

A county-appointed physician had scrawled across the bottom of the form that her small size was most likely the result of malnutrition but that otherwise she was a healthy female with well-healed scars and fractures.

Another form, this one a court statement, reported that the judge felt it was best to leave her in her natural home. Thus, she was released into her father's custody, and a child protection officer was assigned to her case.

As she lay on her bed in the dark, exhausted and still a little raw inside, Angela reflected on Maggie's childhood. Like so many others, Maggie had been haunted with nightmares in her head; every move she made would have been filled with another unknown terror.

Realizing this made Angela feel worse than ever, and she started to cry once more. At the same moment, she heard India crying from the nursery. Sighing, she struggled to get out of bed.

"Rebecca will get her." Nathan turned his head to look up at her.

"There's something about a baby's cry that makes you want to do everything possible to comfort them." She spoke very softly. "I doubt Maggie's parents did anything to comfort her little cries in the night."

"They were damn assholes." His face was stone-hard when he spoke. "I have no respect for anyone who deliberately hurts a child."

Cautiously, she nodded in agreement. "Alcohol, abuse and neglect breeds alcohol, abuse and neglect. And for the most part, people just accept it, not knowing any other way."

"Why don't I go down and get you something to eat. Maybe a cup of tea?" He smiled at her.

"No, I'm fine." She nodded as she pushed herself back against the bed. "Thanks for sitting with me earlier; it felt good knowing you were there."

"You were pretty upset."

"If my dream was any indication of the life that Maggie endured, she went through life believing she wasn't loved. She never had a mother or a father—at least not the type that her friends had. It's sad to say, but it all fits. She was sentenced to live a life which, by our standards, would never be productive or even normal."

Her face went blank; her voice turned cool. "Perhaps her madness now allows the whole truth to be known."

16

The holiday week was quickly coming to a close. The week between Christmas and New Year's was usually a slow week for Angela; it was routinely when she took time off from the salon and relaxed. But this week between the holidays, it was business as usual. With Rebecca working full-time at the salon, Angela was India's caregiver.

India was sitting in her bouncy chair, already fed and bathed for the day, when Rebecca walked into the kitchen. With some time to spare before leaving for the salon, she poured herself a cup of coffee and sat down at the table to play with her daughter.

"I just don't feel right about you staying home tonight—on New Year's Eve—to sit with India while Robby and I go out to a party."

"Nathan and I actually prefer staying home on New Year's Eve. Besides, India gives us the ideal excuse." Angela straightened and pressed the small of her back. "I'm not interested in any of the invitations we got this time around. You and Robby go out and ring in the New Year. India, Nathan and I will be just fine seeing the new year in together at home."

Before Rebecca left, Angela sat down and listened good-naturedly to all of her anxious, first-time-mother's instructions. After she promised Rebecca that she would call if there was any sort of problem, she was finally able to get Rebecca out and on her way.

Angela waited, watching from the living room window until she saw Rebecca's car drive away. Then, grinning, she turned to where India babbled and cooed in her bouncy chair.

"It's just you and me, kid. Come up here to Grammy."

In the den, Nathan attempted to read the morning paper. However, he found himself amused by overhearing Rebecca's anxiety-filled departure and now Angela's verbal love affair with their granddaughter. She spouted off baby gobbledygook, making the inane noises adults routinely make around babies, and from the sound of India's response, that was making her quite happy and content.

When he heard the music start to play, along with India's giggles and the delight in his wife's laughter, he abandoned his morning paper to join them in the kitchen for the fun—but he happened to arrive just in time to answer the telephone.

He sighed to himself that the interlude was over. Reaching for the coffee pot before answering the telephone, he found it empty.

With the coffee pot in one hand and the telephone in the other, Nathan smiled. "Which one do you want?"

"Ah... Lord, let me think." Angela placed a finger up to her mouth and batted her eyes.

"Angela!"

"Coffee. You answer the phone." Amused, she lifted herself up off the floor. "That'll probably be Rebecca checking up on me; hurry up and answer it or she'll panic."

"Hello," Nathan said.

"Nathan, it's Stephen."

"Hey Stephen. Happy New Year!"

"I'm afraid I have some bad news." Nathan held up a hand to Angela as soon as she playfully jabbed a finger into his chest.

"What's going on? Has someone been hurt?"

"No, we're alright. But there's been an incident at the salon—a break in."

"This is crazy. Who'd want to break in to a beauty salon?" Angela jerked her head up and looked at Nathan. Hanging on his every word, she decided not to make a new pot of coffee after all.

"You and Angela need to come down here as soon as possible," Stephen told him.

"Why weren't we notified when the break in happened? We have a security system; didn't it go off?"

"I'm so very sorry," Stephen said slowly, and then finished, "but it wasn't activated."

Nathan rolled his eyes towards the ceiling. "What the hell is that?"

"It's my fault. I take full responsibility. I forgot to arm the system before I left the salon yesterday afternoon."

"How could you forget—" Nathan began but then interrupted himself, saying, "Okay, never mind that. Now, did you at least call the police?"

"They're already here. Paramedics, too."

"I thought you said no one was hurt?" Nathan's expression went grim.

"The fact is, the woman who broke into the salon... Well, she was lying on the floor when I came in this morning."

"What?" Nathan froze. "Dead on the floor?"

"She's not dead, but based the amount of blood she's lost, I'd say she's in pretty bad shape. The paramedics are working on her right now." Stephen's voice shook. "Nathan, I've never seen so much blood. I need to go; the police need to ask me a few more questions."

"Okay." Nathan stepped back and sat down in a chair. "We'll leave now," he said before hanging up the phone.

Nathan rubbed his hands over his face until he was afraid he'd scrub off a layer of skin. Angela rushed upstairs to inform Robby of what had happened at the salon. She left India in Robby's care, and a moment later, Nathan and she were putting on their coats and rushing out the front door.

After twenty minutes, Nathan and Angela pulled up in front of the salon. Angela jumped out of the car just as the ambulance sped away with its sirens blaring and its lights flashing. Quickly she turned and ran inside.

"Oh, Jesus, Nathan." Her knees felt like butter as she braced herself against the door. At first, all she could see was a cluster of police officers. And then, as she looked behind them, she saw blood—a spray of blood as far as five feet from the broken front window, spread on the wall beneath the window all the way across the floor and onto the carpet.

Without thinking, she shoved one of the officers aside. "What happened?" she asked, too frightened to understand or even absorb it all.

"Mr. and Mrs. Roberts, I'm Officer Logan. We met several months ago when you suspected a woman was stalking you."

"Yes, I remember," Angela said, shakily grinning over the memory.

"Why don't we step out of the way?" Officer Logan gestured to the chairs in the reception area. Angela settled into a chair, her arms folded neatly across her body, but she didn't look peaceful. The pungent, foul stench of blood was everywhere. Soon her eyes locked onto a dried blood smear on the arm of Stephen's salon chair, and she figured the woman must have grabbed onto the chair in a desperate attempt to get out of the salon.

Nathan walked over to the window. "We'll need to call the insurance company and get this window fixed," he said as he brought his hand up to knead at the tension just above his eyebrows.

"Mrs. Roberts, I believe the woman who broke into your salon this morning is the same woman you called in a report about several months ago," Officer Logan explained.

"Maggie!" Angela gasped and then shook her head in disbelief.

“Ma’am, she fits the description you gave us the last time we were here,” Officer Logan said. “Has anything happened since then? You’re calling her by name now; did you figure out who she was?”

“Not really.” Angela looked down at her hands. “I didn’t know her name until recently. Turns out she’s an old friend of my mother’s from years ago.”

“Does this bag look familiar to either of you?” Bending down, the officer picked up an oversized bag that had been lying inside the window. A handful of animal crackers spilled out onto the floor.

Stunned, Angela rubbed her arms, remembering the encounter with Maggie the night India was born. She cast a look in Nathan’s direction, remembering that Maggie had asked for the same type of crackers. However, when Angela and Nathan had returned with them, Maggie was gone.

Angela paused before saying, “I don’t know… Maybe.”

“Does the word ‘message’ mean anything to you?”

She had to take a steadying breath before she repeated, “Message?”

“One of the paramedics commented that she kept asking for her ‘message’ while they were putting her into the ambulance.”

Angela nodded, afraid to swallow. “If she is the woman I think she is, she believes I have some sort of message for her.”

Officer Logan gave Angela a puzzled look. “Huh. That’s a new one.” His head stopped moving, and his eyes focused on the report in his hands. “Probably just some kind of game she made up in her head. I’ve been dealing with these homeless people for years; you wouldn’t *believe* what comes out of their mouths sometimes.”

Angela frowned and thought about his comment for a moment.

“From the trail of blood from the window to where we found her, along with the injury to her groin area, it’s safe to say that as she crawled through the window, a piece of glass sliced into her femoral artery.”

Shaking her head, Angela responded, “How terrible. Will she be alright?”

Officer Logan shrugged. “Ma’am, I really don’t know. A person usually bleeds out in a matter of minutes once the artery is hit. It’s almost surprising she’s still alive.”

Almost immediately, Angela leapt to her feet. “If we’re finished, I’d like to go to the hospital and check on her.”

“There’s nothing more we can do here. If I need anything further, I’ll give you a call.”

"That won't be necessary." Angela looked up, totally focused. "Officer Logan, I won't be pressing any charges."

"Mrs. Roberts, this may have been her second attempt at getting close to you," Officer Logan said with a worried look. "This isn't something to take lightly."

As far as she was concerned, there was nothing to consider. Officer Logan hadn't said anything that would change her mind, and she wasn't frightened of Maggie anymore. She thought of the little girl she had seen in her dream and of the mother who was so angry and cruel. Now more than ever Angela had an idea of how hard life had been for Maggie, and it broke her heart. She didn't care what Officer Logan thought or had to say about her decision; she needed to help Maggie, and *that* she was sure of.

"I won't be pressing any charges," Angela said again, then signed her name on the bottom of the police report. As she handed Officer Logan the report, it suddenly occurred to her to ask, "Since I'm going to the hospital, may I have her bag? I'll make sure it's returned to her."

Officer Logan hesitated at first but finally handed it over. "You've been very kind to her," he said, trying to look more comfortable than he felt.

"Oh, wow." The weight of Maggie's bag tugged her arm downward. "What does she have in here?" she quietly asked herself.

"Alright, let's head to the hospital," Nathan said, taking the bag off her hands and carrying it himself.

"Ma'am, if you change your mind, give me a call." Officer Logan handed Angela his business card and thanked the couple for their time.

She smiled back at him. "Thank you."

Angela and Nathan drove to the hospital as fast as they could without running any lights or hitting any pedestrians. Nathan pulled into the first vacant parking space, slammed the car into park, and then they both ran through the emergency room doors and up to the front desk. The nurse told them to take a seat in the waiting room; someone would be in shortly to talk with them. She smiled and walked away before Angela or Nathan could agree or object.

They had been waiting for at least half an hour when finally a nurse came in and stood in front of them.

"I understand you're asking about the woman who was brought in earlier with the leg injury."

"Yes." Angela jumped up from her chair. "Yes, may I see her?"

"Are you related to the patient?" She tipped down her glasses, peering at Angela over the rims.

"Related?" Angela looked at her blankly, as though she were speaking in a foreign language.

"Yes. The HIPAA Privacy Rule protects patients' medical records and other personal health information. You must be a relative or a court-appointed guardian to obtain any information about the patient."

Angela didn't even know what to answer. Who could she call to get permission? And as she tried to make sense of it, Jason Bennett, Kenny's doctor, approached them.

"Angela, Nathan, it's nice to see you. What brings you to the hospital?"

"Jason." Angela looked at him, reassured, as he and the nurse exchanged a glance.

Pausing, Angela looked over at the nurse, her mind racing for ideas. "We're here to check on a family friend."

"Nothing serious, I hope."

"That's why we're here—to find out how she is."

"What's the patient's name?" He reached over the counter to look at the file of new patient charts.

"She was probably admitted under Jane Doe," Nathan said. "Just brought in a little while ago with an injury to her leg."

Angela noticed a change in Dr. Bennett's expression. He looked up from the charts. "Jane Doe? Thought you said she was a friend of the family."

"Yes, we did," Angela said and then mentioned briefly what had transpired that morning at her salon. She went on to explain that the woman was a friend of her mother's and was now suspected of being homeless; she hadn't wanted to make a big deal about it and was only concerned with the woman's condition.

Dr. Bennett didn't say a word; he just listened. He could see the concern on Angela's face and reached over to continue searching through the file of new patients.

"Okay, here's a chart for a Jane Doe." Dr. Bennett quickly scanned the progress notes. "Not much as far as patient information, but physical observation by the physician states the patient sustained a large, deep wound hitting the femoral artery. Status of nerve and vein not known. The patient was brought in by ambulance and immediately admitted to the level one trauma unit and then taken to the operating room. She's still in surgery."

"Thank you, Jason," Angela said quietly.

"Looks like she lost a significant amount of blood; they started a transfusion immediately. More than likely, she will need another transfusion during surgery."

"I could donate blood," Angela said without taking her eyes off Nathan. "My blood type is universal, type O."

"There isn't a blood type listed for her, but your universal O would definitely help your friend."

Just then, Dr. Bennett's pager went off. "I'm needed in the emergency room." He quickly gave Angela directions to the lab, said his good-byes, and then hurried away to call a neurosurgeon he wanted to be available if needed. Once he was gone, a nurse came to ask Angela if she wanted a cup of coffee.

"No, thanks. I'm fine," she said softly, but it was obvious that she wasn't.

An hour later, Angela returned from donating blood and nothing had changed. Nathan and she were just about to get something to eat from the hospital cafeteria when a nurse came into the waiting room. "Mrs. Roberts, your friend has been taken to the ICU. Her condition is critical but stable."

Angela nodded as she listened.

"The doctor is going to give her some time to regain consciousness on her own and then reassess the situation."

"May we sit with her?" Angela asked.

"Come on, I'll take you to her room." Once there, the nurse told her where she could sit, and Angela pulled up a chair next to Maggie's bed.

Angela's stomach tightened and she thought she might have to throw up. In the fading light, Maggie was laying motionless and deathly pale. She had dark circles under her eyes, and her split and swollen lips were parted to reveal the gaps where some of her teeth had fallen out. An oxygen monitor rested on one of her fingers, and another monitor kept track of her heart rate and brain waves. An IV stuck in her arm, administering more blood and medications, and a thick, blood-stained bandage was wrapped tightly around her thigh. Angela just watched, numbed. Maggie stirred in her sleep but didn't wake up.

Angela sighed, leaned against Nathan, who was sitting beside her, and thought for a moment. She sighed again, knowing that her grandmother, Mama Iana, would be beside herself if she had known the fate to which her precious Maggie's mother and father had condemned the sweet little girl. She had no life, no hope, no dreams. She was beaten, abused and detested by parents who she was forced to live with for the majority of her childhood.

Angela fell against Nathan heavily now, pressing her face into his chest. "Please just hold me; I don't want to think."

With a melancholy smile, Nathan pulled her to him, and they sat together in the dim light, waiting for relief and for the strength for what lie ahead.

Hours later, "Happy New Year," wafted into Angela's ears as Nathan leaned over and kissed her on the cheek, waking her from her rather lengthy nap.

"I'd forgotten it was New Year's Eve," she said as she glanced at her watch. "Robby and Rebecca were to go out tonight."

"I spoke to Robby while you were donating blood earlier. They're fine." He gave her a light squeeze around the shoulders. "They said that we should stay with Maggie as long as we need to, and by the end of the phone call, they were planning on popping the cork on a bottle of champagne at midnight." He grinned at his wife, trying to give her a bit of encouragement. "I'm glad you got to rest, but it's ten o'clock already, believe it or not, and I thought you might want me to wake you up."

"Wow, already?" Angela asked, disoriented. Then her eyes settled back on Maggie as she rubbed the soreness out of the back of her neck. "Thank you, Honey," she said, leaning against Nathan again.

Shortly after midnight, the doctor came into Maggie's room. He and Angela both agreed that Maggie's color looked a little better, though even as they spoke, Angela felt a bit self-conscious, wondering if he'd come to the room earlier to check up on Maggie while she'd been resting against Nathan, fast asleep.

"Are you doing alright?" the doctor asked, and Angela nodded.

"Mrs. Roberts, if this is too much for you, go home and get some rest. I'll call you if anything changes."

"I'm not going anywhere," she said firmly.

"She's not out of the woods yet," he said cautiously. "Do you know if she has family? Is there anyone who needs to be called?"

"As far as I know, there's no one to call," Angela said, shaking her head. "Can she hear me if I talk to her?"

"It's unlikely," he said, looking at her with a frown. Then he walked out of the room.

Angela looked intently at Maggie, and although she would have died before she told anyone, she was beginning to feel the room spin slowly around her. It was all too much for her—too terrifying— especially since Manny's death was still so fresh in her heart and mind. She put her head down on the bed, felt a little better and then sat up and began talking quietly to Maggie. And as though Maggie could hear her speaking, she moved ever-so-slowly, trying to turn her head towards Angela, her eyes still closed. Angela started speaking in a firmer voice, pleading with her to open her eyes, to say something, to blink or to squeeze her hand—anything. But there was no sign from Maggie until at last she let out a soft moan.

"Death is here," Maggie whispered.

"Maggie, do you know where you are?" Angela asked.

"In a room... In a house." She sucked in air painfully.

"Nathan, get a nurse. I don't think she can breathe," she said then turned back to her mother's friend.

"Maggie, let me help you." Her voice showed her concern.

There was no response, only a terrified look and straining sounds of desperate breathing.

"She's holding me down," Maggie said as her breathing intensified and became more labored.

"Who's holding you down?" Angela's voice softened. "Maggie, no one can hurt you anymore."

"I would rather die than live like this." She leaned forward.

"That happened a long time ago. You're not in danger anymore." Angela smiled at her warmly and said in a soothing voice, "You're safe now."

She turned her head towards Angela and opened her eyes to focus them on hers for a second. Then she started to close her eyes again.

"Maggie, can you stay with me? Try and stay with me."

Her eyes opened again slightly, their lids heavy. She whispered, "My bag. It's in my bag."

A nurse came running in as soon as Nathan had begun walking down to find her, since the alarm sounded on Maggie's breathing monitor. She checked Maggie's vital signs, looked at the monitors, and ran to get the doctor.

And just as the doctor came in, Maggie sank back into a deep sleep.

"I'm afraid she is moving closer towards death," he informed Angela and Nathan.

Angela turned towards the doctor. "She couldn't breathe."

"As death approaches, breathing becomes more irregular and often slower. 'Cheyne-Stokes' respiration, or rapid breaths followed by periods of no breathing at all, may occur. Congestion in the airway can increase, causing loud, rattled breathing."

"So, how long do you think Maggie has?" Angela asked, her eyes focused on Maggie.

"I've been with many patients in the dying process, which has taught me that death is a personal journey that each individual approaches in his or her own unique way. Nothing is concrete or set in stone. It could take as long as a few days or as short as an hour."

Angela waited a few moments and then smiled. "I like thinking she's on a journey."

"There are many paths one can take on this journey, but all lead to the same destination: the physical departure from this world."

Angela was quiet.

"I'll be here 'til morning. Have the nurse page me if you notice any changes."

Later that night, Angela got up to pour herself a glass of water. Noticing Nathan had fallen asleep in the recliner over in the corner of the room, she walked over, covered him with a blanket and kissed him on the forehead. Seeing Maggie's bag propped up against the bottom of his chair, she bent over and picked it up.

It took her another ten minutes to muster the courage to peek inside of Maggie's personal belongings. Nonchalantly glancing around the room, she then tentatively placed a hand inside the bag and slowly pulled out a black, leather Bible—the one Maggie had been holding the day she stood outside the salon, looking in. Setting the bag down on the floor, Angela laid the Bible on her lap and opened it. Inside the front cover was an inscription: *"To our darling daughter, Iana."*

Angela gasped, "Oh my God," and fought back a tear. "I can't believe I am seeing this," she whispered. Then she drew in a deep breath and blew it out slowly.

Suddenly the air in the room turned crisp and freezing; there was no mistaking it. She turned to Maggie, who could feel it too, as she stared at Angela with wild, frightened eyes.

She looked at Angela for a long time before she finally she spoke. "I wish Mama Iana was my mommy too."

Angela looked at her, astonished. Her mind couldn't cope; she graphically relived the scene from her dream, the abuse that obviously occurred in Maggie's life.

Tears welled up in Angela's eyes and trailed down her cheeks. "Yes," she spoke softly. "But you were friends with Mama Iana."

Maggie's head turned slowly.

"And ya know, friends are better than parents," Angela said and then paused. "Because it means they love you because they want to, not because they have to. We *choose* our friends, but we don't choose our parents."

"I-I'm... a... g-good girl," she stuttered. Her eyes then fixed on the Bible in Angela's hands. "You'll give me my message now, won't you?" There was a dead look in her eyes when she spoke.

Angela said gently, "Maggie, you need to rest for now."

Maggie's breathing slowed, and Angela sensed that she had entered a more relaxed, trance-like state.

Angela resolved to remain at Maggie's bed until things improved or until she reached her journey's final destination.

"Dying comes before death," she thought and continued to gently stroke Maggie's hair while watching her breathe.

Unexpectedly, a wave of light-headedness came over her, and she remembered that she hadn't eaten since that morning. But she had no intention of leaving. More to the point, she couldn't have eaten anything if she'd tried.

Angela leaned forward to assure herself that Maggie was still breathing. Smiling, she reached down to lightly touch Maggie on the arm, and with that, she felt herself begin to peacefully disappear into her mind. Her calm state evaporated as vague images of others—no faces, just outlines and shadows—began to take shape before her eyes. Angela shook her head to clear it and looked up to see a man staring at her with his mouth open, his head slowly shaking back and forth.

Angela sank down heavily in her chair, nervously clutching the Bible in one hand and Maggie's arm in the other.

Although the words didn't come, Angela somehow was able to connect with the man's heart. This man radiated undeniable feelings of love, affection, tenderness and devotion—but for whom, she wondered. Then the sound of a little voice cut through her mind. Angela's eyes followed the frail, tiny voice to a child sitting on the floor, sobbing silently into a yellow blanket.

"Oh my God," Angela whispered. "Is it possible that this man is Maggie's father?"

Angela's eyes traveled back to the figure of the man as his shoulders began to shake, and he closed in on himself, crying a desperate, wounded cry as regret and sorrow spilled out of his heart. As if she could read his mind, Angela recognized this as his confession of emotional attachments to his own self-seeking pleasures that were holding him in bondage, preventing him from expressing the love he held in his heart for Maggie.

Angela combed her fingers nervously through her hair. As the mist faded away, a message came. He simply said, in a low, penetrating voice, "Tell my little girl that I'm sorry. Tell her that I love her and that I will always love her."

An icy wind blew through Angela's mind as she watched him disappear in a swirl. She was barely aware of what was happening; her body felt tight and she heard screams... Frightening, blood-curdling screams.

For a few seconds, she sat frozen with her hand still on Maggie's arm, and then she moved to sit on the edge of the bed. Snapping out of her thoughts, she tilted her head towards Maggie and smiled. "It's come, Maggie. Your message has come."

It was another hour before Maggie made another sound. Her doctor returned to check her vital signs, and Angela briefly explained Maggie's short periods of lucidity throughout the night.

"Mrs. Roberts." He stopped in front of her. "Medically, her behavior is referred to as 'the surge.'"

"Meaning?" Angela asked.

"This is the dying person's final physical expression before moving on. A surge of energy—or the last hurrah—is usually short-lived. Death most likely will occur within the hour."

She took a deep breath, said, "Maggie," and waited. "Maggie, I want you to come back."

And then, with a shudder, Maggie opened her eyes.

Without taking her eyes off Angela, she whispered, "Someone's calling my name. I like his voice."

Maggie and Angela sat quietly for a few moments, holding hands. Maggie gently pulled her hand away and touched Angela's cheek. "I'm so tired."

Angela began softly, "It's okay to go."

Maggie rigidly fixed her eyes on Angela. "Message?" She managed a tiny smile.

"It's from your father." Angela choked back her tears. "Maggie, he loves you, and he always has."

"My daddy loves me," she said in a whisper.

"He does, Maggie," Angela whispered as tears rolled down her cheeks. Maggie made no more sounds, and in a little while her eyes rolled back in her head and she was gone. For the first time in her life, Maggie was at peace.

"You're free now," Angela said gently.

She wanted to tell someone that Maggie had passed, to wake Nathan or call for a nurse, but she couldn't do it. Besides, the alarms from Maggie's monitors would soon alert the staff that Maggie had reached her final destination. So instead she sat down, looking at Maggie and thinking of everything she had seen and heard of her life. Angela was deeply moved; tears welled up in her eyes again as she mourned the life not only of the woman in front of her but also of the small girl she had been, who had given everything a child has to give and had gotten nothing in return.

As she continued to think about Maggie's life, Angela glanced up, almost without thinking. She saw a thin gray mist crawl across the ceiling tiles, and then it was gone. She was no longer sure if what she saw was real or a product of her exhausted imagination.

Settled again, she took one last glance at the ceiling and gasped. She instantly straightened herself in the chair, her eyes wide. Then, through the mist, a swirling apparition spiraled down through a bright and winding tunnel into the softly lit room where Maggie lay. Now, instead of on a hospital bed, she lay on a huge white bed with fluffy, violet-colored pillows. The figure of a man appeared alongside Maggie, and Angela jumped when she saw him. She was in no way prepared for it, however spectacular she thought him to be. He was like a sunset she wanted to watch; his movements were unspeakably beautiful, and she imagined the sound of his voice would be like listening to Mozart. Immediately she realized that he was the most graceful and powerful man she'd ever seen, and at the same time, he was very silent. Angela sat in sheer amazement as his finger reached out and tapped Maggie gently on the shoulder, first once, then twice. "Maggie." Her eyes opened slowly, responding to the tap and the feathery voice.

Angela tried to focus, to see who this captivating man was, but she couldn't.

Maggie had never looked more beautiful, more luminous, Angela thought. And then, with a tired smile, she shook her head. After that, Maggie's body began to lift up from the bed, momentarily hovering midair and then slowly drifting down to the floor, coming to a standing position alongside the unidentified man. With their backs turned away from Angela, the two stood silently for a moment, and although she couldn't see their faces, Angela could feel the warmth, the relief, the happiness—moreover, the tremendous love—they shared with one another. Eventually the pair made their way towards a brilliant white light that was glowing in the corner of the room. Hand-in-hand, Maggie trembling a little bit, and with not a word spoken, they walked towards the light.

Suddenly the man stopped dead in his tracks. And at last, his face turned sideways in front of Angela's. Gasping for air several times, she covered her mouth with her hands and began weeping, her shoulders shaking violently from the myriad of emotions coursing through her body. After a few minutes, her sobbing died down, her chest stopped heaving, and her breathing became more regular. She lifted her head, sniffling, her hair matted against her tear-stained face.

Then their gaze met and he spoke. "I've got this, Mom. I love you!"

"I love you too, son," she whispered, as tears fell from her eyes.

As the monitors started sounding one by one, Angela sat in her own peaceful silence. It all seemed impossible to believe. But in that moment, Angela realized that seeing Kenny again was an amazing gift—and one that her grandmother, Iana Hamilton, had given her.

17

The first Monday morning of the New Year had arrived, and that usually brought about Angela giving a sermon to herself about being sentimental over the previous year. A sense of loss for the time she could never recapture, bits and pieces of remorse and disappointment, regret for unspoken words or acts of kindness... These things usually generated a sorrowful frame of mind for Angela.

Nevertheless, at the stroke of midnight, *old things would pass away and all things would become new.* That was just the way it was. There was no point musing about it or regretting what hadn't taken place. And eventually, with time, Angela would set off on a new journey with thoughts and imaginings above and beyond anything she could fathom—so much so that it would allow her to forget the past and to believe that she was someone different now, rather than the person she was a year ago.

There were no more mysteries in her life, no hidden stories, and no triumphs like hers. She couldn't imagine never speaking of her grandmother, Iana Hamilton, again, or refusing to follow in her footsteps.

She smiled to herself as her heart overflowed with resolve and determination for this new chapter in her life. Above all, Angela's intention was to live her life with purpose; she had been blessed to be a blessing, and she would honor her grandmother's life and gifts with dignity and respect.

As she sipped her morning coffee, Angela noticed her grandmother's Bible had been moved from the box in the garage to a shelf on the bookcase alongside the fireplace. Nathan or Robby must have put it there, she decided, and she got up from her chair and took it from the shelf.

Curling up on the couch, she opened the Bible and turned a page, then another and another. "Look at all these drawings my grandmother must have put in this Bible," she muttered to no one in particular.

As she thought of Iana Hamilton, her heart longed to have known more about her, to have actually seen her, to have spent time listening to the stories she told.

At that moment, another life of Iana Hamilton manifested in her mind—one that was incredibly different and filled with a multitude of unanswered questions. Thinking about the horrors she had survived as a child, and then the woman she had become in spite of them, Angela considered herself blessed and honored to be her granddaughter.

Iana may have had taken her secrets to the grave with her, but Angela sensed with her entire being that there was much more to be told of her life and times, all of which were now a part of the tapestry of Angela's life.

Towards the back of the Bible, Angela came across a section that revealed the first of several pages adorned with a seal. At first glance Angela suspected the seal to be some sort of wax. Being a "pendant style" seal, it was applied to a narrow piece of cord and hung loose after being threaded through a hole halfway down the page. Along with it were hand-written instructions not to turn the page until a particular date had passed.

"That's odd… It's today's date," Angela whispered. Her entire body began to tremble as she sat contemplating her next move. Checking the date again, and then examining the seal once more, Angela found it hard to believe there would be dire consequences should the page be turned before the appointed time. But then again, weirder things than that had happened to her over the course of the past year. Angela sat in silence for a few minutes and then gave it everything she had, everything she could, everything she dared. As she turned the page, before she even broke the seal, an envelope fell out, and it floated to the floor.

Angela bent to pick it up. Inside the envelope was a beautifully designed card with a penny taped to the inside. She opened the card and began to read.

Sometimes our greatest gifts in life
arrive in the smallest of packages.

All my Love, Daddy.

"Angela…"

She quickly wiped her eyes and then glanced over her shoulder.

Nathan came closer. "What's wrong?" he asked, concern covering his face.

"Maggie's father gave her this card. There's a penny inside."

Nathan took the penny from Angela and studied it for a moment. "Huh... 1943. I wonder if this is a real wheat penny," Nathan replied.

"Wheat penny?" Angela looked up at Nathan. "I've never heard of such a thing."

"If it's authentic, it's an extremely rare find."

Casting that notion aside for a moment, Angela gave the card to Nathan, explaining, "Maggie must have slipped the card from her father inside the Bible years ago, and it's remained there for all of these years."

After he had finished reading the card, Nathan walked over to his desk and took a magnet out of the drawer.

"Nathan, what are you doing?"

"My father collected coins. I remember him telling me that the easiest way to tell if a coin is genuine or copper is to test it with a magnet. If the magnet sticks, it's made of steel and worth almost nothing."

They sat quietly side by side while Nathan did his experiment.

"Doesn't stick!" He opened his eyes wide as he said it and then did a search on the computer for a "1943 Wheat Penny".

"Here," Nathan said as he adjusted his glasses and began reading. "If your 1943 copper-colored penny doesn't stick to a magnet, then look at the date carefully." He turned to Angela. "I need a magnifying glass."

"Bottom drawer," Angela quickly replied. Nathan looked over the rim of his glasses at her with a perplexed expression on his face.

"What? I used it the other day to take out a splinter."

Shaking his head with a grin, he reached into the bottom drawer of his desk.

"Okay." Nathan continued to read, "If the tail of the number three doesn't extend well below the line of numbers, it is probably a cut-in-half number eight. A very common fraud involving the copper 1943 penny is to cut away part of the eight in the date of a 1948 penny. If the three in the date looks like half of an eight, your coin is not a genuine 1943 copper penny."

Nathan held the penny under the magnifying glass, examining the coin for any distinguishing traces that would prove the penny to be a fake.

"Wow, Angela!" Nathan looked shocked, and Angela looked up in surprise. "Given what I just read, we may have stumbled upon the real thing."

"Are you sure?"

"I'd say the tail on the number three definitely extends below the line of numbers," he said as he handed Angela the penny and magnifying glass. "Take a look for yourself."

She could hardly believe her eyes. "All right." She sighed deeply and turned to face Nathan. "Now what?"

"First thing in the morning, I'm going to go to a qualified coin dealer for a professional opinion. We'll take things from there."

Later that night, Angela and Nathan went to their favorite Chinese restaurant in the city. He told her about his plans to visit a coin dealer the following day, and then they lightheartedly talked about spending their financial windfall.

The New Year not only brought about a new outlook on life for Angela; after twenty-five years as a practicing attorney, Nathan decided to step back from that demanding career and work only as a consultant on high profile cases. During dinner they talked about the possibility of Angela joining him for a few days in New Jersey while he worked on a case.

Her family was in order; everyone was busily enjoying their lives and doting over Nathan and Angela's first granddaughter, India. Everything was clicking back into gear. Her son was back, enrolled for the spring semester at NYU, living at home and happy to have a break before starting classes. In addition to Rebecca's full-time receptionist position at the salon, she had started taking a few classes at night and was pursuing a career in Cosmetology. Angela knew that there would be some bumps along the way, but she would negotiate them one by one.

"You look happy." Nathan took her hand across the table and held it tight.

"I'm so glad we decided to have our date night."

"Yeah. We needed this," he told her. "I was worried about you; it was a rough year."

She just smiled. "Sometimes when awful things happen, you don't realize it yet, but those trials and tribulations are actually making space for bigger and better things to come into your life."

"Maybe even bigger and better than you know," he said as he offered her a fortune cookie.

She shifted and aimed a fleeting look at him, then cracked open the cookie.

Her mouth twitched into something between a scowl and a smile. Her fortune said she was honorable and patient and had wisdom beyond her years. "Hmmm… Close enough," she said, showing her paper to Nathan.

He told her that his said that he was about to make an excellent deal.

"You never know, Nathan. You have to believe. Answered prayers... You have to believe."

"What I *can't* believe is how much I ate," he said and then promptly had two more bites. He could never resist a plate of chicken fried rice.

"Do you feel like a walk?" she asked, looking up at him. She loved walking in the snow.

"Yeah, it would do me good." He grinned and then patted his stomach.

They walked up Fifth Avenue and along the outer edge of Central Park. Their hair was covered with snow by then, and their faces were red from the cold. It was one of those snows that really stuck and seemed to quiet everything. Angela thought it felt magical walking along with her gloved hand tucked into his arm.

"It's been years since we did this. I miss it," Angela said sadly.

They took a detour through the park and stopped by the edge of a frozen pond. The ice atop the water looked like a pane of mirrored glass tucked into a mound of cotton candy. Light from the streetlamps reflected and doubled in brightness. It really was magical, Angela thought. For as long as she could remember, ice-skating on a pond like this one had been a part of her family's holiday traditions. Here, at this very spot, Angela had taught Kenny to skate, and now she longed for those days when her boys were little again.

"You're looking very serious," Nathan whispered, snuggling closer to her.

It was getting cold and the wind had come up. "Are you okay?" he asked as he nodded and smiled in encouragement.

"I'm fine," she said, smiling back, and then reached into her purse to take out the card from Maggie's father.

"Angela," Nathan said, trying to remain calm. "Why did you bring that with you?"

"I-I don't know," she said quietly. "I guess I didn't want it to get lost."

She was strangely quiet, and Nathan noticed it.

Angela opened the card and held the penny in her hand. "Looks like a regular old penny to me." She took out a tissue from her purse to try and wipe off the snow. Nothing in her behavior even remotely suggested the undercurrents she felt.

Instantly an image flashed into her mind: Maggie's father lying on the floor, his fist clenching and unclenching as a shiny round object lay in the palm of his hand.

"Oh my God." Her face went pale, and she quickly handed the penny to Nathan.

"What's wrong?" he asked as he watched her.

Before she even said the words, Nathan suspected them, and he tightened his grip on her hand.

"You've seen this before, haven't you?" He didn't know how or why he knew, but he did.

Angela took a breath. "Huh… What?" she asked with a small sigh as snowflakes settled on her eyelashes and stuck to her hair.

"Honey, talk to me."

After a pause, she began by saying, "On that fateful day, the day Maggie's father died…" She looked up at him, fear apparent in her expression. "I'll never forget it. In my vision he spoke to me, told me to focus on what was in front of me." She tried to smile but failed. "Nathan, it was this penny."

Nathan felt helpless, and he couldn't take the memory away from her now. All he could do was be there for her, and as always, he was.

Angela wasn't even aware of the tears rolling down her cheeks. "I'm sure of it now."

The following morning, Nathan drove to a part of the city he hadn't visited in years, to a little shop that held a plethora of memories from his past.

Staring at the sign, which read "Historic Deerfield Antique and Coin Shop," he remembered his childhood fascination with the familiar sight. Mr. Deerfield, the owner, had been an American history professor at Harvard, and trips to his shop had been a special gift from father to son on many Saturday afternoons. The tales that Mr. Deerfield told were also gifts in themselves. Nathan had loved hearing the wonderful accounts connected with each of the historical coins and pieces of furniture on display in his shop. It made him suddenly think about his father and his own incredible knowledge of old coins as well.

He smiled to himself, rather overjoyed that he'd stumbled upon the shop's name while looking for coin dealers in the New York City area online. He hadn't thought of the shop for years, and a rush of nostalgia coursed through him as he mentally prepared to go inside.

The Historic Deerfield Antique and Coin Shop was a beautifully built old building, dating back to the early 1800s, and Nathan could see from the window that the front room was filled with lovely antiques and paintings. As he made his way to the front door, he was certain he was exactly where he needed to be. He placed a hand on the polished brass door handle and pushed the door open. Stepping inside, he smiled at hearing the jingle of a bell overhead as he closed the door.

It was a small, quaint little shop and even more charming than he had remembered. There was a fire burning in the fireplace, and a beautiful antique spinet piano sat in the corner, dating back to the beginning of the 1900s, he approximated. The lights were on, but there were no sounds, and a few minutes later Nathan began to wonder if anyone was there.

He had just about given up and had started to turn to walk to the front door when a small, white-haired man, neatly dressed in a gray suit and tie, stepped through the burgundy-draped doorway. He looked at Nathan as if wondering why he had come.

"How may I help you?" he asked.

"Ah yes, I saw the sign... Are you closing?"

"Nope." He smiled at Nathan. "Always open, except Sunday. That's the Lord's day."

Nathan smiled at him and was startled at how alive his eyes were. They almost sparkled, so full of energy and life even though Nathan could tell that the man was well into his eighties.

"Mr. Deerfield?" Nathan asked, extending his hand politely.

"I am. And you are?" He looked at Nathan like an elementary school teacher expecting an answer from his student.

"Nathan Roberts, sir," he said as he shook his hand. "When I was very young, my father, Jason Roberts, brought me to visit with you and this shop on Saturday afternoons. After my father died, I never came back to this part of town."

"Jason Roberts," he said with a smile. "And you're little Nate Roberts?"

"Yes sir, I am," Nathan replied.

Mr. Deerfield smiled at Nathan, and there was something unspoken in his eyes. Nathan couldn't help speculating whether if it was grief at the loss of an old friend or merely a memory.

"I'm sorry, I don't have an appointment."

"Don't apologize, Nathan. What can I do for you?"

Nathan took out a tissue from his pocket, placed it on the glass countertop and opened it to reveal the penny.

"My wife recently came across this coin tucked away in a family Bible, and I was wondering if you might take a look at it." Nathan picked up the penny and handed it to Mr. Deerfield. "I think it may be a 1943 wheat penny. It passed the magnet test—didn't stick—so it's definitely not plated."

Mr. Deerfield looked at the coin for a long time. "You've done your research well." He then lifted his jeweler's loupe to his right eye. "Let's take a look."

Nathan felt a lump grow in his throat as he listened to Mr. Deerfield. It seemed as though there was sentimentality wrapped into his being, and Nathan was just a lucky spectator.

"There were just a few of these 1943 copper pennies ever minted, and all would have been released into circulation by error. Coin analysts suggest that copper plates may have been tested or left mixed among the other steel plated coins from 1942, hence the error." Mr. Deerfield hesitated. "Even in poor condition—meaning that the coin has accumulated a lot of wear and tear through the years—its estimated value is somewhere around sixty thousand dollars."

Nathan staggered. "*Sixty thousand*?" he asked. Laughing, he walked over to the front door and then turned back around.

Mr. Deerfield grinned and then added a bit of fanfare to his professional opinion. "Perfect condition, I'd ballpark the dollar amount at eighty thousand or more."

"No way!" Shock raced into Nathan's eyes first, then he began to feel uneasy about walking around with a coin that could be worth so much money in his pocket.

Nathan stared across the counter, his heart pounding. He leaned forward, picked up the coin and said, "I never would have thought this little coin could be worth so much."

Mr. Deerfield smiled and nodded.

"Just what does one do with a coin of this value?" Nathan asked.

"What happens now is you get the coin certified," Mr. Deerfield replied. "There are several steps to the process; let me look through some books that I have."

He turned swiftly then disappeared behind the curtain that covered the doorway. A few minutes later, he returned with several books in his hands.

He leafed through some of the books with Nathan and then told him, "The Professional Coin Grading Service provides coin certification for a wide variety of coins. There's an office in New York, not far from here."

Nathan took a moment to steady himself. "Then I think I need to pay a visit to the Professional Coin Grading people."

"I'd say you do!" Mr. Deerfield said, smiling at him.

Nathan thanked him, shook his hand once more and promised to return for a visit soon. Clutching the penny tightly in his hand, he got into his car and entered the address for the PCGS into his GPS. Then he headed towards his destination.

By the close of business that day, Nathan held in his hand an authentic and quite valuable 1943 copper wheat penny. The coin was professionally certified, protected and sonically-sealed in a capsule for storage. Enclosed in the capsule was a certification label, allowing investors to have easy access to all the pertinent facts such as the county of origin, the year and mint mark, and, most importantly, the face value of the coin at hand.

Nathan pulled into his driveway just after six o'clock. Exhausted and exhilarated, he stepped into the house, a dozen red roses in one hand and a bottle of champagne in the other.

Angela was relaxing on the couch and reading when Nathan came into the room. She grinned when she tipped her head up to look at him. "Hmm, champagne and roses?" Closing the magazine she had in her hands, she sat up on the couch. "It's either a guilty conscience or you're in the mood to celebrate."

Grinning like a boy, Nathan walked over to her and leaned down to kiss her on her cheek.

"I kicked ass today!" With a laugh, he gave her thigh a quick slap.

"Oh yeah?"

"Oooh yeah." Beaming, he turned and walked over to the china cabinet for two flutes. Then he released the champagne's cork, which gave out a quick pop in celebration. He poured the bubbly liquid and handed Angela a glass.

"Thank you," she said, smiling at him. "So everything went well this afternoon, I take it?"

"I have some news for you," he confessed. "It still feels so weird."

"Well it's not my birthday or our anniversary," she said with a smirk. "Roses and champagne in the middle of the week? You *must* have some sort of good news."

Nathan took a slow breath. "Remember my fortune cookie?"

"Not really. Something about a good deal?" she replied with a slight touch of frustration in her voice.

"Excellent deal—it said I was going to make an *excellent* deal," he said and then poured another glass of champagne.

"Nathan, are you going to tell me, or must I beat it out of you?" She gave him a bland look over the rim of her glass then picked up a pillow and whacked him on his arm, nearly tipping over his glass of bubbly.

It didn't take Nathan long to start telling Angela the whole story. And when he sat down in his favorite recliner, he began describing the meeting he'd had with Mr. Deerfield and the appointment at the Professional Coin Grading Service. Angela felt the excitement like a buzz in the air. Nathan slowly reached into his shirt pocket, pulled out the certificate and handed it to her.

She opened her mouth and closed it again, then took a deep breath to calm herself.

"Are you sure?" Angela asked him in disbelief. "It can't be that much." Angela studied the coin and just beamed. "Eighty-five thousand dollars?"

"I'm not kidding."

"My heart's beating a mile a minute." Angela shifted on the couch and rubbed her shoulders.

Suddenly, she was redoing everything; a new roof, new walls, and the French windows in the kitchen were being enlarged. She'd make a brand new master bedroom for Nathan and herself, and she'd transform India's nursery to look like it came straight out of a fairy tale. She'd even set up a college fund for her.

"You sure aren't wasting any time spending the money, are you?" Nathan asked, half-jokingly, after hearing Angela list thing after thing she wanted to do with it.

"Nathan, a year ago I never would have thought that I'd be sitting here today with blessings chasing us down the street."

Everything seemed to be happening to them at the speed of sound, and she told Nathan he shouldn't wait too long before setting out to locate an investor.

"There's a Porsche out there with my name on it!"

Nathan laughed and promised he would do his best. And as he gently stroked her arm, he reminded Angela that there were no guarantees with all of this.

Angela told him to do whatever he wanted to do to handle it; she trusted him completely. It was pure kismet that they had found the coin in the first place, and she believed that everything would work out as it should.

"So, what's for dinner?" Nathan asked casually.

Over scrambled eggs and toast, and for the rest of the evening, they laughed and daydreamed about what they would do with this slice of good fortune that seemed to have fallen out of the sky and onto their laps. But as they spoke, Nathan began to notice a slight hint of sadness in Angela's eyes.

"Is something wrong?" He could read nothing from her expression as she offered him a cup of coffee.

"I can't stop thinking that if Maggie would have checked into the penny from her father, her life might have been entirely different."

Nathan was in no way prepared for Angela's abrupt change in behavior. "Honey, she was young and naïve," Nathan said as he looked at her strangely. "She never had anyone to advise her; she had scars from her childhood. And from what we know about her, she lived more or less as a recluse."

"I suppose," Angela answered, looking increasingly disturbed.

There was a long silence in the room as the two looked at each other.

"I'm really sorry about what happened to Maggie." Nathan gazed at Angela sadly. "But she is finally at peace—and after learning her father loved her, all thanks to you."

Angela smiled at that thought.

Looking exhausted, Nathan stood up and said, "That may mean nothing to you right now, but perhaps one day it will." He leaned forward, kissed her lips and said goodnight.

Angela waited until Nathan had gone upstairs to shower and had closed the bathroom door. This time alone allowed her to digest and regroup after hearing about his discovery from earlier in the day. Feeling more comfortable, she stood up from the kitchen table and turned out the light. As she walked into the living room, she paused to look at Kenny's picture sitting on the bookshelf.

"I miss you," she said simply and softly kissed his picture.

Not ready to go upstairs and go to bed for the night, Angela took Iana's Bible from the shelf and sat down with it at Nathan's desk.

Putting on her glasses, she opened the Bible to the first sealed page and placed her hand on the seal. She looked up from the Bible, then, thinking it strange that she felt anxious, like her heart was trying to thump its way out of her chest. This definitely was not the response she had anticipated at touching this particular page of Iana's Bible.

Shaking her head in an attempt to rid her mind of all the messy and fear-provoking thoughts, she said matter-of-factly, "I am being ridiculous!" and then took a deep breath and decided to go on.

Tentatively she placed her hand on the folded page and gently broke the seal, turning back the page from left to right. Once open, she rubbed the page with her hand to flatten it out.

Breathing a sigh of relief, Angela sat back in the chair and smiled to herself. "That wasn't so difficult," she said calmly, stunned by the sound of her own voice.

In the fading light, Angela lingered a few more minutes, motionless and on the edge of her chair. Suddenly she sensed something was not right. Something was *very* not right. Powerless to do anything about it, she sat frozen and looked down at her hand resting on the page; it was shaking. Inside—*deep* inside—the words, "*My blood is within you,*" crept into her mind.

"Jesus," she said, quickly lifting her hand from the page.

Her stomach tightened, and she could feel herself coming unglued from the shock of hearing the words. For a moment she thought she might have to close the Bible and run into the bathroom to throw up.

"This stuff... It just won't leave me alone," she said, her eyes searching the room in a moment of panic. "Why won't you leave me alone?" Although she had grown to adore Iana, moments like this one still unnerved her a bit.

Taking a deep breath to clear her head, she leaned forward, picked up a pencil and nervously began tapping it on the yellow legal pad alongside Iana's Bible. After what seemed like an eternity, she stiffened in the chair and directed her mind to press on with whatever was attempting to reveal itself. Angela paused another moment, her stomach churning, and a drop of cold sweat trickled down the side of her face. Sensing no danger, she took a deep breath and then once again timidly placed her hand onto the opened page of Iana's Bible.

Nervously she looked down at the crude illustration: the figure of a man lying on the floor. Immediately she froze, her locking eyes with his, which were haunting and seemed to be pleading for help. Seconds later her previous vision of Maggie as a terrified little girl, locked in a closet, flashed into her mind. She let out a groan, her whole body tight as a wire as she recalled the endless loop of pain and despair Maggie had suffered in her youth. Angela knew that the real tragedy for Maggie was not only that she had trusted and believed in her father, but that she had loved him, and she hadn't felt his love in return. She nodded without looking up from the page and became aware of the shiny, round object lying in the palm of the man's hand. Smiling, she turned her head, fully aware of the identity of that object.

"The penny!" Angela exclaimed.

At that exact moment, she felt strangely peaceful. However, her calm state was short-lived and fled when a gust of wind rattled the storm windows. Suddenly horrified, she looked up, but then she locked her wide-open eyes onto the page again, a dozen questions jockeying for position in her mind.

Drenched in sweat, Angela shook her head, hard. "What just happened?"

Creeping fear and confusion began to fill her mind and body, and she shuddered. "Iana knew," she said softly, amazed by what she had suggested. Angela looked up from the page, distressed and panicked. "Could my grandmother envision, and then predict through her drawings, events yet to come?"

"No, of course not!" Angela snapped, interrupting the thoughts that flooded her consciousness. "How is that even possible?" she asked but then stopped as the memory of Dr. Howard's lecture at NYU shattered her mind.

"Time Travel. We have documented information about people who became both masters of meditation and out-of-body experiences or body travels, which seems to defy all laws known in physics."

Angela sat quietly for a few seconds, contemplating Dr. Howard's explanation. She had never really let herself think about it before, because she had been determined that it was all just a hypothesis mixed with his philosophy. Now Angela couldn't help wondering if everything he had spoken of could be relevant to her grandmother and what she'd discovered in her Bible.

All of a sudden, a shot of adrenaline raced through Angela's body, and she involuntarily jerked forward, almost knocking herself to the floor.

"Whoa." Angela looked at the page, shaking her head.

Her hand was cramping from the tight grip she held on the pencil, but when she tried to loosen her grip, she couldn't. Feeling nothing, but knowing some strange force was guiding her hand, Angela watched from far away as she rapidly began to draw a crude picture on the yellow legal pad. Who or whatever was controlling Angela's body drew the front view of a woman with long black hair, enormous black eyes and huge tears streaming down her cheeks.

"What's happening?" she yelled, gasping for air.

An icy wind blew through her mind as she watched her hand quickly move to the right of the woman and frantically begin sketching the back view of a small child with short, curly, flaxen hair.

"Grandmother!" Angela's breath was coming fast and her hair was drenched with sweat. Her gaze locked on the figure of the unknown little girl.

She looked nervously around the room, breathing deeply and trying to relax. Although she sensed the presence of a power larger than herself, somehow Angela was not afraid, just freaked out by the suddenness of it all. Surprisingly the knot of tension in her stomach began to dissipate and her heartache melted into pleasure. She was totally aware of being in a distant place now, a place that was serene and peaceful. She took another deep breath and wiped some of the sweat from her forehead with the back of her hand. As tears began to well up in her eyes, her hand began to tremble again, and with the pencil still gripped tightly in her fingers, Angela watched in amazement as her hand quickly scribbled the name "*Faith Deveraux*" beneath the drawing of the flaxen-haired little girl.

Angela gasped, jumping up from the chair and dropping the pencil onto the pad. She gasped again and quickly pulled her hands back as if she had just touched something hot. At the same time, what remained of her composure quickly crumbled, and she burst into tears, collapsing back down into the chair.

"This is unbelievable," she whispered.

"*Shhh,*" a voice tiptoed in her ear. "*Shhh. I know it's hard to believe, but denying it isn't going to help. Especially for her.*"

Even though January's brutal chill penetrated the cracks and seams of Angela's home, her living room was suddenly filled with warmth and the deep feelings of affection. Angela shifted in her chair, dumbfounded yet fascinated by the sense of hearing a soft, reassuring voice speaking to her. At once she felt warm and content, and she snuggled in the love that was gathering around her, leading her to a comfortable place deep within.

Then she shuddered at a momentary ripple of anxiety and covered her eyes with her hands.

"I'm so tired. My mind hurts," she said quietly with a look of concern.

Suddenly, a light touch of a hand on her arm startled her. "*Be still my child.*" Slowly, soft hands pulled Angela's own hands away from her eyes and then soothingly touched her cheek. Angela could feel herself begin to disappear into the tender touch of fingertips.

"*Secrets buried alive never die.*"

"I can hear your voice," Angela said thickly.

Then the voice was silent for what seemed a full minute.

"*Take the ashes from the past and allow them to be turned into beauty.*"

As Angela thought about those words, she reached over the desk and turned on the lamp. And as she did, she gave an enormous start. Blinking her eyes to focus, she carefully studied the form of a woman. Standing only a few feet in front of Angela and dressed in a white gown, she had olive skin and intense green eyes, and Angela noticed every detail about her all at once. An odd sense of peace came over her, and there was no question in her mind about who she was.

"Oh my God," Angela said as she sat straight up. She wanted to call her by name, but she didn't dare. Somehow, it was almost as if she felt what Angela was thinking.

She looked right into Angela's eyes and smiled at her. Holding out her hand, she again spoke, saying, "*You are a part of me. I am a part of you. My blood is your blood. Go now; complete the work. Walk in the gift you have been given. Use it for good to bring about an end to the message for Maggie.*"

"Beauty for ashes," Angela replied. "I understand." As she sat thinking about what she'd heard, she whispered Iana's name, but there was no answer—only the gentle feeling of her presence.

Angela could feel her standing nearby. Love saturated her, although there were no more movements or sounds. Then, after a few minutes, the presence of the woman in the white gown was gone—and yet Angela had seen her so clearly. All she wanted was for her to appear again, but she was thankful for what she had seen, for what was already etched in her memory. She knew she would never forget this moment in time.

That night as she lay in bed, falling asleep was harder than she thought it would be. Her head and heart were full of Iana and Maggie. It was as though a door had been closed behind her, and another was opening right in front of her, leading her into a brand new world.

When Angela awoke the next morning, the vision of Iana she'd seen the night before seemed more like a dream than reality. Although she was absolutely sure her grandmother had been there—she had seen her so clearly, after all—she decided not to share this experience with anyone except Nathan. She was grateful for Iana's presence in her life now, her sudden appearance and surprising arrival. It had been an answer to her prayers.

When she came down for breakfast, she still looked tired.

"How'd you sleep?" Nathan asked with a look of concern.

"Oh, I suppose you could say I had a night," she said. She thought about telling Nathan what she had seen, but she was almost afraid to. As Nathan looked at her over his paper, he sensed something.

"Honey, is everything alright?" His eyes were looking deep into hers as he wondered about the previous night, but he didn't say anything more.

"Everything's fine," she said, sipping some coffee as she eyed him sharply.

"Oh?" He tried to look casual as he folded the paper and set it to the side. "I know that look; do you want to tell me now or later?"

"Are you sure you want to hear it?" she asked him. "I thought you ought to have time to enjoy your morning coffee and paper before I shattered all of our dreams." She smiled, although her eyes conveyed something very serious.

"I was afraid of that," he said as she poured herself a second cup of coffee. "I thought you might have had a rough time after I went to bed."

And then she startled him by saying, "I've seen her." Her eyes were deep and sharp as she watched him, and he felt a gentle shiver.

"Seen who?" He looked vague and took a sip of coffee.

"I've seen my grandmother, Iana," Angela admitted to him as she sat back in her chair. She felt relieved to be able to talk with him about what had happened. "I will never forget it. She was beautiful, and she stood looking at me for the longest time in the living room. She spoke, then smiled and disappeared."

"I had a feeling she'd come to you someday," he said, still watching her and feeling a little crazy saying it. "You're open and receptive to her now."

"Well, thanks a lot!" Angela laughed and shook her head. "You should have warned me."

And then he looked critically at her. "Do you suppose she'll come back again?"

"I have no idea." There was a long pause, and then she said, "I wandered around the house afterwards but felt nothing. I was so comfortable and at ease with the whole experience. Just as I was about to fall asleep, I thought I saw the drapes move, but I was too tired to open my eyes. And as I drifted off, I was sure I felt her near again."

"I have a suspicion that you will," Nathan said, smiling. "See her again, I mean."

Angela laughed at the thought, relaxing for just an instant, and she smiled.

"It may take a while, but you will," Nathan assured her.

"I don't know about that, but I *do* know what we're supposed to do with that penny."

"Oh?" he said with fresh interest, an inquisitive tone in his voice.

She hesitated at first but finally began explaining how, by some unseen force, she was able to channel the images of a woman and child onto paper. Feeling like it was almost impossible to explain further, Angela rose from the table and walked slowly into the living room, returning with the yellow legal pad in her hand. She held it out to Nathan, and he took it from her. He examined the drawing carefully, then noticed the name Faith Deveraux written at the bottom of the page.

"What's this?" Nathan looked puzzled as he pointed to the name.

"I know this is going to sound crazy, but I believe that is the name of Maggie's daughter," Angela answered in a whisper.

"Maggie's *daughter*?" Nathan stared at her in astonishment.

She smiled then, and what Nathan saw in her eyes startled him. There was something very unusual about her now, and he was completely unprepared for the passion he saw. Her eyes sparkled as she shared in detail her experience from the night before. Angela believed that Iana had come to give her gift completely to her, to deliver a message through illustrations once again—this time drawn by Angela herself—and to guide her to the completion of the task set before her. That was all Angela wanted. Nathan was certain of it.

"Take the ashes from the past and allow them to be turned into beauty." There was a look of tragedy in her eyes as she said it to him, and then he realized what she meant.

He looked at her long and hard, saying nothing. And then, finally, he asked her one more question: "The penny?"

"Yes, the penny." She smiled at him. "When I saw, when I heard the words... I understood, and my heart ached." Tears spilled down her cheeks. "Maggie's father knew it would bring them luck; he knew the significance of the penny, but his death was untimely and had been unexpected, so the secret was buried with him."

Nathan looked startled for a moment.

"But Nathan, it didn't die with him." Angela gave his arms a squeeze, then eased back. "Secrets buried alive never die; ashes from the past into beauty."

"Does this mean what I think it does?" Nathan asked.

Angela didn't even hesitate for a moment. "It's beautiful, isn't it?" she said, her eyes alive with excitement. "The universe is the great equalizer. Look how the ashes from Rebecca's life have been turned into beauty for her life and for ours." She let out a sigh and smiled. "Secrets will find their way out of the darkness and into the light."

"You never cease to amaze me. After all Maggie did to you, terrorizing and stalking you for almost a year, you still want to help her." He rose to kiss her cheek.

"I promised her that I would. Hamiltons honor their word, and so do Robertses. I'm both."

"Agreed." Nathan smiled and leaned back in his chair.

"Whatever Maggie's mother and father did, Maggie deserved better in life than what she got. It's hardly a wonder that her mind, which already seemed to be somewhat imbalanced, shattered. Let's be honest; in the end, she was mad. She passed away terribly and didn't live much better. Sadly, somewhere along the way, she had a child, Faith Deveraux. And I have a sneaking suspicion that her daughter didn't do any better in life than she did. Another child tossed aside and discarded... The unfortunate product of her environment."

Angela lifted a hand to her throat as it filled. "Nathan, it's not just the money. My grandmother loved Maggie as if she were her own child." Angela's stomach almost turned over as she thought of Maggie's mother. Over time, she had become a monster.

"The thief slithered in to rob her innocent life of the love and security a parent ought to provide," she said stiffly. "But when Iana would take her little hand in her own," Angela continued gently, "Iana again was a beacon of light, loving her and providing a safe haven in the midst of the heartbreaking chaos and darkness in the little girl's life. Maggie and Cilla, two peas in a pod... They were a family."

"I know." Nathan covered Angela's hand with his.

"Maggie is family." A little chilled, Angela rubbed her arms.

"As I look back over the past year, it's as if everything in your life has been leading up to this; both the good and the bad." Nathan let out a breath. He recognized the importance of Angela's words; they showed who she was and who she would be, regardless of trouble—or maybe because of it. Whatever it took to keep her family whole and safe, she would do.

"I owe it to my grandmother to finish this, to complete the work that has been given to me."

Nathan took the penny from his pocket and slid it across the table.

"Now that I know, I can't imagine keeping this penny." He looked up and smiled at Angela. "We need to find Faith Deveraux."

18

The morning after Angela shared her prediction concerning Faith Deveraux, Nathan was up and out of the house by eight o'clock. Driving across town for a nine o'clock breakfast meeting with a former client, he had a sudden idea. He made a quick detour by his former law firm, and not having much time, he gave a brief synopsis of a fictional case he said he was consulting on to his secretary and requested any information she could track down on a woman by the name of Faith Deveraux. She promised to do what she could for Nathan. And an hour later, when he stopped back after his appointment, she handed him the phone number of a Faith Deveraux living in Ridgewood, New Jersey.

By lunchtime that day, Angela felt like it was Christmas Day all over again. She was in remarkably good spirits even though she didn't have a clue as to what she would say when she placed a phone call to the number that Nathan had given her.

Angela sat on the edge of her bed, struggling to find the courage she desperately needed. She picked up the telephone and then put it back down. She couldn't do it just yet. She wasn't ready to make that call.

"*God, please help me. Give me courage I need right now.*"

Following her quick prayer, she picked up the phone again and this time stood up, vowing that she wasn't going to chicken out.

She dialed the number that had been etched in her memory by now. After the third ring, a woman's voice came through the receiver.

"Hello."

Just hearing the woman's voice sent a myriad of emotions coursing through her. Angela took a deep breath and then exhaled slowly.

"Hello." After a pause, she asked, "May I speak with Faith Deveraux?"

Several moments of silence passed, and Angela was about to put the phone down when she heard a voice barely above a whisper say, “Yes. This is Faith Deveraux.”

Her knees buckled, forcing her back down on the edge of her bed. “Hello Faith, my name is Angela Roberts.”

In her mind Angela had gone through a series of scenarios regarding the conversation she would have with Faith. She paused for a heartbeat before continuing and then quickly explained that she’d been a friend of her mother, Maggie Deveraux, and that their mothers had been childhood friends. Angela was completely surprised at how receptive Faith was at hearing about her mother. She listened intently as Angela compared Maggie’s strengths and weaknesses to what she considered to be those of her own mother. As far as Angela was concerned, Maggie and Cilla could have been sisters.

It was difficult at times for both of them, with several breaks in the conversation resulting in complete silence on both ends of the phone. But they talked for a long time that afternoon, and after an hour, Faith and Angela agreed to meet the following day to continue their conversation in person.

It was starting to snow as Nathan and Angela passed a sign on the way into a small town, and they suddenly realized they had just crossed the bridge into the Village of Ridgewood in northern New Jersey. As closely as Nathan could figure it, they had traveled about twenty miles northwest of Manhattan. The Village of Ridgewood was a quaint-looking little town, with its streets lined with small, neatly-tended homes and white picket fences. As they drove further, Angela became enamored by it, the world that was so wholesome and tranquil with everything blanketed in smooth white cotton. And as they continued, she saw rabbits darting through the snow and a deer watching them from the side of the road. It was as though all the people had disappeared, and all that was left was flora and fauna. They reached the edge of town easily, and as Nathan was beginning to feel lost, he stopped the car for a minute and rolled down the window. Unsure which way to go, he saw a street leading off to the left somewhere and turned the car slowly, deciding to try it.

A few minutes later, Angela saw a sign for Regency Woods hanging outside a fence alongside the road. She thought about it for a minute and then told Nathan that was the name of the mobile home park Faith had given to her when they spoke on the phone. Nathan carefully steered the car down the winding, snow-covered road, ultimately ending up at the entrance to a neglected and shabby mobile home park. They continued to drive as far as they could and then pulled into the only driveway that was connected to a mobile home. As it turned out, the number on the home matched the one Faith had given Angela the day before. The lights inside the house were on, but initially Angela felt very uneasy. More than one of the nearby mobile homes were clearly deserted, their doors and windows boarded up. The lots on either side of Faith's home were vacant and in disarray. Shaking her head, Angela thought, *"It couldn't get much worse than this."*

The storm had really picked up, and the wind was blowing. Nathan was worried they'd have trouble getting home, and he suggested their visit be kept as brief as possible. "All right," Angela said quietly, feeling her heart tremble a little bit. She smiled at him as she tightened her coat around herself, and then she stepped out of the car. With her husband by her side, she walked across the fresh snow. All the while, Nathan kept an eye out for any woodland creatures that might want to pay them a quick visit before they could get inside.

Angela only had to climb up one short flight of wooden stairs and knock on the door. For a moment, though, she wasn't sure she could go through with it, losing her nerve at the base of the steps.

"When you start a thing, don't quit until you finish it. You have persevered and have endured hardships. Suffering produces perseverance; perseverance, character; and character, hope."

Remembering those words made her smile. They were like a force of destiny, and Angela felt their power as she stood there in the dark. Feeling as though she had just been given a gift, she knew exactly what she needed to do. Composing herself once more, and with Nathan's firm grip beneath her elbow, Angela walked up the steps and knocked on the front door.

It wasn't long until Faith pulled the door open just a crack.

"Faith Deveraux?" Angela felt embarrassed, almost as if she had intruded on her.

"Yes." She opened the door slightly more to let the dog outside, then looked up at Angela.

Immediately Angela thought her to be around the same age as she was. But she was very pale and very thin, dressed in a black turtleneck and black jeans with no makeup on her face, dark circles under her eyes, and straight blond hair that hung on either side of her head. It was apparent that life had not been easy for her.

"Mrs. Roberts?" she almost looked shy as she said it.

"Call me Angela. And this is my husband, Nathan."

She nodded. "Please, come in."

They entered a small, comfortable room. The dark paneled walls, once polished and glossy, were now dull and beginning to warp, but they were adorned with pictures of a girl Angela assumed to be Faith's daughter, from the day of her birth to the day of her high school graduation. The majority of the furniture was well-worn, and the possessions neatly placed on Faith's end tables and wall shelves obviously each held a special meaning or memory for her.

Faith had seemed so cold to Angela at first, so distant, but this room told a different tale. And so did Faith's eyes when she turned and looked at Angela.

"May I get you a cup of coffee? Maybe some hot tea?"

"I... uh... yes, a cup of tea would be nice." Angela smiled and sat down on the couch.

A few minutes later Faith returned with a tray of hot tea and a plate of homemade Christmas cookies.

"You knew my mother?" she asked as she sat the tray on the coffee table. "For how long? How long did you know her?"

Angela admitted that she hadn't known Maggie well or for a long period of time. She also shared with Faith that Maggie's life story was complicated and appeared to have taken a heavy toll on her as a child. She told Faith about all the things Iana Hamilton had done for Maggie and how she had loved her just as much as her own daughter. She believed those small moments had given Maggie happiness; her illusions had not yet been shattered completely and there was still hope, faith and love in her life. As the years passed, it was almost as if Maggie had died, and a bitter, tired and battered soul had taken her place.

In a way Faith felt compassion for her mother, although it had been difficult for her to cope with never knowing her father and never *really* knowing her mother either. It was obvious to Faith now that her mother had not survived childhood. And somewhere deep inside, Faith suspected that in Maggie's later years, that truth brought her unhappiness. Now there was only bitterness, anger and unhappy silence in their lives.

"Years ago, my mother called about wanting to see me, to spend some time with Caroline and me. But I told her I was too busy."

Angela nodded, easily suspecting that Faith's rejection wasn't just about her being busy. She couldn't help feeling sorry for Faith. It was so unfair of Maggie to take her unhappiness out on her daughter. But she had been a product of her environment; it had become a learned behavior for her.

The truth was that Maggie had been moody and unhappy for such long time that Faith could no longer remember her being a different person, and she no longer had the energy to fight with her. All of Faith's misery and sense of loss had channeled itself into resentment, and the years of disappointment, grief and anguish she'd experienced now generated outrage towards her mother. She had never forgiven Maggie for what she had perceived as her mother's failures in her childhood. Faith had come to hate her mother for her years of being absent and for her seeming lack of interest in her own daughter's life. She was never there for Faith, not even when her daughter, Caroline, was born. That was the final blow to any mother-daughter relationship.

With that said, Faith also had to confess that, year after year, she would fantasize about what it would be like to share everyday moments with her mother. There was always something Faith had wanted to share with Maggie: Caroline's first steps, the anxiety she felt on her first day of school, the time when Caroline had been up all night with a high fever. She just would've liked to have been able to pick up the phone and hear her mother's voice. The normal, everyday things a mother and a daughter typically shared always reminded her, with agonizing pain, how empty her life had been without her. She closed her eyes for a moment, thinking of her, and then forced herself to open them. There was no point in allowing herself to get sucked into the black pit of grief again.

"I wonder if I'll ever get used to it and stop being angry every time I think of her."

"You will." Angela smiled and touched her hand. "Eventually, the heart mends. The scars and the memories remain, but in time, you'll learn to live with the hurt, and even function in spite of it."

By now, it wasn't a mystery to Angela; Faith obviously had been deeply hurt by her mother. She was the third generation with deep-rooted pain, practically destined to fail at life. Angela was concerned that their conversation would stir up emotions that would take days to manage. If that did happen, though, Angela was certain Faith would survive it; she had done it before and would do it again. Her mind would clear, and her heart would not be constantly heavy; it would sink only now and then when she thought of Maggie. Angela had learned that with Kenny.

They sat and talked for a while longer, easily and comfortably. And then Nathan finally glanced at his watch. He hated to leave her, but the condition of the roads was a growing concern for him.

Angela rose to go over and look at the pictures of Caroline. "Your daughter is precious... She has Maggie's eyes. How old is she now?"

"Caroline will be nineteen in a few months. She is studying to be a nurse."

After one last glance at her picture, Angela walked back to her chair and sat.

"Faith, before we go, there is one more thing I need to tell you."

Faith was silent for a long moment. "What's that?"

Angela knew how distressed Faith would be over her mother's death, and she felt badly for having to tell her, but there was nothing she could do. She took a deep breath and began. Looking down for another moment, she then told Faith when and how her mother had died.

As she spoke, Faith's eyes became wet with unshed tears.

"Faith, I believe she really did love you. She just didn't know how to show it."

"I may have been wrong about my mother in some things." She nodded and wiped her eyes, then she glanced over her shoulder. "I suppose you're right; she really wasn't a bad person."

"No, she wasn't. She wasn't a bad person at all."

"Now it seems that nobody really gave her a chance... Except for you, Angela, and your grandmother. But the rest of them... Nobody gave her a chance. Nobody... Not even me." Tears ran down her face. "And now she's gone."

Faith sobbed loudly.

Angela didn't say a word at first but just pulled Faith into her arms and held her tight. It was a long moment before she could find anything to say.

"Please don't be so hard on yourself. You didn't know her life story," she told her softly. "I'm so sorry, Faith... I'm so sorry."

Nathan walked up to Faith and offered his condolences, and he also reminded Angela there was still something else they needed to discuss.

"I don't think I can handle any more." Faith wiped her eyes and then her nose.

"On the contrary," Angela said as she cocked her head and very nearly smiled. "You could use some full strength happiness right now."

"I don't feel like I *deserve* any happiness," Faith said stiffly.

"Oh, but you do." Angela reached into her purse and pulled out a small box, which she then handed to Faith.

"What's in this box, along with this card, were tucked away for decades in my grandmother's Bible," Angela explained. "And both belong to you now."

"A present for me?" she asked, taken aback.

"Call it a long overdue Christmas gift from your grandfather, Gregory Deveraux, by way of his daughter, Maggie Deveraux, and now for you, Faith Deveraux." Angela stretched back in her chair and spoke with satisfaction. "I know they both would want you to have this now."

Curious, Faith turned her head so she could see Nathan. "Go ahead, open it," he encouraged with a smile.

"I can't imagine what it could be," she said, looking touched, and slowly opened the box to find the 1943 copper wheat penny sealed and labeled with its estimated value at eighty-five thousand dollars.

Faith lifted her eyes to meet Angela's, and a slow smile spread over her face.

"Oh, go ahead and let it out," Angela laughed. "I know what it feels like."

"It says eighty-five thousand dollars," Faith said, beaming. "You have no idea."

"Oh, I think I do." Angela slipped her arm around Faith. "From what I've learned about Gregory Deveraux, he knew this would give Maggie a sense of security in her life, something neither of her parents were able to provide for her. And now the gift belongs to you—along with that sense of security."

Faith was struggling not to cry as she held the certificate in her hand. "This is the most beautiful gift I've ever been given."

Angela felt joy welling up within her, and she smiled over at Faith. "Looks like you've got an angel watching over you."

After Nathan explained what Faith would need to do with the penny, Angela and Faith shared a tearful good-bye.

"I'm going to miss you," Faith said, unable to hold back her tears. "I've only known you for a short time, but I feel like we're family."

"I know." Angela held back a tear and thought for a moment. "Ya know, seeing as you and I are about the same age and my grandmother, Iana, was like a mother to Maggie... My mother Cilla, then, was like a sister to Maggie... So I'd say that would make us like cousins."

Faith let her head fall back and laughed. "I think you may be right. And Angela—I'll be very happy being your cousin," Faith said, smiling through her tears.

"It's time to get on the road, Honey," Nathan said gently, trying not to intrude.

Before she and Nathan left, Angela made Faith promise that she and Caroline would come to the Roberts's Family Reunion in the spring. Faith happily agreed they'd be there.

"Are you ready?" Nathan asked Angela softly. She nodded and walked to the front door with Faith following slowly, savoring each final second.

Faith stood on her front steps, waving as Nathan backed the car out of the driveway, and Angela could see her through her tears as they drove down the snow-covered road. Faith continued waving until she could barely see the car anymore. And as the car drove out of sight, she whispered into the wind, "I love you, Mom."

She stood outside for a long time, with tears running down her cheeks, thinking of her mother and her grandfather, and holding the penny's certificate in her hand. She had so much to look forward to, so much to be thankful for. It was a new beginning. She then closed her eyes and thanked God for giving her the family she never had.

That night, when Robby and Rebecca had gone upstairs to put India to bed and Nathan was gently snoring in his recliner in the den, Angela slipped out to the front porch for a dose of her grandmother's spirit. She sat down on the swing, breathed in deeply, and just as she had done in the past, looked up as a bright light streaked across the night sky. The light stopped momentarily overhead, and for an instant, Angela felt the spirit of Iana Hamilton all around her.

"It's only the beginning," she heard in a whisper.

"Your life gave me mine," Angela said as she closed her eyes and settled her mind. "Rest now, grandmother."

Just as quickly as it had come, the light vanished into the night.

Listen to the voice of your true home with a calm mind.
The sea and mountains are extraordinarily beautiful.
Returning to your home, finding your ancient roots.
After having crossed the bridge of understanding,
you will reach the bridge of love.
-Thich Nhat Hanh

Made in the USA
Middletown, DE
16 February 2015